for the

ayou series

"Lila's strength and vulnerability are balanced by Armie's intelligence and humor, making them an easy couple to root for. Blake captures the flavor of her colorful Southern town with a vividly drawn cast. . . . This charming series opener hits all the right notes." —*Publishers Weekly*

"Blake has created a couple to root for, along with memorable supporting characters and story lines with depth. Readers will be eager to visit Papillon again." —*Library Journal*

"Southern delight awaits in *Bayou Baby*. . . . This charming small-town drama is as smooth and sweet as a Louisiana drawl." —*BookPage* (starred review)

Praise for
Lexi Blake

"Lexi Blake is a master!"
—*New York Times* bestselling author Jennifer Probst

"I love Lexi Blake."
—*New York Times* bestselling author Lee Child

"Smart, savvy, clever, and always entertaining."
—*New York Times* bestselling author Steve Berry

"Lexi Blake has set up shop on the intersection of suspenseful and sexy, and I never want to leave."
—*New York Times* bestselling author Laurelin Paige

Titles by Lexi Blake

Bayou Beloved

Lexi Blake

BERKLEY ROMANCE
New York

Berkley Romance
Published by Berkley
An imprint of Penguin Random House LLC
penguinrandomhouse.com

ISBN: 9780593439579

First Edition: March 2023

Printed in the United States of America
1 3 5 7 9 10 8 6 4 2

Book design by Alison Cnockaert

*For my brother, Wes, who will likely never
know this book is dedicated to him.
So much of this book is based on who I was as a kid
and a teen and he had to suffer through that.
So the least he could get is a book
with a cute dog on the cover.
Love you always, brother.*

chapter one

Jayna Cardet glanced down at the watch her grandmother had given her the day she'd graduated from law school and frowned. "Your Honor, it's ten twenty. The trial was supposed to start at ten. I move for you to make a decision based on the fact that the defense didn't bother to show up."

"I'm right here." A thin man in his mid-forties stood, holding up a hand. He was the owner of the gas station and the man who'd made her client's life a living hell.

At least that was the way she was going to argue the case. She firmly intended to make the world understand that taking down that tree on the land that ran up against her client's home had been not only rude but negligent. And she would make that case as soon as the defense counsel bothered to show up. Or perhaps Mr. Abbot could be convinced to defend himself. She could eviscerate the man's argument in five minutes or less and then she would be free to make a whole bunch of calls that would likely lead to nowhere. Certainly not to a job. "Excellent, then we should get started."

"But Quaid's not here." Abbot looked at her like she was some kind of idiot.

Yeah, she got that a lot these days. Once she'd been the

up-and-coming queen of the New Orleans legal scene. She'd been justice in high heels, wielding a designer bag like a shield.

This morning her momma had shoved a PB&J, an apple, and two tiny chocolate chip cookies in a plastic bag from the Fast Mart, and handed her a thermos of instant coffee because only rich people had coffeemakers, and hot water and off-brand caffeine crystals had been good enough for her momma, so they were good enough for her.

How the mighty had fallen.

"Yes, Your Honor, that's my point." She gestured to her client, eighty-four-year-old Geraldine Oliver. "If Mr. Havery can't be bothered to show up on time, then we should either move forward with the trial or you could simply hand down a judgment in favor of my client."

"Whoa," Abbot said with a frown. "That doesn't seem fair. We didn't even get a chance to tell you what happened. Shouldn't we have that chance? Quaid's just running late, like always."

"Mr. Havery is taking up the judge's valuable time," she pointed out. If they'd been in New Orleans, she would already have her judgment and be off to the next client. She would have billed another couple of hours before heading to some fabulous restaurant for lunch where she would schmooze with the bigwigs and bring in even more money.

"My time is not that valuable right now," Judge Brewer said with a yawn. "Can't fish today. I've got a doctor's appointment this afternoon, and if I have to cancel that because Quaid's late, it's fine with me. Why a man can't be left to die in peace, I have no idea. Besides, it looks like Geraldine is having a nice nap. Wouldn't want to wake her."

Sure enough, her client was snoring quietly in the chair beside her. "Your Honor, you can't mean to sit here and wait for defense counsel."

"What else would you have me do, young lady?" The judge's brow had furrowed. Judge Andy Brewer had been the only judge in the parish for over thirty years. He was a thin man with a head of silver hair and thick glasses. "Besides that unfair judgment thing. I'm not going to penalize Mr. Abbot here because Quaid lost track of time. That might fly in New Orleans, but we are different here in Papillon, and you would do well to remember it. Now, if you're bored, we could play a game of some kind."

The court reporter was maybe twelve years old and so shiny it hurt to look at her. She clapped her hands together. "How about Hangman? I could go get the white board, PawPaw."

Okay, so she might be in her twenties, but Jayna still stood by her assessment. She was too cheery. And apparently, she was the judge's granddaughter. The nepotism shouldn't surprise her. Papillon hadn't changed at all.

"Oh, that sounds like fun." The owner of the Last Chance Gas Stop looked enthusiastic.

She should sue him for the name of that business alone. It wasn't the last chance at gas. Not even close. The Fillin' Station was two miles down the road, and they served chicken-fried steak, too. The only last chance one got at Abbot's station was the chance to get overcharged for a bag of chips. She'd heard Abbot had selected the name to scare the tourists into buying from him since the chicken-fried steak brought the locals into the other station. "Your Honor, you can't mean to take up the court's time with word games."

"In my opinion, that's all lawyers do. Take up time playing word games," the judge said with a sigh. "We might as well have some fun with it. Wally, would you help Britney grab that white board?"

The big bailiff walked out with the court reporter, who reminded Jayna of an overexcited toy poodle or one of those other yippy dogs who always looked like squeaky toys for bigger dogs.

Like her Grand Pyrenees, Luna, who was definitely too big for her mother's double-wide trailer.

Sometimes she wondered if Luna wished she'd been left back in New Orleans with Todd. Threatening to fight for custody of her dog had been Todd's way of getting Jayna to give up what little had been left to her after the prenup had stripped her of almost every dollar she had. Still, he'd liked Luna and probably would have hired someone to take care of her. If she'd stayed with Todd, there would have been a yard for her to run around in. Had she been selfish wanting to keep her?

"Miss Cardet," the judge began, "you're Lissa Cardet's youngest, right? Sienna's sister?"

"Lissa has two kids?" Abbot asked, scratching his nearly bald head. "I thought Sienna was her only one."

She got that a lot, too. Apparently walking away from one's hometown and not walking back in for almost fifteen years had an effect on one's memorability. Somehow the people who could remember family members' names back to before the Civil War couldn't seem to recall the high school valedictorian of Armstrong High.

"Melissa Cardet is my mom," she replied. She should have known it would be like this, should have known that Papillon law would be some weird balancing act of family relationships, popularity, and the barest adherence to normal legal protocols. She'd promised herself she wouldn't be here long, that living with her mom was temporary while she tried to find another job and got her license to practice in Texas. "Sienna is my sister."

"Aw, that Sienna is a ray of sunshine," Abbot said with a big smile.

The judge nodded. "Yes, Sienna is an amazing young

woman. After all she's been through, she's still smiling, and her heart is full of joy."

Her sister's heart was full of denial. She was twice divorced with two kids and working at a diner, but yes, she was the Cardet family success story because she was beautiful and smiled even when she should be stabbing someone. That was the Cardet way. At least for the women. The men didn't smile, but had been known to stab people from time to time.

"Your Honor, you can't possibly mean to hold up the court for an attorney who doesn't bother to show up." She was shocked. Not that Quaid Havery would be so arrogant he kept the court waiting, but that the judge would put up with it. Quaid Havery had enough arrogance to serve every single person in the world a double helping of self-confidence.

She absolutely had not been thinking about him when she'd put on her best suit and the only Chanel necklace she hadn't pawned. The one decent pair of heels she hadn't sold weren't on her feet because she needed to look her best for her high school crush. Nope. She'd done it all because wearing these clothes made her feel professional. And spending extra time on her makeup was a thing she always did before appearing in court. It had nothing to do with him.

She hoped that man had a nice potbelly and had lost all that hair he'd had in high school. Quaid had been the prom king and she'd been the nerd who'd tutored him in French. He'd been the rich kid, the one whose family had all the connections, and she'd had two uncles and a cousin in the Louisiana penitentiary system. Her father had only avoided prison because he'd been friendly with the sheriff at the time of his arrest.

Quaid very likely had blown through a couple of trophy wives by now and had a whole bunch of kids who resented the hell out of him just like he'd resented his own work-aholic dad.

The judge waved off her concern. "Quaid's real busy. It's hard to be the only lawyer in the whole parish. He's like his daddy before him, always up to his neck in work. He probably forgot. I'll have Brit call his secretary to remind him. Don't worry. His office is right across the town square. He'll be here soon."

"He's not the only attorney in town. Not anymore." She might not be here for long, but while she was, she intended to show the town what she'd learned.

A brow rose over the judge's eyes. "You're staying in Papillon, then?"

It wasn't like she had anywhere else to go. If she could be anywhere else in the whole world, she would be. "For the time being. From what I understand, Mr. Havery represents the more privileged people of the parish. If I hadn't been around, Mrs. Oliver wouldn't have been able to secure counsel and wouldn't have been able to press her legal claim. So I think I should be a welcome addition to our legal community."

The judge sighed. "If you hadn't been around, Quaid would have already handled the problem and none of us would be here. It's what he does. He settles problems so they don't ever have to reach the court system and I can fish more. I'm not getting any younger, as I'm sure Lila LaVigne will remind me if I have to go in for my yearly physical."

She was going to lose an entire day because the judge wanted to avoid a lecture on his cholesterol.

Geraldine's snoring reached a new, far more audible level, and Jayna realized the woman had left her teeth out. She tended to shove them in the big bag she carried and only put them in when it was time to eat.

Jayna chose to focus on the problem at hand. "Judge, in

all seriousness, Mr. Havery should never be negotiating without other counsel present. He's legally required to look out for the best interests of his client, not those of the opposing party. He's not supposed to be a mediator looking out for both people."

"Of course he is. Quaid's a nice guy. He can do both," the judge insisted.

"Legally he cannot," she argued. How long had it been since the judge had gone to law school?

Dear lord. Had the judge gone to law school? It was Papillon. Anything was possible. One year there were a hundred write-in votes to make Otis the mayor. Otis was the gator who hung around Guidry's Bar and Grill parking lot. There had been real worry that the gator would win, and there was nothing in the town charter that eliminated reptiles from serving in government positions.

It was an oversight.

The judge studied her for a moment. "Now I do recall Lissa having a younger child. You were a smart one, very dedicated to your studies if I remember."

"I still am. I went to Loyola for undergrad and UT Austin for law school, where I was first in my class." Her education was the one thing she could still take some pride in.

The judge nodded like he'd expected her reply. "Yes, I remember you now, Jayna. Your momma was so proud of you. She said one day you'd come back and you'd help people like her, people who couldn't afford Quaid. But that was a long time ago."

She felt her skin warm, a flush of embarrassment running through her system. "I always meant to leave Papillon. I wanted to practice in a city. I worked in New Orleans for ten years. My mom knew I wanted a different experience."

"Well, that's the thing with mommas. They always have hope," the judge said. "I have six grandchildren. Four of them now live in either Houston or New Orleans. My young-est grandson is in the Navy and likely won't leave until he retires. Britney is the only one who stayed, and she's a sweet girl. Not the brightest, though. She barely made it through court reporting school, and sometimes I swear she loses track and makes stuff up. But she needed a job and she stayed here. So many of our bright young people leave us behind. It's why a town like ours never changes. The people who could change things in Papillon for the better go to a city where they have a much harder time having their voices be heard. It's a small town's catch-22. I suspect you're lick-ing your wounds and once you feel strong enough, you'll head right back to the city. Divorce?"

All right. The judge was smarter than she was giving him credit for. "Yes, I recently got divorced."

Divorce seemed like the right word. Divorced from her husband, from her job, from her life.

Exile was a good word, too. She'd been exiled from the life she'd built.

"Well, you're a smart young woman who will likely bounce back quickly, and when you're out in the big city playing by all those rules and getting everyone wrapped in red tape because their lives are so busy and important, Quaid will still be here taking care of the people of this par-ish. He'll still be trying his best to settle some of the most ridiculous arguments you've ever heard and doing it all with goodwill toward everyone. So we're going to wait for him because he would do the same for us." The judge looked up as the door to the courtroom opened again and his grand-daughter charged through with a bright grin on her face.

"We found colored markers," she announced.

"Are they permanent? Because that's a dry-erase board, darlin'," the judge said.

Britney's eyes widened. "Is that bad?"

The judge sighed. "Yes. You can't erase the permanent markers. I'll see if I can find the right ones. Maybe you should grab a snack, Ms. Cardet."

Maybe she should go grab the tardy opposing counsel. "Sure. That sounds great, Your Honor."

Geraldine shifted, her mouth coming open as she began to snore like a water buffalo.

Jayna straightened the blazer she wore and strode out.

It was time to let Quaid Havery know he wasn't the only game in town anymore.

"He's not telling you the truth," Gwen Mallory-Giles insisted. "My mom wanted me to have them."

Stephen Mallory shook a finger his sister's way. "She wanted me to have them. You ignore them. You don't pay a bit of attention to them and you never did."

There were days when Quaid Havery wished his father had been a doctor. A surgeon, perhaps, the kind who spent five minutes talking to a patient and then another two explaining how the surgery went. The rest of the time would be spent in blissful silence.

If his father had been a surgeon, Quaid would have dutifully followed in his footsteps and then he wouldn't be listening to a couple of ornery septuagenarians arguing over a collection of antique dolls.

Unfortunately, he was a lawyer, and he'd been the one to write the last will and testament of one Imogene Louisa Mallory, who had been very specific about every aspect of her estate with one exception.

Some really creepy dolls. There were four of them, and until he managed to negotiate a truce between the siblings, the dolls lived in his office and probably attracted the absolute worst karma because they were obviously cursed.

"Have we considered splitting up the dolls? There are four of them. You could each have two," Quaid offered.

Both siblings gasped as though he'd offered to murder them and post the video online.

"You can't separate them," Gwen sputtered. "How could you even suggest such a thing? What is wrong with you, Quaid Havery? Your daddy would never have thought to do something so heartless."

This was why his daddy had taught him to keep a bottle of Scotch in his desk. "I would never want to be heartless. I can, however, be very ignorant. Why exactly can't we split up the dolls?"

"They are a set," Stephen insisted. "What you are looking at is a perfectly kept set of Loveland Dolls created in the early twentieth century and painstakingly handcrafted by Idella Loveland. She is considered a master."

Of the dark arts, perhaps. He would believe that. He wanted to ask if Idella had maybe channeled any evil deeds she'd done into those dolls, but he knew better than to ask about the religious practices of his clientele. That tended to open doors he didn't want to walk through.

"Momma always told us you can't separate them. They would be lonely," Gwen insisted. "Carmen keeps everyone's spirits up while Justine is the pragmatic one. Shelby, well, they couldn't get on without Shelby."

"And Laurelin is the heart of the sisters," Stephen said with a smile. "She's the one who got them all through the war, you know."

Gwen turned to her brother, a fond smile on her face. "Oh, I remember that. Momma used to tell us the best stories about the sisters."

Stephen dabbed at his eyes. "When our daddy was deployed, we would be scared sometimes at night, but Momma would tell us stories about the dolls and how they would watch over us."

Quaid wouldn't be able to sleep if those damn dolls were in the room with him, but he had to be tolerant. They obviously meant a lot to the siblings.

Gwen had married but was now widowed. Stephen had never married. Neither had children.

What they had were those dolls.

"Have you considered what you're going to do with the house?" A plan was playing around in his head. The siblings had argued over their mother for years before her death, with Gwen insisting that Stephen wasn't taking good enough care of her. Gwen hadn't lived in the house with her mother. The majority of their mother's care had been provided by her brother.

Was Gwen too proud to ask for what she wanted?

Stephen frowned. "Well, it's my home. I wasn't going to do anything with it."

"It's half mine," Gwen pointed out. "Momma left me half of everything, including the house. How are you planning on giving me half the house, Stephen? Have you thought about that at all?"

"You want me to sell it?" Stephen had gone pale at the thought. "We grew up in that home. I've lived in it all my life. I can't sell it and go live in some apartment. What would I do with the cats? I don't think those sad apartments will accept ten cats. Mittens is eighteen years old. She can't handle a shelter. You are killing Mittens, you mean old crone."

Gwen's eyes went wide. "How dare you."

He needed to shut this down and fast. "What if Gwen moved home to help you with the cats? I imagine Mittens requires a lot of care."

Stephen seemed taken aback at the suggestion. "Well, yes. Yes, she does. She's on seven separate medications and needs a special diet. I have to make sure the others don't get in her food. They can be a jealous lot, you know."

"Noodles has always wanted anything Mittens has," Gwen said with a shake of her head. "That one is a handful, and Momma always told me that Sandy and Sparkles should never be left alone together. It must be hard taking care of them all on your own."

"Well, I could use some help," he admitted. "But I know how much you love your house."

Gwen shrugged. "It's a lot to take care of since Tom died. It's awfully quiet."

Quaid was so close to the finish line. He could taste it. He might even be able to fit some writing in before he was due in court if he could get them out of here soon. "You know, you could avoid a lot of problems if Gwen moves in with you, Stephen. You wouldn't have to sell the place to give Gwen half the money. The cats would get to stay in the only home they've ever known. The dolls could stay in their cases. You could maybe even write down those stories about the dolls if you helped each other out."

Gwen's expression went dreamy. "Oh, I always thought those stories Momma told would make a wonderful book."

"We could photograph the dolls so everyone would see how lovely they are." Stephen reached for his sister's hand. "I'm sorry we've been estranged. I've missed you, sister."

Yes, he might get to finish that chapter if they left right now. He was already planning his hero's next steps when he heard the bell on the office ring, and winced.

"I've missed you, too." Gwen squeezed his hand. "Let's go to the café and talk about this. Quaid, you're a good boy, like your daddy. We'll come back for the dolls. You take good care of them."

He let out a sigh of relief. The bell had probably been his secretary coming back from her coffee run.

He could write away for the next . . .

Quaid got a good look at the time and realized he was late. So late.

He reached for his briefcase as the door to his office came open. "Cindy, you were supposed to tell me . . ."

That wasn't Cindy standing in his doorway. No. The woman there didn't at all resemble his sixty-five-year-old legal secretary who wore bulky cardigans even in the heat of summer because she weighed about ninety-five pounds soaking wet and was always cold.

This woman wasn't close to cold. She was hot.

Dark hair cut in a chic bob that brushed her jawline. Pouty, perfect scarlet lips and dark eyes that seemed to zero in on him. She was dressed in a designer suit and some killer heels. That suit had been tailored to show off her every curve.

His writing could wait. Court could wait. The world could wait.

Please don't let her be a client.

"How can I help you?"

Those gorgeous eyes of hers narrowed. "You could have helped me by showing up in court on time." She glanced down at her watch. "Which was thirty minutes ago."

Not a client, but there was no question the woman was irritated. However, he could be quite charming when he wanted to be. "It's all right. The judge is very tolerant, and I think he has his yearly physical today so he'll try to draw things out. It won't work. I heard his wife telling Lila LaVigne to do the whole physical in his office if he doesn't show up. Are you Geraldine's niece? You should understand . . ."

He'd been ready to tell her he already had a plan in place to help Geraldine out since he was absolutely winning this case, but she interrupted him.

"I am Geraldine's attorney, and we would like the courtesy of your presence in court since the judge won't do what he should and give us a directed verdict." Her arms folded across her chest, that glorious mouth of hers turning down into a frown.

That frown should have shut down his libido, but it did not. He kind of liked the thrum that was starting in his system. His life had become a boring cycle of work and family obligations, and a never-ending string of rejections when it came to the one thing he truly loved. This woman had him excited for the first time in years. "Geraldine hired herself an attorney. Now, that I wasn't expecting. Where on earth did she find you? Houma? I know all three attorneys there. Did she go all the way to New Orleans?"

"I live here for now, though I did practice in New Orleans for years," the woman said and then her expression changed, eyes widening. "Dare I ask why you have not one or two, but four Annabelle dolls? There is no way those aren't haunted, and I'm not even a person who believes in those things."

She might be the only woman in Louisiana who didn't. He gestured toward the dolls. "They're part of an estate I'm the executor of. I think I've settled that problem." He needed to get the court thing out of the way so he could ask this woman out. She was new in town, and there were a bunch of men who would take one look at her and try to pounce. He'd like to pounce first and see if this insane attraction led somewhere. He started for the door, briefcase in hand. "I was in a negotiating session over those dolls, and that's why I'm late for court. I'm Quaid, by the way."

He heard the *click-clack* of her heels on the hardwood floors of his office as she followed him. "You don't know who I am, do you?"

He held the door open for her. "I assure you I would remember if we met before."

Her eyes were narrow again, her short hair curling on her cheek as she snapped her head around to glare his way. "I'll take that bet, Quaid."

She didn't wait for him as she took off down the sidewalk toward the courthouse.

Had he met her before? He would remember this gorgeous woman. He definitely hadn't slept with her. He would remember that.

He jogged to catch up with her. "All right, I'm sorry I don't recall where we met. Were we in law school together?"

"No, Quaid. We didn't have a random class together." She could motor in those heels.

"I don't practice much outside of Papillon, so I don't think we've faced each other in court." He was racking his brain to figure out how he was supposed to know her and why she was so irritated with him. Even when he won a case, he was polite about it. He wasn't one of those preening jackasses who felt the need to lord his victory over the opposition. Not that he usually faced opposition in court.

She strode up the steps to the courthouse, and he would bet she spent a lot of time in the gym. He was getting the slightest bit winded keeping up with her.

"My name is Jayna Cardet."

He did know that last name. "Are you one of Sienna's cousins?"

That would explain the law degree. That family needed a lot of legal representation of the criminal defense kind.

Jayna reached the top of the steps and turned on him. "I'm her sister, and we literally went to high school together. I'm the only reason you passed French."

He felt his jaw drop. "No. I'm pretty sure that girl's name was June and she was . . ."

He'd been about to say June the tutor was a total nerd, but her skin had taken on a level of red that was a warning to any man that he'd stepped on a land mine and it was about to explode and take his balls with it.

"What, Quaid? June—which is not and has never been my name—was what?" Her hand was on her hip, eyes staring him down.

Again, he should not be this attracted to a woman who looked like she would strike him down with a bolt of lightning if she possessed that particular superpower. "I was going to say she was a very nice girl who helped me so much. I'm sorry, Jayna. You don't look like you did then. You've grown up."

"Well, you look exactly like the same douchebag high school lothario you always were." She turned again. "Let's get this over with. I expect your client to pay for all my client's pain and suffering."

He followed her as she walked into the courthouse, not bothering to look back to see if he was keeping up. "Pain and suffering? My client took down a tree that was clearly on his property. He had every right. That tree was outside Geraldine's fence."

"But her fence was built a foot back from where her property line ends," Jayna replied, not missing a beat. She turned down the hallway that would lead them to one of two courtrooms. Someone had been optimistic when they'd designed the building. "So the tree was her property."

Did she honestly believe he hadn't studied this? She was absolutely giving him big-city lawyer vibes. They always underestimated him. They saw that he was the conservator for haunted dolls and elderly felines and decided he wasn't up to snuff. Quaid jogged in front of her, getting to the door and opening it like the gentleman he was. "You're right. Let's get this over with."

They had gotten off on the wrong foot. He needed more

information because he hadn't heard the name Jayna Cardet in so many years he'd forgotten it, and that was a mistake.

"Is there an *e*?" Britney asked.

Britney had obviously talked her grandpa into passing the time with a game of Hangman, and Quaid would bet not one of the people in the courtroom saw the irony in that.

The bailiff dutifully placed two *e*'s on the board, and Britney clapped her hands.

A low growl of frustration came off Jayna as she approached the front of the courtroom.

She'd been away from Papillon for way too long if she let something like this get to her. Luckily, he could wrap this up very quickly.

"Your Honor, I'm so sorry I'm late. I was dealing with Imogene Mallory's estate. Her heirs showed up at my office a couple of hours ago and I lost track of time," Quaid explained, taking his place behind the defense table.

The judge set the white board down as Britney dutifully took her place behind the stenotype. "Not a problem at all, Quaid. Were they fighting about those creepy dolls Imogene kept? Or was it the cats?"

"It was the dolls. We have it all figured out now. Gwen is going to move back home so the dolls and the cats stay together," Quaid explained.

"Excellent," the judge said. "Now tell me what this case is about."

"You didn't read the suit I filed?" Jayna stood beside her sleeping client.

Geraldine was getting up in years. She needed her naps.

The judge held up the legal papers that had been given to him. "I glanced through it. Give me the short version."

Jayna's shoulders went back, her chin coming up. "My client's quality of life was damaged when the defendant,

Mr. Abbot, took down a tree that is clearly on her property. Mr. Abbot owns a gas station behind her home, and now the glare from the back lights flood her house every night. It keeps her awake, and quite frankly, my client doesn't have the money to put up a tall enough fence to block out the light. I also believe the fact that you can now watch people pumping gas from my client's backyard has eroded her property value. We ask for a judgment against the defendant of one hundred thousand dollars."

"I don't have a thousand dollars, much less a hundred thousand," Abbot said, a faint whine in his voice.

It took all Quaid had not to roll his eyes. The city slicker was in town, and she thought she could roll over all the bumpkins. She was arrogant, and yet he still wanted to get to know her.

But first she needed to understand he wasn't someone she could steamroll with her gorgeous looks and obvious intelligence. He pulled out his ace in the hole. "Your Honor, before Jimmy Abbot took down the tree, he informed Geraldine he was going to do it. Here is a copy of the letter my client sent along with an explanation and the proof that while the tree is partially on Geraldine's property, the majority of the roots of the tree are on his. I measured it. The trunk and visible roots measure twelve feet around, and nine of those are clearly on the gas station property."

"The tree was partially hers and shouldn't have been taken down." Jayna frowned his way before turning to the judge. "And if Mr. Abbot sent a letter, my client doesn't remember. She's elderly, and he's taking advantage of her."

"I bring her lunch every day," Abbot argued. "I treat her like she's my grandma. Those roots were starting to crack the pavement of the parking lot. Can't she close the curtains?"

"She doesn't have blackout drapes," Jayna replied. "And

honestly, she shouldn't need them because she didn't agree to the tree being taken down."

"She doesn't have to agree. This is decided law, Your Honor. As per *Hollister v. Klein*, whoever owns the majority of the base of the tree makes the final decisions about the tree," Quaid explained. "You yourself made that judgment in 1995."

The judge nodded solemnly. "Yes, I did, and it led to a feud that lasted twenty years."

Abbot stood. "Geraldine don't have twenty years left in her, and I won't feud with any of her kin. I will pay for her blackout curtains. I'll even take her to the Walmart and let her pick them out herself."

"Ooo, can I get some new pillows, too?" Geraldine had magically awakened at this opportune moment. "And I need a few other things for around the house."

Abbot sighed, a deeply relieved sound. "Of course. Miss Geraldine, you didn't need to hire a lawyer. I would have worked this all out with you. I was shocked when I got served with that lawsuit."

Geraldine stood, stretching and then patting down her helmet of steel gray hair. "Well, this young lady here seemed to need some work. I don't know. She talked real fast, Jimmy, and I get lonely at times. But that light is terrible. It's so very bright at all hours of the night."

"Excellent. Then my judgment is for the defense." The judge struck his gavel and stood. "Now, I'm going to hide, and we'll say this took far longer than it did."

Britney was right on top of that. "PawPaw, I can't let you do that. I'm supposed to take you down to Lila's. I'm way more afraid of MawMaw than I am you."

The Brewer family started arguing while Geraldine made her way to Jimmy Abbot, already talking about what a magical place the Houma Walmart was. Jayna Cardet simply stared as though trying to process how her life had taken this turn.

"Hey, why don't we go over to the café? I'm sorry I didn't recognize you, but if you're going to practice here in Papillon, we should probably talk."

"I didn't even get to argue my case." She took the thick file in front of her and shoved it into her Prada bag. "And I'm pretty sure my client intends to pay me in gumbo."

That sounded about right. "There's not a lot of money here, but it can be fun."

She frowned at him. It seemed to be a theme with her. "You seem to be doing fine, Mr. Havery."

"Only because I'm the only lawyer in town and I represent the largest businesses in the area. I've got more work than I can handle," he offered. "Why don't you tell me about yourself and maybe I can hand some of that work over to you."

"I don't need charity." She slung her oversized bag over her shoulder. "I can find my own clients. In fact, I think you'll discover we'll be right back here in no time, and I won't lose again. Good day, Mr. Havery."

"It's Quaid," he called out as she walked away.

He was deeply looking forward to their next encounter.

chapter two

He hadn't even remembered her name.

Jayna sat on the lawn chair on her mom's porch as the sun began to go down. It was a ratty piece of furniture that would likely collapse within the next thirty minutes, but her mother never replaced a thing until it died. She was pretty sure these chairs had been around when she was a child.

Something soft rubbed against her leg and when she glanced down Luna was looking up at her with worshipful eyes. She was pretty sure Luna was the only creature in the world who would ever give her that look again.

She'd paid through the nose to keep custody of that white fluffball. If she'd pressed the issue, she might have gotten half the house, but she'd lost so damn much already, she couldn't lose Luna, too.

The door to the trailer across the way opened and there came another reminder of her childhood here. Her sister stepped out, a trash bag in her hand. From inside she could hear the sounds of giggling children and cartoons playing.

Sienna still wore her Dixie's Café T-shirt from her earlier shift and her hair was up in a high ponytail, her blond tresses bouncing as she crossed the space between her single-wide and their mom's.

Once, she'd felt sympathy for Sienna because she'd never made it out of the trailer park they'd grown up in. Now she kind of envied her sister, because at least she had her own single-wide. Jayna was right back in her old room, in her old bed. On her old mattress that had already been uncomfortable when she was fifteen.

She bet Quaid Havery's bed was comfortable. And probably full.

"Hey, I'm going to make the kids some mac and cheese for dinner. Momma's got the late shift tonight. You want to join us?" Sienna asked, dumping the bag into the can.

Did Jayna want to eat boxed mac and cheese with a couple of grubby kids? "Sure."

Her nieces weren't awful. They were kind of cute. Kelly was a chaotic mess who made her laugh, and Ivy reminded her of herself at that age. She was quiet and liked to read.

Sienna glanced down at the beer in Jayna's hand. "Is that a celebratory beer, or an 'I got my ass kicked in court' kind of beer?"

She sighed and sat back, hoping the chair had another couple of days in it. "It wasn't an ass kicking. It was the weirdest trial I've ever been through. The judge played Hangman while we were waiting on Quaid Havery to finish negotiating a custody agreement for dolls. Or maybe it was cats. I'm not sure."

"Oh, it was both," Sienna said with a nod. "The Mallory twins came into the café and they were talking about those creepy dolls their momma collected and how now that she's gone, they have to take care of them. And then they told me about all those cats and how there was something about them being jealous and seeking revenge for one of them getting better food than the others. I don't know. I just wanted to take their order. I also heard that Britney Brewer chased her granddad all the way to the clinic."

"Yeah, he wasn't looking forward to his yearly physical." It had been an odd, unsettling day. "I should have won that case. Instead my client gave up the whole thing for some curtains and a trip into Houma. And I spent weeks prepping and I'm probably being paid in gumbo."

Sienna's nose wrinkled. "Oh, you should have negotiated better. I'm afraid Geraldine isn't such a great cook anymore. She gets her salt and sugar mixed up. You should have had her knit you a sweater or something."

"I was hoping for some cash." But it wasn't like she'd pressed the old lady. "Well, and I was hoping to get the word out that there's another lawyer in town. It seems like Quaid Havery plays fast and loose with everyone."

"I wouldn't say that." Sienna sat down on the top step. "He's good to the people of this town."

It wasn't so surprising that Sienna would take an optimistic view. Jayna had another perspective. "He represents all the rich people, exactly like his dad did. When he negotiates with a person and that person doesn't have legal counsel, he's not watching out for them. He's getting his client the best deal possible. It's not ethical."

"I don't know about that. He's a good guy. You know he went with our aunt to help cousin Pete when he got arrested for selling weed," Sienna offered.

"For allegedly selling weed. He hasn't been convicted yet," Jayna pointed out. She hadn't even known Pete had been in trouble until she'd come home.

"Well, everyone knows he was selling weed. He was growing it in the backyard."

"Allegedly."

"Aunt Opal tried to burn that alleged weed and she was high as a damn kite because she stood out there with a hose trying to monitor the perimeter to make sure she didn't start a forest fire, as she called it," Sienna explained. "We had to take her to the nurse, but Lila said we should just feed her a bunch of French fries and tacos and she would be fine in the morning. My point is, Quaid went down to the jail with her and helped her get Pete out on bail, and he didn't charge her a dime since she didn't have one to give him. He's not a bad man. He's doing what all of us are."

"And what's that?"

"What he can," Sienna said with a sigh, and then there was a sparkle in her eyes. "How did he take you showing up in court looking all fine and stuff?"

Jayna took another swig of the very cheap beer her mom kept around the house for guests. Her mom wasn't much of a drinker, but she preferred sweet strawberry wine to beer. It hadn't seemed like a strawberry wine kind of day to Jayna. "He didn't know who I was."

"Oh," her sister said, eyes widening. "Well, you do look different. No one's seen you in years, so they remember you as you were in high school. You changed pretty much everything about yourself since then."

That was not true. "I dyed my hair. I didn't get into a *Face/Off* machine."

"You dropped a lot of weight."

"I exercised," she countered. She'd dropped about thirty pounds in law school when she'd discovered how much she liked to jog and work out. It cleared her head and gave her time to think. "Again, no surgery for me. Not even Botox, even though my rat-fink ex suggested I start what he called 'a regime.'"

"Todd wanted you to get plastic surgery?" Sienna asked with a gasp.

Jayna sighed. "Not exactly. He thought we should both start taking better care of ourselves, and one of his suggestions was erasing my frown lines. Apparently I have a lot of them."

"You do not. You are perfectly gorgeous," Sienna said. "Our roles are reversed. I know I was kind of the pretty one when we were young. At least that's what people said. I always thought you were prettier."

Her sister was a freaking saint, and it made her feel guilty that she ever thought bad things about her. And that she'd stayed away for so many years. It wasn't like Sienna hadn't come to see her, but she'd forced her sister and her mom to make the long drive to New Orleans every year because she'd never allowed Todd to see where she'd grown up.

She moved to the top step to sit beside her sister. "Everyone adores you and you're stunning. That's what I hear when they realize I'm your sister. *Sienna is a bright light in all the darkest night* and some shit."

Sienna snorted and grabbed Jayna's beer, taking a sip. "They do not."

"They do, too." She wasn't about to let Sienna get all maudlin. That was Jayna's job, and she wasn't giving it up anytime soon. "The judge practically glowed when he talked about how wonderful you are. He didn't remember me, either."

"That's because I sneak him an extra piece of bacon every now and then," Sienna admitted. "It's probably a sin. I know the man has a cholesterol problem, but he tips well. I'm sorry Quaid didn't remember you. I know you had a little crush on him."

A little? Quaid Havery had been the most beautiful boy in the world, and when he'd focused in on her she'd felt like the center of the universe. Of course, now she understood that it was all charm and he likely pulled that crap on everyone he met. "He thought my name was June."

Sienna passed her the beer back. "Well, it's been a long time."

"You know, I didn't think anyone was here missing me or anything, but it would have been nice if someone remembered who I was," she admitted. "I guess the people who would have remembered me are somewhere else now."

She'd been thinking about what the judge had said. All the smart, ambitious kids left, and Papillon stayed the same.

Although sometimes the smart, ambitious kids took a wrong turn and wound up right back where they started.

"Do you want to sit around the dinner table and talk about how to kill Todd Shale? I've watched a lot of *Dateline*, and I think I know how to avoid the pitfalls. We need to lure him out here and then we'll feed his ass to Otis and no one will ever know," Sienna offered.

Her sister knew the whole story around her divorce. It wasn't a pretty one. It had started with a flare of conscience that led to Jayna losing damn near everything but her dog and a wardrobe that didn't fit into her new life. "No. I knew who he was when I married him. I didn't love Todd. I thought we would make good partners. And we did, right up until I became slightly inconvenient."

"Well, hell. I loved both of my exes and it all ended the same way, so maybe Granny was right and we're cursed," Sienna said with a sigh. "I don't have real good taste in men. I think the new deputy is cute, so I'm staying far away from the man because if I like him, he's got to be bad news. I switch tables with whoever is working with me when he sits at mine. No way. No how. I am not going there again."

That was news. "You like the deputy?"

Sienna shrugged. "I just think he's cute. Like I said, I'm not going to get to know the man. I'm done with all that. It's me and my girls now."

Sienna was living their mother's life. Her whole world would be her family and that job at the café where she was on her feet eight to ten hours a day and beholden to tourists for tips. Her girls would grow up and there would be no money for college if they couldn't get scholarships or take on a godawful amount of student loan debt. Instead, they would find jobs and promise themselves they would save money and go to school next year and oops, they were pregnant and the cycle started all over again.

"I don't think I'll be able to work in New Orleans after everything that happened." She had to be practical.

"But you were doing the right thing. I don't understand," Sienna replied.

"I know. The legal world is not black and white. What I did when I turned my client in was technically legal." She didn't like to think about the case that had ended her marriage and career. "But no one wants to touch me. I'm still embroiled in various ethics complaints, and until I clear those up, I don't think I'm going to find a firm willing to take me on."

"How long do you think that's going to take?"

It could be years, but she wasn't willing to admit that to herself yet. "A couple of months, hopefully. Six, tops. I was thinking I could help out around here in the meantime."

"Help like you did with Geraldine?"

"Yeah, I know it's a small town, but the area around it is pretty big. I would bet the public defender comes from at least an hour away." She'd been thinking about this for a while now. She couldn't sit in her momma's trailer until she found a new job. She had to make a job for herself. "I would need to find clients and rent some office space. I'm not sure I can afford that, though."

Sienna's eyes lit up. "No. You don't need an office. You need to be in the place where everyone can find you, where all the gossip flows. Where a person who hears every sad-sack story in town can direct potential clients to you. Though you should know I'm going to expect at least ten percent of that gumbo."

"I thought you said it was awful."

"Ten percent of awful is still ten percent," Sienna pointed out. "If we can get money, we'll take it, but I know how to work this system way better than you. You be the brains, sister, and I'll handle negotiating payment."

"I don't know."

Sienna turned her way and there was a hint of desperation in her sister's expression. "I want you to give me a chance, Jayna. I know everyone thinks I'm just working until I find a new husband. They throw men at me all the time, but I really am done. The trouble is I can't find anything beyond waitressing and taking odd jobs. I need a chance at doing something that might give me some experience I can put on a résumé to get a better job."

Jayna's chest suddenly felt too tight. Somehow she'd thought Sienna was okay with her lot in life. Sienna never complained, never faced the day without a bright smile on her face.

Because that was what she'd been taught. That was her place in the family. In some ways she'd had to be that way, because Jayna was the rebel.

"You want to try to handle the business end of my job?" She kept the question simple, trying not to make a big deal out of the emotional moment they were having. Her sister was asking her for help.

"I do." Sienna nodded.

"Well okay, then," said Jayna.

The look on her sister's face softened as though she was content with having a chance to prove herself. Jayna could start applying for corporate jobs again in a few months, and until then, make some money working in Papillon. That money would help her sister, too. It was time for Jayna to admit that she was stuck here for the time being.

It would also be great to eviscerate Quaid Havery in court. She simply needed the right case.

When she left town again, maybe her sister would be in a better position.

And that man would remember her name. "You've got a deal."

Quaid was still thinking about that gorgeous, irritable woman who'd stormed into his life as he made the drive back to the big house he'd grown up in.

"Quaid, are you there?"

Unfortunately, he was also on the phone with one of his best friends and longtime clients, Rene Darois. "Of course. I'll get that contract to you tomorrow."

Luckily he knew this particular deal backward and forward. Rene simply needed to talk before he made a big move, and all Quaid needed to do was listen. Well, absentmindedly listen.

A sigh came over the line. "I'm being annoying."

If there was anyone in the world who didn't annoy him, it was Rene. Rene was the only person in his life who truly understood what it meant to have the weight of a whole family on your shoulders. Rene had also had his path in life laid out for him at a young age. He'd taken over the company that had been in his family for decades, working in the position his father had held.

Quaid had often thought that Rene had the harder road since he'd had that massive family of his to look after and all Quaid had to deal with was his mother and younger brother. But then Paul had lost his damn mind and become harder to deal with than all of Rene's kooky aunts and uncles and cousins combined.

Rene's family just fought about money. Paul's demons were far more demanding, but he'd been in LA for the last two years and seemed to be doing well now. With the exception of holidays, he saw little of his brother, and that was how he liked it.

Rene, Armie, and Remy were his brothers. His friends had become his family.

"Not at all," Quaid replied. "You're being thorough, and I'm being distracted. Tell me something. Do you remember Sienna's younger sister? She was a year behind us in school."

"Jayna Cardet?" Rene asked.

"Why did I think her name was June?"

"No idea, since if I do recall, she was the one who got you through French," Rene replied. "She also had a big crush on you and you barely noticed she was there."

Damn. No wonder the woman had been irritable. "She's back in town and she's a lawyer. I faced her down in court today. I probably should have read whatever she sent over but I'm lazy when it comes to these cases. Honestly, I was surprised Geraldine sued. Jimmy always meant to get her some blackout shades. I think that woman convinced her to take this thing to court. Are you sure she had a thing for me?"

A chuckle came over the line. "I'm sure. She did half your homework for you and got that dopey, glazed look in her eyes anytime you walked in a room. I'm surprised you don't remember her. She was a whiz kid. I'm pretty sure she was the valedictorian of her class. She was the editor of the school paper and president of the debate team."

He hadn't paid attention to any of those things. High school had been a blissful time to play football and drink beer and date cheerleaders. He'd known his path. His place at Tulane had been assured by all the work his father had done for the school, and then he was on to Harvard Law, where he'd frozen his ass off for three years before coming home. High school had been his time. He hadn't bothered with things like extracurricular activities to pad his résumé in hopes of getting into a good school or looking attractive to a scholarship committee.

Yeah, he'd been an overly privileged asshole now that he thought about it. "Well, I didn't remember her and that is a mistake on my part."

"She looks good, doesn't she?" Rene asked. "She was at Guidry's the other day when Sylvie and I took my momma and Louis to dinner. She doesn't look like a down-on-her-luck divorcée."

"She's divorced?" That was some interesting information. "Do you know what happened?"

"How do you not know this?"

"How do you know it? You're not exactly the town gossip."

"I suppose I spend more time in New Orleans than you do." Rene's company had an office there. "It was something of a story about six months ago. She was involved with some client who ended up going to jail when she turned him in. I'm not sure what she turned him in for, but it was a bit of a scandal."

"Yes, it would be." He wanted to know the rest of that story. "Attorney-client privilege is the holy grail in our world. The client would have to have done something criminal. Her firm fired her?"

"Yes, and from what I understand, she was married to the son of the head of the firm. He divorced her, and I think she's being blackballed. She couldn't find a job in New Orleans so now she's back at her momma's," Rene explained. "Sylvie's thinking of hiring her to do some city work."

Quaid winced. "Yeah, I'm sorry I haven't gotten to that yet."

"We know how hard you work, and the parish doesn't

pay much. As your biggest client I certainly appreciate you prioritizing me, but Sylvie wouldn't hate having someone who could work faster."

Rene's wife was the mayor and one of the smartest people he knew.

"Give it to Jayna. I'm fairly certain she won't get anything like cash out of Geraldine, and if she's living with her momma, she's in that trailer park." The thought hurt his heart. She'd been magnificent in her designer suit and heels. A goddess in Louboutins.

How much of a blow to her pride had it been to come home?

He wanted her whole story. Preferably told to him after he'd gotten her into bed and given her a couple of orgasms. Then they could lie there, well-satisfied, and she could tell him how her life had gone off the rails.

The fact that he was as interested in the story as he was the sex was likely a sign of his impending old age.

"I'll let Sylvie know." There was a pause over the line. "Do you want me to get a report on her?"

Rene had a couple of private investigators on his payroll who could get him every bit of information on Jayna Cardet that he could ever want.

"No." He wasn't going to invade her privacy. He wanted the story from her, and only when she was ready to give it to him. "Don't sic your PIs on her. If she's still practicing, then what she did wasn't a disbarrable offense. I suspect she did the right thing and it cost her firm money, so she got the boot. Do you know the name of the husband?"

Rene paused for a moment. "I want to say it was Todd something."

Quaid groaned. "Shale. Todd Shale's father runs one of the biggest corporate firms in New Orleans. I would bet a lot that's who we're talking about. He's also a nasty piece of work. If he's been married up until recently, he's also had a girlfriend on the side because he was with a woman at the last conference I went to, and it wasn't Jayna."

The woman had been a blonde and looked to be barely twenty years old. She hadn't held a candle to the magnificent creature who'd looked like she'd wanted to claw his eyes out earlier today.

"You sound like you're already invested in this woman," Rene pointed out. "I hope you didn't admit to her you couldn't remember who she was. Please tell me you didn't."

"I wish I could." He wished he could take back more than just that. Including the fact that she'd caught him with demonic dolls in his office. "It gets worse. I kept her waiting in court and then had a judgment for my client within ten minutes of walking into the place. Then I asked her out. She turned me down."

"How surprising. Well, I don't suspect she'll be here all that long. Jayna was one of those kids who left and almost never came home after she went to college. She wanted out of Papillon."

And now she was home and was trying to find something to do while she put her life back together. He could understand that. "I can be her rebound guy."

Rene snorted over the line. "You're too old to play these games. You're not twenty-five anymore."

He knew that. All of his friends were married with kids, and it wasn't that he didn't want a family. He'd just never found the right woman. "Well, even if she is my dream woman, she didn't walk back into town to stay, so I have to take comfort where I can. And Jayna Cardet looks like she could use some comfort, too. I see no reason why we can't comfort each other while she's here. And if she can take some work off my plate, I might have a chance to look for someone who can come in and help me."

"I've been telling you to bring someone in for years," Rene said with a sigh. "Good luck with Jayna."

Quaid pulled down the long driveway that led to the big, Creole-style house his grandfather had built back in the thirties when he'd settled here in Papillon. That house represented all of his family's happiness and prosperity and all the backbreaking responsibility that came with it. "I'm going to need it. Talk to you later."

Luck wasn't something he'd had a ton of lately. Quaid hung up and he could fully concentrate on driving down the paved road that took him home.

His heroine had long hair, but suddenly that didn't make a ton of sense. She was a spy. Short hair was probably better to have in a fight. He could give her a fashionable bob, one that drew a man's eyes right to her lovely lips.

If he was lucky, his mom had some function to go to this evening. If she wasn't around, he could eat dinner in front of his computer without his mother giving him grief about working through a meal. Of course, once she realized he was working on his latest novel, the grief wouldn't end.

Why on earth would you waste your days away in some fictional world, Quaid? You've been given everything you need to have an amazing life. Why subject yourself to rejection? You're a lawyer, not a writer.

He would reply by telling her half the time he lied for a living anyway, so didn't see the difference. Four finished novels and fifty-two rejections later, he had to think she might be right. Still, writing those books was the only thing that kept him sane sometimes.

He realized his luck wasn't running any better when he saw the Porsche in the driveway.

He didn't know anyone who would drive a Porsche around Papillon with the singular exception of the one person he didn't want to see.

The front door opened and his mother waved from the porch. "Quaid! Quaid, come inside. Your brother's home!"

Paul stepped out next to their mother. His brother had dropped weight. His elegant clothes now looked slightly too big for his lanky frame, but he was sure his brother still did well with the ladies. He'd gone to LA to pursue a modeling and acting career. At least that's what he'd said. Quaid had always thought what his brother was pursuing was an easier way to get high.

It was a cycle with his brother. He got some money and times were good for a while, then the money ran out and he came home.

Quaid's gut tightened. The last time his brother had come into some money was when he'd gotten access to his trust fund at the age of twenty-five. That had been five years before.

Had his brother run through ten million dollars in five years?

He might have bigger problems than seducing Jayna Cardet.

chapter three

⌒

Four days later, Quaid sat at the breakfast table, and still had zero idea why his brother was truly there.

After that first night Paul had been home, Quaid had been called away to New Orleans to deal with a problem at Beaumont Oil's headquarters. The company was his second-biggest client, and the issue had been over drilling rights. He'd spent several nights at Rene's house in the Quarter poring over international law and making calls to experts.

He'd solved the problem, but he was irritable since he was running on very little sleep and hadn't had a second to write or read or even watch an episode of television. The last thing he needed was his brother's bullshit, and he was getting a big dose of that this morning.

"I was at this party with one of the biggest producers in Hollywood and he tells me the problem is I'm too handsome. Every director is trying to go a more natural route," Paul was saying.

Their mother shook her head. "That's not right. Movie stars have always been attractive. It's one of the reasons the movies are so enjoyable."

"Who wants to watch normal-looking people?" Paul

replied. "It's hard to find work when all the directors are looking for average-looking people. It's a real problem for me."

"Sure. All the movies I've seen lately are filled with average-looking people." Quaid took a long drink of the coffee Caroline had set in front of him. "We recently had a movie filmed here. Lots of ordinary-looking people."

They hadn't been. The two leads had been far too beautiful to play an aging small-town sheriff and his angry deputy daughter, but that was Hollywood. Of course, the actress who'd originally been set to play the daughter had dropped out to run off with one of Papillon's deputies.

Paul sat up straighter in his chair. "I'm good friends with the actress who played the daughter. Ally Pearson. Such a fun girl. We've gone out a couple of times."

His mother put a hand to her heart. "Really? She was such a sweet thing when she was here. Oh, I never imagined she was your girlfriend."

"Because she's not." His brother was full of crap, and he'd likely been filling their mother's head with it for days. He would butter her up with all kinds of stories of how close he was to breaking through, and then he would go in for the kill. He only needed some money—not much—and then when she gave it to him, he would disappear from their lives again, breaking his mother's heart. "You know her sister lives here. Ally is often in town. She's very friendly and I suspect she would bring her boyfriend with her. If she had one."

Paul sat back, the omelet on his plate untouched. "We're casual, not serious. We see each other at clubs and when we're out for dinner. You know I have to focus on my career."

"I'm sure you would. Again, if you had one." Quaid was well aware he sounded like his father.

"Quaid, don't be so rude to your brother. You know he's

in a tough business. It's not like being a lawyer," his mother admonished.

This was the other thing that happened when his brother came home. Suddenly Quaid had everything easy while Paul couldn't catch a break. "Yes, it's so easy to be a lawyer. It's easy to work sixty hours a week and be expected to handle every legal trouble this town has. I'm sure going on auditions is much more difficult."

"You have no idea, brother. You aren't the creative type so you don't understand rejection," his brother replied.

He wanted to reject his brother's face. "How much do you need, Paul?"

His mom gasped.

"I need a lot of things, brother." Paul took a sip of his coffee. "If you're talking about money, I don't need any. I've been careful with my trust fund, and I'm growing my investment portfolio."

"You never come home unless you need money or you're in legal trouble, so which is it?" Quaid didn't want to wait for the other shoe to drop. How many damn times had he been through this?

"Quaid, you stop this right now." His mother still had the same stare she'd used on them as children. "We are having a nice visit with your brother, and if you can't be civil then perhaps you shouldn't join us."

"Now, Mom, I don't want to cause trouble," Paul said, proving he was capable of acting when he wanted to. "Maybe I should cut this trip short."

And just like that, Quaid was in a corner again. This was what always happened. He needed to remove himself from the situation or he would end up being the bad guy. Again.

He pushed back from the table. "I think I'll head into the office."

"Quaid, maybe you should stay there until you can be nice to your brother," his mother said, her lips pursed.

There was no mention of how he was the one who took care of her, who ensured she maintained the standard of living his father had provided her with; no mention that this house literally belonged to him because he'd bought it from her and then let her stay in the same room she'd lived in for years. Nope. Paul was back and everyone had to cater to him or face her wrath.

Being the dependable one meant nothing.

Quaid stood. At least he had a ton of work to distract him. "Give me a call when it's all right for me to come home, Mom. Paul, don't give me a call at all."

He was feeling tired and mean as he started toward his bedroom. He would pack some clothes and simply take himself out of the equation. His office had a small apartment on the top floor. He would stay there for however long it took for Paul to get bored and ask for whatever he needed this time around.

"Quaid?" Caroline stopped him before he went upstairs. She moved toward him, rolling one of his suitcases along the way. "I packed it the night he came home. I'd hoped you wouldn't need it."

He sighed. This woman had taken care of their house since he was a kid. She'd been part-time mom and full-time friend. Caroline had been the one to give him his first science-fiction and thriller books, since his parents thought fiction was a waste of an intelligent man's time. He took the suitcase with the full knowledge that everything he would need would be in it and leaned over, brushing her cheek with an affectionate kiss. "Thank you, and call me when things go bad."

She nodded. "I will. Do you want me to make you a thermos of coffee?"

He shook his head, picking up his laptop bag. At least staying at the office meant he wouldn't have to entertain his mother and her friends, and he might get some writing in. Positivity. He was going to be positive. "Cindy will already have a pot on. I'll see you in a couple of days."

He walked out the door with a heavy feeling in his heart.

Twenty minutes later he was walking into the café across the square because Cindy, in fact, had not made a pot of coffee. That machine she had insisted on getting for the office was intensely complicated, and he couldn't handle it this morning. His legal secretary had left him a note reminding him that she was taking the month off to help with her new grandbaby. Her daughter had gone into labor early and now he was down a secretary, but he also seemed to be down a bunch of work.

The city project he'd intended to start was now off his plate, having moved to the new lawyer in town.

And three of the negotiations he'd had on the calendar had been canceled.

He intended to find out why after he had some coffee.

"Hey, Quaid." Dixie had owned the café for the last thirty years, and the menu never changed. "Come on in and find a seat. We're at a lull right now. You want your usual?"

His usual was coffee, egg whites, and turkey bacon with a side of whole grain toast. It seemed boring today, but he nodded anyway. "Sounds good."

The breakfast crowd had already left, so the café was pretty quiet. The lunch rush wouldn't start for another hour or so. It was nice. He could find a table and read through the stack of mail that had come in while he'd been in New Orleans.

Sienna Cardet walked out of the kitchen with a pot of

coffee in her hand. She took one look at him and her eyes widened in a deer-in-the-headlights way that made him worry he'd offended her. Or scared her.

"Hey, Sienna. How's your momma doing?" When in doubt, the Cajun boy always asked about family.

She seemed to think about that for a moment. "Great. Just great. Were you picking up an order? I can get that for you."

That was odd. He heard the bell announcing another customer but kept his attention on Jayna Cardet's sister. He'd been so busy the last couple of days, he'd almost forgotten about the new lawyer in town. He wondered if she was struggling with the legalities of the new park Sylvie wanted to build. Maybe he would ask her to dinner to talk it all over. "No. I was going to sit in the back and eat. Don't worry. Dixie already took my order. I'll find a booth."

Jimmy Abbot brushed past him with a nod. "Morning, Quaid. Hey, Sienna. I'm here for my appointment."

Sienna flushed but pointed toward the back of the café. "She's waiting for you."

Jimmy started for the booth Quaid had been planning on using, but now he saw it was taken. A woman sat at the table, her cap of glossy brown hair clearly visible over the seat. She turned slightly as Jimmy approached, and Quaid watched as she shook his hand and offered him the seat across from her.

"Sienna, is your sister holding office hours at the café?"

Sienna's jaw went tight. "She's just . . . you know . . . meeting people."

Oh, she was not, and suddenly the problems with Paul and his mother got shoved aside. It would be so much more fun to figure out what Jayna was doing. And with one of his clients.

He set down his files at a booth close enough to Jayna to eavesdrop, but far enough away to not arouse suspicion.

"She can't keep this up," Jimmy was complaining. "I did everything she wanted me to. I bought her blackout drapes, and when she said she wanted help with her hot tub, I fixed it. It's an aboveground tub she hasn't used in years. I helped fill it and made sure the chemicals were all right. I didn't know she was going to . . . It's too horrible. It's affecting my business."

Dixie placed a mug of coffee in front of him.

"How long has she been holding office hours here?" He asked the question in a whisper, a hint of a smile on his face.

"Oh, she's been here for three days. Every day from at least eight to two," Dixie replied. "I would kick her out, but Sienna asked politely, and it's not tourist season, so we've got the space. In a couple of weeks, though, she's going to need to find another office. You know, I practically forgot Sienna had a younger sister."

Yeah, apparently the younger Jayna had been a bit forgettable, but this Jayna was completely fascinating to him. Dixie promised him his food would be out soon and he went back to listening in.

"Well, it is her own property, Jimmy," Jayna was saying. "I believe that property line was used to your advantage in the last case."

"Well, I would have thought differently if I'd known what that tree was really hiding," Jimmy replied in a desperate tone. "She's got that thing on her raised deck. Everyone can see her. All of my customers are complaining. Well, almost all. I'm real worried about the ones who aren't."

Quaid was confused. Jimmy had been his client for years. He wasn't on retainer or anything, but Jimmy had always come to him when he had legal issues with the gas station. It was time to ask a couple of questions. He slid out of his booth and moved to theirs. "Hi there. Jimmy, is there a reason you didn't come to me? Ms. Cardet, you should know

Jimmy Abbot is my client. It's not proper for you to talk to him without his attorney present."

Jayna looked up at him, and she was every bit as gorgeous as he remembered. He'd nearly convinced himself that he'd been wrong about how good-looking she was. It had been a while since he'd had a girlfriend, and he'd decided it was his lonely state that made it seem like she was glowing.

Nope. Those lips turned up in a challenging smirk, and he was right back to nearly drooling.

"Mr. Havery, I think you'll find you've been fired. Mr. Abbot put me on retainer two days ago," she replied. "And I'm having a private meeting with my client. You should understand attorney-client privilege. If you don't, I can send you some materials to help educate you."

"I'm sorry, Quaid. She's way cheaper than you are. She's willing to do all the legal stuff in exchange for three free fill-ups a month," Jimmy said, an apologetic look on his face. "And from what I can tell, that car of hers won't last long, so I think I'm coming out on the good end of that bargain."

"And Cheetos." Sienna refilled her sister's mug. "Don't you forget, she gets free Cheetos and two slushies a week, and those slushies will be brought to her by my kids. But they're for her."

It was good to know Sienna's girls were getting something out of this deal. He turned to Jayna. "You dumped Geraldine?"

"Geraldine never paid up," Jayna replied. "No money. No gumbo. She has conveniently forgotten our agreement in the same fashion that she forgets her swimsuit during her new daily hot tub time."

Quaid snorted, the humor of the situation hitting him. He should have known that stubborn old lady would have her revenge. "Are you telling me Geraldine Oliver is skinny-dipping in broad daylight?"

"It's not right." Jimmy's eyes glistened with unshed tears. "No one's supposed to see that. I'm not sure which parts are which. They all hang so low."

Jayna's lips pursed. "I think you will find that my client has been traumatized by Ms. Oliver's flagrant violation of public decency laws."

"Well, I say good for Geraldine," Dixie said, putting a plate of food on Quaid's table. "That will teach you not to take down trees. The city code only allows eight-foot fences, and Geraldine's backyard was raised years ago because of flooding. You have to be a good neighbor, Jimmy Abbot. You didn't care when the lights from your station flooded into her backyard. Now the lights from Geraldine's boobs will flood yours."

It was good to know Dixie had an opinion.

"Oh, I have to get in on this. Consider me Geraldine's counsel. I could use some gumbo." What he could use was some more time across the aisle from Jayna. It would also be fun to argue this particular case in front of the judge.

"Did you hear the part where I didn't get the gumbo?" Jayna shot back.

"I'll take my chances." He grabbed his plate and stared at Jimmy. "I think you should let the lawyers handle it from here."

Jimmy practically ran out of the café.

"I had more to talk about with him." Jayna sighed and sat back, her hand on her mug.

"Now you can talk about it with me." He sat down across from Jayna with his food. When he glanced up from his plate, he saw Sienna was still standing there. "Has she eaten yet or is she surviving on coffee and her rage at the world?"

"I'm not hungry," Jayna insisted.

"Her stomach is growling loud enough to shake the booth, but she doesn't have a deal with the diner for free food." Sienna seemed far chattier now that Quaid was aware of the new business arrangements.

"I'll pick up the tab. It's the least I can do for all the help with high school French," he offered. "And I'm feeling like something sweet. Are there any cinnamon rolls left?"

"I'll take one, too," Jayna said. "And some pancakes and bacon. And grits, but only if she still puts cheese in them."

Oh, she wasn't going to be a cheap date, but he liked that. Not that he would do anything at all to imply that this might kind of, sort of, be a date, because she would almost assuredly turn him down. After she'd eaten the free breakfast.

"I'll get that going for you," Sienna promised.

Quaid had his appetite back. "Now let's talk about how to get Geraldine in her swimsuit."

Her stomach was pleasantly full of yummy sugar and carbs and bacon she would never have touched a couple of months before. She would have to add another mile to her jog, but she hadn't been able to resist some comfort food this morning. Especially when Quaid Havery was paying.

She wished the man wasn't so pretty. He had sandy blond hair, and his shoulders still went on for days. His youthful, cute-boy look had been replaced with whole grown-man handsomeness. If she wasn't careful, she would end up right where she'd been in high school—mooning over a man she couldn't have. Shouldn't have.

He hadn't even remembered her damn name.

"So you're taking over the park project?" Quaid asked, laying out his napkin over the plate.

"I finished it." She'd been surprised when the mayor had shown up on her mom's sad doorstep earlier in the week.

Sylvie Darois explained that the parish had a few projects their normal attorney was behind on and offered her the work. She'd taken it immediately and gotten it done quickly thanks to the tiny library's Wi-Fi, which was so much faster than her mom's. She was fairly certain her mom's provider was only one step away from dial-up. "I've moved on to a few of the other parish projects. I've got depositions for the suit against the sanitation department scheduled for next week."

It seemed like the whole world waited on Quaid. Before Jayna took them over, the depositions hadn't been scheduled because they weren't sure when Quaid could get to them. The fact that a whole parish's legal system was dependent on the whims of one man seemed like a mistake.

His eyes flared, surprise plain on his face. "You're moving fast. I thought discovery would take a while."

"What am I supposed to discover, Quaid? The sanitation worker is suing over a raccoon taking over the cab of his trash truck. He shouldn't have left the door open with his half-eaten sandwich on the seat. In fact, he shouldn't be eating on the job at all. He literally handles trash. He should wait until his break. If he hadn't left food on the seat and the door open, the animal wouldn't have snuck in. If he'd been paying a lick of attention, he would have noticed he had a friend. And if he hadn't panicked, he wouldn't have lost control of the vehicle."

It was one of the silliest suits she'd ever been a part of, and she had to try to convince the mayor to let the sucker go to court. Apparently, the former counsel preferred to settle out of court. Always.

"Who did the driver get to represent him?" Quaid asked, sitting back, and she tried not to notice how the sun hitting his hair made it even more golden than usual. "I hadn't gotten around to that file yet."

"Someone from Houma." She glanced down at the file. "Lionel Carter."

A huff came from Quaid that she shouldn't find so charming. "He's an ambulance chaser."

"Doesn't surprise me," she said. That was the only type who would have taken on this crazy case. "I'm not sure how they think they can prove the parish is responsible for a curious raccoon."

"Oh, they'll tell you it's Brian," Quaid explained.

She'd already heard this story. "I refuse to believe that a raccoon leads a band of woodland creature thieves that the parish has failed to round up." She picked up a second folder. "Nor do I believe there is a Cajun werewolf eating pet rabbits. That is a clear case of a lazy dad who forgot to secure the cage. He's trying to get out of his guilt for letting his baby girl's pet hop away."

Quaid's lips curled up in the sweetest grin. "Yeah, the parish gets a lot of crazy claims. Did you work out a deal for Sylvie to pay you in chocolate chip cookies?"

"No." It wasn't optimal to get paid in barter, but most of the potential clients she'd seen couldn't afford her and, damn it, she was bored. She could only send out so many CVs a day, and sitting and waiting for her phone to ring had become beyond annoying. "I'm charging a project rate to the parish. They can't afford my hourly rate."

"Very few people around here could ever afford a lawyer's hourly rate," he admitted. "It's pretty much why I negotiate instead of letting things get to the court."

Here was where they completely differed, and she didn't mind telling him what she thought. "You know it's not ethical to negotiate for both parties."

A brow rose over his deep green eyes. "For most of the negotiations I help with, I don't receive payment from either party. Any negotiation where I'm the counsel of record for one of the parties, it's disclosed, and the opposition is able to decide whether or not they wish to seek counsel. Do you always walk into a situation and immediately question a person's ethics?"

It was good to know she could irritate the man. He seemed so very calm, so laid-back.

"Not usually. You're special. You know they can't afford counsel and even if they could, they would have to look outside the parish," she pointed out.

"What exactly do you think I get out of these negotiations? Do you know how many times I've had to convince the LaMont brothers that they can't turn their mechanic shop into an amusement park? I'm not joking. They had an annual park pass and a bunch of used cars they wanted to turn into rides. It comes up at least twice a year. What do I get out of that?"

"Some people get off on the power." She knew many people like that, including her ex-husband. He'd enjoyed being the heir to his father's throne, loved having power over every single person in the firm.

A deep chuckle came from Quaid. "Power? You've been living in the city for a long time if you think I have a lick of power. I don't even have it in my home. I serve this town, not the other way around."

"Then why stay?" She'd understood that Quaid had been raised a prince waiting to take his daddy's crown, but it wasn't like the man didn't have choices.

"Why did you go?" Quaid countered.

"For the same reason everyone leaves. There wasn't any opportunity for me here." She'd been thinking a lot about this question lately.

"And I stayed because the only real opportunity I ever had was here."

"That's so untrue. You could have gone anywhere. Done anything."

"From the time I was old enough to understand words, I knew I would follow in my father's footsteps."

Oh, the poor little rich boy. "Well, following in my mother's would have meant a mindless, never-ending job at a plant, so I guess you got the better end of that deal."

His lips curled down. "Of course I did. I was wealthy so I never had a single problem in my life and everything fell into place for me."

"I didn't say that. I was only saying you had a good opportunity here and I didn't. So I left and you stayed." She wasn't surprised he was getting annoyed with her. She annoyed a lot of people. "You still have all your opportunities, and the world has become one giant garbage dump for me."

He relaxed a bit. "What happened?"

"You don't know? I shouldn't be surprised. I guess I'm not interesting enough for anyone in this town to know anything about me." She'd thought the man would at least ask around to try to find out more about her after they'd faced off in court.

He sat back. "I know you turned in a client and that it cost you your job and your marriage, but I asked my friend not to tell me the whole story. I thought that should come from you. I've met your husband a couple of times. I know you probably don't need to hear this, but you're better off without him."

She didn't feel better off. "Just so we're clear, I'm not crying over the loss of my great love. I didn't love Todd, and he didn't love me. We made sense, and his father wanted him to settle down. He also needed women lawyers to parade around to show he wasn't a sexist. So I fit the bill and we got married."

"If you didn't love him, what did you get out of it?"

This was the part she often felt bad about though she knew it happened all the time. She wasn't going to lie to him. "Marrying him meant I got the job I wanted and I got a seat at the table I wanted to sit at. I also thought I was getting a partner who wanted to work toward the same goals. That was how I viewed marriage. It was supposed to be a good partnership. The way you're looking at me, I would suspect the last time you saw Todd he was with a woman who wasn't me. I knew about that, too. I didn't care."

"Didn't care? So you had an open marriage?"

Her heart constricted a bit, and now she was the one getting annoyed. "Not at all, but I knew who he was when I married him."

"So it was all your fault?"

She didn't like the sound of that. "Of course not."

"Then why excuse him? You're putting the blame on yourself. I find it interesting that you frame your whole marriage as a marriage of convenience."

"It didn't turn out to be convenient for me." The cheating had started fairly early on, but she'd told herself it didn't matter since they weren't in love.

So why had she never cheated? Why had she stayed true to a marriage that was basically a sham? Why had she spent years without the consolation of warm arms around her?

For a career that ended so easily?

"What did happen, Jayna?"

It was far easier to talk about this than her marriage. "We had a client who I believe blatantly used insider information to make money on the stock market."

"Then you had to turn him in. You informed the partners of your firm, right?"

"Of course." She'd followed all the rules and still gotten burned. "I presented them the evidence of the crime and my father-in-law told me it was a gray area and I should step down as his counsel. I still had the duty and obligation to report the crime, so I did."

Quaid whistled. "That took some guts."

"He was a horrible human being, and I'm absolutely certain there were other, more unsavory crimes the man committed. I couldn't prove those, but I could prove he committed this crime." She hated the fact that she could feel tears forming in her eyes. It wasn't because of sorrow. It was anger. She'd felt so helpless. She'd done the right thing and it cost her a life she'd . . . She hadn't loved it, but she'd worked hard for it. "I could stop some of the things he did by putting him in jail for insider trading. So I did it. I knew it was likely the end of my time at the firm. I knew it would be the end of my marriage."

"He was hurting people?"

"I couldn't prove it, but my every instinct told me the man was a predator, and now every eye is on him because unlike my father-in-law, the federal prosecutors didn't see any gray area at all." Getting eyes on the man she'd been certain was involved with the Mafia was the whole point of the endeavor. "They arrested him, and he'll go on trial next year."

"Then you did the right thing."

She sniffled and nodded, wishing those stupid tears away. "I did, and I would do it again. And that is probably why no law firm wants me. I didn't play ball. I'm also being investigated for misconduct. It's just a nuisance because there's nothing for them to find, but it's going to cost me a whole lot of time and a bunch of money I no longer have."

"Who's your attorney?"

"I haven't decided. I have a couple of weeks. I'm hoping to get together enough money to be able to hire someone. I'll do all the work, of course, but it doesn't look good to have me represent myself." She probably shouldn't admit she didn't have the money for a lawyer, but the man already knew she was working for gasoline and chips, so it wouldn't come as a surprise.

"Todd Shale is very wealthy. Did he wrap you up in a prenup?"

"Yes, though I should have been able to take half our assets." She'd been a moron to sign that paper, but she'd thought their marriage could work. "The house was still in his father's name, so that was covered."

"What about your accounts? Investments?"

She chuckled, but the sound wasn't a humorous one. "He protected those as well. Mostly by spending everything we had. I didn't realize how much debt we were in. I got half of that. I basically sold everything I had to pay it off and be able to keep my baby."

His eyes went wide. "You have a kid?"

She bit back a smile because he looked like he was ready to run. Scaredy-cat man. "Luna is the love of my life. The only good thing Todd and I ever did together."

She watched as he seemed to consider the issue. It wasn't lost on her that the man was flirting. He was definitely attracted to her, but it would be a bad idea to give in. Still, having Quaid's attention was nice, but she would be fine with losing it if he was the kind of guy who couldn't handle a woman with some baggage.

He rallied, losing the confused look and bringing back the smooth, earnest expression he'd been using on her before. "Luna's a nice name. How old is she?"

Ah, so he'd decided to pursue her despite the perceived child. "She's three."

"A toddler. That must be hard on you." He frowned suddenly. "Is she with your mom right now?"

"Probably." Luna was having a hard time adjusting to trailer park life. There was a tiny chihuahua who lived two doors down that scared the holy crap out of her big baby every time they went for a walk.

"Probably?"

"Mom had some shopping to do and Luna doesn't love cars, so she stayed behind." It was fun to tease this man. He looked mortified.

"Jayna, are you telling me . . ." He stopped, and a rueful smile lit up his features. "Are we talking about a dog or a cat?"

Sitting here with him was legitimately the most fun she'd had in forever. "She's a Great Pyrenees. She was a Christmas present a few years ago. I told my father-in-law I'd never had a dog as a kid and I'd always wanted one. When I got her, she was this tiny ball of fluff, and I had all these visions of keeping her in my handbag. I didn't know how big she'd get."

"Hah, then she was forty pounds in a couple of months," Quaid continued.

"And now she's eighty pounds and it's her lunchtime." She glanced down at her watch. "I should head back and feed her. I don't have another appointment until tomorrow, so I should get some work done. I've got a suit to file because your client won't wear a suit. I need to do some research and that means heading to the library because my mom's Wi-Fi is awful."

He grinned. "I've got some space. If you're going to work in town, you might as well have an actual office."

"I can't afford rent right now. I'm afraid this booth is it for me for a while."

"Look, the truth of the matter is you're helping me out by taking the city work off my plate. The least I can do is give you a place to do it. I own the whole building. The first floor is the office, and it's got space for a partner."

Jayna raised her eyebrows in question.

"My father always meant for me to work beside him, but that only lasted a few years. He retired when he thought I was ready to take over, but I expected to be able to consult with him for a long time." The bittersweet tone of his voice let her know how much he missed his dad. "There's a second floor with a full apartment. Dad used to rent it out, but I've kept it empty since I took over. I like to be able to use it when I'm working late or I need a place to be alone."

"Living with your mom a drag?" She realized that could sound like she was ragging on the man when she wasn't. "I get it. I love my mom, but I did not expect to be in my thirties and stuffed on the twin bed that was already too small when I was fifteen. And Luna tries to share it with me."

"Then the least I can do is give you a place to work," he offered. "In fact, my legal secretary is off for the next four weeks. Her daughter had a baby and she's helping out. You could answer phones and act as an assistant when you have time. You are the only qualified person around."

"She's a legal secretary. She shouldn't be answering your phones, and neither should I." An idea played around in her head.

"Well, my last receptionist ran off with one of my clients, and I haven't been able to find a reliable replacement. I would call a temp agency in Houma, but no one wants to drive that far every day," he admitted. "We could take turns answering the phone?"

"Or you can take a chance on someone." It was time to pay her sister back. Sienna would never think to apply for a job like working for a law firm, but she was smart and she learned quickly. The woman could take a ten-person order and get it perfect without taking down a single note. "How about I'll answer the phone today until Sienna's shift here is done. She can be your receptionist until three o'clock when she has to pick up the girls. If she works out, she can quit the diner and work full-time for you. That way your legal secretary won't have to act as your receptionist anymore. Sienna's going to need good insurance and two weeks' paid vacation."

"Whoa. How did I go from being the nice guy who offered you free office space to hiring your sister and paying for insurance?" Quaid asked.

"You got lucky because she's going to be excellent and she's going to be reliable. She's got two kids to support, and if I can find a way to make sure that they don't spend their entire childhoods with a mom who works two or three jobs to barely make a living, I will do it," she vowed.

"I would typically require an associate degree. Even for a receptionist."

Jayna shrugged. "Then she's going to need tuition assistance. Quaid, how old is your legal secretary? Because if I'm correct and we're talking about Cynthia Dobson, she's in her sixties. How long before she wants to retire and hang out with her grandkids all the time?"

He sighed. "She's already told me she intends to retire in five years."

"Are you willing to take the chance that you'll find someone qualified who'll want to move here?" She could win this particular negotiation. And that's what they were doing. Quaid Havery had a problem. She had a problem. There was a simple solution that only required something Quaid had plenty of—money. The other part might be harder. She had to convince her sister to believe in herself, but she would deal with that. She would make Sienna see how perfect she was for this job. "Or you could take on someone who needs a break and give it to her. You could lift someone up."

He stared at her for a moment and then Sienna was standing next to him, a fresh pot of coffee in her hand.

"Am I interrupting?" The smile she'd had on her face faltered. "Are you about to fight? Because I heard it got heated between the two of you at the courthouse the other day."

Quaid simply turned Sienna's way, and for a moment Jayna worried she'd way overplayed her hand.

"What would you say if I told you I'll pay for you to go to school to become certified as a paralegal?"

Her sister's eyes went wide. "Why would you do that?"

"Because I'm going to need one when Cindy retires, and it was recently pointed out to me that it's going to be difficult to import one. This same person might have convinced me that I should look around and find a smart, hardworking person to train, someone willing to stay in Papillon for a long time," Quaid continued. "So here's the deal. You work for me from eight a.m. to three as my receptionist and office manager. You pick up your girls and then you do online classes or night school. You might have to do both, but I'll pay for the tuition and the certification process. You don't have to rush, but I'll expect you to get that certification before Cindy retires in five years, and then her job will be yours and we'll find another receptionist."

"I . . . I have a job," Sienna stammered. "A couple, actually."

"This one will pay better and has actual medical and dental." She wished Quaid hadn't hit Sienna like this. She'd been planning to ease her sister into the idea. With blunt force, if necessary, but a little more time to let her adjust.

Sienna's hand tightened around the coffeepot handle. "I'm not qualified."

"You would be after you finished the classes," he pointed out.

Jayna's gut twisted. "Maybe Sienna and I should talk about this."

Quaid shook his head. "No, this is between me and Sienna. If I'm going to make this investment, I need to know she's serious about it. This would be an important job and will require discipline and hard work. It's also a job where you can make enough money to support your kids without a side hustle. You won't have to work weekends unless we're on a big case, and we don't usually have those. Now that I think about it, I like the idea of having someone who knows the town."

"Yeah, and they know me. They know I'm not some paralegal. I'm the girl who brings their breakfast and pours their beers on weekends," Sienna replied, her voice soft.

Quaid sat back. "Sienna, this is an opportunity that could work out for both of us, but you have a decision to make, and I know it's a hard one. You can stay the girl everyone loves who brings them their breakfast and pours their beers. Or you can be the woman who believes enough in herself to take the chance to better her life. Her daughters' lives. Do you honestly believe you can't get through the classes?"

Sienna's jaw went tight. "I can do it. I was good at school. I liked school."

"Are you uninterested in the type of work?" Quaid asked.

"I am fascinated with all of it. I just never thought I could . . ." Sienna's shoulders went straight. "I can do it, Mr. Havery. I would like to talk to you about salary, but I agree to all your other terms. When would you like me to start?"

Relief flooded Jayna. She'd thought for a moment that Sienna's insecurities would hold her back, but her sister had been brave.

"As soon as possible," Quaid replied. "Especially since you'll be working for two of us in the beginning. Your sister has agreed to move from this incredible location to my extra office. She'll be answering the phones until you get there. Please come as quick as you can before she has the firm taking goats in exchange for legal services. Or running off clients with her intense personality."

"I can be nice." She wasn't inte . . . Well, maybe a little.

"Do you feel like being nice?" Quaid asked.

"Not most of the time," Jayna allowed.

"Are you serious, Quaid Havery?" Sienna ignored their byplay, her eyes on the man who might be her boss. "Are you telling me I can answer phones for you and take care of the office and you'll pay for me to become a paralegal?"

"Yes."

"Why?"

"Your sister pointed out that if we don't want our town to die off, maybe we should make opportunities for people to stay and thrive and grow. Maybe if your girls see how their momma made a great life for them here, they'll want to do the same for their families. Because your sister reminded me that sometimes our lives turn on the whims of fate, and today I wanted that to be a good thing." Quaid reached out. "Do we have a deal? I can be a handful."

Sienna shook it. "I've broken up bar fights on a Saturday night. I can handle anything. I can start tomorrow. Dixie's got too many servers for the off-season anyway. Madison and Alice will be more than happy to pick up my shifts."

"Then we'll see you at eight sharp. And tell your girls that one of the perks of the job is your boss will buy them snow cones at least once a week during the summer should they come to visit their mom," Quaid promised.

Sienna grinned. "They'll be thrilled." She winked Jayna's way. "I'm going to go talk to Dixie."

Jayna watched her sister go and then stared back at Quaid. "I thought I would have to push you. I thought I would have to push her, too."

"You made sense. I'm a reasonable guy."

She knew she shouldn't, but she reached out and put a

hand over his, warmth immediately spilling through her. "You are a kind man, Quaid Havery. I guess I didn't truly understand that until now. Thank you."

He flipped his hand over, taking hers in between his. "You're welcome, Jayna."

To her horror, she was about to cry. How long had it been since she'd seen someone act out of pure kindness?

He was taking a chance on her sister, and that was all the more reason to not make a fool of herself.

"Hey, Quaid. Your office was locked so I thought I might try you here." Herve LaMont stood at the end of the table, saving her from going on instinct—which was to offer Quaid a hug and then oops, our lips met and we should kiss while we're here.

And that was a good thing because she wasn't going to go there with him.

Quaid let her hand go. "I was just having brunch with Jayna here. She's going to be helping out with the legal work around town."

Herve was a slender man who still believed in mullets. His was spectacular, flowing past his shoulders and cut far too short up front. He wore his mechanic overalls. "Nice to meet you, Ms. Cardet."

Jayna frowned. She'd known the man since she was a kid. Her mom would take Jayna with her to get their old sedan checked. "You, too."

Quaid snorted like he knew exactly what had gone through her head. He picked up the bill and slid out of the booth.

"I was talking to my brother, and we have a new idea for Rev It Up," Herve said. "But someone pointed out that there's this parish ordinance against using old mattresses as trampolines. That seems like overreach to me. I want to file a protest."

Thank god she didn't have to deal with that. She'd gotten a free breakfast and bargained her sister into the perfect job, and she was getting Wi-Fi until she could find a real job. All in all, not a bad day.

"Jayna here will be taking over your case," Quaid said smoothly. "She's handling some of the parish's cases, so she'll know exactly what to do. And, Herve, I have it on good authority that her car's a piece of crap and she will likely work for auto parts."

"You bastard," she whispered under her breath.

He gave her a smile that damn near set her panties on fire. "See you back at the office. And you're definitely answering the phone this afternoon."

She watched the man walk away. He looked fine in a pair of slacks.

Herve slid into the seat recently vacated by that weasel, rat-fink, magnificent bastard. "See here, lawyer lady, I was planning on hollowing out some antique cars and putting old mattresses in them and voila—bouncy house. I'm recycling and making a fun place for kids to play."

And germs to infect them all. "Yeah, I think we're going to be looking at more than mere parish ordinances. We might have the feds to deal with. But hey, I never say no when there's billable hours on the line. Let's talk about batteries, because mine won't hold a charge."

She got down to business.

chapter four

"What do you want me to do about it?" Armie LaVigne sat back, a beer in his hand.

Rene put down his cards and sighed. "Well, it seems mean, but I think you should at least talk to Geraldine. Do you have any idea how many complaints city hall dealt with today? Tourist season is going to begin in a few weeks. How are we supposed to explain 'Don't use one of the only two gas stations in town because Geraldine and her friends have decided to start a nudist spa'? I'm all for free expression and for every person feeling good in their own body, but this is taking it too far."

Quaid sat in his usual seat, the one across from the window. He wasn't sure why he'd picked that seat years before, but it had been his at every weekly poker game since he and Rene had come back from college. Rene had started the weekly game, and though some of the players had changed over the years, Quaid found a deep comfort in the ritual.

It started with a single glass of Scotch, and then he would have two beers. Any more and he wouldn't be comfortable driving home, so he stopped at two no matter what the time was. In the beginning, Rene's housekeeper had been the one to come up with platters of food, but now it was usually Rene's wife, Sylvie, who brought the snacks and inevitably stole a couple of kisses from her husband.

"I don't see the problem." Remy Guidry had been a couple of years ahead of him and Rene. Both he and Armie had left Papillon for many years before coming back to raise their families. Armie had come home and run for sheriff while Remy had come back to take over his family's bar and grill. "I say good for Geraldine. I hope I'm as comfortable with myself as she is when I'm her age. I know I definitely don't want anyone telling me what I can do behind the confines of my own fence."

The new guy sat back, his cards still in hand. Landon Price was a deputy with the county. He'd taken Major Blanchard's place when the former deputy had married and requested a leave of absence to spend time with his father. No one actually believed Major would come back. He would follow his wife out into the world.

"But the problem is, it's not behind her fence." Landon was a transplant from Beaumont, but he'd fit right into the Cajun community. "She's got this weird yard that slopes down. She told me it was something about flooding and she had to have the patio raised so the water would flow into the creek that runs between her and the gas station. The gas station is also raised, so you can see right into her backyard. She's fully on display, and now her friends are, too."

"She didn't use to be." Quaid felt the need to argue his client's point. Not that he was going to get paid. Jayna at least was going to get gas out of this case. "She used to have the natural protection of the tree. Jimmy took that tree down so he wouldn't have to pay for yearly pruning. It used to completely block any view of Geraldine's backyard."

Armie frowned his way. "I thought you were Jimmy's

lawyer. Didn't you successfully plead his case? I thought he had the right to take the tree down."

Quaid shrugged. "He did and I was. Jimmy has found other counsel for this case and I am representing Geraldine, so I will tell you all that while Jimmy's actions were legal, they, like all actions, have consequences. For some reason the parish has a rule stating that no fence can be more than eight feet tall."

Rene mucked his cards, choosing not to call Remy's bet. "That happened because way back when, Gene's father decided to secede from the United States and built his own wall around his farm and then had to be evacuated because he put the lock on the wrong side. That wall was twenty feet tall and he couldn't climb it. So the former city council put in the ordinance. Geraldine's fence is eight feet tall but because of the slope it sits somewhat below her deck."

"So change the ordinance or give her an exception." It was precisely what he'd talked about with Geraldine today. When she hadn't been napping, she'd agreed that being able to build a twelve-foot fence would give her the privacy she required. Of course, she wanted Jimmy Abbot to pay for it, and that was why they would end up in court again.

The judge was going to get irritable if it prevented him from getting his fishing in.

"You know why Sylvie can't encourage that outcome," Rene argued. "I think in this case the law needs to weigh in."

Armie took a swig of beer. "I did. I went out to Geraldine's, asked her a couple of questions, and came to the conclusion that she's not breaking the law."

Remy nodded his approval. "That's very forward thinking of you, Sheriff."

"Yeah, well, we'll see how forward things get now that she's invited a bunch of friends from the assisted living home to join her." Landon pushed a couple of chips toward the pot. "Jimmy is going to get dicks on display in a couple of days."

And the result would be the same because most people didn't fully understand obscenity laws in Louisiana. "Nudity is only illegal if the person is baring their genitals or breasts with the intent to titillate the public. Geraldine is choosing to be naked in her own backyard, which has a regulation-height fence. She gets into her hot tub to enjoy the benefits of the spa for her arthritis. Most law enforcement would arrest her anyway, but Armie appreciates the full extent of the law."

Armie sighed and tossed a couple of chips in. "Armie knows there's more to this, and if I arrest Geraldine, I get a whole lot of protestors. What are you planning on doing, Quaid? Jimmy can't plant another tree. The one he took down was at least twenty years old. Geraldine needs some privacy."

"I'm going to keep the pressure on until city hall gives her an exemption," Quaid admitted. "I promise you, in the end both the judge and opposing counsel will beg Sylvie for that exemption."

Rene practically growled his frustration. "And then every time someone wants the council to change something we'll get nude protests."

"And then maybe we'll be a happier society," Remy argued. "Let people be who they are and don't body shame them. I assure you running around naked will get old fast. Let them eff around and find out. I promise you the first time one of the protestors sits on those metal benches in the park and burns their asses, they'll find another way to express themselves. Geraldine is literally in her yard. She should be able to do what she wants."

"Yes, that is going to be my argument." Quaid glanced down at his cards. Normally he would be all about the game. He loved poker and played the players as much as the cards, but he was completely distracted this evening, and it was all Jayna's fault.

She'd arrived late in the afternoon and he'd shown her around briefly before she'd disappeared into the office he only used if he was working with another lawyer. Sometimes lawyers who specialized in something his clients needed would come in for days at a time and he offered them a place to work.

It had been his office for the few years he'd worked with his dad. He wondered what his father would think of Jayna Cardet.

"Who exactly are you arguing against?" Landon asked. "I thought you were the only lawyer in town."

Rene perked up, going from slightly annoyed to bright and shiny in an instant. "Oh, Quaid is no longer the only lawyer in Papillon. He's going to have to work for it now. Jayna Cardet is back in town, and she's willing to take Quaid down a peg or two."

He could remember the way her eyes had shone when he'd offered Sienna the job, how she'd reached for his hand and suddenly the world had felt like a warmer place.

He'd forced himself to walk away from her because he'd started to realize how dangerous the woman might be to his heart.

"Jayna Cardet? I don't know the name," Landon replied. "I think there's a Cardet who lives in the trailer park on the edge of town, but I don't think she's a lawyer."

"Jayna is Sienna's younger sister." Remy sent Quaid a pointed stare. "You in or out?"

Quaid sighed and mucked his cards. His brain wasn't focused this evening. Not on the game, at least. It was interesting that Remy remembered her. "You knew Jayna?"

"Wait, Sienna, the waitress at the café? The one who will not even look me in the eye?" Landon asked.

"Yeah, though she's not a waitress anymore," Quaid explained. "She's my receptionist, and I'm going to have her trained to take over as my paralegal when Cindy retires. So, what did you do to her to make her not like you? Sienna is one of the nicest women I know."

"Whoa, when did you decide to hire Sienna?" Rene stared at him for a long moment. "Did you hire Jayna's sister to get closer to Jayna? What's going on, Quaid? It's not like you to make impulsive decisions."

"Maybe I've been thinking about it for a while."

"If you'd been thinking about it for a while, you would have mentioned it to me," Rene pointed out. "You are one of the most careful human beings I know. You would have made a decision matrix and gone over all the pros and cons of hiring someone who isn't qualified."

"When I'm done, she will be qualified." He'd been swayed by Jayna's belief in her sister, by the way she'd advocated for her. He'd liked the fact that she'd trusted him with her sister's future. It was the first time he'd felt like she didn't think he was some privileged kid she had to put up with.

"She's not working at the café anymore?" Landon looked like a puppy who'd gotten kicked.

"You'll have to excuse Landon," Armie said. "He's a glutton for punishment. Sienna doesn't want anything to do with him but he still goes in every day and moons over her."

"I do not moon. What does that even mean?" Landon frowned. "Sometimes Armie talks like we're still in the sixties or something. I expect him to say 'groovy, man.' I think she's cute. That's all."

"Well, she's also got two kids, so she's serious," Quaid pointed out.

"None of which explains why you suddenly decided to take on a whole new employee." Rene obviously wasn't letting this go.

"Shouldn't you deal another card?" Quaid was starting to wish he hadn't opened up this line of conversation.

Armie sat back. "Nah, he's good. I think we should get to the bottom of this particular mystery."

Remy nodded. "Oh, yeah. If this is about a woman, we should definitely talk."

"Uh, I thought we were playing poker." Landon looked around as though unsure of what was really going on. "Why does everyone care Quaid hired a paralegal?"

"He didn't. He hired a waitress with nothing more than a high school diploma. One who's never shown a lick of ambition professionally." Rene suddenly sounded like he was Sherlock Holmes on the scent of a mystery. "A man as careful as Quaid Havery doesn't do that unless he's trying to impress someone. I know I'm not particularly impressed, so it's not me. How about you, Remy?"

"I think it's great he's giving Sienna a chance, but I don't think he cares what I think," Remy admitted.

"Anyone gotten a good look at Jayna Cardet these days?" Armie zeroed in on the kill.

"We should be playing poker. What is the sudden interest in my hiring practices?" Yes, he definitely shouldn't have mentioned this.

Armie pointed Quaid's way. "Because it's obviously your turn, brother."

"His turn?" Landon asked.

"Yes, you're new here so you don't know how much hell Quaid can give a man when he finally decides to settle down," Rene complained. "He put me through the ringer when I fell in love."

"I'm not settling down." He barely knew the woman. He wasn't thinking about playing house with her. Except he was bunking at the office for now, which meant he'd literally invited her to work at his house.

"I would hope not, since we're talking about Jayna." Remy's face settled into a concerned expression.

Quaid knew he should simply agree and let it all go, but he was curious. "Why would you say that? Do you know her? I didn't think she still had friends here."

"Sienna was in my class. We were pretty good friends. We even dated briefly, but I liked the hell out of her. My group of friends spent a lot of time hanging out at her place," Remy explained. "And the one thing we all knew was that her sister hated everything about this town and utterly disapproved of Sienna."

"I wouldn't say that. Jayna seems close to her sister. It's been a long time since high school." Nothing about the way Jayna had treated her sister today had been condescending. She'd been her sister's champion. "Jayna was the one who pointed out that Sienna deserved a chance."

"Hah." Rene pointed his way. "I knew this was about Jayna. I've known since you first asked about her."

Remy held a hand up. "Look, I just know how she was back then. She always had her nose in a book, and there's nothing wrong with that, but it was obvious she thought she was better than her sister, and she definitely thought she didn't belong in this town."

"Well, she's not the only one who left for years and years," Rene pointed out. "I seem to remember a young man who enrolled in the Navy just so he could get out of Papillon."

"I was getting out of a very bad marriage," Remy countered. "And then I stayed away because of problems between me and my cousin. When I had a chance, I came home. I don't think that's why Jayna is back. I heard she got divorced and got in trouble with her firm."

"She got in trouble with her firm for turning in a criminal." He'd studied up on the case that led to all of her troubles. It hadn't been hard to find. The New Orleans papers had covered the story extensively. "It would have been easy for her to hide behind attorney-client privilege and call the whole thing a gray area, but she did the right thing. She did the ethical thing and she lost her career and marriage because of it, and now she's facing a bar hearing on the status of her license. Don't make it sound like she's running home because she screwed up."

Armie's brow rose. "Rene's right. He's got a thing for her."

"I don't . . ." Maybe he was going about this the wrong way. Maybe he could use some advice. "All right, I find her intriguing. She challenges me, and it's been a long time since someone did that. She was right about her sister. Sienna deserves someone taking a chance on her. Like your wife decided to take a chance on Zep. Who would have guessed that Zep Guidry would turn out to be one of the most reliable figures in parish government?"

Zep's older brother snorted. "Well, definitely not me," Remy said. "It wasn't until he got close to Roxie that he got his life together. And I'm not saying Jayna's a bad person. I'm trying to tell you that I don't know she'll stay in town for long. She'll look for a better opportunity and she'll take it when it comes around. Unless you believe she can't come back from this career hit."

He didn't think that at all. "She's smart and good at her job. Once she gets past the bar review, she'll be able to find some firm willing to take her on. Or she can find government work, perhaps even in a prosecutor's office. She didn't specialize in criminal law, but she could learn fast."

"Then she won't stay around," Rene said gently. "And I would hate for you to get your heart broken again."

"I thought we were going to play poker and drink beer," Landon said with a frown.

"Hush," Armie admonished. "It's not your turn yet."

"If my turn means talking about my private relationships like we're a bunch of teenage girls, then I don't want a turn," Landon complained.

Remy ignored the deputy. "When did Quaid get his heart broken? I thought he was kind of the player around town since my brother got married."

Quaid snorted at the thought. "I have never come close to Zep's level of womanizing. I will admit to a few wild nights, but that was years ago. I've been happily single for a long time. I'm married to my work." Except lately he'd wondered what it would be like to have a family, to have a woman he could talk to. He'd dated around but never found anyone he could connect with here in Papillon. "I believe Rene is referring to the one and only time I asked a woman to marry me. It was back in law school. I thought we would make a good team. She decided she could find a better team to join in New York."

He'd had visions of him and Alison taking over his father's firm. She'd taken one look at the town and broken off the engagement.

Just so we're clear, I'm not crying over the loss of my great love. I didn't love Todd, and he didn't love me. We made sense, and his father wanted him to settle down.

That was how Jayna had explained away years of a loveless marriage without shedding a tear. At that moment, he'd wondered if she was as cold as she sounded.

But wasn't he doing the same thing? He didn't want to acknowledge the hurt, the weakness, so he made his previous engagement sound like less than it was.

"I'm lying. I was crazy about that woman," he admitted. "When she left, I ached for a very long time. I threw myself into work, and it might be why I haven't been serious about anyone else."

"And that's why I'm worried." Rene put a hand on his shoulder. "I think you should be careful when it comes to Jayna because Remy's right. I don't think she's going to stick around. Sylvie said she's very impressive but that Jayna told her she was absolutely not staying in Papillon long-term. She said she'd be happy to work for the parish as long as she was here, but she intended to get her license to practice in Texas and be there sometime next year."

Quaid hadn't expected her to stick around, but this news oddly still felt like a kick to the gut. She wouldn't want to work in a place that tried to pay her in gumbo and gas for long.

He was more invested than he'd thought. "Well, you should know that I offered her my free office while she's here. She was going to get kicked out of her booth at the café in a couple of weeks when school lets out and the summer tourist season kicks in."

"So now you're taking in her and her sister?" Remy whistled. "You must have it bad, Quaid. Never thought I'd see that happen."

"All right, fine, I like her." If he went into a relationship knowing it had an end date, he wouldn't get hurt. And maybe getting hurt wouldn't be the end of the world. Hell, it had been so long since he'd felt anything that maybe getting twisted up over a woman was exactly what he needed. He'd watched his friends find what they needed. Jayna wasn't what he needed, but they might be good for each other in the short term. "But I will think about what you've said. Armie, you should also know my brother's in town."

Armie's head fell back on a groan. "I worried that damn Porsche was going to be trouble." He brought his head up and took a long draw off his beer. "I saw that car rolling around town yesterday and prayed it was one of Major's new relatives visiting. Is he on anything?"

"When is my brother truly sober?" Quaid asked and then shook his head. "I don't know. He swears his last rehab took, but I'm almost certain he's here to get some money out of our momma. And like she always does, she's taking her baby's side. So you'll excuse me if I drown my sorrows in that gorgeous woman. If she'll let me."

Rene picked his cards up. "I'll back off. Just know that I'm here if you need anything. You want to stay with me for a couple of days? I know how toxic your brother can be."

His brother was toxic but charming as hell, which was precisely why his mother fell for the act every single time. "I'm staying at the office while he's here. It shouldn't be long. Our mother will write him a check and he'll head back to LA and then I'll pick up the pieces again."

Maybe that was why he was so interested in Jayna. She was a distraction, and one he could feel all right about. She wasn't interested in staying around. She wouldn't expect anything from him, and he would have no expectations of her.

It could be a nice time for both of them.

When they dealt another round, Quaid tried to get his head back into the game.

Jayna sat back on the lounge chair and wondered if Quaid was going to give her keys to the office tomorrow. Would he still give them to her if he knew how much she wanted to sneak back in and get some work done tonight and maybe bring a sleeping bag and her dog and live there for a while?

She could live off ramen noodles and coffee and excellent Wi-Fi until she figured out the rest of her life.

Yeah, she wasn't going to mention that to him or he might rethink the whole letting-her-use-the-office thing.

Luna's head came up, her attention focusing on the trailer

opposite her. The door to Sienna's trailer came open and a slight figure slipped out.

Ivy wore pajamas and fuzzy slippers on her feet. She looked around as though seeking something and then lasered in on Jayna. Luna's tail thumped and she moved down the steps to escort the young girl across the yard between them.

"Aunt Jay, what did you do?" Ivy whispered the question.

"A lot of things." She wasn't sure what her niece was talking about. She'd gotten home about an hour before and found a note from her mom saying she would be over with the girls until Sienna got home. About thirty minutes later, Sienna's car had pulled up and she'd waved Jayna's way, holding up the new outfit she'd bought for her first day of work. Sienna had been bubbly and full of optimism. "What's going on?"

"Momma and Granny are fighting, and they're saying your name a lot." Ivy moved to sit on the second chair, her feet not brushing the floor.

"What would they fight about?" She hadn't even talked to her mom today. Over the weeks she'd been home, they hadn't spent a ton of time together. Her mom had begrudgingly let her stay. Sometimes she thought the only reason she'd done it was so she could say *I told you so*. And Luna. Her mom seemed to love having Luna around.

"Momma told her about the new job with the lawyer guy and Granny said she's got her head in the clouds and she's going to ruin everything."

"What?" Jayna stood up. She should have known her mother would have an opinion. She always did and it was always negative. "Your mom got a new job, a better job with better pay and better hours. She doesn't even have to work weekends. How is that ruining things?"

"Mom could be home on Saturdays?" Ivy asked.

"Every single one, and Sundays, too. Her new boss is even making it so she'll be able to pick you guys up from school. I think you'll like him. He's pretty nice." And dangerous to her peace of mind. Quaid was all her high school dreams rolled into one sexy, "couldn't she get rid of all her frustrations with him?" man trap.

She'd closed the door to the office he'd given her because it was way too nice to think about the fact that he was right across the hall, and she could go poke him any time she wanted.

She'd worked with a man she'd been involved with once and wasn't going there again.

"I don't think it matters if he's nice." Ivy shook her head. "Granny doesn't think Mom can do it. She said she should have known you would come in and put ideas in her head." Ivy sniffled.

"That is not right. Your granny shouldn't have said those things because your mom *can* do it." She was going to have such a talk with her mother. What had she been thinking? Even if she'd put the girls to bed, she had to know they could hear everything in that tiny space. The walls were paper-thin. Jayna should know. She'd grown up being able to listen to every word her mother said about her.

Ivy's honey blond hair shone in the moonlight. "Aunt Jayna, do you really think I can go to college and be a doctor? Because I don't think Granny thinks I'm smart enough, either."

Anger bubbled up but Jayna shoved it down. She'd dealt with this so many times when she was a kid. The idea of sweet, smart Ivy going through it made her heart ache. She got on one knee. "You can do anything you put your mind to, Ivy."

Her niece's bottom lip trembled. "Granny says it only makes it worse when you say things like that. She says it's cruel to tell us we can do things we can't. There's no money for college. Momma worries about money all the time. My dad . . . he doesn't help at all. I barely see him since he got a new girlfriend. He's not going to help me, and college is expensive."

"I promise you that if you work hard and make good grades, I will make sure you go to college. It might not be your dream school, but it will be a good school. I'll pay for what I can, and we'll find every scholarship and loan we need. I will not let you down. There was no money for me to go to school, either, and Granny wouldn't sign for loans. I had to do that all by myself. And I made it. I worked my way through law school."

"Granny says you're up to your ears in debt and it would have been better if you'd stayed in your place." Ivy put a hand on her cheek. "Do you think my mom would be happier if she hadn't had me and Kelly?"

Oh, her mom had so much to answer for. "Never. Your mother loves you so much, and that's why she's getting a better job. She wants to be able to spend more time with you. She won't be on her feet all day, so she won't be as tired as she is now. She's going to get a certification that she can use anywhere she wants to go, and she'll get insurance. This is a good thing, and she's doing it because she loves you and wants to give you the best life she possibly can. Now, let's get you back in bed and I'll have a talk with your granny about being nicer."

Ivy sniffled again, and her arms went around Jayna's neck as she hugged her.

Emotion swept through her, and she felt that guilt again. She'd spent so much time staying away, and they'd needed her. Her nieces and her sister needed her for more than the money she'd occasionally given them. She walked Ivy back toward her sister's trailer, Luna trailing behind. The door was unlocked, and she could hear her sister crying as she walked in.

"It's okay. Everything is going to be all right. You've done nothing that can't be fixed." Her mom was sitting beside Sienna on the sofa, her hand on her knee. "You can talk to Dixie and get your job back. I'm sure she'll understand."

"Hey, I found this one out wandering around. Thought I'd bring her back." Jayna had to keep a happy attitude around Ivy, but inside she was seething. How many times had her mom tried to talk her out of something she wanted because she "wasn't being realistic"?

How many times had her mother cost her an opportunity because she didn't want her daughter being arrogant?

Sienna gasped and stood up, wiping her eyes. "I didn't see her slip out. Ivy, you can't do that. It's dangerous out at night. Hey, baby, everything's okay. Your granny and I were only talking."

She moved in to take her daughter's hand.

Ivy yawned and wrapped her small hand around her mom's. "You were arguing."

"Naw, honey. We were discussing something that you shouldn't worry yourself about," Jayna's momma said. She was still wearing the jeans and T-shirt she'd worn to work, her gray-streaked hair back in the same ponytail she'd worn for as long as Jayna could remember. Her mother was a slender woman, but there was a worn and tired expression on her face at all times, as though the years weighed heavily on her. "You get some good sleep and everything is going to be back to normal tomorrow. You don't worry about nothing, girl."

She was not going to correct her mother's grammar because that was rude, but she was going to correct a few things. Just not where the girls could hear her. "Mom, I'd like to talk to you over at your place."

Her mother's lips pursed in that stubborn way of hers. "Yes, I think we should."

"They're going to argue, too," Ivy said as Sienna walked her back to the bedroom she shared with her older sister.

Oh, they were absolutely going to argue.

Jayna could barely contain her anger as she made the short walk that proved exactly how *not* far her sister had come. A whole lot of that was their mother's fault. "What the hell, Mom? What were you saying to Sienna to make her cry?"

Luna followed her up the porch steps, her tail wagging like they were going on a fun walk.

"I was pointing out a few truths to her," her mother replied, crossing her arms over her chest. "I was making sure you don't walk in, get everyone's hopes up, and then walk right back out to your perfect world and leave the rest of us here picking up the pieces."

She turned on her mom, her hand still on the door. It appeared this was going to be a porch discussion. She was sure some of the neighbors would be listening in, but her mother never minded being the subject of a bit of gossip. "Perfect? I never said it was perfect and it obviously wasn't or I wouldn't be right back here."

"Exactly. Which is precisely why you shouldn't be giving your sister advice. Why are you trying to screw up her life?"

This was what she couldn't understand. She truly had expected her mom to be excited. She wasn't shipping Sienna out of town, merely getting her better pay. "I'm not screwing up her life. I'm helping her. Do you know how much more money she can earn working for Quaid? He's willing to pay for her to get her paralegal certification. She'll be able to work anywhere she wants."

Her mother's head shook. "And that's another thing. She would not work anywhere she wants—she would be working for a Havery. They're practically royalty in this town. It's one thing to work for Dixie, who understands where Sienna comes from. The Haverys never worked a hard day in their lives."

"Just because they don't work with their hands doesn't mean they don't work hard." She felt crappy about how she'd thrown Quaid's privilege in his face so casually, like he'd never had a bad thing happen to him, like he could control who his parents had been any more than she could. From what she'd learned, the man used his privilege to help the people around him.

"Well, I assure you his mother never worked a day in her life. She came from old money, and that brother of his thinks he owns the world," her mother argued. "Quaid Havery works for the Beaumonts and the Darois family. Do you honestly think Sienna is going to fit into that world?"

Jayna felt her hands fist at her sides. "It's not another world, Mom. It's literally across the street from the world she's in now. She's going from working in the café where she makes below minimum wage plus tips to a hundred yards away where she'll have a salary and flexible hours so she can take the girls to the doctor without worrying about how she'll pay for it. That's the only world she's going into. She still comes right back here at night."

Her mom leaned in, voice going low. "We are doing fine. We have been doing fine all along. You think I don't take care of those girls? Those are my grandbabies. I'm the one who was here when they were born. I'm the one who helped Sienna change their diapers because their daddies sure weren't going to do it. I make sure they get exactly what they need."

Her mother wasn't thinking of the big picture. "Ivy's going to need braces. How do you expect Sienna to pay for that? It's thousands of dollars."

"Her teeth are fine."

"Like mine were?" She'd had to suffer through half of law school looking like she was thirteen because her parents hadn't been able to afford the braces she'd desperately needed.

Her mom waved off that. "Your teeth were fine, too. You're just vain, and you always were."

"Mom, my mouth was too small for those teeth." Frustration welled hard and fast. "I couldn't floss properly. I couldn't keep them clean. I was going to lose them at a very early age."

Her mom's hands went to her hips, squaring off. "Then you would have gotten dentures like the rest of us. Look, I know you think I was a failure. You made that very clear throughout your childhood, but I won't have you coming in here and making me look bad in front of my grandbabies."

Jayna's gut got tight. "I didn't think you were a failure. I think you never once tried."

"Never tried? I worked sixty hours a week to keep a roof over your head, to give you a good life, but you always had to have something better. Well, you got it, and like I always knew it would, it ruined your life. Now you're trying to ruin Sienna's."

"My life is ruined?" Had her mom been spreading this all over town? "I got divorced. I had some trouble at work. I hit a speed bump. I'll rebuild my life."

Her mom pointed her way. "No. You'll try for something far out of your league, and it will fall apart again. You're thirty-three years old, Jayna, and what do you have to show for it? A whole lot of debt and a failed marriage. You don't have a life. I had two teenagers when I was your age."

A completely unamused laugh huffed from Jayna's chest. "Because you got knocked up at eighteen. It's not a thing to be proud of."

"And it's not a thing to be ashamed of, either," her mom

countered. "I had a family. I had babies to love, and I had a roof over my head. I had friends who had my back. I knew what my life would be, and I accepted it. I was grateful to my momma and daddy for everything they gave me. You know I had a brother who was just like you."

Hadn't she heard this story before? Her uncle had been a sore point for her mom all her life. Uncle Ron had been the only member of the family to get the hell out of Papillon. "Yes, he was a lawyer and he moved to the big city and drank himself to death. I'm not an alcoholic, Mom."

"Not yet you're not, but when you realize you can't find what you need out there, that everything that would have made your life good was right here and you were too ambitious to see it, that's when you'll turn to the bottle. You'll end up exactly like my brother, who walked away from his family and never offered us anything. He only invited us to visit so he could show off how much he had. He wanted to show us his fancy wife and his fancy kids and a house that had a bathroom bigger than our whole trailer. He made our parents feel ashamed of what they had. I won't let you do that to Sienna. She's always been a good girl."

Her mother was being a complete hypocrite. "If my divorce ruined my life, how is Sienna better than me? Twice, Mom. Two times she got married and two times they failed. She's renting a single-wide across the yard from where she grew up, working two jobs to try to barely make ends meet, but she's the success story? She's the smart one?"

"I didn't say smart. I said good," her mom replied. "Sienna is a good girl who thinks of others first. She cares about other people, not just herself. You've always been a selfish girl who couldn't be happy with what she had. Nothing was ever good enough for you. You had to have more. Sienna's doing fine and has been for years. She doesn't need anything from you. Not money or advice, and she definitely doesn't need a job that moves her into a world she doesn't belong in. Nothing from you. If she needs something she can come to her momma because I won't expect anything from her."

"I did need her money when she had it." Sienna stood at the bottom step, her eyes weary. "I didn't tell you but after I divorced Donnie, I was dead broke. I told you Donnie paid the first and last month on this place, but it was Jayna, and she never asked me to pay her back. I told you both my exes were making their child support, but Donnie doesn't have a job, and Austin sends about half of what he owes every other month. Jayna's paid for a lot and now she can't, so I'm scared about what happens if I get sick and can't work a full week or if the tips are bad. At some point the bar I work at on weekends is going to find a permanent bartender and I'll lose my shifts there. I walk on a knife's edge, and if I lose fifty dollars of income a week I'll get cut and so will my girls."

Her mother's shoulders straightened. "You should have told me. I would have handled it for you."

"You can't go and fight with my exes, and you don't have the money to help out," Sienna said with a weary sigh. "But you're probably right. I wasn't good at school in the first place."

Jayna's heart ached for her sister. "You weren't bad at school. You are smart, Sienna. You can do this."

Sienna wiped a tear away. "Yeah, well I'm not feeling like I can tonight. I'm going to bed. I'll talk to Quaid tomorrow and let him know I need to think about it. And, Mom, Uncle Ron offered to help all the time. You were just too proud to take it."

"Because he would have held it over my head to show me how much better he was," her mother insisted.

"Or he actually just wanted to help. He was willing to

pay Jayna's tuition to college and you turned him down," Sienna said with a frown.

Jayna felt those words like a kick to her gut. "What?"

Her mom had flushed. "He wasn't serious."

"He was." Sienna turned to Jayna. "I was there, and he was absolutely serious. He thought you were smart, and our cousins had already started to get into trouble by then. He said he knew his own kids weren't going to go to college, so he might as well pay for the only kid in our family who would. He offered to pay for everything and Mom turned him down, told him if he ever said a word to you about it she wouldn't see him again."

"Sienna." Her mom managed to make her name an accusation.

Sienna shrugged. "Well, you basically called me dumb and now I'm feeling mean. I'm going to bed."

"Sienna," her mom called out.

But Sienna kept walking until she disappeared inside her trailer, the door slamming behind her.

Jayna stood there, completely floored by what she'd just learned.

"I think you should go," her mom said, her jaw so tight that every word ground out. "It was wrong for you to come back here. When you left, you left, and no matter what, you shouldn't have come back to a place you hate so much."

"I never said I hated it." How could this be happening? How could her mom have turned down tuition? It wasn't like she would have used the money to buy new clothes.

"You might not have said it out loud, but I got that message loud and clear."

"I can't believe you . . ." Why was she wasting her energy arguing? If she wasn't welcome here, then she shouldn't be here.

"Can't believe I wouldn't willingly send my daughter out

in a world that I knew damn well would eat her up and spit her out?" Her mom moved up to the door, shaking her head. "No, I wasn't going to make that easy on you. I wasn't going to have my daughter taking money for pipe dreams."

"I got my degree." She wasn't sure why she was even talking at this point. Luna sat beside her, her head tilted up. "I became a lawyer."

"And now you're fired and don't have two nickels to rub together and you're putting all kinds of ideas in Sienna's head. You're going to ruin her life and those kids lives, too. You need to go, Jayna. I can't do this anymore. I'm tired and I can't . . . can't feel like I'm failing every minute of the day. That's how you make me feel." Her mother walked away.

Jayna followed her inside without saying another word, grabbed her overnight bag and her dog, and prayed her car kept working because it looked like she would be living in it for the time being.

Quaid closed the door to the office as the rain started coming down. He stretched and looked around the space. Someone had cleaned up, and by someone he meant Jayna since she'd been the only one around. He'd rushed them both out of the office in his haste to make it to Rene's in time for dinner before they played poker, so he hadn't seen what she'd done.

She'd reshelved the books, every one of them in the proper place. She'd neatly stacked the files on Cindy's desk, and it looked like she'd prepared the actual reception desk for her sister.

He should have thought of that, but he was deeply dependent on his support staff.

He'd turned into that guy—the one who could barely function without an assistant to do all the everyday chores.

He didn't even know how to use that crazy coffeemaker Cindy had bought.

He would bet Jayna wouldn't bring him coffee in the morning. She'd barely talked to him all afternoon beyond telling him he was an asshole for giving her the LaMont brothers as clients. She'd spent two hours explaining to them that there was no way the parish fire marshal would sign off on a roller coaster made of used auto parts and some piping they found at the dump.

She'd been awfully cute when she'd explained her conversation with Herve. *Sexy* was a better word.

Damn it. He'd just had this conversation with his friends and decided that he shouldn't pursue the woman, and here he was thinking of her again.

His cell buzzed, and he slid it out of his pocket, accepting the call before looking at the screen. "This is Havery."

"Quaid, it's your mom."

His mother never understood that he recognized her voice. "Hello, Mother. What can I do for you?"

"You can stop being so stubborn and come home to be with your family," his mother said. "This is ridiculous, Quaid."

"I've got some work to do tonight. I'm going to stay here in town for a couple of days and give you and Paul a chance to catch up." It was best not to tell his mother that until her precious baby boy left town, he would stay right where he was. He knew damn well that Paul wouldn't show up at his office. His brother was allergic to actual work, so he would keep far away.

His mother sighed over the line. "I don't know why you have to be so jealous of Paul, honey."

"I'm not jealous."

"You've always been jealous, and I don't understand it. I know that I spent more time with him, but that was because you were your father's obvious favorite," his mother explained needlessly. He'd heard this before. "It had an effect on him. It's why he has so much trouble with authority. Your daddy didn't pay much attention to him because he was so different."

Because whenever his father had tried to spend time with Paul, Paul acted the fool. Every summer when they were in high school, they worked at the law firm for a few hours a day. Paul had spent that time flirting with every female in sight and stealing money from the petty cash fund. He'd also stolen a key to the office and snuck a bunch of his friends in for a party that had almost killed his father's career. Still, there was no way to convince his mother that Paul's problems had always been caused by Paul. He was her baby, and she would protect him even if it meant rewriting history. "It's because he's so attractive. I didn't get his looks so I'm jealous. It's best I stay away so I don't get depressed having to face my own flaws."

"Don't be sarcastic, Quaid. I want my sons to get along. Do you know how long it's been since I had the two of you under one roof? I don't understand why you can't allow us all to have a nice visit."

"Is it a visit? When is Paul planning on leaving?"

"Well, he's not sure. He's taking some time off, and he wants to spend it with his family."

"Taking time off from what?"

His mother sighed. "I know his job isn't like yours, but when he works it's days and days on set."

"Momma, what movies has Paul been in? What TV shows? Why haven't we actually seen this work he says he's doing?"

"He can't help what the movie studios and networks air. He's had some bad luck."

"Yes, it's unlucky that the play he was in shut down the

day before we were supposed to go out and see it." He stood in front of the window, watching the rain. Was this how the rest of his life would go? Would he spend it either working or dealing with his mother? In some ways, she was like the town. He'd picked up where his father had left off. He'd taken over his father's never-ending responsibilities to the town, and he'd become the person his mother relied on without thinking about what it cost him.

He was in a rut, and he worried if he didn't get out of it soon, he never would. He might be stuck right here for the rest of his life. Not in his physical location. He loved the town, loved having friends he'd known his whole life. But he couldn't get stuck in this place where he was always on the outer edge of every circle. How had he ended up here? He certainly hadn't meant to.

"You are just like your father. You have to question everything and see fault in everyone," his mother said, and he could practically see her shaking her head.

He wanted to go to bed. Maybe in the morning he would have a couple of hours to write before he had to start planning his answer to the suit Jayna would absolutely file against Geraldine's new nudist resort.

There it was. There was the spark of excitement he'd felt the first moment he'd seen the woman. It was the light that illuminated the gloominess that was taking over his life.

"Mom, I'm going to hang up. It's getting late and I have to work in the morning. I'll come by for dinner tomorrow night, but I think it's best if Paul and I don't spend a lot of time together right now."

His mom got quiet for a moment. "Is this about that Cardet girl?"

Now his every instinct flared to life because his mother could win a gold medal in meddling. "What does that mean?"

"It means people are already talking. Paul went out with some of his friends and they were all saying that you're sniffing around that woman."

What a way to put it. "She's a colleague."

"She's a scandal waiting to happen. Quaid, I understand that you're lonely and it's time for you to settle down. It's past time, honestly. You are not getting any younger, but you have to think seriously about who you associate yourself and this family with. The Cardets are not our kind."

His mother could also be a snob. "What kind are they? You know the poor aren't actually a different species, Mother."

The lights from a vehicle rolling down Main Street illuminated the road and the rain that was still falling softly to the ground. The car began to pass by the office and then stopped suddenly and backed up.

It was dark so he wasn't sure he recognized the make or model, but it pulled into a parking space in front of the office, right next to his own Benz.

She huffed over the line. "They have a bad reputation. Those cousins of hers are in and out of jail all the time."

"So is Paul. Maybe someone should warn the Cardets not to have anything to do with us."

"It is not the same," his mother insisted. "Your brother is fine now. He had a spot of trouble when he was younger, but he's from a good family."

His brother had been a whole eight months younger when he'd last gone into rehab, but his mom acted like it was years and years ago.

A massive white dog appeared, pulling on its leash as though ready to run as fast as it could, and then there she was. Jayna caught up to what had to be Luna. She had a big bag slung over her shoulder, and her hair was plastered to her face. She knocked on the door.

What the hell was she doing out this late?

"I have to go." He hung up over his mother's vociferous protests and strode to the door, unlocking it and throwing it open.

Jayna looked more vulnerable than he'd ever seen her, makeup off and in her comfy clothes. She was shaking from the chill as she looked up at him with big, glorious eyes. "I got kicked out. I was hoping I could stay here for the night. I know it's crazy, and I'll be out by morning."

He stepped back, allowing her inside. He didn't like the idea that she would be *out* by morning. What did she mean by *out*? "What happened, Jayna?"

He didn't want to think about how much he cared about the answer to that question. She walked in, still shivering, with her dog beside her.

Luna immediately shook her big body, sending the water that clung to her coat everywhere.

"I am so sorry. Luna, stop." Jayna shook her head. "This was a dumb idea. I'm going to go."

He got the feeling that if she left, he wouldn't see her again. That might be for the best if he took into account the conversation he'd had with his friends and the fact that his mother would disapprove and potentially cause trouble for Jayna.

He couldn't stand the thought of not seeing her again. Even if he never made a move on her, he wanted to get to know this woman. Something deep inside told him that no matter where the relationship went, it could be important. "Don't go. Let me get you a towel." Luna was staring up at him. "A couple of towels. And maybe some tea."

That was when one of the strongest women he'd ever met burst into tears.

He didn't care that she was soaking wet. He hugged her,

half expecting her to shove him away. "It's okay, Jayna. Whatever happened, it's going to be okay."

Her arms wrapped around him and despite the fact that the world always seemed to depend on him, for the first time in a long time, he felt needed.

chapter five

◡

Jayna accepted the glass of Scotch Quaid passed her. "This is a whole apartment. What did your dad do up here?"

Shortly after she'd completely fallen apart, he'd guided her to the stairs that led to the second floor of the building. She'd noticed them earlier but had thought they likely led to a storage room. Nope. No utilitarian storage spaces for the Havery family. Despite the fact that their palatial estate was only twenty minutes outside of town, Quaid had explained they'd kept this two-bedroom apartment for decades and he'd offered her one of the bedrooms as shelter for the night.

"It goes back to my grandfather. He and my grandmother lived separately toward the end of their lives. The Haverys do not have a long history of happy marriages." He had his own glass in hand as he sat down across from her. "My dad spent a lot of time here, too. He claimed he kept this place up because he often had to host some of the lawyers he worked with or negotiated with. It's a long drive back to New Orleans, so they would often stay here, and at the time there wasn't a B and B."

"Why wouldn't they stay at your place? It's big enough." She felt calmer now that she was here, and she rather thought it was more about the man than the fact that she had a roof over her head.

Quaid snorted as though the thought was ridiculous. "Because my mother won't allow what she calls 'shop talk' in the house. Not at the dinner table. Not at her cocktail hour."

Okay, that was a ridiculous thought. She didn't know a single person in their profession who wasn't obsessed with their job. "And she married a lawyer?"

"Oh, yes. And it wasn't like my father didn't have an office at home, but if he was working on a case with someone from out of town, they stayed here. He avoided a lot of arguments with my mother that way. Sometimes I think she was lonely. We live outside of town, so we didn't have close neighbors. There's also the fact that my mother was a debutante and only wanted to associate with certain kinds of people. She still believes there are 'good families' and, well, she would never call a family bad, but there are families that supposedly don't belong in her sphere."

"So she's a snob." She shouldn't have said that. Quaid was being wonderful to her, and she insulted his mom. "I'm sorry. That was rude."

"Not at all. It was honest, and yes, she's an awful snob," Quaid agreed, seemingly not offended at all. "She splits her time between here and her sister's place in Biloxi. That's her hometown. I sometimes wish she would move in with her sister. I think she'd be happier. She enjoys what she calls 'society.' I'm afraid society here isn't high enough for my mother. Oh, she'll spend time with the Junior League and she'll go to all of Celeste Beaumont's teas, but I believe she still thinks it's all beneath her."

"Then why marry your dad? Also, I've never been able to figure out what a Junior League does," she admitted, sipping on Quaid's very fine Scotch and running a hand over

Luna's once-again-puffy fur. She'd looked like a large drowned rat before she'd shaken all that rain off onto their savior.

Quaid had gently run one of his towels over Luna, drying her fur.

It had made her wonder what it would feel like to have those big hands on her.

Instead of finding out, she'd taken a shower and changed into the PJs and robe she'd shoved in her overnight bag. She would pick up the rest of her things when her mom was working.

"It's a volunteer thing," he replied. "I don't know. I don't understand it, either. And she married my father because she hadn't married anyone else. At least that's what I suspect happened. She went to college to find a husband because that's what wealthy women did in those days."

She wrinkled her nose at the incredibly sexist idea. "That's so hard to even think about."

His lips quirked up. "Of course it is to you, but it still happens. Especially around here. Anyway, she made it through and graduated, but without a husband, and for her that was a horrible failure. I once heard her telling a friend that she was perfectly horrified that she might have to get a job, but then my father came along and saved her from the ignominy of employment."

The sheer irony swept over her. "Yes, well, my mother firmly believes that using anything but your hands to work is elitist and makes you one of those arrogant rich people."

"What happened tonight, Jayna?" Quaid asked, turning serious. "What did you fight with her about? Your job?"

"She doesn't think I do work at all. No. We fought over Sienna's new job. It's stupid and she's done this all my life, and I still don't understand it." She wasn't going to cry again. The minute she'd seen Quaid standing in that doorway, she'd felt safe and she'd lost it. Everything that had happened crashed in on her, and she'd hugged him tight.

She kind of wished she was still hugging him.

"She doesn't think Sienna should take the job?" Quaid asked. "That doesn't make any sense."

"No. It's completely illogical. I never once thought my mom would be a problem. I knew she would fight like hell if she thought I was trying to get Sienna to move or something, but that's not what's happening. She's still going to be right here in Papillon, so I have to wonder what my mother's problem is. Then I find out that my uncle offered to pay for my college tuition and she turned him down. Do you have any idea how hard I had to work to make it through school? How long it took me to pay off my student loans?"

"Do you think she did that to try to keep you in town? There aren't a lot of kids who are willing to bet on themselves the way you did."

"I worked hard. I wasn't about to go to community college. I had scholarships and grants. All I needed was like eight thousand a year. It took everything I had to get my degree. She could have made it easy on me. She could have . . ." She was close to breaking down again. "I guess it doesn't matter. You know, I never once considered the possibility that my mom is a mean person. I always thought she didn't understand me and I excused her behavior because life was pretty hard for her. But what she did to Sienna tonight, I don't think I can ever forgive."

He seemed to think about the situation, the quiet sitting easily between them. Shouldn't it be awkward? Shouldn't she feel odd sitting here with a man she didn't truly know?

"She's a single mom, right?"

"Yes, our dad left when we were kids, though I think my mom was relieved when he was gone." There was more to the story that she normally didn't tell anyone, but somehow she wanted him to know. "He died in prison. I found out because I went looking for him to help me pay for college. I was pretty much willing to do anything. He was in for involuntary manslaughter. The DUIs weren't enough to stop him."

He nodded, absolutely no judgment on his face. "That had to be hard on your mother, and it likely made her feel some shame."

"My mother's never felt an ounce of shame." Her mother was the most prideful woman she'd ever met.

"Honey, you can't believe that." He winced. "I'm sorry. I shouldn't have said that."

"It's okay. It's nice to hear an endearment. Most of the time if someone isn't calling me by my name, it's not affectionate. And yes, I can believe it. She thinks she's better than everyone else."

"Or she puts on a show because she knows there are people who look down on her because she's poor. There are people who strike first if they think they're going to take a hit. Even if no one was ever going to hit them in the first place. I suspect your mother's like that. And my mother is a shining example of why."

She would have to think about that. Was her mother's identity so tied up with her class that she couldn't see past it? Quaid's mother certainly didn't seem to be able to. "So why aren't you? Like your mom, I mean."

His lips curved slightly, but it was a bittersweet expression. "I was not a debutante, and I was not raised by a debutante."

"You didn't live with your mom?"

"Of course I did, but she didn't exactly raise us," Quaid corrected. "She was an affectionate mother who enjoyed having us around the dinner table and showing us off to friends, but Paul and I were raised by nannies and my father, when he was around. Mom was more interested in us when we got older, but by then I was my father's shadow. In some ways Paul became her playmate. And growing up rich in a place like Papillon is different than in the city. It wasn't like there were fifty kids with my parents' kind of money to socialize with, so I played and hung out with kids of all kinds. My father used the money he made from working for the wealthy to fund his pro bono work. He was very comfortable around all kinds of people. He used to tell me that the law, when properly applied, was the great equalizer. The law in its purest form should see neither race nor sex nor economic disparity."

She wished that was true. "Your father was a dreamer."

He shrugged. "He was an idealist. But he always put that 'should' in there because he also believed we can't fix problems if we don't acknowledge they exist."

"Your father was a good man." She owed a lot to Wilson Havery. Many people in the town had, and it appeared Quaid was carrying on that tradition.

"He was. He was also a little rough around the edges, so he thought my mom could teach him how to be more comfortable in society, how all of us could. My grandmother on my dad's side wasn't prepared for any of it. She came from a family of eleven, straight off the islands. She was a Drummond."

"Oh, wow. I didn't realize that." The Drummonds were one of the poorest families in the area. They worked as shrimpers and fished, and the newest generation sometimes got into trouble running drugs. "I guess I thought all of the Haverys came from money."

"Like I said, it can be different in a small town. My grandfather married her after she got pregnant. At least I don't think my father was two months premature. He weighed nine pounds," Quaid said with a chuckle. "He saw my grandmother struggle and didn't want that for his kids.

So he married a woman who did, in fact, make sure Paul and I could easily move through even the wealthiest circles, and my father taught me not to think that made me better than anyone else. Just luckier."

She was fairly certain Quaid didn't realize she had a connection to his dad. "Your father is the reason I wanted to be a lawyer."

He sat up a little straighter. "Really?"

"Yeah. My cousin got in trouble when I was in junior high, and it looked like she was going to jail for a long time. Cassie was my favorite cousin. She was our babysitter when I was a kid, and I couldn't stand the thought of her being in jail. I heard them talking about how bad public defenders were, so I marched into your dad's office. I had saved up five dollars and fifty-two cents."

Quaid gasped. "You were that girl? I remember this. I couldn't remember who he ended up defending, but I remember him telling my mother it was some of the best money he ever made. She couldn't understand because it was next to nothing, but he said money was relative. What meant nothing to him meant the world to the young lady who'd hired him, and he would honor that by doing his best."

She was so emotional this evening. She could remember the moment so clearly. She could feel the way the air had changed from the heat outside to the air-conditioned office, hear the slight rattle of the ceiling fan, taste the sweet tea the secretary had offered her. "Your dad and his secretary didn't treat me like a dumb kid. He talked to me like I was smart. And he dealt with the situation. He negotiated a deal so she only got probation. The public defender had told my aunt she better be prepared for Cassie to serve at least three years. And that was when I knew I wanted to be a lawyer."

"I'm glad he was able to do that for you. How is Cassie today?"

"She's married with three kids. She moved to Houston and works for an insurance company, and she has a good life that I don't think she would've had if it wasn't for your father." She wiped away another stupid tear. "I thought I was going to go into criminal law. That was my plan when I started. Sometimes I think about how far I've drifted from where I thought I would be."

"And I think about how I never even once drifted, and that means I never got to figure out if there's anything beyond right where I am." He set down his glass and leaned toward her. "I'm sorry I didn't recognize you."

"I've changed a lot since I was that kid. It's okay."

"I promise I'll never make that mistake again."

The silky sound of his voice did odd things to her libido. She was surprised she still had a libido. She'd kind of thought she wasn't that woman, but Quaid Havery was reminding her that she had all the right parts and hormones. He made her understand she'd been fooling herself all these years, shoving her physical needs aside.

It was a bad idea.

It would be so much easier on her if she hadn't stopped at the office. She had enough money for a couple of days at a motel. Especially if the motel needed some legal representation, because then she could barter for a room. She could sell the last of her handbags and find a job. Any job that didn't keep her in the same space as the most tempting man she'd ever known. She couldn't go down this road again. Quaid wasn't Todd, but their families were similar.

"I should go to bed." If she stayed up any longer, she worried she might end up in the man's arms. Arms would lead to lots of other mingling body parts. "I'll answer the phones tomorrow if I can't convince Sienna to come in, but if I can't find a place to stay soon, I'll have to move on. I've got a friend in Dallas I might be able to stay with until I can deal with the bar situation."

"Jayna, you can stay here for as long as you need. And I've got the bar situation handled. I was going to talk to you about this tomorrow. I found an attorney who specializes in bar complaints. We can call her tomorrow but she's going to be at a conference I'm attending in New Orleans in a couple of weeks. I was hoping you would come with me and meet her."

More and more temptation. "You want me to go to New Orleans with you?"

"That's where she'll be," he replied as though it was a very simple situation and not one fraught with a never-ending minefield of sexual tension. "I suppose we could drive separately, but it's a networking conference so you might get something out of it, too."

She knew that conference well. She'd signed up for it before the divorce. "I've got tickets. I go every year. Todd and I split up those conferences so we didn't have to do them all. And so that he wasn't uncomfortable banging every blonde in sight."

He completely ignored her quip, nodding her way. "Excellent. I've got a suite."

A suite in one of the most romantic cities in the world with a man who made her mouth water. "I don't know if it's such a good idea that I stay with you."

"I would try to get you your own room, but I believe the hotel is full. You'd have your own room in the suite." He studied her for a moment. "You do realize I was planning on staying here tonight, don't you? That's why I was here so late."

"I thought you were working." How she'd gone from being thoroughly annoyed by the man to kind of wanting to be around him . . . a lot . . . she didn't understand. Kind of? She needed to stop lying to herself. She still had a thing for him, and it wasn't merely sexual. She liked him.

"I'm avoiding my brother and his problems," he replied in a manner that let her know he did not want to talk about it.

He could keep his secrets. She'd met Paul Havery a couple of times and he'd seemed like an okay guy, but she didn't know him well. She would trust that Quaid had good reasons for wanting to stay away.

The problem was she couldn't trust herself. Jayna stood. "I should go, then."

Luna's head came up but her big body didn't move, as though she was totally comfortable and her mom's worries about making a fool of herself weren't going to change her situation. She gave Jayna a nice side-eye that told her, "Don't screw this up."

Quaid stood as well, getting into her space. He put a gentle hand on her shoulder, a friendly gesture. "Jayna, I can go home. The last thing I want to do is make you uncomfortable. Well, maybe not the last thing. The last thing would be sending you out into the night without a place to stay."

"I don't want to kick you out of your own apartment." She had to tip her head back to look at him, at his strong jawline and lush lips. Men shouldn't have lips like that. He might mean that hand on her shoulder as an indicator of a simple, friendly connection between the two of them, but she felt heat where he touched her. "But I don't think this is a good idea."

A confused expression crossed his face. His hand came off her, and he seemed to think for a moment. "Jayna, what exactly are you worried about? There are two bedrooms. There's plenty of space."

She felt herself flush.

His hand moved, brushing a lock of her hair out of the way. She hadn't straightened it after her shower so her normally perfect bob was a wavy mess. "Jayna, are you worried I'm going to force myself on you?"

"No." She trusted him on a base level. Even when she was annoyed with him, she knew Quaid was a truly good man.

"Are you worried you're going to try to force yourself on me?" He asked the question with a glint of humor in his eyes.

She frowned. "No. I would not force myself on you. How would I even do that?"

"You could wait until I'm asleep and very gently tie me up, and then I would be at your complete mercy. You could get me tipsy and have your wicked way with me. There are any number of ways you could trick me into an intimate encounter with you."

He was right back to annoying. And sexy. And funny. "I just think it would be a bad idea if either one of us decided to make a move on the other. We're going to be working together and on opposite sides of the courtroom."

"That's why we're going to agree to keep a nice strong ethical wall up when it comes to representing opposing clients. No talking about the case. No listening in. I promise I will honor that wall and make sure it's got strong bricks, so that's not going to be a problem."

She should move away from him. *Move. Take two big old steps back and save yourself, girl.*

Her feet stayed in place. "It's still a bad idea."

"Then don't make a move on me, Jayna." He was so close, and that voice of his had gone warm and silky.

The room was suddenly way too small. "*You're* making a move on *me*. Right now."

The sexiest smirk hit his lips, and his hands cupped her elbows. "No. I'm standing in one space that happens to be close to the space you're standing in. You're the one who went up on her toes to get her mouth closer to mine."

She had totally done that. Why had she done that? "Well, you're the one who is touching me."

"I don't want you to fall."

Falling was exactly what she was afraid of and yet she couldn't make her feet move, couldn't pull her arms away from those big hands of his. "And you called me honey."

"You said that was fine," he argued. "I think you said that because you're under the mistaken impression that I'm one of those old-school Southern males who calls every woman in his life honey. I don't. I'm very professional. I'm not particularly affectionate with my friends. I called you honey because there's a part of me that's dying to figure out just how sweet you can be under all that armor of yours."

"See? You can't say things like that when we're working together."

"Are we? Because I don't remember putting you on the payroll. I can't say that to your sister, and I won't because I'm not interested in your sister. You and I are merely sharing a workspace."

"And going against each other in several important cases," she pointed out even as he moved in closer.

"Yes, the *Last Chance Gas Stop v. Geraldine's Boobs* is going straight to the Supreme Court. I'm not going to allow our personal relationship to influence how I try that case in any way. Are you saying you can't do the same?"

He was challenging her. She knew and she still couldn't resist. There was something inside her that couldn't back down when tested. "Oh, Quaid, if I decided I wanted you, it wouldn't matter. I could sleep with you wrapped around my body, kiss you good-bye in the morning, demolish you in court fifteen minutes later, and you would still do whatever you could to get back into my bed that same night."

Now his hands moved to her hips, his mouth barely hovering over hers. "And I promise that when I crush you in court, I'll make sure to soothe your wounded ego by buying you dinner and taking very good care of you."

She moved to bring their lips together because this was inevitable. This might be fate, and there was nothing she could do about it but give in and enjoy the ride while it lasted. It was foolish, but she wanted him, wanted everything he'd promised her.

Except the beating-her-in-court thing. That wouldn't happen, but he would find her a gracious winner. Mostly.

His cell phone trilled, a sound that seemed to blast through the room. It was a phone call, ringing loudly.

It was a wake-up call.

"Damn it." Quaid stepped back, reaching for his phone. "I'm sorry. That's the tone I use for the sheriff's office. I have to take this."

She nodded, stepping back from the precipice. Quaid spoke low into the phone while she realized how close she'd come to jumping on him and throwing away all semblance of sense and decorum.

Quaid's jaw was tight as he turned around. "I have to go down to the station. I'll be back in a little while. Take the room closest to the bathroom. You should get some sleep."

"I can come with you." If he was meeting with the sheriff, it was likely because someone had been thrown in jail. She could help with the paperwork that came with bailing someone out.

He shook his head, all warmth gone. "No. You stay here. I'll talk to you in the morning. Does Luna have food?"

"She already ate but I'll have to get more in the morning." She'd left a lot behind that she would have to deal with.

"I'll get some from the station house." He reached for his jacket. "They always have extra. Roxie and Armie bring their dogs in all the time. Feel free to use anything you need. There's toiletries in the bathroom and snacks in the kitchen. I'll see you in the morning."

"Is everything okay?" She hated him leaving like this. Something was obviously wrong.

"Everything is perfectly normal. Exactly the way I thought it would be," he said, and walked out.

Well, it wasn't normal for her. Not at all. She was supposed to be focused on herself, on fixing her problems, not taking on his.

And still she moved to the window and watched him get into his car, watched him pull away as the rain beat down softly on the windows.

Luna moved beside her, resting her head down on the windowsill as if she, too, was disappointed Quaid had left.

Jayna took a deep breath. It would be damn near impossible to sleep after the day she'd had. Despite the deep weariness she felt, her mind was still going over and over the fight she'd had with her mom. She would sit up all night thinking about what she was going to say to Sienna in the morning. The last thing she was going to do was give up on her sister. No matter what her mom said.

Her best—and worst—distraction was gone now, and she seriously doubted he would show up anytime soon and want to pick up where they left off.

But he had a lot of books. There were bookshelves on either side of the window, and unlike the shelves downstairs, these weren't lined with scholarly legal tomes. She glanced through the titles. There were classics and then there was row after row of mysteries and thrillers.

Quaid Havery liked to read. She wouldn't have guessed it. He hadn't been interested in school when they were kids. He'd been into sports, and she'd been the kid with her nose in a book. But she would bet these were his books since she recognized some recent bestsellers.

She ran her fingers over the spines of books by Agatha Christie and David Baldacci and Gillian Flynn. He seemed to love Grisham. He had all of his books in hardcover.

And then there were several bound books, but these didn't have names on the spine. They were bound in plain black, like the legal papers she used to have assistants bind together.

Jayna pulled one out, expecting to find Quaid's legal papers bound into a couple of volumes.

The Man in the Black Hat
An Armand Landry Mystery
By Q. A. Havery

She stopped, holding the book in her hand.

Did Quaid Havery write mystery novels?

She pulled out the others and it appeared that Q. A. Havery had written at least five Armand Landry novels.

Oh, she should put that sucker back and walk away.

Except he had put them on the bookshelf. He'd also told her to use anything she needed, and she suddenly needed to read this book.

She picked up *The Man in the Black Hat* and made her way back to her room, Luna following behind.

At least she had something to distract her. She climbed into bed with her dog and a book.

Life wasn't so bad.

He should have turned his phone off. Better yet, he should have thrown the sucker away because if he had, he could be in bed with Jayna Cardet instead of walking into the Papillon Sheriff's Department in the middle of the damn night.

It would probably have been a terrible mistake, but one he could live with. Like literally live with for at least a couple of months. The idea had been firmly lodged in his brain the minute he'd realized why she was hesitant to stay with him. She didn't trust herself to keep her hands off him, and realizing that had been the best thing that had happened to him in a long time. The whole earlier conversation with his friends about guarding himself and being careful had been tossed in the garbage bin, and he'd been ready to see if it could work. After all, she needed a place to stay. If she got into the habit of sleeping with him, living with him, working with him, she might decide not to leave at all.

That had been his true mistake. He'd let an optimistic thought in, and that was the moment the phone had rung.

Roxie Guidry was in uniform, and her hair was in the neat bun she always wore when she was on duty. She stood in the middle of the hall as though waiting for him. Since she'd been the one to call, she likely had been. "He's not under arrest."

"Then why didn't you let him walk home?"

Roxie sighed. "Because he's your brother and Armie would have my head if I hadn't called you. You know you didn't have to come down. I could have given him a ride back home."

"What happened?" He hadn't even asked. He'd heard the deputy stating that Paul was at the station house and his brain had gone to the worst—or in this case most likely—scenario. "I thought for sure you'd arrested him."

"No." She shook her head. "He actually called us out. He was at the bar on the edge of town. He was meeting with some friends and when he came out, his car was gone."

"He's lying. Paul doesn't have friends." What was his brother up to now? "Did you ping the GPS?"

She winced. "He says he had the service turned off a couple of months ago."

"He had the security on his hundred-thousand-dollar vehicle turned off?" Quaid felt his blood pressure tick up.

She held her hands up as if to say she wasn't involved in that. "I'm going to look into it, Quaid."

"Here's what you have to understand, Deputy. Armie will likely explain all of this to you in the morning since this is my brother's first time in town since you started working here. My brother is an addict of the first order. He's a liar and he'll charm the pants off anything he can if it means he can get a little more money. You can't trust a word he says."

"Well, the car is absolutely gone," Roxie replied. "I've got proof that he drove up in it. There are several witnesses to Paul arriving at the bar. There are no cameras out at the Back Porch, so I need eyewitnesses. I'm going to call the highway patrol and see if they've got footage of a Porsche on any of the highways going out of town. Right now I'm writing up a report so he can file it with his insurance company."

"Let's hope he still has insurance." Quaid didn't say that this might be a whole new scam. As much as he couldn't stand his brother, he wasn't going to throw him under the bus for committing insurance fraud until he was sure he was right. "I would assume a Porsche will stick out like a sore thumb around these parts."

She shrugged. "Absolutely. If some kids took it for a joyride, someone will brag about it. I've got one of the other deputies monitoring social media because they often film themselves and put it online. He's in there finishing up. I'm actually kind of glad he didn't drive home. When we got out there he was definitely not in a condition to drive, if you know what I mean."

"My brother is well acquainted with DUIs," Quaid said with a huff.

"His record is clean," she pointed out.

"Only because Armie wasn't the sheriff when Paul was living here." He was well aware that the old sheriff had been willing to sweep indiscretions under the rug when it came to the wealthy people of the town. What was "kids getting in trouble" for the Beaumonts, Daroises, and Haverys were felonies for the Cardets of the world. "I assure you he's been arrested in LA."

"Not in years, Quaid." His brother stepped out looking far less polished than he normally did. "I did my community service and I did my time in rehab."

"And you were in a bar tonight," he countered.

"Well, alcohol wasn't my problem," Paul replied. "It's not like anyone expects me to go without a drink for the rest of my life."

"The rehab counselors would disagree." Quaid looked to Roxie. "Hey, can I get a couple of cans of dog food? I have a canine guest and she's going to need to eat in the morning."

Roxie nodded. "Of course. I've got some in the back."

Paul looked him over. "You got a dog?"

"I have a guest who has a dog."

Paul's brows rose over his eyes. "Ah, you have a woman. That's a surprise. According to our mother you've practically been a nun for a year. She says you're not dating."

"And I'm not dating this one, either." He wasn't about to give his brother gossip to take to his mother. The last thing Jayna needed was a sixty-eight-year-old mean girl coming down on her. "She's a professional contact. We're working on a project, and she brought her dog along."

"So you're using the place for exactly what Dad used it

for." Paul's head shook. "Work and to get away from our mother."

"I was getting away from you," Quaid pointed out. He was about to start questioning his brother when Roxie showed up, a bag in her hand.

"Here you go." She passed him Luna's breakfast before turning to Paul. "I'll let you know if we find anything out about the car. If it was stolen for a joyride, we'll likely find it soon. If someone is breaking it down for parts, it's probably long gone, but we'll look into it."

"You're not looking for it tonight?" Paul asked, his jaw firming. "What kind of place is this? I'm not sure what else you have to do. It's an expensive vehicle. It can't have simply disappeared. Someone has to have seen what happened."

"This isn't LA." He needed to make it clear to his brother that he wasn't getting special treatment. "There isn't a camera on every corner here, and Roxie is one of two deputies working the night shift at this time."

Paul seemed to realize he wasn't winning anyone over because his expression shifted from angry to apologetic. "Of course. I'm sorry, Deputy. I wasn't thinking. And honestly, it's not like I would get better help in LA. They would write a report and tell me to file it all with insurance. I've had an upsetting evening, and I shouldn't take that out on you. I appreciate everything you can do for me."

He held a hand out in that purely Southern-gentleman style.

Roxie shook it. "I promise I really will look for it, but we have to consider the possibility that it's being taken apart as we speak. Car theft isn't usually a big problem around here, but it does happen from time to time. We'll do everything we can."

"I appreciate it very much, Deputy." Paul stepped away. His shirt was wrinkled and missing one of the buttons, which made Quaid wonder what exactly his brother had been doing. "Quaid, I thank you for picking me up. I didn't want to bother our mother, and it would have been an imposition to get a ride back home from the deputy."

And imposing on his brother was one of Paul's favorite things to do. "Let's go. I've got work to do in the morning. Thanks for the dog food, Rox."

She nodded and Quaid turned, ready to get his brother out of here as soon as possible.

Would Jayna be asleep by the time he got back? What would he say to her in the morning? If she was even there in the morning. She might decide to turn tail and run. The woman was skittish around him when she wasn't challenging him in court.

She was going to drive him crazy, but he couldn't stand the thought of her not being there when he got back.

"I'm sorry, Quaid. I know you won't believe me, but I didn't go out looking for trouble tonight," Paul said as they made their way outside.

At least the rain seemed to be over. "You never do."

"I'm trying this time." His brother jogged to keep up with him. "Look, I know I've caused trouble for you in the past, but you're my brother. You're the only brother I'll ever have, and I want us to be okay with each other."

Quaid turned, stopping in the middle of the street. "All right. Then tell me why you're really here."

Paul could sound very reasonable when he wanted to. He knew how to make people like him, how to get them to want to help him. He was excellent at looking like the good son, especially since their mother insisted he was. This meant that most people who met Paul thought Quaid was the problem. How could Quaid not see how nice his brother was? How polite and charming?

He was always made out to be the monster who couldn't

appreciate how creative Paul was. Paul was creative, all right. He was an excellent, creative liar.

"I'm here to see Mom and to spend some time with you," Paul insisted.

Like he was lying right now.

Quaid turned again because he wasn't buying that line of bull. He would take his brother home and then pray that Jayna was still awake and waiting to finish what they'd started.

What had they started? A kiss. A flirtation. Two people who could use some affection spending time together.

An all-raging-hot affair that would lead to . . .

"All right. I came because I got in some trouble."

Quaid groaned, a deep weariness sweeping over him. If Paul was willing to admit he was in trouble, it had to be bad. "What happened?"

"I just . . ." His brother started to pace, moving back and forth behind the Benz. "I owe some people money."

Quaid felt his gut tighten. His brother knew a lot of unsavory characters, dangerous people. They were the type of people Quaid liked to write about, not have in his life. "Drug dealers?"

Paul's head shook in the negative. "No. I told you. I'm off the stuff. That last stint in rehab took. I've been clean for a long time now."

"But not sober." He didn't see the difference. His brother had an addictive personality.

"I still drink," Paul explained with a nonchalant air. "Drinking wasn't my problem. And it's weird to go to a bar and order water or soda. You know I like to fit in. I met some people I knew in high school tonight, and I ended up kind of hooking up with an old friend. Deena Kenmore."

Quaid knew where his next divorce case was coming from. "She's married with three kids."

Paul held his hands up. "I did not know that."

"Did you ask before you got with her?"

Paul shrugged. "Not exactly. I'd had a couple of beers by then, and is it really my problem?"

"It will be when her husband gets back from his rig and kicks your ass." Deena's husband was a roughneck, and he wasn't known for his calm demeanor.

"Well, I'm not his wife so I don't see why what I did is all that wrong. I'm not the married one." Paul huffed. "Look, none of this matters. Like I said, it's not drug dealers. But I might have borrowed some money for a movie project that never actually happened."

"Well, then you should have the money to pay the bank back. How long was the term of the loan?" Quaid was waiting for the other shoe to drop.

"I didn't exactly borrow it from a bank, and I had bills," Paul admitted. "It's why I had to turn off the security system on my car."

"Who did you borrow the money from?" Quaid could feel his eye start to twitch.

"A guy I know," Paul said, sounding exasperated. "Look, all I need is a couple of weeks to get the money and then everything will be fine. I'm going to lay low here. That's all."

None of that answered Quaid's principal question. "Why the hell do you need money when you have a trust fund? Please tell me you still have a trust fund."

Paul was silent for a moment. "Things are expensive in LA."

Quaid cursed and felt his hands fist. It was every bit as bad as he thought it would be. "Millions of dollars, Paul. You went through millions of dollars. Did it all go up your nose?"

"No," Paul said through gritted teeth. "It went into my career. It went into acting lessons and the clothes I need and the networking that goes on, and it went into a couple of projects that might still pay off. I produced two movies with friends of mine. One of them is good, Quaid. It's a great movie but it's tied up in a bunch of legal shit that could take years to deal with, and now I've got to sell my house to pay off this guy who might break my legs if I don't."

Naturally his brother had gotten involved with a loan shark. Maybe even the mob. That tracked perfectly. "How much do you owe?"

Paul took a long breath, his hands going into his pockets. "I told you I'm handling it. I'm working on selling the house, but it takes time."

"How much?" He wasn't about to back down until he knew exactly how bad the situation was.

"A quarter million."

Quaid cursed under his breath. "What the hell were you thinking?"

"I was thinking I needed to do something." Paul proved he could act out an overly dramatic scene. "I was betting on myself. You can't understand because you're not an artist."

Because even if his brother knew he wrote novels, that wouldn't be art. No, that would be commercial fiction that anyone could produce. "No, I'm just the one who cleans up your every mess."

"I'm not asking you to clean up this one, damn it," Paul shot back. "I needed a place to stay while I'm selling my house. I've got a real estate agent working on it but it's better if the place is empty."

"That's not why you came back."

"I drove all the way from California to here because I needed to be home," his brother argued.

He wanted this situation over with as soon as possible, and allowing Paul to drag it out would only cost them all more pain. "Give me the guy's name and I'll handle it."

"I told you I would take care of it."

His brother wasn't thinking at all. "Have you considered for one second that they might follow you? That this person you owe money to might decide to look you up and figure out who you are? Or did you think he would shrug and say, 'Well, I guess he's gone—too bad'?"

"He wouldn't come out here," Paul insisted. "He doesn't know where I grew up."

"And that's hard to find out?" It was time to hope his brother could grasp logic. "It's not. A simple skip trace will connect you to both me and our mother. It'd be pretty easy for him to figure out you're here. I think taking that car of yours might be an excellent start to getting his money back."

"No." Paul had paled. "No. He wouldn't do that. I told him I would have his money back and soon. I bought that house for cash. It's worth at least three million. The market is hot right now. I just need a couple of weeks. He knows that."

"He agreed to wait?"

Paul went silent.

Quaid pulled his keys from his pocket. If he didn't start for home now, it could be after midnight before he got back to the office. "I want his name. I'll pay him off so he doesn't come after our mother, who would have no idea how to protect herself. I might be able to get your car back or at least negotiate for him to take it off your bill."

He was so sick of having to save his brother.

"I can do this. I'm not trying to get out of it," Paul insisted. "I need time. I have the money but it's invested in property, and that takes time to sell."

"Your house is worth three million. Where did the other seven go? It can't all be acting lessons." He was floored by the fact that his brother had wasted everything their parents had given him.

"I was never good with money the way you are. I like enjoying my life. Sue me." Paul's expression turned sullen, and he moved to the passenger side of the car.

"Oh, I wish I could, brother." Quaid opened the door and slammed inside, forcing the seatbelt over his torso before turning the car on.

"I didn't mean to run through it all. I thought I would do better than I have," Paul admitted quietly. "Everyone always told me I could be a star, and then things went wrong. I did spend a lot while I was high. I know you think I don't have feelings, but you can't imagine how much I regret putting Mom and Dad through that. I suppose you can't understand because you were always the perfect child."

"Don't turn this around on me." He wasn't going to sit here and listen to Paul whine about how easy he had it. "I didn't have it any easier than you did."

"You were handed the career you wanted."

"You think I wanted this? I'm not complaining. But it might shock you to know that it wasn't exactly my choice. I was basically told what I would do. You had choices."

Paul was quiet for a moment as Quaid pulled onto the street. "You could have said no."

"Really?"

"Yes. It's a powerful word. You say no and then don't do whatever the thing is you don't want to do."

"And then when Dad died, I would have left the whole town with no one to look after them." He wasn't properly explaining himself. He wasn't sure why he was explaining at all, but the least he could do was be precise. "I didn't mind law school. I enjoy the job, I do. I wouldn't change the course of my life, but you pretend like it wasn't hard work or that I never wanted to be anything except what I am right now. You pretend like I never had a single dream."

"Well, I suppose I didn't think you did," Paul replied. "What did you want to do?"

He wanted to write, and he did write.

He wanted someone to read what he wrote and enjoy it.

He wanted to walk into a bookstore and see the world he'd always had inside his head being shared with others.

He wanted to make a lot of money off books so he didn't have to spend every second of every day working, and he could travel and see the world and fictionally murder people in international settings.

"It doesn't matter." Telling Paul would only give him a weapon to use when he needed it.

Paul fell silent and the miles rolled, the night flowing around them.

"I'm not the same asshole I was in high school." Paul leaned his head against the passenger-side window.

"You just had sex with a married woman, you're on the run from a loan shark, and you lied about why you came home." He was exactly the same.

Paul sighed. "I didn't know . . . I'm not going to win with you, am I?"

"There's nothing to win because we're not playing a game," Quaid replied, turning down the long drive that took them home.

"No, we're not. I spent a long time thinking we were, that we were competing." Paul sat up as they approached the circular drive in front of their house. "Every class I ever took I had to deal with comparisons to my brother. I wasn't as smart or as athletic as Quaid. So I tried to be more artistic, more charming. But we don't have to do that anymore. We can just be ourselves."

His brother seemed to be working out something, and Quaid wasn't sure he liked the sound of it. Paul's voice seemed to gather excitement as he continued.

"We don't have all those expectations. We can enjoy being brothers."

"I'm not enjoying myself."

"Because I never gave you step eight." Paul sat back, a hand on his head like he'd made a true revelation. "I never made amends to you."

Oh, that was twelve-step stuff Quaid did not need. "I'm fine. We're good."

He brought the car to a stop in front of the big Creole mansion they'd grown up in.

"We're not," Paul replied. "Not even close, and if I don't do something about it, we'll never have the kind of relationship we could have."

What the hell was happening? "Don't worry about that. Like I said, if you tell me who you owe money to, I'll handle this and when you sell your house you can pay me back and we'll be even. Now get inside. I have to go back into town. I have work in the morning."

Paul opened the door and stepped out, but then turned to look back at Quaid. "I have to think about this."

"No, you have to give me the name of the guy who is going to find you and break your legs if he doesn't get his money," Quaid returned. "That's all you have to do."

Paul slapped the top of the car. "No, I have a lot of work to do, and I'm going to fix this problem. I promise. I'll talk to you tomorrow and we'll figure out how to fix this."

"I told you how to fix it."

Paul stepped away. "Nah. You told me how to fix a temporary and, in the end, meaningless problem. I meant how to fix our family. You're right. This has gone on far too long, and it's my problem to fix."

"I did not say that. At all. Not even once. Just give me the name and we all go back to our lives." The idea of Paul trying to fix something was unsettling. Unbelievable, too.

"I think I need to reevaluate my life, brother. Starting here and now. I'll see you tomorrow." He began to walk away.

Quaid lowered the window, his panic rising the tiniest bit. "You don't have to see me. You can text me that name."

"Good night, brother," Paul called out, not looking back.

Quaid took off for town again. When he got home, the lights were out and Jayna's door was closed.

It had not been his night.

chapter six

Jayna yawned and rolled over, reaching a hand out to pet Luna. "I'm getting up. I promise."

Then she fully opened her eyes and sat up because her dog was absolutely not lying on the bed next to her.

"Luna?" She glanced around the small bedroom and did not catch even a glimpse of her dog. The clock on the bed side table read 8:35 a.m. Luna never lasted that long without whining and licking her face to get Jayna to let her out and feed her some breakfast. Luna was better than any alarm clock.

Where the hell was her dog?

She'd been up way too late reading that book of Quaid's, but that wouldn't have mattered to Luna. Her dog's bladder didn't care that she'd needed to know if Armand Landry, Cajun private investigator, had been able to figure out who had killed his high school girlfriend at their twenty-year reunion.

He had, and she'd kind of fallen for the super-smart Armand and wondered if he was going to get together with the police detective he'd battled with over the course of the investigation.

None of which solved the case of her missing pup.

The door was slightly ajar. Had Luna learned how to open a door and decided to go wandering in the middle of the night? And if so, how many of Quaid's belongings was she going to have to replace? Luna could be klutzy. That big tail of hers could do some damage, and Quaid probably had a bunch of nice stuff in here.

She wrapped her robe around her and prayed she didn't look too bad before heading out into the living room.

The good news? The place didn't look like it had been ransacked by pirates—or a curious dog's massive tail. But there was no Luna.

"There you go, girl," a deep voice sounded from the kitchen. "Here's hoping that's fairly similar to your usual food or we'll be going for walks all day."

She moved into the kitchen, and there was Quaid in athletic pants and a T-shirt. Luna's leash was hanging over the old landline that was still mounted to the wall. "What happened? She usually wakes me up."

Quaid sent her a smile that threatened to melt her. "I heard her scratching and figured out what she needed. I hope you don't mind I opened your door and took her out for a morning walk. I promise I did not look inside. You want some coffee? I got a couple of cups from the café while we were out."

She gratefully accepted the travel-size cup emblazoned with the café's name. "Thanks, but you have a perfectly good machine downstairs, and by perfectly good I mean spectacular."

She'd noticed it during her tour yesterday. It was one of those super-expensive machines that usually required a barista. It made all kinds of hot drinks.

Quaid took a sip from his own cup while Luna munched down. "I am not smart enough to work that thing. Cindy had it brought in, and I can't even get it to make regular old coffee."

"Well, then it's good for you that I worked at a Stirbucks for three years while I was in college, and yes, you heard me right. It was Stirbucks, and yes, it had a slightly different logo from Starbucks. The owners had found an old Starbucks sign, and they put a patch over the mermaid's eye. It was one of the first court cases I ever helped on. We totally lost that one, but I did learn how to make a killer latte. I'm sure I can figure it out." The owners had also had a Duking Donuts store they claimed was nothing like the national chain because their donuts all had a fighting theme. Upper Cut Crullers, Knock-Out Old Fashioneds.

Yeah, she'd lost that one, too.

"I look forward to it. You're staying, then?" Quaid asked.

She hadn't thought much about it the night before. She'd been too busy reading. "I'm staying at least until I've read the other four books. Are there only five?"

He frowned. "Five books?"

"Yeah." This was the part where he might get mad, but she wasn't going to hide it. She'd done the potential crime. She wanted to know if she would be doing any time. "Armand Landry. I needed a distraction last night so I read *The Man in the Black Hat*."

His jaw actually dropped. "You read my book?"

Yeah, that didn't sound good. The night before it had seemed like a good idea, and she'd liked the book, but now she could see where it might be a slight invasion of privacy. "You told me I could use whatever I needed, and since you weren't around to distract me with what would have been the start of an ill-advised sexual relationship, I had to settle for a good book."

"Those are private," Quaid said, his expression going blank.

"They were on your bookshelf, not like hidden in your office or anything." She pointed to the shelves. "They're right there. In the open. With all the other books that I would assume people are allowed to read."

"Jayna, you had to know that . . . You said it was good?" Quaid asked.

Thank god. The writer's ego was totally going to save her and keep the nice hot man from kicking her to the curb, where she would have to live because she was pretty sure her car had died in the parking lot the night before. She gave him what she hoped was her brightest smile. "It was so good. I did not figure out that it was the jock. I was shocked when I found out he killed the cheerleader because she'd figured out that he'd purposefully thrown the state championship all those years ago to get his father out of trouble with the mob."

In the book, the ex-cheerleader had threatened to go public with her evidence and the now-big-time NFL player had strangled her to death rather than trying to survive the scandal.

"Really?" Quaid got the sweetest, goofiest grin on his face. "I was worried it might be too obvious."

"Not at all. I was absolutely certain it was the nerdy science guy who became a billionaire." He'd been hiding the secret that he'd stolen the idea for his groundbreaking invention from his lab partner in high school and given the partner no credit.

Quaid nodded. "Yeah, I thought that was a pretty good red herring."

Was he blushing? "It was good, Quaid. I couldn't put it down. Is there a reason you haven't published it yet?"

He was definitely blushing, and now he groaned. "I'm glad you liked it. No one else does. I've been trying to get those published for almost seven years now. I have over fifty lovely rejection letters downstairs in my office."

"Why?" She wasn't joking. She'd genuinely enjoyed the book and the setting. Quaid had done an excellent job writing what he knew—Southern Louisiana and quirky characters. "What reason do they give you? I read a lot, and that was a fun, well-thought-out mystery."

"No one wants to take a chance on a new guy, I suspect. I've gotten a lot of 'This isn't what we're looking for at this time.' A lot of acquiring editors have told me they're looking for something a little darker."

"The humor was why I liked it so much." Mysteries often had very dark tones, and Quaid's lighter touch had been a welcome change.

"And some others wanted me to pump up the potential romance in order to draw in women readers," he explained. "But I don't think I should do that. I think I should concentrate on the mystery."

That's where he was wrong. "Armand is so into the police detective it hurts."

"He is not."

"Yes, he is. Their chemistry flies off the page, and that is the one criticism I have. It feels like you're holding those characters back. It's very clear they're attracted to each other."

"They're professionals," Quaid insisted. "If anything, he's annoyed with her stubborn nature. He's certainly not attracted to someone who annoys him."

She stared at him for a moment. He wasn't being very self-aware.

"You don't annoy me that much."

"Only because you haven't read the latest draft of my suit." She sipped her coffee, feeling strangely optimistic.

She liked being here with him, the morning light streaming through the windows. "And I think we're going to get to court later this week. The judge is fast-tracking us because he uses the gas station on a regular basis and he nearly had a heart attack when he saw that Geraldine had invited half the nursing home to a hot tub barbecue party in the middle of a Saturday afternoon. His secretary called and asked if we could be ready by Friday. I said yes."

Quaid frowned. "Well, now I am very annoyed."

Beyond optimism, she was now feeling flirty. Her confidence was coming back. Or rather showing up. She was absolutely sure she was a badass in the courtroom, but now she could see that ten years of a loveless, mostly sexless marriage had done a number on her when it came to men. "And?"

He looked her up and down, a deeply grumpy expression on his face. "Yeah, I'm still attracted."

But he made no move on her. Had he rethought his stance from the night before? Or perhaps that moment had been a turning point and they'd missed their shot.

Or something crappy had happened to him since he'd gotten called to the jail.

"You want to talk about the call you got last night?" She moved into the kitchen, going to the refrigerator.

"I don't think I have time to talk about it," Quaid shot back. "I apparently have a suit to respond to."

"If you don't want to talk about it, that's okay." She wasn't going to push him. He could be touchy. She found eggs and butter and strawberry jam. "Do you have bread for toast? I'm thinking eggs and toast, unless you want to go over to the café."

He reached up to one of the cabinets, opening it and pulling out a loaf of bread. "I picked up basics yesterday afternoon. It's mostly stuff for sandwiches and some protein bars. I'm not much of a cook."

"Then we're lucky I'm a pretty good cook." She pulled out the eggs and butter. "Scrambled or fried?"

"So I shut you out and you offer to cook breakfast for me?"

"You think you shut me out?" She wasn't sure why that shocked him. "Just because you don't want to talk about what happened last night? It's none of my business."

"I've found that women I'm involved with tend to view my silence as shutting them out."

She chuckled. "Well, first of all, we're not involved. We didn't even kiss last night. You are a nice man who can't let a colleague or her super cute dog sleep in her car." It didn't bother her that he'd clammed up. He could have multiple reasons for not talking about what had happened the night before. "I was merely offering to be a sounding board if you needed one. As for breakfast, I'm offering you your own food. It's kind of a good play for me because otherwise I have to go to the café and pretend I'm not hungry because I have no money and hope someone gets tired of listening to my stomach growl."

He was quiet for a moment. "My life is very complicated. My family dynamic is complex and with my brother back in town, I worry it's going to get worse. It might be better to not involve you in that situation."

Well, that was a kick in the gut, but he was right. It was complicated, and the last thing she wanted him to think was that she would sleep with him so he would help her. Still, she didn't like the fact that this warmth she felt would end so quickly. "I agree. So we'll be colleagues. I can find a place to stay. I would like to keep using the extra office here if that's okay, because I need to keep an eye on Sienna. I hope you can be patient with her. I'm going to convince her to take your offer. I just need a few days."

He held up a hand, stopping her. "Hey, I wasn't asking you to leave. And I wasn't saying I'm not interested. I was saying that my life has become more complex than it was before last night and I don't want to expose you to something that could be distasteful. I would go home and let you stay here by yourself, but I'm pretty sure I would end up needing to secure your services if I do. I don't think I would be able to restrain myself from punching my brother."

That actually wouldn't be a terrible thing. Quaid could pay in cash.

"Are you thinking about the fee you would charge me?" Quaid asked, his lips quirking up.

She shrugged. "Well, you would be the first private citizen in town to not try to pay me in barter. I've been told the absolute best I can hope for is gift cards to the place that sells chicken-fried steak in the middle of the convenience store, or a goat."

Sienna had explained that the goat would be nice because she was the one who had to mow the lawn, and the goat could take care of that chore for her. Also, they were cute, and she'd promised to train Luna to herd them if they could get two.

Such a weird place to find herself in. She'd gone from Louis Vuitton shopping to treating herself for a job well done by hoping for goats.

Quaid shook his head. "I think I'll stay here for now. Both places are dangerous for me, but I think I might prefer one outcome to the other. And I'll eat whatever you put on my plate. I won't be picky. We can go buy more groceries this afternoon."

She found a pan and placed it on the stove top. "Danger?"

"Well, the way I look at it, if I go home I will be opening myself to all of my brother's drama. If I stay here, I'll probably end up letting you seduce me and get my heart broken when you sashay right back out of town."

Oh, his brother wasn't the only dramatic one. "Heart-broken?"

"I think I could get used to having you around," he admitted. "You've already taken on quite a bit of the city work, for which I get paid very little compared to the corporate work. You've taken roughly half my Papillon quirk claims, as I like to call them. I got paid nothing for those and you've managed to maybe get a couple of livestock out of them."

"Don't forget the gas and chips, and that Herve has to fix my car." She melted some butter and cracked four eggs in before adding in a fifth. Quaid looked like he could eat. "I might need to find out if the tow truck driver needs legal help because I think my car died last night, along with my dignity."

"Your dignity didn't die, but I'll call and get your car towed if we can't get it started," he promised.

"I cried on your shoulder and I looked like a wet cat," she pointed out. "My dignity definitely took a hit, and that's why I assert that I am no danger to your heart."

"I don't know about that," he replied in that slow Cajun accent. He sighed and opened the bag of bread, taking out two pieces and placing them in the toaster. "But like I said, I'm more willing to take the chance that you can't keep your hands off me than risking the scenario where you have to represent me in a murder trial."

"Yeah, it's going to be me, big guy." She stirred the eggs, feeling perfectly comfortable with their banter. It was fun, probably the most fun she'd had in a long time. She was going to spend her whole day preparing to sue an old lady for showing her boobs, but it was okay because it would be fun to face off against Quaid. "So you'll stay here and not murder your brother. That will save you a lot of money, because I would charge you my full rate."

"You're not going to press me about what's going on with my brother?" He sounded like he couldn't quite believe it.

"Who hurt you, Havery?" Someone obviously had made him believe he had to open his soul in order to be friends with a person. "Because no, I'm not going to press you. You're an artist. You work out your problems on the page."

"I do not." He scoffed at the idea. "Those are nothing more than stories in my head."

She chuckled because he clearly didn't do a lot of self-reflecting. "Armand has a brother who is constantly in trouble. He's also got an overbearing mother who thinks his job is beneath him. He wanted to be a lawyer but had to take over his father's private investigation firm after his dad was mysteriously murdered. Now, the murdered-dad part isn't real life, but the rest of it seems to be close to it. Do the brothers make up?"

Quaid leaned against the counter, a thoughtful look on his face. "Pierre dies in book three, and Armand has to solve the mystery."

"Was it a painful death?"

One big shoulder shrugged. "He was beaten to death with an Academy Award. Damn it. He's Paul."

She barely stopped her eyes from rolling. "Of course he's your douchebag brother, Paul. See. You don't like to talk about your problems. You put it in your art. But I'm here if you do want to talk. Though you should know that for the most part I'll just tell you that sucks and ask you what you're going to do about it. I've found giving people advice almost never works out. No one listens to me and even when they do, they screw it up and then I get blamed. So I really would be a void to shout into. Like me telling you to amp up the romance since Armand obviously needs a woman who challenges him."

The toast popped up. "I'll think about it. I always saw it

as more of a one-sided thing between them. Shannon is incredibly attracted to Armand, but I think it's because she can't have him."

Now she couldn't stop her eyes from rolling. "Oh, that's such bull. He wants her bad."

"*I* wrote the character, Jayna."

"Yeah, well, you didn't even realize you were writing you," she countered sweetly. "So I think you should listen to me, pump up the sexual tension, and resubmit. Which you won't do because you know better than me, and even in your brain right now you're all 'She's not a writer. She knows nothing about publishing.' So I will simply read the next book and let you go on about your business after I finish your eggs and we have a perfectly nice morning. Before I find a way to eviscerate you in court."

She moved in, and his hand came up to touch her cheek. "And that is why I'm going to get my damn heart broken."

He leaned over and brushed his lips against hers, the moment seeming to stop and lengthen, everything else shutting out. It didn't matter that the eggs might burn or that Luna had put her paws on the countertop so she could sniff the toast and jam. It didn't matter that she wasn't dressed properly and didn't have a hint of makeup on. All that mattered was how soft his lips were, how warm the world suddenly seemed.

And then a chime swept through the place, a light jingle that let them know someone was at the door downstairs.

Quaid growled. "If that's my brother come to perform step number eight on me, I'm going to need you on retainer."

"Step eight?" She turned off the burner.

"Make amends," he replied.

Ah, his brother was a twelve-stepper. That did not surprise her. Paul had been wild in high school. He'd been two years behind her, but it hadn't taken him long to find his way to her trailer park and the dudes in the back who sold every-thing under the sun and who her mother had prayed every day didn't blow them all up.

How hard had that been on Quaid? He'd been the golden boy, always expected to be the best, to follow all the rules and be a role model, while his brother had been the bad boy.

That had to have killed their father, who had a sterling reputation. The man had practically been a saint. "Then you should finish up that toast. Luna, no, baby. You do not need that. I'll go see who's here." She glanced at the clock. "We're not open yet, right? The office, I mean. The office isn't open."

"No, we're not open until ten." He pulled out two plates. "I know that's Paul at the door. I'll let you buy anything you want at the grocery store if you manage to get rid of him."

"I'm incredibly tenacious." She made sure her robe was properly belted and that she had perfectly respectable fuzzy bunny slippers on her feet before she headed downstairs. "Luna, come."

She'd found if she wanted to scare off a man, having a massive well-trained dog at her side helped. Unfortunately she only had Luna, so she would have to make do with a massive dog. She got to the bottom of the stairs and could see a shadow at the door. Paul was taller than his brother, but he didn't have Quaid's muscle. She remembered him being fairly slender for a man. He pressed the bell again, proving he really wanted in.

It was sad that sometimes a man simply didn't get what he wanted.

She unlocked the deadbolt. She checked the alarm and saw that Quaid must've turned it off when he'd taken Luna out for her morning ablutions, so she threw open the door and there was Paul Havery.

He was one of those guys who technically looks handsome but whose privilege was so stamped on his face that she could practically smell the frat party that went on around him. His expression went from determined to surprised in a heartbeat. "Well, hello. You are not what I was expecting. My name is . . ."

"No." She slammed the door closed and watched through the opaque glass as Paul put a hand on his chest as though deeply offended by the gesture.

He knocked this time. "Hey. You can't tell me no. I'm here to see my brother."

She opened the door again. "He doesn't want to see you. He doesn't need amends. He's good. Go away."

Paul put a hand out to stop the door from closing. "I need to talk to him. It's about a case."

She bet he had money, too. "Excellent. You can talk to me. I handle half the cases here now."

He looked her up and down, but not in an assessing way. "You're a lawyer?"

"Don't let the bunny slippers fool you. I've practiced for years."

"And you have a dog. You're the colleague Quaid is working with." Paul laughed like that was the funniest thing ever. "When he told me he was working with someone here in town and they were staying over, I thought for sure you were a man. You must be Jayna Cardet. I heard you were back in town and got your law degree. No wonder Mom is worried. But you are not my brother's type. I'll tell Mom she doesn't have to worry about you making a move on him. Damn, you look good, girl. You can be my type."

Yes, he'd also been a high school lothario. "How can I make a move on your brother if you keep interrupting us? Since you heard Quaid has a guest and I wasn't staying here until last night, you must be the reason he got called to the sheriff's. Did you get arrested?"

"No," Paul replied, seemingly offended. "Why on earth would you think that?"

"I don't know, maybe because you got arrested a lot when you were younger. Also, logic." She could logic a lot of things. Having to deal with his brother being arrested would absolutely put Quaid in a bad mood and lead him to think his life had gotten more complicated.

"None of those charges stuck," Paul pointed out. "And I haven't been arrested in more than three years. I went to rehab and I graduated and everything. That's why I'm here. I'm going to make amends with my brother."

"He doesn't want amends. He wants breakfast."

"Well, I could eat," Paul replied.

"What kinds of amends are you making?" She wanted to find out exactly what she was dealing with.

Paul seemed to think about that for a moment. "Well, I thought I could spend time with him. Keep him company while he works. Rebuild our relationship so he knows the new me."

That felt like a powder keg waiting to explode. She also noticed Paul had managed to center the "amends" around himself. "No. Come up with better amends."

Paul's hands went to his hips as he stared her down. "Look, Cardet, he's my brother and you can't make me leave. Don't try to intimidate me with that big fluff ball of yours. That dog might lick me to death, but that's the worst danger I'm in. So you might as well move that cute ass of yours and let me see him."

That was not going to happen. If he wasn't intimidated by her fluff ball, she would see how much he remembered about living in Papillon. "If you don't leave Quaid alone, I'm going to tell everyone I can that Paul Havery came home because he's lonely and really wants to meet a nice girl."

Paul's eyes went wide, and his jaw dropped. "You wouldn't."

"I would," she vowed. "I'll sit in that café and tell every grandma who walks in that there's a single man in town and he is looking to change his luck. I'll say the name Havery and they will drool, Paul. Then I'll give them your phone number."

His hand went to his pocket as if to guard his phone. "You don't have my number."

"Oh, but I bet Quaid does," she replied. "Imagine it. Every momma and granny with a single daughter will flood your phone. You won't be able to hook up with a single female because you'll be surrounded by all the ones who want to marry you. The casseroles sent to your house will be never-ending."

Paul took a long step back. "You are a monster."

Jayna followed him out, not caring that there were people on the street all gawking her way like they'd never seen a lawyer in PJs threatening one of the town's scions with the possibility of true love. "I am a woman who has lived off mac and cheese and peanut butter and jelly sandwiches for months. My mother still makes tuna casserole and thinks Spam is a breakfast food. Your brother promised me I could buy whatever I want at the grocery store if I could get you to leave, and I want steak. I want shrimp, and I want actual vegetables that didn't come from a can. I am desperate, so yes, I will rain my vengeance down on your overly coiffed head."

Paul stared at her like she might attack. "Well, then. Tell Quaid that I'll talk to him later. I hope you enjoy your steak."

He turned and practically ran away.

Everyone on the street was staring at her. She nodded to the blond woman with the toddler. "Good morning."

The woman smiled. "Well, not for Paul it wasn't. You go, girl. He's an asshole." She looked down at the stroller. "Don't you repeat that. That's a momma word. Morning, Quaid."

"Morning, Hallie."

Jayna turned and Quaid was standing in the doorway, an amused look on his face.

"I take it we're having steak for dinner tonight," Quaid said, one hand coming down to pet Luna. "I look forward to it." His eyes moved above Jayna's shoulders. "Well, look who it is. I'll keep breakfast warm for you, Jayna. Good morning, Sienna."

Jayna turned again and then her heart threatened to seize because her sister was walking down the street in the peacock blue power suit she'd bought the day before. She'd done her hair and makeup and wore her good three-inch heels, the ones she wore when she wanted to impress people.

She ran to her sister, bunny slippers and all, and threw her arms around her. "You came."

Sienna hugged her tight. "I can do this. I can. Mom is wrong."

"She is." Jayna felt tears pool in her eyes as she realized Sienna was serious. "You took off the tags."

If she'd been hesitant, she would have left those suckers on.

"I'm going to be a paralegal, so I need to look professional," Sienna said. "Tell me I can do this, Jay."

Jayna stepped back and put her hands on her sister's shoulders. "You can do anything you set your mind to, Sienna. Anything, and I will help you. You are not alone."

Sienna hugged her again. "Thank you. Where do I start? Uhm, and is this the dress code? I was thinking professional, but I might be overdressed. Did you stay here last night? I was worried because you didn't text me back."

"I told you I was safe and then I'll admit I got caught up

in a book I was reading. Yeah, I'm staying here, but Quaid is in a separate room so put that out of your mind." Jayna smiled and wiped away her tears. "I will get dressed and then we'll have Quaid show you around the office."

She threaded her arm through her sister's, ready to start the day.

Quaid sat in his office, still thinking about how the morning had gone.

He'd followed Jayna downstairs, ready to deal with his brother when Paul inevitably got through Jayna's defenses. He wasn't sure if Paul would charm his way past her or simply walk around her, but he'd known Jayna wouldn't be able to keep his brother out.

He was wrong. She'd been an immovable wall in pajamas and slippers, her hair all soft and curly. She'd faced down his brother like a Valkyrie wielding small-town meddling as her sword.

There might not be any way to protect himself now. He had it bad for that woman.

She was both a distraction and a much-needed help.

He glanced out the open door of his office and watched Jayna handing a file to her sister, who seemed both nervous and eager. Sienna was starting to get a handle on the phone, and she was already a pro with the coffeemaker. Between the two women, he was fully caffeinated and ready to work.

If only he could focus on the file in front of him. He was due in court in a few days, where he would be facing off against the wiliest opponent he'd had in forever and all he could think about was kissing her again.

It hadn't been a passionate kiss that morning. The kiss hadn't gone hot and heavy, and yet somehow that kiss had been meaningful. He'd gotten lost in the kiss, in the way she'd softened against him, in the sigh she'd made when her arms had gone around him.

Then there was the fact that she'd actually read his damn book and wanted to talk about it. He didn't even talk to his best friends about his writing.

She was wrong about the whole romance thing. That wasn't a road he wanted to go down. The police detective was there strictly as a foil to his protagonist. He'd even brought in another police officer in subsequent books. A new police officer or federal agent kept things focused on his hero and the mystery he was trying to solve. Jayna was flat wrong.

Of course, she'd probably been right about the whole "using his writing as a way of processing his emotional state" thing. Now that he thought it through, he had given Armand a version of his own history and family.

Was he about to make a huge mistake? She could get under his skin like no one ever had before. The only other time he'd felt this way about a woman had been Alison, and it had taken years to get over her.

Jayna turned and started walking his way.

He tried to pretend to be doing something other than watching her like a lovesick teen.

Why the hell hadn't he seen how amazing she was back in high school?

She knocked on his doorframe. "Hey, Britney from the courthouse called. We're on for ten a.m. Friday, but she's begging us to settle out of court because her granddad's heart can't take a long trial about a nudist colony."

Only in Papillon would the court reporter beg for her grandpa judge. "Well, if the judge doesn't like the view, he can buy his gas somewhere else."

"Apparently he also buys his bait there," Jayna pointed

out. "He's not willing to give that up. There's something magical about Last Chance Gas Stop's worms. I got a whole lecture about it."

"Then maybe your client should think about planting some shrubbery or something at Geraldine's." It was handy to have opposing counsel right down the hall. He didn't have to schedule a call to go over the little things. "My client merely contends that she's an old lady who should be able to use her backyard in peace."

Jayna was back to her usual fashion perfection in a pencil skirt and a silk blouse. Her feet were now in designer shoes instead of the bunny slippers she'd used to run his brother off. Her hair was straight, the edge running just below her jaw.

He found both versions of Jayna incredibly appealing. He liked the distinct differences in the woman who'd negotiated with him over breakfast and the one who stared him down now.

"I know the sheriff is reluctant to arrest Geraldine, but eventually he'll have to," she pointed out. "Wait until the tourists show up in a couple of weeks. When Geraldine's protests start costing the town money, he'll do something about it."

"The sheriff is properly interpreting the law." She'd been gone for a while. She might not remember how things tended to go here in Papillon. "And he's smart enough to know that if he arrests Geraldine, he'll get a bunch of geriatric protestors after him all hours of the day and night, and they do not mind using a walker on a man."

She growled, a sound that shouldn't be so sexy. "You have to see that it's unreasonable to ask my client to pay for . . . what? Screens? I don't even know how we'd get around the town fence code. Even if we could, he's not paying for a new fence. He had every right to take down that tree, and he's done what he could to mitigate the light coming into her house at night."

He didn't point out that last week she'd argued the opposite. It was a given in their world. The argument was the point. "He took the tree down, so now he gets a front-row seat to all of Geraldine's parties."

"Well, we'll see what the judge thinks." She frowned, her arms crossing over her chest. "He should recuse himself, if I'm being honest. He's too close to the case. Those worms give him a real stake in how this whole thing goes."

"And then who hears the case?" he asked. That was the problem with being so remote. They didn't have a lot of choices. "If this gets bumped to New Orleans, it could be years before there's any legal relief."

"You think he'll be able to be fair even though his heart health is apparently at stake?" she asked.

"I've known Judge Brewer since I was a kid. He's a solid guy. I worry about what happens when he retires. I don't know anyone who'll want the seat."

Her nose wrinkled. "I wouldn't. I can't imagine having his job. They'll have to bring someone in or we'll get a totally unqualified judge."

"Mr. Havery." Sienna stood behind her sister.

"It's just Quaid, Sienna." Mr. Havery was still his father to him. Only very young people called him mister. The ones who remembered his dad usually still treated him like he was a newbie trying to replace the old man.

"I got a call from the courthouse, and it looks like the public defender from Houma isn't going to make it today. They've got two arraignments this afternoon," Sienna explained. "I actually know what that is because so many of our cousins get arrested. Yeah, I probably shouldn't mention that."

He let his head fall back. He'd hoped to get some writing

in this afternoon. He'd cleared his schedule and everything. But he couldn't leave people sitting in jail. Usually it was for minor offenses, and if it took too long they would end up transferring the prisoner to a larger jail. It wouldn't be the first time some kid who'd been caught smoking pot got lost in the system.

The weight of responsibility pressed down on him.

"I'll take it." Jayna slapped a hand on his desk. "It'll be fun. I don't have a lot to do since I'm perfectly ready for our Friday showdown. I'm going to win, by the way. And if I don't get back in time to go grocery shopping, you need to buy those steaks. I'm not joking. Remember what I promised Paul? I can do the same thing to you."

"I will have them ready or I will take you out tonight and buy you the biggest steak I can find." He believed her. She could be mean. The last thing he needed was the town deciding it was time for him to settle down.

But wasn't it? Was that what this restless feeling was deep inside? He'd had it for a couple of years now, this feeling that he was missing something in his life. Jayna had turned that whisper into a voice that threatened to scream.

She grabbed her briefcase. "Oh, that's even better. That way I don't have to cook. I want a place where I can get a decent martini. I've heard Guidry's makes a good one. Oh, and I'm going to need . . ."

He tossed his keys her way. "Do not bang up my car, Jayna."

She grinned, catching the keys. "I promise nothing. Be back in a bit."

She turned and walked out.

"You gave her the keys to your Benz?" Sienna looked at him like he'd gone a little crazy.

He hadn't even thought twice about it. "Is she a terrible driver?"

"Well, no. Although she drives pretty fast." Sienna frowned as she thought about the situation. "But you don't know her very well. She could run off with it."

"I have her dog as collateral." Luna was hanging out in the office, her big bed near the front door. The pup wasn't a problem. She liked to nap and sniff things. She gave the office a homey feel. He sat back. Jayna had bought him a whole afternoon, and the evening was suddenly looking up. He seemed to remember Remy talking about how they were going to have live music tonight. He might be able to get Jayna on the dance floor. It was one way to get his hands on her. "Somehow I don't think your sister is going to run off with my car."

"Well, she wouldn't, but some people think we would," Sienna pointed out.

"We?" He wasn't sure what she was trying to say. He didn't know Sienna well enough to read her yet. It was funny because he could already tell Jayna's moods from the set of her shoulders, the way her lips pursed.

"People like me and Jayna and my mom. Like my cousins. I'm worried, Quaid."

"Worried about the classes? You know there is going to be plenty of time for you to study. We aren't all that busy."

"No, it's not that," she replied with a shake of her head. "I'm going to do my best. I promise you that. I appreciate this opportunity, and I know I'm going to make it work for me and my girls. I'm worried about the way my sister looks at you."

"How does she look at me?" His walls crept back up. He wasn't sure how he felt about Sienna warning him off her sister. He thought he could be good for Jayna. He knew she was starting to be good for him.

"The same way she did when she was seventeen."

"I feel bad that I didn't recognize her. In my defense,

she's changed quite a bit. I overlooked her in high school, but I also overlooked anything that wasn't football and whatever cheerleader I was dating at the time. And beer. I drank a lot of beer in those days." Those had been the last days of his freedom, but then that was pretty much the point of high school. When he'd gone to college, he'd had to buckle down and do the real work. He'd put football behind him and studied and worked with his father.

His writing had become the only outlet he had, and he hadn't shared it with anyone except unknown editors and now Jayna.

"She's being a drama llama about people not recognizing her. She looks nothing like she did in high school. That is so not her natural hair color. She made sure she didn't look like she used to and honestly, she was pretty obnoxious back then. Jayna couldn't wait to get out and didn't mind letting everyone know how fast she was going to run."

"A lot of kids feel that way."

"Probably, but they also likely weren't as vocal as Jayna about how awful everything was. But she was a kid. She's gotten far better at hiding her disdain." Sienna sighed. "Or maybe she's older and wiser and not as disdainful as she used to be. I know our relationship is much better now. Sometime after she got married and I had Kelly and then Ivy, she reached out and we got close again. She wouldn't come home, but she called and invited us to New Orleans. She became someone I could depend on. So I need to look out for her."

He could understand that. If he was close to his brother, he would likely do the same. "I see her quite well now. I'm not the same idiot I was back then."

Sienna's lips pursed in almost the same expression Jayna got when she was about to get stubborn. "No, but you're still a Havery and she's a Cardet."

"Why would that be a problem?" He wasn't sure where she was going. "I'm going to admit that I'm attracted to your sister. I would like to have a relationship with her while she's here in town. We've talked about it, and she's been upfront about the fact that she's going to leave at some point."

Sienna nodded. "She worked so hard to get out of this town when she was a kid. She'll leave as soon as she possibly can."

"Or maybe she'll see that this isn't such a bad place."

"I doubt that very much, but that's not the problem. The problem is your mother. I know that you don't care that the Cardets aren't exactly the town's elite family, but your mother will. She's not going to be happy about you pursuing Jayna."

Of course. He should have known. "What has she done?"

"Nothing yet, but she will. Do you remember a couple of years ago when you were dating a woman named Sally La-Bon?" Sienna asked.

Sally had worked at the local bank. She'd been fun to be around, but it hadn't gone anywhere. Like most of his relationships. "Of course. Sally was a nice woman. We went out for a couple of months but it didn't get serious, and she broke things off. I think she married and moved to Houma with her new husband."

"Yes. She got married two years ago. But she didn't break things off with you because she didn't think you were moving fast enough. She broke it off because of all the talk that she wasn't good enough for you, that you would never get serious about a woman of her class."

That got his brows to rise. "Her class? That's ridiculous. Do people still think that way?"

"Some do. There was a lot of talk when Rene Darois married Sylvie Martine. Some people wondered if she married him for his money."

"They shouldn't wonder that around Rene. Or me for that matter." He didn't like the thought of anyone questioning Sylvie.

"Sylvie's family is well thought of. Marcelle is a pillar of the community, but there was still some talk. It was the same when Seraphina Guidry married Celeste Beaumont's nephew, and everyone loves the Guidrys. It's going to be worse for Jayna because our family has a bad reputation. We're mostly considered trash since our relatives are in and out of jail. Jayna's the first Cardet to ever go to college, much less law school."

He hadn't thought about her family beyond the fact that she obviously loved her sister. "I don't think that at all. There's not a concern in my mind that Jayna Cardet wants my money. Well, she's serious about the steak. The woman is hungry, but I'm not concerned about it if that's what you're worried about."

"I just have to think that part of why my sister wanted out of here was because of how we were perceived growing up. We were those trashy Cardets. It's better now, but things change slowly. One of the reasons I'm here is I want out of that trailer. I want a different home for my girls."

"There's nothing wrong with living in a trailer."

"Says the man who grew up in a mansion," she replied quietly. "I know that poverty isn't a moral failing, but some people treat it like it is. Jayna worked hard and got herself out. Having to come home with her tail between her legs has been difficult on her. I would hate for there to be a bunch of gossip that would make it worse."

He tensed, realizing what she might be saying. "Are you asking me to stay away from your sister?"

"Would you fire me if I said yes?" The question came out with a quiet strength, as though the answer wouldn't change the outcome, but she would like to know.

He didn't even have to think about it. "No, I wouldn't fire you, partly because I'm afraid of what Jayna would do to me if I did."

"So what would you say if I asked you to stay away from her?"

That he did have to think about. "I would tell you that I don't want to hurt your sister. I would also tell you that I don't give a damn about gossip, and I don't think Jayna will, either. If we decide to go for it, the rest of the world can go straight to hell."

Sienna's lips curled up. "Good. Then you're ready. You should expect my mother to try to scare you off at some point."

A sense of relief swept through him. He could handle that. It would be much harder to progress with Jayna if Sienna was against the relationship. On the other hand, knowing her mother didn't approve would likely send Jayna into his bed immediately. Of course, he had a family, too. "Jayna should probably expect to have to deal with my mother as well."

Sienna waved that worry off. "Oh, Jayna will not care about what your mom thinks. She won't care about what anyone thinks, but you should know that she also won't care if the world hates her. If gossip isn't going to bother you, then you'll be okay with my little sis. I had to make sure. Jayna could get upset if you're upset."

He'd grown up surrounded by gossip. The town ran on it, and Sienna seemed to be tapped in. "Are they already talking?"

Sienna chuckled. "After this morning? Yes. When I went to the café to pick up lunch, the whole place was buzzing."

"Dare I ask?" He should probably know what people were saying because it would absolutely get back to his mother.

"Well, given the way Jayna ran off Paul this morning, some people think she's seduced you and your family is trying to save you from her," Sienna explained. "But she knows she's got a good thing and isn't letting you even see your family. You are a captive to passion."

So he needed to take his mother somewhere public for lunch this week or he would likely be considered a prisoner. "Anything else?"

"Oh, there's always another side. People in town love to argue, so they need a counterpoint. In that case, you're the villain. You are taking a woman who is down on her luck and making her do all your work and possibly also taking advantage of her physically. But I'm pretty sure it was my mom spreading that rumor, and not many people listen to her."

He'd barely even had a chance to kiss her yet. "I'm paying her in steak, Sienna. Let everyone know that. She's got expensive tastes. I don't suppose anyone is talking about the fact that we're two single adults with very similar interests who happen to like each other, and that the dynamic of our relationship shouldn't be anyone's business?"

"No. No one has said or thought that," Sienna said with a shake of her head. "And you should not expect that to change anytime soon."

"Good to know."

Sienna slid a hand into the pocket of her blazer. "There are some things she likes about this place. I think she likes being around my kids. I also think she's enjoying being in court. She used to talk about how boring all the corporate stuff had gotten. She's been more energized in the last week than I've seen her in a long time. Maybe if we show her how fun this place can be, she won't leave."

Would she enjoy dancing at Guidry's? Or would it pale in comparison to the lights of New Orleans? Would the quirkiness of this place rub her the wrong way, or would she see it with different eyes now that she was older?

The phone rang and Sienna turned to get back to her desk.

"Hey, Sienna, if that's for me, tell them I'm out. I'm going to work on a special project, and I don't want to be interrupted." Jayna was taking one for the team. He wasn't going to waste her efforts.

"Will do." Sienna closed his office door on her way out.

He sat back. So everyone was talking.

It might be time to give them something to talk about.

He was supposed to work on his latest book, but some instinct deep inside made him pull up the folder that contained *The Man in the Black Hat*. He would look through it and see that Jayna was wrong.

Except at some point while he read, the police detective with the long blond hair morphed into a raven-haired woman with a chic bob.

He started to rework some of the book. Maybe there was some flirtation between the characters, some emotion he hadn't mined. He could make a few changes and see what Jayna thought.

After all, what could it hurt?

chapter seven

Jayna stalked into the office as the sun was going down. Earlier in the day, she'd been preoccupied with thoughts of steak and shrimp and a couple of martinis at Guidry's. She'd dreamed that tonight they would dance and maybe come back here and he would kiss her again and she could lose herself in him.

Not anymore. She was going to murder Quaid Havery.

Her sister's desk had neat stacks of files and notes for the next morning. She'd texted Jayna that she was heading to pick up the girls and would be back tomorrow. It was a good thing Sienna had left since that meant she didn't have to witness what was about to happen.

The door to Quaid's office was closed. She thought about looking for the password to Sienna's computer. Quaid had given her one earlier and told her to memorize it, but it would take Sienna a while to do that, so she'd almost certainly written the sucker somewhere. She could find it, get her hands on the file she needed, and then plot how to take the whole evil scheme down.

That would get her sister in trouble and make her every bit the unethical attorney she was accused of being. She couldn't look through his files. She would just make sure whatever plot Quaid had failed.

She would go straight to the source. She opened his door.

His head rose from staring at his laptop screen and his eyes lit up. "Hey, how was court?"

She'd spent the afternoon dealing with the criminal system, and it hadn't helped her mood. She'd helped an eighteen-year-old plead no contest to a misdemeanor possession charge in hopes that the judge would be lenient. The other defendant had pleaded not guilty to assault when he'd been clearly guilty. He'd told her he was sure his wife would drop the charges when she'd had time to think about it.

Sometimes it was hard to be a lawyer.

"Tell me you're not tearing down the only library in town."

He stared at her for a moment as though he had to flip through the files in his head to find the right answer. "I'm not personally tearing it down, no."

"But you're representing the asshole who's selling the land out from under the library."

"It's a complex situation, but a clear one. The Hillyard family owns the land. They've leased it to the city for one dollar a year for the last fifty years." Quaid pushed back from his desk. "The agreement with the mayor at the time was when Grant Hillyard passed, he would leave the land to the city for as long as the library stood. However, he never wrote that into the will and the agreement was never written down. So now Hillyard's daughter inherited everything and she's selling the land to an investment firm."

"It was an oral agreement. It counts."

"If you can prove it, it counts. Hillyard's written will was simple but clear. Everything went to his only heir, Peggy Hillyard. She wants to sell the land. I'm not sure what you expect me to do about that."

She should have known that would be his defense. He was doing his job. Nothing more. Simply representing his client to the best of his ability. It didn't matter that the client was taking away something precious.

The day had started so well, but now everything seemed to be crashing in again, and she wasn't sure she could handle it.

"Jayna, what happened?" He moved toward her, his eyes narrowing. "This can't be about the library closing. Sylvie's already looking into a new site."

She was sure the mayor was. Sylvie Darois cared about her community, but the wheels of bureaucracy turned slowly. "That's years away. What happens to the kids who need that library now?"

He stopped in front of her, his hands going to her arms and holding her. "What happened?"

She moved away. She couldn't think when his hands were on her. "I found out you're closing the library."

"I'm not closing the library," Quaid insisted. "I wrote the will. I'm enacting the last wishes of my client. Besides, the city's not fighting it. The librarian is retiring next year, and they can't find a replacement. That's one of the things they'll do as they're working to build a new one. Now tell me what's wrong."

Closing the library was wrong. The email she'd gotten was wrong. The text from one of her only friends back in New Orleans was wrong. Her life was wrong, and it wasn't his job to fix it.

She shook her head. "It's not your problem. I think I'm going to skip dinner tonight. I'm going to take Luna for a run, and then I'll head to bed early. Is she upstairs?"

"I think you need to tell me what happened today."

"It's none of your business." She turned to walk away but his hand came out, gripping her elbow.

"Baby, tell me what's got you in this state. Jayna, calm down. This is not you."

Did he think he knew her? She'd been careful around him. He hadn't even started to see her crazy side. "You have no idea who I am. None. You think you know me because you've spent a couple of days with me? Because you've kissed me and thought about hopping into bed with me? This is exactly who I am. I'm the woman who gets mad. Do you know how many times I've been told to calm down?"

"That was wrong of me. I shouldn't have said that, but I'm worried about you."

She didn't want to hear his apologies. She wanted to fight with him, wanted a knock-down, drag-out fight, but he didn't deserve that from her. "I won't be here long enough for you to worry about, Quaid. I'm leaving this place as soon as possible."

"You going to leave your sister after you promised to help her get through school? You going to leave after you took on clients here in town who no one else will serve? Maybe the things I've heard about you are right."

"Maybe they are. Maybe I'm exactly what my mother told me I was. An arrogant social climber who didn't appreciate anything I was given. Maybe I was bound to fail and end up right back in the dirt I came from."

His expression softened and he moved into her space again, his hands going to her hair this time. "Baby, tell me. I'm sorry I got my feelings hurt when you said you would leave. You are not arrogant. You are confident in your abilities, and you should be. You are not a social climber. You couldn't care less about what anyone thinks. And you are not a failure."

That was where he was wrong. "They've moved my ethics case up."

The email she'd received had explained that the complaint was being viewed with urgency. As though she was some kind of criminal who'd conspired to cheat her law firm instead of being the person to report actual criminal activity.

"Then we'll move our meeting with the attorney up," Quaid replied, as though it was a simple thing. "I'll call tomorrow."

She shook her head. "It could cost thousands of dollars, especially since I need help fast. Money I do not have."

"I told you I would take care of it."

"Then everyone will think I'm sleeping with you for your money. I know you think I don't care about my reputation, but I can't stand the thought of everyone looking at me and thinking I couldn't cut it so I'm back here using a man for his cash." Tears welled. She'd thought about this the whole way home. Every scenario she'd come up with had led to one conclusion. She couldn't let Quaid pay the lawyer for her. "The only people who remember that I was ever in this town only remember me because I was obnoxious. I thought I would one day waltz into our twenty-year reunion and show everyone how successful I was, but the truth is they would have looked at me and wondered why I was there because no one would know who I was. I'm just as forgettable now."

"That's not true."

"Tell that to Todd Shale, who recently announced his engagement to a woman who is barely out of high school." The final blow of the day, the one she would have thought wouldn't affect her, had damn near brought her to her knees. "She's pregnant, too. He told me he didn't want kids. I guess he just didn't want mine. She's from a good family, of course. One of the wealthiest in New Orleans. I think he was planning on dumping me before I made the mistake of giving a crap about men who worked with the mob and hurt young women."

He started to pull her into an embrace, but she didn't want his sympathy. She pushed away from him.

"It doesn't matter. I knew what our marriage was. I didn't love him. You know, now that I think about it, maybe I did use him. I used him to get into a big law firm."

"Jayna, of course you loved him. You thought you could build a future together. I'm sure that logical mind of yours worked out a way to explain the relationship you had with him in a way that protected you, but deep down you loved him. He hurt you and you're not helping yourself by rejecting the fact. You're not helping yourself by taking the blame."

"I don't take the damn blame." What was he talking about? If there was one thing she knew for a fact, it was that her husband's prolific cheating wasn't her fault.

"Yes, you do. You tell yourself you knew who he was. You tell yourself you were okay with the cheating because you knew what you were getting into. You say all those things because you think it's better to be cynical and smart than to have gotten your dumb heart broken, but, baby, it's better to have a heart that breaks than to have one encased in ice." He caught her again, dragging her close. "You are not icy, Jayna. You are warm, and your heart works fine. Stop thinking and let me show you."

He lowered his lips to hers, and all that toxic energy inside her morphed into something wild, something primal and necessary, something she wasn't sure she'd ever felt before.

Want. Not need. She'd known so much need, but this longing was beyond anything. It was scary, and she couldn't turn away from it. She knew she would likely ache later, but it didn't matter in the moment. Now, all that mattered was him.

She needed this after the day she'd had. It wouldn't last forever, but these moments with Quaid might save her sanity.

She wrapped her arms around him as he deepened the kiss, his tongue surging into her mouth and sending heat through her system. Quaid was right. She'd been cold for so long. She'd wrapped herself in cold logic for years, and it felt so good to be warm again.

His hands stroked down her back, moving toward her backside, and she pressed herself against him.

"Damn it, Jayna." Quaid took in a shaky breath as he brought his hands back up to her waist. "We need to take a minute."

All she heard was a rejection.

Quaid didn't want her. Well, Todd hadn't wanted her, either, and she'd survived that. She pulled away. "Take as long as you like. I'm going to find a motel."

"I don't think we should do this when you're so emotional."

"Fine. I won't do it at all, Havery. Like I said, I'll find a motel and we can both go back to our regularly scheduled lives." She couldn't stay here with him and listen to all the reasons why they couldn't work. She hadn't asked for some long-term relationship. She'd wanted to spend some time with him. That was all.

And he felt sorry for her. They all felt sorry for her. Well, the ones who didn't actively loathe her. Like her own mother.

God, she was such a fool to have thought he would actually have a sexual interest in her. Hadn't she learned she wasn't that kind of woman?

"I'm starting to believe my life will never be normal again," Quaid growled her way. "I know this is a mistake. I know we should take our time, but you're not going to let that happen, are you?"

She was about to argue with him, to tell him he could go to hell, when he kissed her again. His hands went to her hair, holding her in place while he ravished her mouth. Even if her bruised heart had wanted to fight him, her body didn't care. Her body simply needed, and it had found the one man she would put aside her ego for.

He kissed her for the longest time and then she was in his arms, being carried up the stairs.

She'd never been carried anywhere. "Quaid, you should put me down."

"And lose you again? No." He stared ahead, climbing the stairs. "I've wanted you from the moment you walked into my office. I wanted to go slow because I want this to last as long as it can, but I'll take you any way I can get you, Cardet. Any damn way."

He managed to get the door open and then Luna was staring up at her from the couch with wide doggy eyes.

Luna was going to have to learn that the humans sometimes closed the doors and did things she couldn't be a part of. The big dog had started wagging her tail, but Quaid ignored everything as he strode toward his bedroom.

He kicked the door open and closed again before setting her on her feet.

"I'm going to show you how unforgettable I find you." He smoothed back her hair and then he was kissing her again.

No one had ever kissed her like Quaid did, like he'd been hungry for years and only she could satisfy him. He devoured her mouth, and all thoughts of how awful the day had been fell away. She let herself feel something other than anger and anxiety, and it was magnificent.

When he tugged at her blouse, she brought her arms up, letting him drag it over her head. She kicked off her shoes and was suddenly so much shorter than he was. Or perhaps he was just bigger than he'd been before. Bigger, stronger, safer than she'd believed.

"I was right," he said as his hand came up, fingers brushing her shoulders before running down to skim the tops of her breasts. "You're even more beautiful without your clothes on."

Had he been thinking about her, too? Had he spent these days distracted by thoughts of what it would be like if she wrapped herself around him? She couldn't fool herself anymore. High school Quaid had been a pale comparison to the gorgeous, smart, kind man in front of her.

He thought he was going to get his heart broken, but she would be the one left aching, and she couldn't stop herself. She went on her toes and kissed him, pressing her body hard against his.

It had been so long since she'd had strong arms around her, and she was willing to drown in his attention.

Somehow her skirt came off, his hands sliding it over her hips to pool on the floor below. Cool air hit her skin, but she was warm all over, her body tensing in the sweetest way. She watched as he shrugged out of his dress shirt, taking in his muscular chest and broad shoulders.

He tossed his shirt aside and got his hands on her again. He kissed her, making his way from her mouth to her neck, lighting up her skin everywhere he touched her. She felt his fingers twist at her back and then her bra fell away.

"I've thought of nothing but this for days. You've made it hard for me to think about anything or anyone but you," he whispered as he kissed his way down her torso. His arms were around her and he lifted her up, his mouth on her breasts. He licked her nipple and then sucked it inside his mouth, sending a flash of heat through her.

She gasped as he nipped her, her fingers clutching at his shoulders.

He moved, never setting her down. She was caught between the sweet cage of his arms and the hot pull of his mouth. Quaid maneuvered his way to the bed and settled her down on the soft comforter.

"Tell me you want me as much as I want you." The words were a low growl coming out of his mouth, but she sensed the vulnerability behind them.

He needed her. This wasn't a random hookup, and it wasn't merely sex. He would try to tie her to this place she'd always wanted out of, this place she'd started to enjoy for the first time in her life. He'd been right. They should take things far slower. "I want you so much."

Her whole life had been about discipline. She'd had to work twice as hard, be better than everyone around her to get half as far as her counterparts. She had to make herself fit in, make them forget where she'd come from in order to move ahead. She'd sacrificed her personal life, her primal needs, at the altar of proving she wasn't her mother.

She couldn't sacrifice him. Not him. Even if this only lasted a few nights, it would be worth the heartache.

Jayna watched as Quaid hurriedly undressed, getting rid of his loafers and socks, his slacks and boxers hitting the floor in record time. He was the gorgeous one, built on athletic lines. The high school football player had been replaced with a man she couldn't take her eyes off.

He gripped her ankles and dragged her across the bed before dropping to his knees. He eased her panties off and spread her legs wide. She gasped as warm breath caressed her sensitive flesh.

"I told you I'd show you how sweet you are."

He proceeded to make a feast of her, every stroke of his tongue driving her higher and higher. She fisted her hands around the comforter, holding herself in place for his torture. All of her self-consciousness fell away, and she was left with nothing but pleasure as he managed to send her straight over the edge.

Every muscle tensed and released, satisfaction flowing through her.

This was where she'd needed to be since . . . since forever. "Jayna?"

She looked up and Quaid stood there, staring down at her like he needed her permission. Always the gentleman. He'd given her everything and still made sure she wanted more.

Now would be the time she could let her fear back in. She could still protect herself. It wasn't too late.

"Please, Quaid." She reached out for him.

Protecting her heart was overrated.

With shaking hands, Quaid pulled the condom out of the drawer of the nightstand.

If she'd refused him, he might have died of sheer wanting. She was gorgeous, every inch of her body calling to him. He knew it was a mistake, that she wasn't ready for what he wanted, but she'd pushed him. He'd realized in that moment that he would take a single night with her if that was all he could have, and damn the consequences. The only thing he couldn't take was letting her be alone tonight.

She needed him, needed to know how much she was wanted, how much he craved her.

He could still taste her on his lips as he managed to roll the condom on.

He was glad he still had half a brain to remember to put the damn thing on because his whole being was focused on her.

But then hadn't it been since that moment she'd walked back into town and his world had amped up to Technicolor?

She'd said yes and he was going to convince her to keep saying yes. All he needed was a little charm, a bit of luck, and a whole lot of pleasure.

He pulled her up. The last thing he intended to do was fall on her and have everything end in mere moments. No.

He had a feeling she'd neglected this part of her life, that she hadn't had a lover who indulged in her. He intended to make her need him. Even if it was only in bed.

All of his life he'd been the good guy, the responsible one, the dependable one. He was going to show her the good guy could also be a bad boy.

She looked up at him with sleepy eyes. "Is this where you bring all your dates? Your booty call room?"

He needed to make things perfectly clear to her. "I haven't had a woman up here in years." He moved to the bed, lying back and helping her straddle his hips. "I bought those condoms today and put them up here in the desperate hope that we would get to a place where this was a good idea."

She sat back on her heels, that soft, wet part of her so close to where he needed it to be. "But you think it's a bad idea."

He was so deeply aware that he could still lose her. It might be for the best. They could reset and go to Guidry's and they could work on their relationship before they got physical.

Her skin was so soft under his hands. "It's a great idea."

One hand came out, brushing down his chest. "I'm serious, Quaid. Why do you think this is a bad idea? Because you don't want people to know we're involved?"

He flipped her over because it was obvious he needed to take charge. When she was on her back, he rubbed himself against her, every move getting him harder. "Baby, everyone thinks we're already sleeping together. You confronted my brother in the middle of Main Street looking all soft and sweet in your PJs, and not a person in town is thinking I let that gorgeous woman sleep in the guest room. I would like everyone to know we're together, but I think you might use me for sex and then get some revenge by forgetting my name in the morning."

The sweetest smile made her face glow. "That would be fun."

Maybe he'd been wrong. Maybe this was exactly what she needed. Intimacy. He pressed up, bringing them together, biting back a groan. She felt absolutely perfect. "That would not be fun. Not in any way. This means something to me. You mean something to me."

Her legs wound around his waist, her arms circling his neck until she was wrapped around him. "You mean something to me, too. Kiss me, Quaid. I need this so badly. I need you."

It was all he wanted to hear. He lowered his lips to hers, giving her what she needed. He kissed her as he pulled out and thrust back in, loving the way her silky heat encased him. He kissed her while he made love to her.

He was in far too deep, and it no longer mattered.

He kissed her until she groaned against him, tightening around him and bringing him over the edge with her.

When he fell against her, he held her for the longest time and prayed this could last.

"Do you want to get dressed?" An hour later, Quaid was still in bed, his arm cradling her to his chest. "I owe you a steak. You never told me how court went."

"No, because I was too upset about the library." She rubbed her cheek against his chest. "I don't suppose we can get something delivered."

"I can run across to the café, but the only steak they sell is Salisbury."

She turned, her chin now on his chest and eyes on him. "I think I'll stick to a burger and fries, but the idea of leaving this bed is not an ideal one. It's nice here."

He reached out and smoothed back her hair. "It is." They'd

spent the last hour making love and exploring each other's bodies. Hugging. Kissing. Playing. It might be time to get serious. "Are you all right? Do you want to talk about it?"

She laid her head down again. "About what? The fact that my career is over or the fact that my marriage was a complete failure?"

"Anything you want to talk about, Jayna."

She shifted, sitting up in bed, the sheet around her. "Or we could talk about the fact that you're depriving an entire generation of knowledge by closing down this town's one and only library."

That wasn't what she needed to talk about. "Your career isn't over. Let me take care of your legal fees. You can repay me either by handling cases for me or in cash when you get back on your feet."

Or she could just let him take care of her. She could stay in town, right here in his apartment, and years could go by and she would forget there was a time it had felt weird to let him help her.

She frowned and he hated the fact that she was tense again, but they needed to figure this out. If her case had been moved up, someone was putting pressure on the bar association. She couldn't fool around. Proper representation was absolutely necessary.

He reached out and threaded his fingers through hers. "Baby, you know I'm right. The bar doesn't move things up unless someone is pressuring them. They want you on the ropes so you make the mistake of not hiring a specialist. They know the only way they can possibly win against you is to get you to make a mistake."

"They know how little money I have," she countered. "They think if they can get me to represent myself, I'll screw up something procedural that allows them to judge against me. If I have a judgment against me, that will help any suit they file."

"Then we can't let that happen."

She stared down at their joined hands and sighed. "I'm going to pay you back, and not in sex."

He tugged her down and kissed her forehead, cuddling her close. "However you want to reimburse me is perfectly fine with me. Do you think they're going to sue? What's the point if they know you don't have any money?"

"They made sure I don't have any money. And I lied when I said I thought *maybe* Todd had been planning to leave me. I'm certain he was. Our prenup only covered the first ten years. After that it was dissolved, and we were about to hit year nine. He was going to make sure he got rid of me before then."

"That's not your fault, either."

"It feels like my fault. It feels like I should have realized what would happen. All I hear in my head is my mother telling me it wouldn't work, that it was all a mistake, and turns out she was right."

"You can't look at it like that, Jayna. You went into the marriage because you thought it would work. You couldn't know how it would end up. We learn from every relationship we have."

"Well, I learned my mother was right, and I should have accepted the life I was born into."

"You know why she's that way," he prompted.

"Because she hates anything she doesn't understand."

"Because she's afraid that you'll look down on her, that she'll lose you. It's why she tried to talk Sienna out of taking the job. She thinks if Sienna gets educated, she'll lose the only kid she has left, and her grandkids, too."

"That's ridiculous. She didn't lose anyone."

"You didn't come home for years," he reminded her. "Did you come home during summer breaks?"

"No." Her arm moved over his waist as she sighed. "I worked during the summers. Something I wouldn't have had to do if she'd let my uncle pay for college."

"Well, you have to decide if you can forgive her for that." He understood that conundrum well. "You don't owe anyone forgiveness, but she is your mother. You have to figure out if the good part is worth the toxic part."

"Is that what you did?"

"It was easier when my father was alive," he admitted. "He took care of everything when it came to my mom. And then when he got cancer, she became an entirely different person. She was always so flighty, always dependent on him, but when he got sick . . ." He had to take a deep breath because this was why he didn't talk about his dad in anything but fond memories. He got emotional when he thought about those last days. "She let that all fall away, and she was focused on him. My mother, who couldn't stand the sight of blood or talk of any bodily function, learned how to change bedpans in the middle of the night and how to make sure his IV was properly placed. I was always confused about that. On the surface, they never seemed close."

"Maybe our parents are like trees and we only see what's above the surface. Some of it's pretty. Some of it's cracked and broken, but we don't truly know how strong and deep the roots are," she said quietly before her tone turned to wisecracking. "Unless you're my parents, and then it's all out in the open."

She hid behind sarcasm so often. "I'm sure your mom has some pretty deep roots, too."

"Yeah," she replied. "They're all buried deep, and there's no room for movement."

The problems with her mom seemed to be one of the

reasons she wouldn't consider staying in town. "Did you always fight this way with her? Even when you were young?"

"Oh, no. When I was a kid she was . . . she was the one who made things fun. She would take us places with her. Dumb places like the grocery store or to Miss Marcelle's to get her hair done. When she had to work on the weekends, we would go with her, and she and some of the other single moms would turn the breakroom into a playroom. They would bring sheets and pillows and we would make these big forts." She was quiet for a moment. "Then the manager found out and we weren't allowed to go with her anymore. Of course, they didn't stop making her work weekends. Instead they made her find and pay for a babysitter. Then Sienna was old enough and we stayed alone in that trailer."

He'd never once had that problem as a child. There was always someone dedicated to making sure he had something to do, somewhere to be, that he was safe. "I'm sorry about that. It sounds like she was in a bad place."

"And she wanted me and Sienna in that bad place, too." She sat up again, though this time she didn't bother covering herself. "I know what you're doing. You're trying to get me to feel sorry for my mom."

She was so beautiful, and his instinct was to drown in her. He could get her under him again, and they didn't have to talk about anything except the things that made her smile. But that wouldn't start to solve her problems, and keeping Jayna close suddenly seemed like the most important thing in his life. "I'm feeling out your relationship with her because it seems important."

"It's not. I haven't been close to my mom for years."

"But when you got in trouble, you called her."

She sighed, her shoulders coming down. "I called my sister. I needed a place to stay but she doesn't have an extra room. She's only got the two bedrooms, and the girls are in one. I would have been on the couch. My mom's was a compromise."

"Did she know that? Did she know you didn't want to come home?"

"Probably. It's not like she met me with a party or anything. We barely talked and then she kicked me out."

He sat up, getting closer to her. How long had it been since he sat in bed with a woman and talked, their intimacy a warmth that blanketed them both? It had never felt like this. "Do you want a relationship with her?"

"I don't know. Maybe. It's hard."

If she was on the fence, then he had a chance to help mend that rift. "Then you need to talk to her. I think one of the reasons my mother is meddling in my life right now is that she spent all those years taking care of my father and now she's not sure what to do with herself. She's not in a place where she can concentrate on herself, so she focuses on me and my brother, and not always in a good way. And she doesn't understand why I get upset. Maybe that's what's happening with your mom, too. She worked hard all her life for you and Sienna, and she feels like you don't appreciate who she is."

She was quiet for a moment.

"Do you, Jayna?"

"Of course I appreciate what she sacrificed for us. But I shouldn't have to prove that by not using the gifts I was given. She wanted me to join her at the plant she's worked at for most of my life. She set up an interview when I was a senior. She knew I was applying to colleges, but she didn't think I would be able to afford it, so she arranged a job for me. When I refused to go to the interview, she was furious."

"That was presumptuous of her, but I'm sure she thought she was being helpful."

"No, she thought she could trap me."

"She thought she could keep you," he corrected. "I know you don't want to hear this, but you should put yourself in her shoes. She watched you grow up and pass her by. That had to be hard."

"I'll think about it if you'll think about talking to your brother."

"It's a completely different situation."

"I don't see how. We both have family members who've hurt us. You think I should give mine a second chance," she pointed out.

"Paul's had a hundred chances." His chest suddenly felt tight. He didn't want to talk about Paul. He wasn't sure what Jayna knew about his brother, but if he could avoid the worst parts of it, he would.

There was a scratch on the door that saved him.

"I think Luna needs a trip outside." He eased out of bed and grabbed his pants. "Why don't I take her out and grab us some dinner at the café? Unless you changed your mind. I'll still take you out for a steak."

For a moment she looked like she was going to argue with him, but then her expression softened. "No. I think I'd like to stay in. Especially now that I know you bought condoms today, which means everyone in town will know we had sex."

He buttoned his pants and pulled a T-shirt on. "They'll still know tomorrow."

She shifted, her legs dangling off the bed. "I'll be okay with it tomorrow. I'm a bit raw tonight. It's been a while since I had a . . . I don't know what to call you. It's too early to say 'boyfriend.' 'Lover' is a weird word. And I wouldn't say that was a booty call."

"It was not." He moved into her space, reaching out to tilt her head up so she had to look in his eyes. "I know it's early, but I like you, Jayna. I like you far too much for how little time we've known each other. I don't have any interest in seeing anyone else. So call me whatever you like, but know I'm serious about this relationship for however long it lasts."

Her lips curled up but there was something wary in her eyes that made his heart clench. "And that's why I'll be okay tomorrow. Get me some onion rings while you're out. Do you mind if we watch a movie tonight?"

He leaned over and kissed her forehead. Lucky for them he'd had his father's old TV replaced with a smart one. "Pick whatever you like. I'll be right back."

Luna barked, proof that she was ready to go, regardless of whether or not the humans were done.

He shoved his feet into loafers, not bothering with socks, and opened the door.

He was a coward for not talking to her about Paul, but it didn't matter. His relationship with his brother wasn't the problem. Paul would be gone soon. His brother wouldn't surface again for a year or two, and by then his relationship with Jayna would be on solid ground or completely dead because she would be in New Orleans or Houston or Dallas.

He clipped the leash on Luna's collar and started toward the stairs.

"And pie, Quaid." Jayna stood in the doorway of his bedroom, leaning her gorgeous body against the frame without a stitch on.

She was going to be the death of him. "Pie it is, then."

He was rapidly discovering he would do just about anything to keep her.

chapter eight

❧

"Your Honor, this is not a case about private property laws."
Jayna faced the judge, not looking her opponent's way at all.
Quaid looked far too hot in his tailored suit, and she would
remember how he looked even hotter without the suit on,
and then she would stare at him and maybe drool a little. It
was better to pretend he didn't exist. "This is a case about
what we owe to our neighbors. This is a case about community and kindness."

Onc full week of living with Quaid and she was already
getting used to how nice it was to have an actual partner.
The last few years of her marriage, she and Todd had barely
been roommates. They'd talked about nothing beyond the
firm and how to get another step up the ladder—usually
with her being the one making the sacrifice to help him up.

Quaid took Luna out on walks every day so Jayna could
sit and quietly have coffee in the mornings or read her book
in the evenings. He'd bought groceries without her when she
had a meeting, carefully getting everything on her list and
then cleaning up the kitchen because she'd cooked. He
hadn't brought up the fact he'd bought everything or that she

was living rent free in his house. He'd simply taken the dishes and done them after refilling her wineglass.

"There are social contracts," she continued. "And Geraldine Oliver is breaking her social contract to her neighbor Jimmy Abbot."

The judge held up a hand. "Wait, I thought you were Geraldine's lawyer and Quaid was Jimmy's. I'm confused."

Britney looked up from her stenotype. "They changed, PawPaw. Now Quaid is representing Geraldine and Jayna is here to present Jimmy's case."

"Why?" the judge asked.

"I think Quaid wanted to charge Jimmy too much and Jayna was willing to be paid in chips or something, and Quaid didn't want to get left out, so he agreed to take on Geraldine's case pro bono," Britney explained.

Geraldine raised a hand. "I'm paying him by knitting him a sweater, Your Honor."

"And I'm paying her in gas, too," Jimmy interjected. "I'm not being cheap or anything."

Sure he wasn't. She hadn't taken him up on the gas offer since her car was in Herve's shop and Quaid drove her where she needed to go. Although, apparently the girls had gotten their weekly free slushies, and went in for chips every day after school. Sienna was making sure they used that bit of compensation.

The judge frowned. "I don't like it. It's confusing. Also, I would like to point out that the two of you have requested not one, not two, but four different court dates."

"Yes, Your Honor." She wasn't sure what the problem was. "We have four cases, so we need four court dates."

"But we only had two civil court dates all last month," the judge pointed out. "When am I supposed to fish?"

She bit back a groan because she wouldn't get anywhere

yelling at the judge to do his damn job. Things moved differently in Papillon. Everyone here expected to have some kind of a life outside of work.

She'd even started thinking it was nice to not work eighty hours a week. It was kind of fun to sit with Quaid at night and eat popcorn while watching a movie, or read a book while he wrote on his laptop. She'd rarely done that before, since her firm had demanded every second of her time.

Next week they had plans to go to one of Papillon's many festivals together. They would walk around the park grounds and eat yummy food and listen to music.

"I'm sure we can't keep up this pace for long," she promised.

"Oh, we can keep it going for a long time," Quaid countered, his voice going all low and sexy despite the fact they were in court. "You will find I have an enormous amount of stamina when it comes to my work, Your Honor. Up until now, I haven't had a worthy adversary, but Ms. Cardet is proving to be a fine opponent. The citizens of Papillon should understand they now have two champions, and we're willing to get into the ring anytime they need us to."

He made every word sound like a temptation, like a promise of pure pleasure, and she was blushing.

"Are you sure you're all right, Quaid?" Judge Brewer adjusted his glasses. "Your voice sounds funny."

His voice sounded like he was hot for her and ready to take her to the nearest private place and throw down, like he couldn't wait to tear off her clothes and get inside her.

God, she hoped no one could see how hard her nipples were. That man could get her hot with nothing more than a look, but he wasn't supposed to do that in the courtroom. They had a deal. Because they were on opposite sides of most of the cases they were working on, they didn't talk about the cases together. When they left the office and went upstairs, they didn't talk about work. They talked about his books and what she was reading. They talked about the news or TV shows and movies.

Even when they weren't together, she was thinking about him all the time. Every minute of the day, he was there in the back of her mind. She was in high school again, and he was the object of her affection.

Except this time, he seemed to be right there with her.

"I am perfectly fine, Your Honor. More than fine," Quaid said with his confident smile. "And we're ready to go because Ms. Cardet is right. This case is about what we owe our neighbors and how we treat each other here in Papillon."

"Well, it seems to me Geraldine there treats her neighbors to a whole lot of skin," the judge shot back.

That got the people in the courtroom laughing.

"You're welcome, Andy," Geraldine said with a wave. "You should come out on Friday. We're having a party. Everyone is getting so tan. You know you could use a little vitamin D."

"Is there any way you could settle this out of court?" The judge looked a bit desperate. "I'm supposed to fish on Friday."

"What do you say, Cardet?" Quaid liked to use her last name when they were working. "Do you want to settle?"

He was so annoying sometimes. "If by settling you mean your client ceases to scare off my client's customers with her adults-only parties clearly visible to the public, then yes. We can settle. I even have damages drawn up. Also, I have witnesses who can clearly show that it's not merely adults who are being affected by Geraldine's protests."

Ivy and Kelly were ready to be sworn in and hoping it would be during school hours.

"Yes, I saw that you're bringing in your nieces." Quaid chuckled. "I'm ready to show that Geraldine's protests are also of a feminist nature, proving that body shaming is damaging. Showing girls and women that they are beautiful at any age is important."

"Oh, that is such BS." She turned Quaid's way. "Geraldine is not trying to lift up women. She's trying to milk my client into paying for a new fence, a fence that isn't even legal."

"Well, your client sends invasive light into Geraldine's backyard all night long." Quaid didn't miss a beat.

"Which is why my client paid top dollar for blackout drapes and then went the extra mile and installed them himself at no charge to your client." She was stretching the term *top dollar*, but they had been the most expensive ones at Walmart.

"So is my client not allowed to enjoy an evening outside?" Quaid asked with an innocent expression on his face that she didn't trust for a single second. "Judge, do you spend every evening in your home? Hidden behind drapes and not enjoying the evening air?"

"Of course not," the judge replied. "There's nothing better than sitting out in my backyard listening to the sounds of the night. We live in a beautiful place. We should enjoy it while we can."

Quaid gestured Jayna's way. "I guess Ms. Cardet doesn't have the same belief. Maybe that's because she lived in New Orleans for all those years, or perhaps she believes the gifts of nature we've been given aren't important to the elderly."

Asshole. "I never said that."

Jimmy held up a hand. "Neither did I. My momma's Geraldine's age. She loves the fire pit I built for her."

Yeah, courtroom protocol wasn't much of a thing here in Papillon.

"No one is saying Geraldine shouldn't enjoy her backyard. I literally did not say that." She felt the need to put that on the record or she might find herself with protestors of her own. And she probably had enough of those already since she'd heard from her sister that Quaid's mom wasn't happy with his current choice of roommate.

He ignored her. "And she now has to look at the back of his gas station, which is not pretty. She has the trash dumpster to look at, and that same light floods into the backyard all night long. Imagine not being able to enjoy a spring or summer night because you're blinded by the harsh lights of the business that took down your precious trees."

He was so dramatic. "It was one tree. And if she didn't want to look at the gas station, maybe she shouldn't have moved into a house that was behind a gas station." She could counter his every argument. "There has been a gas station or convenience store in that exact location since 1952. Geraldine didn't purchase that home until 1974."

"And I have pictures of what the backyard looked like the day she moved in. You can't see that gas station because of the trees planted behind her fence. Those trees cut out noise and light," Quaid explained in an annoyingly patient tone. "She was completely unaware that the gas station was actually right behind her house."

"I was very surprised to find that out," Geraldine said, her lips pursed.

"But my daddy used to hand your order over the fence when you needed milk but didn't want to make the walk around the block," Jimmy countered. "Where did you think he was coming from?"

"I think you'll find that Geraldine was unaware of what she was buying because the owners of the gas station cleverly hid their location," Quaid announced.

She put her hands on her hips, outrage plain in her tone. "Hid? Behind a tree that had been there forever? Also, you know these are the exact arguments I made when I was representing Geraldine."

"They're very good arguments," Quaid replied smoothly.

The judge threw up his hands. "And this is why I'm so confused. I'm hungry and it's time for lunch. We're in recess until two p.m."

But they'd just gotten started. She bit back frustration as the judge gaveled out and then he was talking to his granddaughter about how long to microwave the leftover meatloaf he'd brought with him.

"Those two are going to kill me," the judge said as Britney led him out of the courtroom.

"I do think he's talking about us," Quaid said, a glimmer of humor in his eyes. "So I was thinking we could go home and spend our lunch hour together."

"Seriously?" She stared at him, aware that the courtroom was emptying and Geraldine and Jimmy were walking out together.

"I was thinking about asking your mom to come to one of my parties, Jimmy," Geraldine was saying. "It's been an age since I saw her."

"You can't do that, Geraldine. She's my momma. I never thought you would play so dirty," she heard Jimmy say as the door closed.

"I don't think they should be talking without us." She started for the door.

Quaid reached for her hand, tugging her back. "Hey, are you annoyed with me?" He didn't look worried at the prospect. "They were good arguments. That's why I used them."

"Good arguments I didn't get to use because the judge ruled in your favor without even hearing them," she countered.

"That was a completely different case, baby." He put his

hands on her hips, drawing her in close so she had no choice but to look into those warm eyes of his. "That was all about property laws. This is different and you know it."

"It's lazy to use my arguments." Her body was already warming up, and she was less annoyed with him when his hands were on her. "You're spending all your time working on your new book."

He stared down at her for a moment, a soft smile on his face, as though he liked what he saw. "I'm not working on the new one. I've put it on hold."

That was news to her. "Hey, I'm almost done reading the last book. I need the next one in the series, mister. It's not fair to keep your readers waiting."

She'd been making her way through Armand Landry's adventures. The night before, she'd finished the one where Armand had to solve the particularly vicious murder of his brother, Pierre.

"I'm not working on a new one," he admitted. "But only because I'm revising. I'm going through *The Man in the Black Hat* and strengthening Shannon Wright's character because I'm going to put her in every book as Armand's love interest."

It was her turn to smile. "Are you serious?"

He dragged her close. "I thought about it and you're right. They spark off each other. I can see it now. Armand deals with the police in almost every book—I can replace those police officer side characters with Shannon and slowly grow that relationship into something good. Hell, I'm thinking at some point Armand will have to save Shannon from a killer and will be forced to confront his feelings about her."

She snorted and didn't care that it wasn't a ladylike sound. "Like he would have to save Shannon. She's a badass."

"Oh, she needs saving," he teased, his mouth swooping down to cover hers. "Just like you need saving. Come on, baby. Let's go back to the apartment and I'll save you real good."

She was almost ready to give in because he was completely irresistible, until she heard the dainty sound of a woman clearing her throat, a polite but icy request for attention.

She turned and then practically jumped back from Quaid, because his mother stood beside the last row of benches. She was dressed in slacks and a vibrant green jungle-print jacket, with pearls around her neck just waiting to be clutched.

"Quaid, I was hoping we could talk." Marian Havery had her eyes on her son, refusing to acknowledge that Jayna was even there.

Quaid turned his mother's way, but not before threading his fingers through Jayna's. "Of course. Jayna and I were about to go to lunch. We've got to be back in court in an hour or so. Will this take long?"

"Quaid, I need to talk to you about some family business."

"Fine. You can join us for lunch."

It was completely obvious to Jayna that his mother did not want her in this conversation. "I've got some work I can do. I'll grab a sandwich back at the office. You need to talk to your mom."

He frowned down at her. "Then you go and have lunch at the café and I'll take my mother back to the office. After all, she'd like to talk about business."

He leaned over and kissed her briefly before turning away.

He said nothing to his mother as she followed him out the door.

She couldn't remember ever seeing Quaid so cold, and she wondered what was going on between them. He didn't talk about his family, and certainly didn't talk about the problems they had—despite the fact that he constantly pressed her to deal with her mom.

Yet when she asked about his family, he always distracted her.

She wasn't sure if his problems with his brother were "the bastard slept with my girlfriend" serious or simply due to a regular sibling rivalry.

Her stomach rumbled. She was eating way more now that she had sex on a regular basis. All that physical activity made her hungry. She could go over her notes and try to turn this fiasco of a trial around. Maybe she should open another couple of buttons on her shirt and distract opposing counsel with her boobs.

She made her way out of the courthouse and into the bright light of day, the sun warming her.

She stopped and breathed in the spring air and the sweet scent of daffodils. They were blooming all around the courthouse.

"Hey, I finally get you alone," a deep voice said.

Jayna turned, and her quiet lunch went all to hell.

Quaid opened the door to the office and allowed his mother to enter first, the habit of a man raised to be a gentleman.

Sienna looked up from her desk, a smile dying on her face as she realized it wasn't her sister who'd come back with him. She straightened up. "Good afternoon, Mrs. Havery."

His mother looked Sienna up and down and instead of replying, turned his way. "Where is Cindy?"

This woman had raised him to be a gentleman but wasn't bothering with politeness herself. "She's on . . . I don't know what to call grandparental leave. She's home with her daughter who had a baby recently. Sienna Cardet is going to answer the phones and run the office until Cindy retires. Then she'll take over as my paralegal."

"Cardet? As in Jayna?" His mother managed to make the question sound like a condemnation.

Sienna stood, picking up her purse. "Jayna's my sister. She's a lawyer and a smart one, too."

"Well, I'm sure she's fine, though from what I can tell she's simply taking the cases Quaid doesn't want."

He was about to scold her when Sienna's brows rose, and she stood right in front of his mother.

"Quaid is lucky to have her. My sister can run rings around him when it comes to the law. She had to do everything he did during law school while working thirty hours a week to pay her way through school. I assure you those cases Quaid doesn't want are in good hands." She looked Quaid's way. "I'm going to lunch."

"You feel free to take a long one, Sienna." He gave her what he hoped was a reassuring smile.

Sienna was going to work out just fine. She was already finding her feet and emulating her sister's confidence.

It was really the only way to deal with a woman like his mother.

"Well, you should think about firing that woman. She's rude," his mother huffed.

"You were the rude one. I think you'll find that Sienna has beautiful manners when the person she's with is worthy of them. You're a snob, Mother, and I'm not putting up with it when it comes to my staff. You can be polite or you can leave."

Her face flushed. "I am perfectly polite to Cindy. I was simply surprised that you hired someone new. Your father never needed more than his secretary."

"Because Father was happy to work eighty hours a week.

I'm willing to spend the extra money so we're not over-whelmed." He opened the door to his office. It was apparent he wasn't getting out of this meeting. He would have to make a sandwich or he'd be hungry all afternoon. "What do you need, Mother?"

She stared at him for a moment before taking the seat in front of his desk, placing her purse on her lap, hands holding the handle. "I need for you to be reasonable. This is ridiculous, Quaid, and people are starting to talk."

"I didn't realize they'd ever stopped."

"Quaid, you're going to cause a scandal."

"Mother, don't pretend like it's Regency-period England and our family name is going to be tarnished because I'm dating a woman outside my financial class. I've done that a lot, you know. Most of the women I've dated have not had our money, not that it matters."

"But they came from solid families. The sister of hers, the one you hired, has been married not once but twice. Her daughters have two different fathers."

"And one loving mother," he argued. "That's all that matters. She's going to be excellent at her job once she's fully trained."

"Did she even go to college?"

"No. And that is not a requirement for her to become a certified paralegal." He was curious. "You know she's raising two children on her own and working hard to better herself. What exactly is your problem with her? Beyond that she doesn't have the amount of money you require to view someone as a human being?"

"That is not true, Quaid, and beneath you," his mother huffed. "I do plenty of charity work. I've done it all my life to help people like the Cardets, and they still end up in trouble. She's raising those kids herself because she made bad choices, the same kind of choices I see you making.

How well do you know that woman who's moved in with you after what? A week? How do you know she's not trying to trap you into marriage?"

He laughed at the very idea. "I assure you Jayna's not trying to trap me. If anything, I'm the one trying to trap her. You think I should get her pregnant? I've been trying to tempt her with my helpful nature and mystery novels. Maybe I'm going about this the wrong way and I should poke a hole in one of the condoms I bought."

His mother gasped. "Don't you dare."

He decided it was time to get serious. "I want you to stay out of my relationship with Jayna Cardet."

"Tell me you aren't serious about this woman," his mother said. "I'm worrying myself sick over this. Did you know she's the subject of an ethics review?"

"Most lawyers get complaints," he countered. "Dad had to answer a couple himself."

"That was different and you know it."

"No, I don't know it. I know why Jayna is being reviewed, and she'll be cleared as long as she's got halfway decent counsel."

"And where would she get the money for that? I've been talking to some of my old friends in New Orleans. She lost everything in the divorce. It's why she crawled back here. The Shales were smart enough to protect their family money from her with a prenup. Now she's looking for a new sugar daddy."

Quaid laughed at that one. "A sugar daddy implies that the daddy—in this case I believe you would be referring to me—takes care of everything financial so the woman doesn't have to work. Let me tell you, that woman's work ethic is outstanding. I've been working hard to get her to relax and take some time off."

"But you're paying for everything."

"She's bringing far more than money to the table. I've heard she's almost closed a deal to get us a couple of goats." Sienna was still working behind the scenes, acting as Jayna's . . . did lawyers have agents? "And she takes care of the paperwork so I can write."

A long-suffering sigh came from his mother's chest. "You and that writing . . . Quaid, I love you, son, but I do not understand your obsession with writing pulp novels. You need to leave the artistic endeavors to your brother. I don't understand why you can't be happy with your place in the world."

"And I don't understand why you can't let me be, Mom." He was tired, too. "Did you honestly come down here to warn me off Jayna? If so, then you've done your duty and you should feel free to go."

He might be able to hustle over to the café and still have lunch with Jayna. If she wasn't too annoyed with him.

"I think your brother is in trouble, and I need you to fix things."

Well, of course this was about Paul. It was always about Paul. "I've already tried. I know about his debts. I've offered to pay them, but he won't give me a name."

She waved that off. "I'm not talking about that misunderstanding."

"Is that how he put it?" His brother was certainly creative when it came to explanations.

"Of course. He's paying that man back, but you know how banks can be. You know your brother. He's got a lot of balls in the air."

He had a set of brass balls, that was for sure. "Then what are you talking about?"

"Has Paul talked to you about the film he recently produced?"

"The one that's being held up because of a lawsuit?" He wasn't getting involved in this. Not in any way.

"Yes." His mother confirmed his fear. "Paul wants to show his film around to some important people and he can't because of this nuisance lawsuit. I want you to fix it for him."

"I know I wear a lot of hats around this town, but I'm not an entertainment lawyer and I'm not licensed to practice in California, where I'm sure the contracts were signed and the lawsuit is being litigated," he explained. "And you know that. You were a lawyer's wife for decades."

"I know that your father would have looked into it for him."

"Then send Paul in here to ask for help." He would love to tell his brother to pound sand. "Like I said, I've offered to help him. He's refused. I don't think he wants my help, and I would appreciate it if you would stay out of that relationship, too."

He felt a twist of guilt when his mother's eyes shone with tears. They glimmered but did not fall.

"I can see you don't want me in any part of your life, do you?"

"That's not true, but I think it's for the best right now that I keep a certain distance."

"It's because of that woman."

The guilt he'd briefly felt fled. "I left the house before I started dating Jayna."

"Is that what you call it? Because from where I'm sitting, there's no dating about it," she said primly. "She's your mistress, and everyone in town knows it. It's embarrassing. You're a grown man who should be looking for a wife, not a playboy."

He'd never been a playboy and he wasn't one now, but she might have a point about the whole dating thing. The days had been long, and they'd been content staying in. They faced off at work, battling it out, and then went upstairs and battled it out in a different way.

Was their whole relationship about sex? Was that how Jayna saw it?

Was he Jayna's booty call? She didn't even have to call. He was right there waiting for her to need him.

"Get used to her, Mom. I'm not joking. I'm serious about her, more serious than I've been about a woman since college." He needed her to understand that he wasn't going to be moved on the subject. "If you can't get along with her, we're going to have problems."

"So you're giving me an ultimatum?"

"I'm telling you that I won't accept any insult to her or her family. Not from anyone. If you can't be polite to her, then stay away."

"I'm trying to look out for your best interests, son. Do you honestly believe your father would approve?"

"I think Dad would have adored Jayna. He would be deeply amused by her quick wit and impressed with how hard she works." Why wasn't he showing her off? He was being self-involved. He was taking advantage of the fact that she didn't mind quiet evenings. He was also indulging in the way she enjoyed his books.

"So you won't help your brother?" His mother stood, her chin coming up. "And you won't help your family?"

"I can't help Paul if he won't even give me the tools I need to help him. And if you think I can help the family by breaking things off with the only woman who's moved me in forever, then no, I won't help the family and we need to make some decisions about our living arrangements."

"Are you saying if I don't accept that woman, you'll throw me out of my home?"

His mother could be dramatic. "No, but I might buy another house. The apartment is all right for now, but we'll need some more space if only for the dog."

Luna poked her nose in. She hung around the office, which was nice because she reminded him to get up and move around from time to time.

His mother looked down at the dog, and her expression softened. "Your father was allergic. I always did like dogs."

"She's Jayna's. She gave up a lot of what her husband owed her so she could keep Luna." He reached out, and Luna came to sit beside him. "Does that honestly sound like a woman who's only out for money? There's always another side to every story. I know your rich friends in New Orleans are going to spout whatever the Shales want them to say, but I believe Jayna. You know, Todd is getting married again. A whole two months after his divorce was finalized, and according to what I've heard, his fiancée is at least three months pregnant."

He could fight gossip with gossip.

His mother looked scandalized. "He was cheating on her?"

"Pretty much through their entire marriage." He would use sympathy if that was what it took.

His mother stared for a moment. "If I consider giving your . . . girlfriend a chance, will you think about talking to Paul?"

It was as much as he could expect her to bend, and talking to Paul wouldn't change a damn thing. "Yes."

And she'd only asked him to think about it. He could easily do that.

His mother nodded and walked out, the bell over the door ringing when she exited the office.

Quaid sat back with a sigh, watching out the window as his mother strode down the street. He wondered if he should go over to the café. There might still be time to grab some lunch with Jayna, but some of what his mom had said was still sinking in.

He hadn't taken her on a single date.

He grabbed his cell and dialed up his best friend. "Hey, Rene. I need to know what the word is about me and Jayna. What's the town saying?"

A chuckle came over the line. "Are you sure you want to know?"

If he was going to convince Jayna that staying in Papillon might be a good idea, he had to remind her there was life beyond the office and the courthouse and the café. "Not at all, but hit me."

Quaid petted Luna as his best friend gave him the lowdown.

chapter nine

"You should talk quickly because as soon as I'm finished with lunch, I'm going back to the courthouse, and you will not be allowed to follow me," Jayna said as the waitress who'd replaced Sienna bounced away. She was likely in her late teens and looked so young and perky it hurt.

She was fairly certain she'd never once been that perky in her life.

Paul Havery watched the waitress, too, a smile on his face. "I forgot how nice this place is."

"She's barely out of high school. What do you want, Paul?" She'd ordered soup and half a turkey sandwich because they wouldn't take long to make and she could inhale them both, thereby cutting down on the time she was forced to spend with Quaid's brother.

He frowned her way, his brows meeting over blue eyes. "What has my brother been saying to you to put you off me? You know you can't believe a word he says about me. We're a bit estranged, you see."

The trouble was Quaid didn't say much of anything about his brother. Or his mother. Or his friends and family. When she thought about it, they talked a lot about her family and past and not much about his. "Yeah, I got that, which is why I shouldn't be having lunch with you. Is this some kind of setup? Your mom shows up wanting to talk to Quaid and now you're going to put me in some compromising position?"

There was a part of her waiting for Marian Havery to walk in, followed by Quaid, and "catch" them in the act of not yet eating lunch. Jayna rather thought Quaid would see through that plan, but she could be wrong.

"Why would I do that?" Paul asked.

She could think of a hundred reasons they might give it a try, but she went with the most obvious. "So I can't get my poor grubby hands on the Havery fortune. To save your mother the embarrassment of having her son date trailer trash."

That insult had been thrown around when she'd first married Todd.

Her heart ached at the thought because Quaid had made her deal with the real truth of her marriage. She'd thought she'd been in love with Todd, and over the years as the marriage had disintegrated, she'd allowed that young, naive girl to morph into a mature, hardened woman who couldn't acknowledge the girl's heart.

It was weird. Accepting the truth hadn't made her angrier. It had the opposite effect. It made her softer, more tolerant of her own past mistakes.

"Oh, she probably does think that way," Paul agreed. "I love my mother, but she's an unconscionable snob at times. I think you're going to be good for Quaid. He needs someone who'll challenge him. Also, I think you might be far more reasonable than he is about certain things, so I am going to be incredibly nice to you so you'll put a good word in for me."

"I'm not doing that. I'm walking away from this table and immediately telling your brother everything that happened here." She was still suspicious. She wasn't about to let Paul drive a wedge between them.

"You can tell him anything you like," Paul agreed. "But I want you to hear me out. You owe me that."

"I don't owe you anything."

A smirk hit Paul's face. "Sure you do. If I wasn't here, Quaid would be living at home and then he wouldn't have been at the office the night it rained, and you would have left town after your momma kicked you out because you're trying to lead Sienna . . . I'm not clear on where you're leading Sienna and why that's wrong. Also, Sienna looks damn good. Did I hear she's single?"

"Oh, you stay away from my sister." She did not need an extra niece, and that was what happened when Sienna got involved with an attractive douchebag. "How do you know my mom kicked me out?"

"Everyone knows because your mom told Darlene Denis, who told the whole story to her sister who works at the Back Porch, and she was telling it to everyone last night," Paul explained with obvious relish. "You came off as very full of yourself and elitist."

"Says the guy who had his Porsche stolen," she pointed out.

Paul shrugged that off. "Fine. That isn't what I wanted to talk to you about anyway. I simply wanted you to understand that my mother can be on the judgmental side, and while I adore her, I do not carry the same prejudices as she does. Like I said, I think you're good for Quaid. He seems happy."

"How would you know?" From what she knew, the brothers hadn't seen each other in at least a week. They certainly weren't hanging out and talking about their love lives.

"Oh, I'm excellent at following people, and I watch him quite often."

"You're stalking your brother?" Now she was starting to understand why Quaid found the man annoying.

"I like to think of it as keeping up with a man who doesn't want to talk to me."

"You know I'm going to tell him you're watching him, right?"

"Maybe you will. Maybe you won't. How else am I supposed to figure out how to make amends with him? You won't let me in the office. He won't talk to me unless he's picking me up from jail, and then it's all one long lecture. It's all 'you can't do that, Paul' and 'why don't you get a real job, Paul?' He does not understand my artistic nature," Paul complained.

"Your brother is very artistic. He's creative and smart, but he understands that he has work to do as well. He has a whole town depending on him, and he isn't going to let them down." She'd been thinking about how much weight had been placed on Quaid's shoulders at a young age. His father should have been around for years to take on part of that weight, but he'd died far too soon, and Quaid had been left to handle everything. From what Sienna had told her, Paul had moved to California years before and Quaid had been left to take care of his mother and keep the law firm going.

"He used to be. You know when we were kids, he would tell the best stories. Sometimes when it stormed, I would sneak into his room because I was scared and Quaid would tell me stories about how the storm was nothing more than the clouds playing games up in the sky." For the first time, Paul seemed serious. "He was my hero when we were kids."

"What happened?" She knew she shouldn't ask since Quaid didn't seem to want to talk about his brother, but she couldn't help herself. "You're obviously not close now."

"Time happened. Distance. Life. Me screwing up about a thousand times and making his life harder than it had to be," he admitted. "He was only a couple of years older than me, but he was always more mature. A therapist will likely tell you that it has something to do with the way our parents treated us. Quaid was the responsible one and I was the charmer who entertained everyone. Quaid had his path set, and I rode the wave in his wake. Quaid belonged to our father, and our mother became my champion. It split our family in a way I don't think they intended."

"That's a very astute observation."

He grinned, lighting up the whole café. "I played a therapist in an off-off-Broadway show. I say off-off because it was actually in Anaheim. I studied and everything."

She wasn't buying his charm, but she did understand his appeal. He was a pleasant companion. If she wasn't sure it would irritate Quaid, she would be enjoying herself. "That soup isn't going to take long."

He waved off that worry. "I ordered the quiche because they ran out earlier and that sucker just went in the oven. I made sure the waitress knew we wanted to eat together so she'll have the kitchen hold your order until mine's ready. We've got plenty of time. Wow, that is a very intimidating look. Do you use that in court? I need to remember it in case I play a lawyer. My dad smiled a lot."

His eyes narrowed, jaw going straight. He looked slightly constipated. She did not look like that.

He was so annoying. "What do you want, Paul?"

His expression went smooth and pleasant again. "I want to have a nice conversation with a woman who is obviously important to my brother."

She stared at him.

Paul sighed. "Fine, I need a lawyer."

Oh, that was an easy answer. "No."

"You haven't heard why I want to hire you," Paul replied, a pout coming over his face. He was very emotive.

"I don't need to." It was likely nothing more than a way to screw with Quaid, and she wasn't going to be a part of that.

"I can pay you," Paul said quickly, as though he was afraid he was about to lose her.

It was a good call because she was weighing her need to eat against her need to get away. Money might be the one thing that could get her to stay. Still, she had to think about Quaid. "Your brother wouldn't be happy with me taking you on as a client. You need to talk to him."

"He won't take a meeting with me. He literally sent you out in your jimmy jams to make sure he didn't have to talk to me," Paul pointed out. "There isn't anyone else I can trust with this. I need a lawyer."

"There are one point three million lawyers in the US. We are legion. Go find one." She reached for her purse. She would take her lunch to go and eat at her desk. Hopefully Quaid and his mom had closed the door to his office so she could sneak in unnoticed. If this was all some kind of setup, she wasn't going to fall for it.

"Jayna, please."

He'd lost all the affectation, and his expression seemed open and raw.

She let go of her bag. "What do you need a lawyer for?"

"I need you to review a couple of contracts for me," Paul explained. "The first one is a simple real estate contract. I'm selling some property I own in LA. I've never worked with this real estate agent before. He's a guy who was recommended to me, and I'm not sure I trust him."

"Then get another agent."

"Not really an option."

Something about his tone was setting off alarm bells. She'd been a lawyer long enough to know when a client was about to tell her something she didn't want to hear. "What's going on, Paul?"

"I might owe some money to a guy."

Yep, she didn't want to hear that. "How much?"

"Well, I told Quaid it was a quarter million, but it's closer to half."

"Half a million?" She lowered her tone because it was the lunch rush and this was gossip central. "You owe some guy half a million dollars?"

"It started at three hundred, but he's serious about the interest."

Jayna took a deep breath because this was way worse than she'd imagined. There might be a real reason Quaid didn't talk about his brother. How much trouble was he in? No legitimate lender would charge him that much interest. Banks could be predatory, but not like this. "Paul, are you telling me you owe some mafioso half a million dollars?"

Paul glanced around as though trying to make sure no one was listening. He leaned forward. Jayna waited for what had to be a lengthy explanation. "Yes."

Paul sat back.

"You can't just tell me yes. I need more than that. Why would you borrow that much money from someone who likes to break arms and legs?"

"Well, I didn't know he liked to break things," Paul admitted. "I only knew I needed the money and no bank was willing to give it to me. Film is not cheap. This was a business loan. I needed it to finish my film. I'm the producer, so it's my job to finance the project."

"Usually that's done through banks or production companies."

"I would have had to give up control," Paul explained. "And if I brought in other producers, they would want part of the profits. This all happened very quickly. There wasn't a lot of time to think. We were going to lose our shot at hitting the festival circuit. Which, I mean, we lost anyway when the script got caught up in a lawsuit. I went to this guy who came highly recommended for short-term loans. The plan was to finish the film and put it up on the festival circuit, where we would absolutely have been snapped up for distribution. The film is great. It's the best thing I've ever done. Probably because they convinced me not to act in it. I'm a terrible actor. But I'm a good producer, and I'm pretty good with a script. I took that money because I believe in myself."

"And it didn't occur to you to ask your mom for the money? Or Quaid? You have a very wealthy family."

"I ask my mom and Quaid gets mad at me. I would never ask Quaid for money. Never. He would accuse me of wanting to buy drugs—which I haven't done in a long time. You have one little cocaine addiction and Quaid never lets you forget it."

"Okay, so because you didn't want to fight with your brother, you went to a loan shark."

"I didn't know he was a loan shark. I thought he was a film enthusiast who wanted to help me out in exchange for thanks in the film's credits and a potentially insanely high interest rate that I never thought I would have to deal with. There was a balloon payment, but I was sure I would pay it back before then."

A sudden thought hit her. "Your car wasn't stolen, was it?"

"Oh, it was stolen. I've been informed that it pays off a portion of my debt, but that car is worth a hundred K and he's only giving me half credit," Paul complained. "That's not fair. Do you think you could negotiate with him?"

He wanted her to negotiate with his loan shark? "I don't think that's a good idea. We need to go to the police."

"No. That is a very bad idea. It's not that big a deal. Look, the car's worth a lot. I've already started the paperwork for the . . ."

"Don't complete that sentence. I'm not kidding. I do not want to hear the words 'insurance fraud' come out of your mouth."

"I wasn't going to say that. Is it fraud? It was totally taken from me," Paul began.

She held up a hand. "Not a single word more. I cannot hear about any crime you've committed or are planning to commit."

"Is it a crime?" Paul seemed deeply confused. "He stole it right from a parking lot. I didn't know it was him until way later."

"That's great. That means you didn't file a false police report. But filing that claim with your insurance company is a crime, and so is the loan you took out, so let's go to the cops. We can explain the situation to the sheriff's office, and he can put us in touch with someone in LA."

Paul's head shook. "I can't. I took out the loan. I knew what would happen, but I was betting on me, you know? I was saying yes to myself."

"And now some guy will also say yes to breaking your limbs." Quaid had gotten all the brain cells. All of them.

"No, they won't because I'm going to pay them off when the sale of my house goes through in a few days," he said with confidence. "And then I'm going to play it safe from now on. I'm going to settle down here in Louisiana and get a real job. I was thinking about opening an acting studio in New Orleans."

Yeah, that would work out for him. It was blatantly obvious to her that Paul was in trouble and was totally naive about everything in the universe. It was probably a terrible idea, but she couldn't let Quaid's brother go without advice. "So all you need is for me to read over a property contract?"

He hesitated, and she knew she was in for way more. "That, and I was hoping you would look over another contract for me. It's the one for the film I produced. It's a fabulous story. I worked with a friend of mine on the screenplay. It's about these brothers . . ."

"I don't need to know the plot." Where was her food? The café was usually very quick. This felt like torture. "What do you want me to look for? If I actually agree to do any of this. Which I have not."

"The movie is caught up in a legal situation, and they're saying I can't release it until it's done. I was hoping you could advise me on how long you think that will be. I've got all these documents, and I don't understand any of them. It's so many papers. I think I'm supposed to do something about them, but it's a lot of words."

"Have you gotten served?"

Paul gestured to the empty table between them. "No, Jayna. Neither one of us has, but I told you the quiche is going to take a while."

She bit back a groan. "Did you receive a notification that you were being sued?"

"Oh, yeah. I think that's part of the paperwork."

"What does your lawyer in California say?"

"I didn't hire one because by then I was trying to pay him off," he admitted.

"'Him' meaning your mobster?"

"The guy who gave me the loan."

She'd thought dealing with two lawsuits involving Geraldine was rough. Paul was going to be even more difficult. She hoped he didn't decide to host nude swim parties to scare off his loan shark. "So you don't have a lawyer because you don't have any money, and now you're here in front of me promising you can pay me."

"Well, it might take a couple of days, but once the sale of

the house goes through I'll have three million and I can pay everyone off, including you."

He was oblivious to so many things normal people would know. "You do know that the money from your house isn't coming through in a couple of days, right? Unless you're already in escrow. I thought you hadn't signed the contract."

"Once I sign it I'll get the money, right?" Paul asked.

"When you close. I don't mean a door. I'm sure you already closed the door." She had to cut him off at the pass. "There's usually some time between when the contract is signed and when the actual property is transferred along with the money. Usually a couple of weeks. It's called 'closing.' There's paperwork to be filed, and the person who's buying your house typically has a loan and the bank checks things out before finalizing."

Paul had visibly paled. "I'm not getting my money anytime soon, am I? The Porsche is only going to hold him for so long. Do you think he's going to break my legs? I use my legs. Jayna, please, you have to help me. I know I don't have the money now, but I will. That's what you would be doing, getting my money so I can pay you."

This was absolutely the worst idea ever, but the truth was she could use the money and she couldn't imagine that Quaid would want his brother to get his legs broken. She was only looking over some contracts. "Get me the paperwork."

He handed over a tote bag. "It's all in here. I can't tell you how much better I feel."

"You shouldn't." It looked like he'd stuffed the contracts in, and maybe not in order. Excellent. "Do you even want to know what my normal rate is?"

He shrugged. "Doesn't matter. I'll pay it. You're the only lawyer in town who'll take my case. Mom is over at the office right now begging Quaid to fix things for me and he's going to tell her that he'll think about it if she'll think about being nice to you. They will both think about it, and then neither will change their minds. I know them. You're my only hope. Hey, that was like *Star Wars*. Help me, Jayna Cardet. You're my only hope. Ooo, lunch is here. I don't actually like quiche. Let's switch."

He had her turkey sandwich halfway down his throat before the waitress could finish putting the plate down.

Yep, huge mistake.

Quaid locked up his office since Sienna hadn't come back from lunch yet. Jayna hadn't shown up, either, so she was either still at the café or she'd returned to the courthouse. He was betting on the café, and that was fine with him.

It was time they sat down and discussed a few things.

Talking to his mother had made him restless. Talking to Rene had made him a little anxious.

Mostly because talking to Rene had made him think his mother was right and the town wasn't properly viewing his relationship with Jayna. They were talking about them like it was some kind of crazy sexual affair between a woman on the edge and a man who hadn't gotten any in a while.

It was more than sex. And he was going to prove it to this whole town. He was going to take her out to dinner and they would dance. A double date with Rene and Sylvie Darois would prove to everyone that he was serious about Jayna Cardet.

He was halfway across the square when he saw the door to the café open and the object of his affection walk out.

Jayna was frowning as she settled a tote bag over her shoulder and shoved her sunglasses on. Damn, she was pretty when she frowned. And pretty when she smiled, and all the expressions in between.

How would she handle his mother? The last thing Jayna

needed was a woman who would look down on her and make her feel small. If it had been anyone else judging her, he would cut that person out of his life, but this was his mother. He'd promised his father he would take care of her, but he knew his father hadn't meant that he should give up his whole life because his mother couldn't get along with one of the kindest women he'd ever met.

Jayna was kind. Maybe not nice, but kind. She could be grumpy as hell and still do the right thing.

The door came open again and his brother strode out, moving right up to Jayna and giving her his biggest Hollywood smile.

Ah, if there was anyone in the world that smile wouldn't work on, it was Jayna.

Except she shook her head and seemed to laugh at something Paul said. Then a long sigh went through her and she pulled her phone from her purse. She unlocked it and passed it over to Paul.

Was she giving him her number?

He felt like his feet were glued to the ground beneath him. He should be moving, walking right over to where Paul was passing back her phone and putting his hand on her shoulder.

Jayna stepped back, waving her hand and dismissing his brother as she turned toward the courthouse. She walked away, not looking back while Paul stared after her.

Paul shook his head like he'd really enjoyed the view.

That was what got Quaid moving.

Paul started to walk across the square, and it took him a moment to look up. A big smile crossed his face as he saw Quaid. "Hey, brother. You already get rid of Mom? I'm supposed to meet her in thirty minutes."

"What were you doing with Jayna?"

Paul's eyes went wide. "Nothing. We were both at the

café and it was full. It's lunchtime, you know. So we shared a table."

He was lying. "Jayna wouldn't have lunch with you."

"Why? She's a nice person and she's dating you. Is it such a surprise she would be curious about your family?"

"Jayna doesn't care about my family. I don't know what crap Mom has filled . . ."

"Hey, Jayna's cool. I like her. I think she's good for you. Mom will come around." Paul put a hand on his arm. "You're a lucky guy, but you need to get her out of that apartment and show her off or the whole town is going to think you're her rebound booty call."

"So you randomly met Jayna at the café."

"Okay, I might have been hoping to see her since I knew Mom was planning on having one of her special talks with you. Did she tell you all about how Jayna went after Todd Shale's money by signing an ironclad prenup and then working her ass off to help his dad's law firm?"

He snorted because at least Paul knew their mother. She could take a situation and rework it in her head so it fit her own personal world view. "I might have pointed out that Jayna's actions weren't that of a woman after a man's money. They don't usually sign prenups and work hard when all they want is cash."

Paul's eyes rolled. "I love our mother, but she is living in some weird feudal world where we're all nobility and the peasants are trying to kill us or something. Why are you looking at me like I grew an extra two heads? I am not unaware of our mother's flaws. I know you think I kiss up to her constantly, but I've genuinely tried to get her to stay out of your business."

"What are you up to?" His brother hadn't sounded so reasonable in years.

"What is that supposed to mean?" Paul asked.

"It means you stopped trying to charm me years ago."

"I'm not trying to charm you, Quaid. I'm trying to have a relationship with my brother. I know I've been an ass in the past, and I hurt every single person I care about. I know you think I can't change, but I've done the work this time," Paul said, his voice tight. "I'm a screwup and I continue to make dumb decisions, but I'm making them without the influence of cocaine or any other drug. If I have to give up the occasional beer to prove that to you, I'll do it. I'm not the same brother who left here years ago. I want another chance."

"This is not the first time I've heard this speech, Paul." He wanted to believe his brother, but he was tired. He'd been through this at least ten times. Paul would go to rehab and Quaid would get his hopes up and it would start all over again—the lying, the stealing. He was weary when it came to his brother.

"But I promise you, it is the last. I don't know why it worked this time, but it did. I can't say I won't ever use again. That's not how this works. I have to wake up every day and make the choice. I made the choice today." Paul seemed to struggle to keep his tone calm. "I will do everything I can to make the choice tomorrow. I know my promises don't mean much and that I've managed to make a mess for myself again, but it's an honest mess this time. I'm not going to take any money from Mom. I'm not going to put you in a bad position for helping me. I've got a plan, and you'll see I've changed."

Quaid's gut had tightened. He didn't want to fall down this rabbit hole, but he wasn't sure he could avoid it. "Mom asked me to help you."

A ghost of a smile hit his brother's lips. "And you said you would think about it."

Well, at least his brother knew him. This was a terrible idea, but he didn't see a way around it. "Send me the contracts and I'll look them over."

Paul shook his head. "Don't worry about it. I've found a good lawyer, and she's going to take care of it."

Suspicion rose again. "She?"

"Oh, yeah." Paul winced. "Should I have said that? Is that covered under the attorney-client thing where they can't talk about each other?"

His brother had never grasped legal terminology. "That's not how privilege works. You can and should tell me the name of the attorney you hired."

Paul actually took a step back. "I think I should talk to her about that first."

He wasn't going to play this game. "Did you or did you not hire my girlfriend to represent you?"

"She's looking over my contracts," Paul said quickly. "And maybe making some phone calls, but that's all."

Of course. That whole "I've changed" speech was all bull to cover the fact that he was using Jayna. Quaid wasn't sure what Paul intended to do, but it almost certainly had something to do with his mother's plotting. "She's not helping you."

"It's not really help," Paul replied. "Help is something a friend does for free. I like Jayna, but she's not very friendly. And she was annoyed when she had to pay for lunch because my credit card got declined. I think she's going to put it on my bill. It's a job. She's assured me she's going to charge her full rate. Should I be worried? How much is that?"

He turned away from his brother, anger rising in his gut. He wasn't about to allow his family to put him in this position. They'd figured out their normal manipulations weren't working, and now they'd changed their play. He wouldn't let it happen. They weren't going to use Jayna this way. "It doesn't matter because you don't have any damn money. You leave her alone or we'll have trouble, you and I."

"I thought we already had trouble. That's why you moved out. I'm going to have money. I just have to close something," Paul called out. "At least that's what my lawyer says. I'm not sure what I'm closing."

He didn't care. His brother was a manipulator, and he'd found a way to force his way into Quaid's life. Again. He would use Jayna and drag her into their trouble, too.

Had his mother come up with this plan? Or was it all Paul? It was a good play, but it wouldn't work.

He jogged back across the park to the courthouse as Jayna went inside, the door closing behind her. She was about to turn down the hall when he managed to catch up.

"Give 'em hell today, Quaid!" Jerry Nichols owned the gardening center and rented out heavy equipment. He stood with his daughter, LaTonya, beside the reception center.

LaTonya frowned at her dad. "You are not going to one of Geraldine's parties, Dad. Quaid, can't you see how crazy this is?"

He thought it was a little crazy that this case was drawing bigger and bigger crowds. "See you two inside." He had to catch Jayna.

"Hey," he called out, making her stop and turn.

A bright smile hit her face before she glanced down at her watch. "Hey, you. How did things go with your mom? Don't tell me now. We need to hustle. We're supposed to be in court in five minutes."

He didn't need five minutes. "They went about the way I thought they would go. I just found out my brother forced you to have lunch with him and then convinced you to take on his case. I'm sorry he put you in a bad position."

Her hand went to the tote bag around her shoulder. "I

wouldn't say 'forced.' It's no big deal. It's a couple of contracts. Your brother's not the brightest bulb, you know. Also, he needs a serious lesson in organization. I think there are two separate contracts in there, but they might have bred. And one of them has some jelly on it. I think it's grape."

That sounded like his brother. "Don't worry about it. I'll take them and get them back to Paul."

"Why would you do that?" Jayna asked.

How should he put this? He'd avoided most talk about his family with her, wanting to leave her out of their drama. It was far too soon in the relationship for her to find out how nasty his family dynamic could be. "Because he's not truly interested in hiring you. He doesn't have any money. This is his way to force me to do what he wants."

"So he doesn't want me to look into his contracts even though contracts are my specialty?"

Somewhere in the back of his mind, distant alarm bells had started to ring. Maybe it was the tone of her voice or the way her brows had risen. He still plunged ahead, his anger with his brother far greater than those warnings. "No, he's trying to force me to do it."

"But you don't have to, because I'm going to do it." She took a step back. "It's a couple of contracts, Quaid. It'll take me a few hours tops to go through them. Well, once I get them in the proper order. It's a pretty simple situation."

That was where she was wrong. "It's never simple with my brother."

"He needs to sign the paperwork on his house so they can set a closing date and get the ball rolling. He needs the money from the sale of that house, and he doesn't understand how it works in any way."

Ah, but Paul understood how *he* worked. "You can't believe a word he says, baby. I know that he's in trouble, and bringing you in is his way of dragging me into whatever scheme he's working on. My mother asked me to handle this for Paul. That was why she was here."

He wasn't about to mention the part where his mom had told him all kinds of rumors about Jayna.

"That's what Paul said she was going to do, and he said you would tell her you would think about it," she mused. "He also said you wouldn't really think about it."

"Of course I won't think about it." He hadn't considered it in the moment, and after this play of his brother's, he wouldn't think about helping him in the future. How dare he bring Jayna into his plans.

Her arms crossed over her chest, a sure sign she was about to get stubborn on him. "Did she also try to talk you out of seeing me?"

He wasn't getting into this. "None of that matters. What she says doesn't mean a thing to me. She lives in her own world, so don't worry about it. Give me the contracts so I can give them back to my brother and you can be out of this."

Her hand tightened on the strap. "Why should I do that? He's my client. If I hand over his contracts to you without his permission, I'm violating attorney-client privilege."

"There's no privilege because he didn't give you any money. In fact, he stuck you with the bill for lunch," he pointed out. "And that's what's going to happen when you deal with my brother."

"There is the assumption of privilege," she argued, and then sighed, relaxing a bit. "Quaid, I'm not sure what's going on, but I don't think this is about hurting you. I think Paul needs some help, and he doesn't think he has the right to ask it of you."

Paul had worked his magic on her. "Jayna, I'm asking

you to give me that bag and walk away from this. Don't ask me any more questions. I need you to believe that I know what I'm talking about."

She frowned, looking more confused than he'd ever seen her. She glanced around, and that was the moment he realized everyone in the courthouse was watching them. There were a bunch of people who'd been milling about and now they'd stopped to watch the drama playing out.

"Is it because you think I can't do it?" The question came out as a whisper.

"It's because I don't want you involved with my family." It would be a disaster if she worked for Paul, and he had no idea what his mother was up to, but he knew what she wanted. She wanted Jayna gone, and he wasn't going to allow her to chase off the only woman he'd truly wanted in years.

Her face flushed, and she drew in a shaky breath. "All right. I'll give the contracts back to your brother, but I'm not turning them over to you. I'm not going to open myself up to another ethics complaint I can't afford to defend. Now, we have a court case to deal with, and I hope that you can handle it with the professionalism I expect from you, Mr. Havery."

"Jayna, baby," he began. She didn't understand what he was trying to do.

She turned away from him. "It's Ms. Cardet when we're in this courthouse. And keep your voice down because everyone is listening to us right now."

"What's wrong?" He wasn't sure why she'd turned so cold on him. "I'm doing this to spare you trouble. I'm not trying to take something from you. If it's about having more work, I can find that for you."

He wasn't sure why she needed the work. It wasn't like she had any bills to pay, and he was handling the ethics complaint. They'd even talked to the attorney together, and she was incredibly certain this would all be cleared up in a matter of weeks.

"No need to find anything for me." She started toward the courtroom. "I can get my own work. If there's anyone else in this town who's off limits, you should give me a list."

Maybe he hadn't handled this as well as he could have. He was making a scene. The whole town was already talking about them. He shouldn't give them more to discuss.

He hurried to keep up with her. "Baby, this is a family thing. It has nothing to do with you and me."

"I told you what I was willing to do. I'll turn the contracts back over to Paul, grape jelly still intact." Her heels clicked against the marble floors, the sound seeming as irritated as the woman herself. "I'll leave your family alone. No one will think for a second that I have any connection to you outside of work. No one will misconstrue our relationship in any way."

"What is that supposed to mean?"

"It means people will draw the proper conclusions," she explained. "Look, it's fine. I thought I was helping you out. I thought if I handled Paul's trouble you wouldn't have any pressure to do it yourself. I also thought I was potentially making some money so I can find a place of my own. You don't want me around your family, so I'll give the contracts back and find the money some other way. I'm sending out CVs as fast as I can, and I'm going to look into a prep course so I can get licensed in Texas."

He stopped in the middle of the hall, her words shocking him. "Hey, I was not asking you to leave. I don't want you to leave. I was actually going to ask you to go out with me tonight."

"To where? You want to head into New Orleans where no one in Papillon can see us together?"

"No, I was going to see if you wanted to go out with some friends of mine."

"Sure you were." She stopped, her hand on the door. "It's fine. I knew when we started that this wasn't some hearts-and-flowers relationship. We're both lonely, and the sex is good. We have similar interests. I thought we were friends, but if you can't even stand the thought of me being around your family, then we're just two people in close proximity with nothing better to do. I can handle that. Honestly, I'll probably still sleep with you because I am lonely and you're good in bed, but let's not pretend we're anything more."

"That's not true." This was exactly what he was trying to avoid.

She stared at him for a moment. "I'm a realist, Quaid. I take a look at the evidence and I come to a conclusion. You refuse to talk to me about anything truly important, but you demand I bare my soul to you every night. You want to know everything about my family and my relationship with my mother, but I can't even read over your brother's contracts to see if I can help him. You don't think much of me."

"I know you're good enough to help him. He's not good enough to deserve your help. That is what I'm trying to tell you. This isn't about you not being good enough for them. They aren't good enough for you," he insisted.

She sent him the saddest look. "We should get inside."

She pushed through the doorway, where everyone was already waiting for them. The crowd had grown again. It had started with a few curious onlookers, and now half the town was in there, eager to watch the proceedings.

What had happened? How had he gone from getting ready to ask her to go out with him to the door slamming in his face?

His brother had happened. Naturally.

Of course, he could have handled it with more finesse. He certainly hadn't meant to make her feel like he was trying to hide their relationship.

Quaid took a deep breath because he couldn't do what he wanted to do. He couldn't walk in, throw her over his shoulder, and take her back to their room so he could show her exactly how serious they were.

She was sending out CVs? He'd thought she wasn't going to do that until after her ethics case was settled. He'd thought he had more time to convince her to stay here in Papillon and give them a shot at a real relationship. Hadn't he set everything up so she didn't have to worry about money?

Damn it. That was likely part of the problem.

How hard was it on Jayna to let him pay for her legal fees? She was a proud woman and had been raised to believe she shouldn't accept what her mother would likely think of as charity. It wasn't. It was one friend helping out another friend.

It was one man who couldn't stand the thought of her being hurt in any way making sure she had what she needed.

Except this time he was the one who'd hurt her.

He pushed through because there was nothing to do except work at this point. He would have to find a way to make her understand how much he cared, because the one thing he couldn't lose was her.

chapter ten

"So you walked out and left him?" Sienna leaned toward her, practically yelling over the raucous music reverberating through Guidry's. She picked up the two beers they'd ordered and handed one to Jayna.

It was seven p.m. on a weeknight, but Guidry's was packed.

Jayna glanced around the place and had to admit that it had a vibrancy and energy that could compete with any restaurant or nightclub she'd been in. Like many establishments in a small town, Guidry's served more than one function. There was a dining room, a bar section with big TVs playing whatever game was on, and a patio for quieter dining. There was even a dance floor, and it was hopping this evening. A zydeco band played, and she recognized some of the people swaying on the floor.

Sienna tugged on her elbow, nodding toward the door. It was too loud to talk in here, and her sister seemed done with waiting for explanations.

Jayna took a long swig before starting for the big patio. Out here the music was softer, the air warm. Edison lights were strung around, bringing a soft ambiance to the setting.

In front of her, the bay was laid out. Here at Guidry's one could dine on some delicious Cajun cuisine and also rent a boat to fish. There was a marina down the hill.

"Hey, Aunt Jay!" Ivy called out before throwing her body down the long slide.

The girls were playing on the big playground that had been around since Jayna was a kid. It was attached to the patio by a wrought iron fence she'd been told had recently been installed when Otis, the alligator, had grown attached to sunning himself on the merry-go-round. She waved to her nieces.

"You two be careful," Sienna called out. "Dinner should be here soon."

Ivy and Kelly ignored their mom, preferring to giggle with the other kids as they raced around the fenced-off playground.

She and Sienna had done the same thing while their mom had met with her friends and had dinner and danced and talked. Later, when they were older, they'd sat at their own table with friends.

Well, Sienna had friends. Jayna had Sienna, but it had still been fun. It wasn't the kind of thing they would have been able to do if the community hadn't been so tight. She would never allow her nieces out of her sight if they were in New Orleans, and the restaurants there wouldn't let a bunch of preteens sit away from their parents in a big obnoxious group, but they all knew each other here. In her day, if she'd misbehaved, LC or Glendola Guidry would have marched her right over to her mom's table and she would have gotten in trouble. Now that was Remy or Lisa Guidry's job.

Like it was Quaid's to take care of the town's legal needs. Sylvie Darois had come back home to be the mayor. Sylvie's father had worked in the government, too.

So many people in town followed in their parents' footsteps, working side by side and taking over when it was time.

"Jayna? Are you okay?" Sienna asked once they'd gotten to a place where they could hear each other.

She shook off the odd thoughts she'd been having since her fight with Quaid. Though it hadn't been much of a fight. He'd told her what to do and she'd figured out her place in his world, which was beyond limited. "I'm good. I told him I had something to do and I walked out. Then I went to your place and convinced you to actually give me something to do."

Her sister had been surprised when she'd shown up, but she'd been game to take her to her friend Angie Jones's birthday party at Guidry's. Like most of her life here in Papillon, she was going to a social event because her sister took her along.

Because no one liked her. Not even the man she'd been sleeping with.

"Angie didn't mind at all. The more the merrier, you know," Sienna said, pulling out the chair to the table they'd claimed. "It's pretty much just a get-together, though she'll serve some cake in an hour or so. I'm sure you'll see a lot of people from school."

Angie Jones worked at the post office, and she'd gone to high school with Sienna. She'd barely nodded Jayna's way when they'd stopped at her table to say hello. Jayna wasn't sure if it was because Angie didn't recognize her or because everyone here knew she was sleeping with Quaid Havery with no expectation of any kind of relationship with him outside of bed.

"People from school don't like me." She took another drink of her beer.

"That's not true. You had plenty of friends, but they all left Papillon," Sienna pointed out. "They're all across the country now, and you didn't keep in touch. It's normal, you know. Most of us don't keep in touch with the people we knew in high school. I'm still friends with Angie because we live close by. Now stop procrastinating and tell me what happened with Quaid."

She didn't want to talk about Quaid. She certainly didn't want to think about the way he'd looked at her when she'd walked away from him. He'd seemed genuinely surprised that she didn't want to talk to him.

Likely because women didn't argue with Quaid. Quaid was gorgeous and sexy and rich. He could have any woman he wanted, but he also lived in a small town where his choices were limited. That's why he'd fallen into bed with her. She was a change of pace.

"Nothing happened. I didn't want to spend another night in that tiny apartment, that's all."

Sienna's fingers drummed along the table. "Liar. You know, you think you're an excellent liar, but I can tell. Something happened with Quaid and it's bothering you."

She was an excellent liar and there was no way her sister could tell, but there was another way to get information here in town. "You heard we had a fight."

Sienna shrugged. "I might have heard something about a disagreement at the courthouse that didn't involve Geraldine's state of dress."

"It was nothing." Like their relationship was nothing. That had been such a kick in the gut. She'd been thinking about how she was going to tell Quaid she was working for his brother. She was going to tell him everything, and then he'd opened his mouth and she'd actually felt her damn heart break.

She hadn't thought it could break. Not that way. What Todd hadn't managed to do with years of cheating, Quaid had done with a few careless words. He'd made her feel small.

"It had to be something or you wouldn't have shown up on my doorstep," Sienna pointed out. "You walked all the way from the courthouse to the trailer park. It's two miles. If it was nothing, you would have had Quaid drop you off."

She hadn't exactly enjoyed the walk, but she also hadn't wanted to listen to Quaid tell her she hadn't understood him and he didn't mean what he said the way it had come out. "I don't think it's working out between me and Quaid."

"What happened?" Sienna asked again.

Her sister could be stubborn when she wanted something. "Paul Havery asked me to look through some contracts for him and Quaid objected. Quite adamantly."

"Was that what you were doing earlier?"

While she'd waited for Sienna to get ready for the party, she'd casually browsed through the contracts. Not a deep dive, but she could already tell the agreement to sell Paul's house was in order. He should be able to move forward with it, and in a few weeks he could sign closing papers and have the money he needed. He'd paid cash for the house and was making a tidy profit given he'd only been in it for a couple of years, but that was West Coast real estate.

There were a few things about the production contract she would like to check out. She'd like to read the suit surrounding production. Something was off there, but she would need to delve into the text to figure it out. Every instinct she had told her he was getting scammed and the proof would be in the details. She could figure it out.

And she wasn't going to get that opportunity because she was meeting Paul in the morning for breakfast where she would hand it all back over to him and be done with the Havery family. Like Quaid wanted.

"Yes, I probably shouldn't have looked through them since I'm giving them back tomorrow, but you know I can't stand to leave anything that disorganized. He threw both contracts in the tote bag without separating them, so I had to put them back together again." She wondered what Quaid was doing. Probably writing or hanging out with his actual friends. He'd been stuck in the apartment with her for days, so he was probably anxious to get out. Had it been hard for him to lock himself away from the world with her? He was too polite to go out without her. That was the only possible explanation she could find. Or he was enjoying the sex but Paul's offer had screwed things up for him.

"Did Quaid want to look into it himself?" Sienna asked. "I would be surprised to hear that."

"What's surprising about it?" She knew Quaid didn't intend to look into it for Paul, but she wanted to know why Sienna thought it would be surprising for him to.

Sienna straightened her blouse before waving to a friend walking by. She leaned in. "They don't get along. At least that's what I've always heard."

"Why?" She knew what Paul had told her, but all Quaid would say was they didn't get along. "Paul talked a lot about how Quaid was closer to their dad and he was closer to their mom, but I didn't really get it."

"Oh, I think it's more than that," Sienna assured her. "You know Paul got into a lot of trouble when he was younger, right? You might have already been in college by the time it got real bad. I know the old sheriff smoothed things over and Paul doesn't have an arrest record here in Papillon, but I've heard rumors things went bad when he moved to Los Angeles. There wasn't a friend of the family out there who could fix things for him."

"Paul told me he had a drug problem." Paul had seemed open and honest in their conversation. She'd been surprised since his brother didn't talk about him at all. Well, beyond telling her not to fraternize with the man.

"A big one, from what I understand," Sienna explained.

"I think he had a couple of DUIs in California, and Quaid had to bail him out of jail. He's been to rehab more than once. I don't hang out with him, but I know some people who do. They all say he's a nice guy when he's not using, but when he is, life gets complicated around him. You know how that kind of thing can tear apart a family."

She'd watched it happen. "I know what it did to our aunt, but she was willing to talk about it."

"Because Mom got her some therapy, though don't mention it to anyone," Sienna said, her voice low. "You know how the rest of the family feels about therapy."

Jayna sat back with a sigh, a weariness coming over her. "They think therapy is for rich people who can't handle the world. I'm surprised Mom was willing to help her do that."

"She's not a monster. I think she was worried she could lose her sister. After her brother died, Aunt Opal was all Mom had left of her siblings. That last time our cousin went to jail sent Opal into a bad spiral," Sienna said. "But she went to a doctor who got her some antidepressants and a whole lot of therapy. Mom drove her every week. Still does. I know you think she's cold . . ."

"I don't think she's cold." Cold wasn't her mother's problem. "I think she's closed-minded. I've heard all my life how strong people don't need help."

"She's one of those people who struggles to understand a concept until it happens directly to them," Sienna replied. "It can make things difficult, and sometimes getting her to understand can take a while. She's set in her ways."

That was the understatement of the year. Still, she couldn't stop thinking about the concept of passing along a legacy. Quaid's father had passed on his. The café had been in the Halford family for years. It was the way Papillon worked. "Did Mom ever try to get you a job at the plant?"

Sienna snorted. "Pretty much every time I quit a job she

tried to get me on at the plant. I always tank the interview on purpose because the last thing I need is to work where Mom does. She would drive me crazy."

"She's worked there since she was a teenager," Jayna mused.

"Yes. That was when she got pregnant with me and dropped out of high school and Grandma got her a job at the plant working next to her. Why are we talking ancient history?"

"I was just thinking about the fact that everyone who stays in town tends to follow in their parents' footsteps."

Sienna seemed to think for a moment and then nodded. "I suppose if the family has a business, they tend to pass it down to their kids. Although there are exceptions. Sylvie isn't a hairdresser. When Marcelle retires, she's planning on handing over the salon to her nephew. He's a stylist in Baton Rouge. But mostly, yes. Even Angie. Her dad used to run the post office. She got hired on after high school and worked with him for fifteen years. He retired and she took over. What's your point?"

"What if Mom sees that plant as something she could pass on to us, as some kind of legacy? It's not easy to get a job there. They don't have much turnover." The plant didn't pay great, but it was steady work and the overtime could add up.

"That's a crappy legacy," Sienna said with a frown. "But you might be right. It would explain why she was so against me taking the job with Quaid."

"He thinks she's afraid of losing you the same way she lost me." She'd been thinking a lot about what he'd said.

Sienna's gaze went soft. "She can't lose me. I'm her daughter. She never lost you. You called. You invited her to visit you."

"She didn't feel comfortable at my place, and I wasn't comfortable here." She certainly hadn't been comfortable bringing her husband here. In later years, coming without him had felt like she would be admitting defeat, so she'd tried to get her family to come to New Orleans. It had led to spending holidays surrounded by people but feeling utterly alone.

"Well, I'm not leaving Papillon." Sienna resettled herself on her chair, glancing over at the playground.

"Tell me you aren't already thinking of finding a new place to live." She'd seen Sienna looking through online real estate ads on her breaks.

Sienna rested her head in her hand. "It would be nice to have a house with a yard. There are a couple of duplexes and townhomes for rent that I could afford. I would like the girls to have their own rooms. Kelly's going to be an actual teen soon. She's going to want some privacy."

"She's going to want to not share a room with her bratty younger sister." Like Sienna hadn't wanted to share a room with her, but they'd been stuck together for years. Until Sienna had moved out after high school to live with a group of friends in an old house they rented.

"I think it would be nice for them to have their own space. You know I didn't hate sharing with you."

"But you want something better for your kids." This was what she'd never understood about her mom. "I don't think she wants that for us or for Ivy and Kelly. I think she wants us to be right where she is, always. I think she resents the fact that we wouldn't take jobs at the plant. Even before I screwed up my life, she wasn't ever proud of me."

Sienna reached out, putting a hand over hers. "I think she was, but she doesn't know how to show it. She doesn't handle change well, and you have always been this chaotic agent of change. It was easier with me because she understood me. I wasn't as smart as you were. I didn't have your ambition. You confused her. The two of you have never known how to communicate. I worry if you leave, you'll never have a good relationship with her."

"Do I need to?" She wasn't sure it was possible to have a good relationship with her mom.

"No. You can have a great life and not have a relationship with your parents, but I think deep down she means well. I know you do," Sienna said, getting emotional. "Whether you reconcile with her or never speak to her again, you will always have me. Always, Jayna. And you didn't screw up your life. You did the right thing, and you got your butt kicked for it. You got knocked down, and you're getting back up. I'm worried Quaid knocked you down again today, and he didn't mean to do it."

Sienna's words made her blink back tears. At least she'd also given Jayna a point to argue. "Oh, he meant it. Not the knocking-down part. He wasn't trying to be cruel, merely making himself plain."

Sienna sat back. "I don't think you understood him. I think you heard some words and put your own spin on them."

"He said he doesn't want me around his family."

"Because he has a strained relationship with them. Do you want him around Mom?"

"I wouldn't tell him to stay away. If she needed help and he was the best choice to help her, I would ask him to." She'd thought about this all afternoon. Even while she'd battled it out with him in the courtroom, she'd gone through a million scenarios and realized she cared more about him than he did her. She was at risk of getting into yet another unequal relationship where she pined for a man who couldn't love her.

"Your experience isn't his," Sienna said. "You can't know why he wants you to stay away unless you ask him and discuss the problem."

"He doesn't talk much about his family. He'll talk about

his dad some but not his current situation." She needed her sister to understand. When she talked to Quaid, he would listen but was always silent about his own problems. "I hear you, but I also know that I have to take the evidence in front of me and reach a logical conclusion. He's not serious about me and that's okay. It's not like we've been together for months and he's made a ton of promises. The truth is we got into this relationship because we're both lonely. It was never meant to be meaningful. I'm the one who put that on him, and I'm going to apologize for making him uncomfortable."

Sienna's eyes went wide. "You're going to apologize?"

She'd thought it through and this was the best course of action. She hadn't been fair to Quaid. He'd been lovely to her and honest. He hadn't promised her anything. She was the one who'd overreacted, and it was up to her to put their friendship on a good footing. "Yes. If he's awake when I get back tonight, I'm going to ask him if it's all right for me to stay and I'll apologize. I'll get Paul's contracts to him in the morning and we can go back to being friends."

"I would like to be there for this apology because I don't think he wants to be your friend."

That hurt. "You think I screwed that up, too?"

"No. I think he's crazy about you, and from the way he's looking at you right now, he's the big bad wolf and you're going to get eaten up if you tell him you want to save your friendship. That man has it bad."

Jayna turned and sure enough, Quaid was sitting at a table not twenty feet away. Rene and Sylvie Darois sat with him, though he wasn't paying them any attention. All of his focus was on her.

She wasn't sure if he was angry or . . . hungry. He looked hungry, and not for food. Was he upset that his booty call had walked away from him? Maybe she'd misjudged the man. She'd thought he was a nice guy, but sometimes nice guys didn't like it when a woman denied them. Sometimes they got mean.

"Do you want to run?" Sienna asked. "Because I can grab the girls. Kelly's real good at distracting people I don't want to talk to. She sits down in front of them and starts crying. I've gotten away from Mom's lectures many times with that play. We just have to circle around and pick her up in the back."

Why would she run? She wasn't a runner. She was a face-the-music kind of girl. Besides, Sienna was reading him wrong. He was upset and likely because she'd left him with her dog and refused to talk to him when he wanted to. Men could be touchy about things like that. Oh, he didn't like to talk about his feelings, but he would get mad when she didn't want to talk about hers. It had been a misunderstanding on her part, and she should have handled it better than she had.

She was the one who'd made the relationship more important than it was. It was best to see if she could salvage some politeness out of it. After all, they still had to work together. For a few weeks, at least.

"No. I'll get the hard part over with." She pushed back her chair. "Are you okay with taking me over there later to get Luna? He might say no. If he does, I have to find a pet-friendly motel, so I might need a place to stay tonight."

"Oh, I don't think I'll see you again tonight," Sienna said. "One way or another. Remember that part about Kelly if you need a quick getaway."

Her sister was being overdramatic. She turned and made her way to Quaid to see if there was any way to salvage her dignity.

Quaid watched as Jayna walked out of the dining room and onto the big patio where it seemed most of Papillon was hanging out tonight. Though Jayna didn't seem to see him, all of those nosy bastards out here did. Much of the small town's population was whispering, their gazes moving between him and the gorgeous brunette who'd walked out on him this afternoon, leaving him with all the work and a dog who'd whined the day away.

He'd felt a lot like Luna. He'd stood beside the big dog and watched her walk away and wondered if he'd been abandoned.

Surely she would come back for her dog. He could keep Luna with him at all times and then she would have to talk to him.

"Did you know she was going to be here?" Rene had a glass of sauvignon blanc in front of him. He claimed it paired perfectly with Remy's gumbo.

"No." He shouldn't have come. He should have stayed in his stupid, tiny apartment that seemed too big for him once she was gone. "I mean I wasn't sure."

Sylvie chuckled as Rene refilled her glass. "For one of the most talkative men I've ever known, you have said all of ten words tonight, Quaid. Maybe you should go over and talk to her."

She didn't want to talk. She'd made that plain to him. She hadn't wanted to talk when they'd had a break in the afternoon session, hadn't wanted to talk when they'd walked back to the office, hadn't wanted to talk when she'd changed her clothes and left him behind.

"I think she walked all the way to her sister's." Because she didn't have a car. It had taken him a while to figure out where she was going. He'd thought she'd gone to the café to grab a drink. She'd made sure she'd taken the contracts and left. When he'd gone looking for her at the café, one of the regulars said they'd seen her walking along the road that led to the trailer park.

"It's only a couple of miles," Rene said. "Doesn't she run a couple of miles a day?"

"She's incredibly fit. I see her running by city hall and I feel lazy," Sylvie replied. "Not that it gets me to actually exercise. I cheer her on from my comfy chair."

Jayna jogged every day. He'd gone with her a couple of times and barely kept up, but that seemed to be the way it was with Jayna. She excelled at anything she wanted to do. Except relationships. Or maybe she didn't want the relationship with him since she'd taken the first exit ramp she could find.

"Now, you do yoga every Wednesday in the park." Rene winked his wife's way. "I know because I like to take Lady and Marci for a walk right around that time. I love the view."

Sylvie chuckled and leaned over to kiss her husband.

Their ease with one another was exactly why he'd wanted to bring Jayna on a double date with them. He'd thought about who to go out with and Rene and Sylvie had made the most sense. They were affectionate with one another and easy to talk to. Armie and Lila had two insanely chaotic boys, and half the time their dates ended with them running home to save the babysitter. Roxie and Zep usually ended up going at it in a closet somewhere. Harry and Seraphina were a great couple but Harry was too handsome, and Quaid wasn't secure enough with Jayna to deal with that yet.

Rene and Sylvie were perfect, especially since Sylvie was a great example of a smart woman who'd had success in the big city and managed to be happy coming home.

But no. He was sitting here alone, and she was looking gorgeous and enjoying a beer with her sister. She was likely telling her sister what a dirtbag he was for trying to save her from his brother's manipulations. Though he was sure she didn't put it that way.

"Is he going to stare at her all night? People are starting to notice," Sylvie whispered her husband's way.

"Oh, they've been noticing." Rene didn't bother to keep his voice down. "Did you hear about the big scene Quaid made today at the courthouse? He practically tackled her when he heard she was having an affair with his brother."

That got Quaid's attention. Had the gossip gotten that bad? "She is not."

"Well, of course she isn't, but you know how the rumor mill goes." Rene appeared infinitely amused. "I believe it started with the two of you arguing over her working for Paul, but after the story made its way across town, little details changed."

"Oh, some of the interns told me that Quaid was upset because Jayna is planning on joining Geraldine at her next protest party, and she's not bringing her swimsuit. I think that was wishful thinking on the interns' part because they were planning on gassing up their trucks that day."

He wanted the names of those interns. "Who?"

Sylvie's head shook. "They're just kids, and Jayna is gorgeous. Get used to it. You can't beat them all up."

He bet he could. He was surprised at how much this fight of theirs was bothering him. Any other woman and he would likely have written her off for being unreasonable. He'd handled things all wrong, but she wouldn't talk to him about it. She'd shut him down and then walked away. It wasn't how he dealt with relationships. The logical thing to do was to let it all go.

There was nothing logical about the way he felt about Jayna Cardet. He wanted to walk right over there, throw her over his shoulder, and run away with her.

She was turning him into a caveman.

Or worse. He was becoming one of those people who

said they hated drama and then turned right around and made a whole lot of it.

"So I take it the fight was about her working for Paul?" Sylvie prompted.

He wasn't sure what had made him come out tonight. He'd thought seriously about calling Rene and canceling, but then he'd caught sight of Sienna's open calendar. She'd written in *Angie's party 7 p.m.* Angie had to be Angela Jones, and she held her party every year at Guidry's.

She was turning him into a creepy stalker, too.

"Paul is using her for some reason. I already called and left him a message telling him to stay away from Jayna," he explained. "Naturally he hasn't called back. I'm sure he's out somewhere partying it up."

"Or he feels bad that he got Jayna in trouble," Sylvie mused.

"He doesn't feel bad. He's thinking up another way to get what he wants," Quaid explained.

Sylvie started to say something, but Rene put a hand over hers and she went quiet.

"Do you want to talk about what happened?" Rene asked quietly. "It's okay if you don't, but it's obvious you're upset about it. How did you screw up?"

"Rene," Sylvie admonished.

But Rene was right. "I didn't properly explain why I was concerned about her working for Paul, so I'm afraid she misunderstood my motivations."

"Why does she think you don't want her to work for Paul? And what exactly was she going to do for him?" Sylvie asked.

"He gave her a couple of contracts to read, but that was only the start. That's how Paul works. He starts with something small and drags you in deeper." He'd thought about it all after Jayna had left. Paul knew unsavory people. Paul owed money to some guy out in California. He could see his brother asking Jayna to help him deal with that. *Oh, could you just make one little phone call for me?* And then she would be dragged into whatever plots Paul could come up with. It wouldn't be the first time Paul's connections had landed someone in a hospital. "And Jayna thinks I don't want her around my family."

"You don't want her around your family," Rene countered.

It was true, but she was wrong about one thing. "She thinks it's because I don't think she's good enough."

That got a loud laugh out of Rene.

Sylvie sent him a pointed stare.

Rene held out a hand, trying to stave off his wife's complaint. "Baby, you have to know how hard Quaid's mother is on everyone. She's an awful snob. And we all know how he feels about Paul. If he's doing anything, he's trying to keep her from figuring out what a hot mess his family is."

At least someone knew him. "That is exactly why. But she wouldn't listen to me. She told me I obviously wasn't serious about her and that she now understood I was only seeing her for sex, and then she walked into the courtroom and refused to talk to me about anything but work."

"How did you ask her to not work with Paul? Were you polite about it?" Sylvie's eyes had narrowed as though she knew the answer to that question.

Rene sighed when he didn't reply. "Tell me you asked her and didn't order her."

"I would love to be able to tell you I took that rational course," he admitted. "But I did not. I did tell her she wasn't going to work for him and then I pretty much ordered her to turn over the contracts to me. I was going to go shove them in my brother's face. In my defense, I had just had to deal with my mother, who wanted me to be the one to handle my brother's numerous problems. She showed up this afternoon, and I didn't realize she'd done it so Paul could get a shot at Jayna."

"I thought she didn't want Jayna around." Rene seemed confused.

So was he, but he knew one thing was true. "She's got a plan. In a way, she wins no matter what. If Jayna turns Paul down, Paul tells everyone what a bitch she is. If she takes him up on the offer, I'll be upset with her and the whole situation causes a rift between us. I guess I walked right into that one."

"There's a third option," Sylvie offered. "You could let her do the job and trust her to know when she's being used. I've worked with her. She's one tough cookie. She's very sensible. I don't think she's going to allow Paul to drag her into something bad."

"I think that's iffy." Rene backed him up. Likely because he was the one who knew exactly how bad things had gotten with Paul. After all, Rene had been the one to fly out to California with him a couple of years before when Paul had hit rock bottom. Rene had been with him when he'd bailed his brother out of jail and taken him straight to rehab. "Paul can get into trouble with some dangerous people. If I were Quaid, I would be worried."

"Then watch her carefully. Or offer to help her." Sylvie's pretty face had turned serious. "Look, Quaid, you know I adore you, but I want Jayna to stay in town and become the city's lead attorney. I've got plans for us, plans that require a lawyer with four rows of sharp teeth she's willing to use."

He was a bit wounded at the thought. "Since when do I not do what you need?"

"Your heart isn't in this and you know it," Rene replied, his voice tinged with sympathy. "I know you're good at your job, but you want to be writing. You told me you've gotten to write more with Jayna here."

"That's not why I'm crazy about her." He enjoyed the time she'd been able to give him, but he didn't like the thought that he'd been using her.

"I think that's a perfectly good reason to be crazy about her," Sylvie countered.

"I'm not using her so I can write," Quaid insisted.

"No, but you're writing because she's here. You're writing because she's inspired you, because she's supported you and unlocked that part of you that's been buried for a couple of years now," Rene replied. "Tell me you're not excited about it again."

"I can't. I had gotten to a point where I was ready to quit. I was sick of getting rejected, and the whole 'I write for myself and don't need an audience' thing was starting to feel like a lie I told myself." Jayna had changed that simply by reading what he'd written and then challenging him to do better. He was suddenly thinking about his characters again, and that was all because of her.

"She's good for you." Sylvie smiled, a bright expression, before sending him her "I'm the mayor and I will get things done" frown. "She's good for all of us, so you should do what you need to do to keep that woman here."

"Offer her a job." Quaid knew it probably wouldn't work. "But you should know she's overqualified."

Sylvie sat back, a satisfied smile on her face. "Aren't we all. And I'm putting together a proposal that would offer her a permanent position as the city's attorney. I'm working with a couple of the small towns in the parish. If we pool our resources, we might be able to offer her enough to make it tempting. But she's used to city life. She needs more than a job to stay. She needs someone she wants to stay with. That's you. So step it up, Havery. I don't want to lose this resource. We need her."

Because she was better than him when it came to the hard-core legal work. He would have thought the insinuation would bug him, but it didn't. He was proud of how smart she was, how hard she worked for her clients even when they were paying her in gas and chips and gumbo that never actually got made.

If she'd fumbled the way he had this afternoon, he would have listened to her. He would have shoved aside the pain and tried to understand her. He would have given her a second chance.

Damn it. He was in love with Jayna Cardet.

"Is he okay?" Sylvie asked in a whisper.

"That's his thinking face," Rene replied smoothly. "He's working some stuff out in his head. He's going to come up with a plan, and then she won't stand a chance."

He wasn't so sure about that. The more he thought about it, the more . . . angry wasn't the word. Irritated. Unsure. Vulnerable.

He was in love with her, and she'd walked away from him. The smart play would be to protect himself.

He didn't want to be smart. He didn't want to protect himself. He didn't want the world to view him as some manly man who didn't take crap off anyone.

He wanted her.

Her eyes widened as she caught sight of him, and she quickly turned back to her sister.

If she thought she was going to run, she was in for a surprise.

"Okay, now you've got some crazy eyes going." Rene sounded worried for the first time. "Maybe we should talk about this."

Jayna stood, and Sienna leaned over and said something

to her before she turned and carefully schooled her expression. He knew what she was doing because he'd watched her do it in court. She put on that bland, professional countenance when she was going to make a logical point.

He should have known she wouldn't run. He should have known that his baby would walk right over and likely tell him she got here first and he should leave.

She was about to find out that he wouldn't walk away so easily.

"Quaid, could we speak for a moment?" Jayna asked in that oh-so-polite tone of hers that still somehow held an edge of challenge. Like she halfway expected him to say no because he was a scaredy-cat.

He stood. The good news was he was friends with the owner of this place and knew exactly where they could talk.

"Of course." He slipped his napkin on his plate and stepped aside.

"Quaid, remember your manners," Rene warned.

Manners didn't matter. It was obvious she wasn't going to respond to his gentlemanly side.

It was time to let the bad boy come out to play.

chapter eleven

Jayna followed Quaid into the dining room. "Uhm, I thought we should talk outside. It's loud in here."

She wasn't sure where he was going. Did he need a drink in order to have a conversation with her? This might go worse than she thought. She'd expected a short conversation followed by some awkwardness and then they would get on with their lives.

"I know a place where we can talk and not have everyone in town listening in," Quaid said, his voice rising over the sound of chatty diners and the music from the dance floor. "Or watching."

She glanced around and sure enough, almost every eye in the room was on them. That was exactly what Quaid wanted to avoid. She'd screwed up again. "Maybe I should return to Sienna. You can get back to your friends. We can talk tomorrow."

His hand came out, grasping hers and basically challenging her to pull away and create even more drama than they had now. "I don't want to get back to my friends. They were supposed to come out with us tonight to get to know you. If you're not there, there's no reason for me to be there, either, so let's talk. And I don't care what they say about us, Jayna. You should understand that right now."

He turned and started walking again. She pretty much had no choice but to follow unless she wanted to make things worse. No matter what he said, he did care about gossip. It was precisely why he wanted to keep her away from his family. They were in Papillon's upper crust, and no matter how many degrees she had, she was still one of those Cardets. She didn't even have her father's surname because her mom hadn't been married to her or Sienna's dads. Two kids. Two different fathers. No marriages.

Was her mother afraid of losing her to more than distance?

Quaid pressed through the big stainless-steel doors that led to the kitchen. The smell of frying food made her stomach rumble, reminding her that she hadn't had dinner yet. One of the waitresses picked up a tray with two orders of chicken strips and French fries, one salad with crawfish bisque, and that big old po' boy with fried shrimp she'd planned on eating her feelings with. Yep. That was her order walking away.

"Lisa, I need to use the apartment," Quaid said to the petite woman in a Guidry's shirt and jeans.

Lisa Guidry's gaze moved between the two of them, her big eyes even wider than normal. "Sure, but it's kind of bare right now. We only use it when Remy's working overnight."

As if saying his name made him appear, Remy poked his head out from behind the row of shelves, frowning their way. "Hey, Quaid. You know there's no condoms up there. We're trying to get pregnant."

Now she pulled her hand away. Whoa. Someone misunderstood. "We don't need condoms. We're going to talk for a couple of minutes and then I'm going to rejoin my family and Quaid is going to get back to his life."

"I've got some on me. Don't worry about it," Quaid said, and then nodded her way. "Not that we would need them because of what she just said. But you should tell everyone in town that I hauled her up there because I couldn't stand a single afternoon of her being mad at me and I'm going to do everything I can to make it up to her. You tell them all that."

He gripped her hand again and started for the back of the kitchen and the stairs tucked back there. She would have pulled away but she felt warm for the first time in hours.

"Quaid, what is going on? You basically told Remy and everyone in the kitchen that we're going to have sex. Which we're not. We're going to talk. Or rather I'm going to talk and you're going to listen."

"And then we'll probably have sex. I was serious. I snooped Sienna's calendar and saw that she was going to be here." He took the stairs two at a time. "I made a bet you would come along with her."

She had to jog to keep up.

"You didn't think this was a coincidence, did you?" Quaid asked, his voice rough.

Was he going to be more difficult than she'd imagined?

"You wouldn't talk to me this afternoon," Quaid continued. "You walked away without giving me the chance to explain. I'm not going to make the same mistake. You want to talk, I'll listen, but you're going to give me the same courtesy."

"I didn't think there was much to say. You gave me an order. I'm following it. I'm giving Paul the contracts tomorrow. I won't have anything further to do with your family, so there's nothing for you to worry about and all of this is not necessary." She allowed him to lead her inside the tiny apartment over the kitchen.

Quaid closed the door behind her and turned on the light,

revealing a room that was nothing more than a bed, two nightstands, and a small closet.

It was too small for the two of them. Or rather Quaid was far too big.

He loomed over her. "Do you care about me at all, Jayna?"

What kind of question was that? "Of course I do. I wouldn't have slept with you if I didn't care. And that's why I'm apologizing. I was going to tell you about working with Paul. I wasn't planning on hiding it. I thought it would be a fairly easy way to make some money, but I didn't take into account how it would make us look to the town or your feelings about me being involved with your family. I misread some signals, and that's my fault, not yours."

"Your fault." He said the words with no intonation, as though he couldn't quite recognize them.

"Yes, mine." She needed to make herself clear and maybe they could find their footing again, this time on even ground. "I should have asked for clarity about our relationship rather than assuming we felt the same way."

His jaw went tight, a stubborn look coming into his eyes. "Didn't you do the same thing with your ex? His behavior was your fault because you knew who he was. Is that what you're saying?"

The last thing she wanted to do was talk about Todd. However, he had a point. "Not exactly, but it's similar. I knew going into it that this would be a short-term relationship with you, and I made too much of it. I shouldn't have been surprised by your reaction. We're two consenting adults who don't have any connections beyond sex and work. Your mother has made it plain to you that I'm not a right fit for your family. Not that any of that matters."

"Because we're only sleeping together and you're going to leave as soon as possible."

She felt pinned by his eyes even though he was feet away from her. She wasn't about to admit to him that she'd lied. In the last few weeks, she hadn't paid much attention to her job search. "I'm going to find a job, Quaid. I've always been planning on finding a job as soon as the ethics complaint is finished."

"I happen to know that you're going to receive an offer from the city," Quaid replied.

"I don't think that's such a good idea." The idea of working for the city made her happier than she would have believed a month or two ago. The first thing she'd do would be to figure out a way to save the library from the clutches of Quaid's client.

But she couldn't take that job. She wasn't going to stay in town and watch him find someone his mother approved of, watch him start a family, watch him be happy. She wanted him to be happy, but she couldn't watch it.

"Because you think I want to please my mother?"

The problem was she knew he had trouble with his mother, but she also knew he'd promised his father he would take care of her. That wasn't a promise Quaid would break lightly. "I think you're devoted to your family."

He nodded as though he'd expected the answer. "And I asked you to not represent my brother because I'm . . . what? I'm afraid to let you near him?"

This was starting to sound like he was questioning a witness. "What is going on, Quaid?"

"I'd like to understand what you're thinking," he admitted. "Since, according to you, this is all your fault."

She put her hands on her hips, frustration welling because he was deliberately misunderstanding her. "I didn't say that. I said I misunderstood a few things."

He took a step toward her, head tilting down so he could

look into her eyes. "So we don't want any more misunderstandings. Why did I not want you to work for my brother?"

They'd gone over this, but he seemed to need to play this out like a case he was prosecuting. "Because you don't want me near your family."

"And why don't I want you near my family?" he asked, moving in again.

Emotion welled because she didn't want to go over this. There was so much tension between them, and it was time to ratchet it down. He needed to understand that she wasn't going to make trouble for him. "Quaid, you're making a big deal out of something that's not. It's okay. We're not in a serious relationship. It's normal that you wouldn't want a casual fling to get tied up in your family's business."

"You are involved in a casual fling, Ms. Cardet," he said, his voice going deep. "I am not, and that's where you went very wrong."

"What is that supposed to mean?"

He moved closer to her, and this time she backed up because she could sense the well of emotion in him. "It means that you were right about you misunderstanding the situation but wrong about who was serious and who was not. I've been serious about you since the day you walked into my office. You—I'm starting to believe—viewed me as an opportunity."

That made her stop because she wasn't taking that from anyone. She hadn't slept with him so he would take care of her. She'd slept with him because . . . well, because she wanted him. "An opportunity to what? You should understand that there are knives downstairs, so I would watch what you accuse me of."

He didn't miss a beat. "I think you were crazy about me in high school, and I was a moron who couldn't see how amazing you were. And now the tables have turned and you've come back for revenge. Is it going to be fun for you to break my heart?"

She barely managed to not roll her eyes. "That's ridiculous and you know it. I did not sleep with you to get revenge for my high school self."

"And I didn't ask you not to work for my brother because I'm ashamed of you or because this is some fling that should be kept to the bedroom," he said in that same tone he used when he made a point in court. "It's the exact opposite. I need you, Jayna. I can't stand the thought of my brother and mother running off the best thing that ever happened to me."

He'd backed her up against the wall, taking up all the space, and she could barely breathe.

She'd thought the idea of him sending her away and not wanting to continue their friendship had scared her. This scared her even more.

What was he saying? Could she believe a word of it?

He put a hand behind her head, palm to the wall, and his eyes narrowed as he stared down at her.

"You just don't want to lose your friends with . . ."

"Don't you even say it. I understand that you've come out of a bad relationship and you don't want to trust me. I can wait, but don't tell me how I feel. Don't make this less than it is. For me, this is it, Jayna. I don't think this feeling goes away. I don't think I'll ever get over you, so don't lump me in with Todd, and don't you dare say it's your fault because you should have known. I'm telling you straight how I feel about you. I'm in love with you, Jayna Cardet, but I'm afraid you're going to realize how hard my family can be to deal with and you're going to walk away."

"Quaid," she started, her heart threatening to seize.

He shook his head. "Don't. Don't say a thing because I know you're not ready. That's all right. I need you to understand that I am. But I'm willing to be patient and I'm willing to be braver than I was this afternoon. You want to represent my brother? All right, but I'm your co-counsel. Not because I don't think you're smart enough. We both know you're twice the lawyer I am. It's because my brother gets into dangerous situations, and I won't have you hurt."

He was right. She wasn't ready to believe him. He wanted to keep his convenient lover for a little while longer. If he helped her, she did the same for him.

Did she want to leave? She'd started to enjoy the town, seeing it through a different filter than she had when she was younger. There was a lot to like about Papillon.

Quaid was here.

"Do we have a deal?" He stared down at her, the question another challenge. He seemed to be doing that a lot today— challenging her.

It was dangerous. He was dangerous. No matter what he said, she knew a man could change his mind. Right now, she was new and shiny and he didn't mind her annoying habits. She wasn't ever going to be the "stand by her man and make him look good" type. It was fun right now and it seemed to make sense to him, but he would figure out that she wasn't easy. In the end, he would want some twentysomething who could spit out a couple of kids while he built his career.

Women didn't get to have it all. She'd known that from the time she'd been able to understand how hard her mother had to work.

"Jayna." His voice had turned soft. "Don't get scared on me. You tell me you don't want me, and I'll be able to walk out of here. You tell me you can't love me, and I'll likely stay with you and try to change your mind. But don't make me leave because you think I'm going to turn into Todd. I've been waiting all my life for you. You aren't a piece of the puzzle that will get me the next rung up the ladder. You aren't some tool that will help me win a prize. You are the prize."

Tears pierced her eyes at the sweetness of his words. Quaid knew exactly what to say to get her into bed.

Or he meant every word and she'd finally found the right man.

She shoved that thought out of her head because she couldn't deal with it right now. Later she would pull it out and examine it, searching for the truth, but for now she needed to live in the moment.

She went on her toes and wrapped her arms around him and thanked the universe that Quaid was a man who came prepared.

"That's my girl," he whispered, his hands finding her hair. "You won't regret taking the chance. I promise."

She was going to argue with him, tell him she wasn't taking any chances and hadn't decided anything, but his mouth covered hers and she couldn't think at all when he kissed her.

He wasn't playing around this evening. His tongue surged in and stroked against hers as he pressed her against the wall. She was caught between the hard wall and Quaid's big body.

She wrapped her arms around his neck and gave herself up to the kiss. Nothing mattered except this moment and this man. Yesterday couldn't be fixed and tomorrow was a problem for another day.

Tonight she could be his.

Tonight he could be hers.

Quaid picked her up and carried her, though they didn't have far to go. The room was small but it had a bed, and that was all he needed. Not that the lack of a bed would have changed his course. He would have done what it took to make her comfortable, but he had a point to make.

He'd known the minute she'd said it was her fault that he was being stubborn. She had real reasons to be worried, real recent trauma, and he was being petty. He'd been wrong. It was up to him to make it right, to show her he wasn't going anywhere.

For the first time in his life, he genuinely considered leaving Papillon. If she needed a city to feel complete, he would do whatever he could to find someone to take over his practice, but he would follow her.

He held her close, pressing her body to his and reveling in her softness. "When I realized where you'd gone this afternoon, I should have marched right into your sister's house, picked you up, and brought you home."

"You would have had to fight two preteens," she whispered between kisses. "I've been teaching them not to allow men to treat them like objects."

So feminism had come to Papillon Gardens Trailer Park. Jayna could shake up the whole town, bringing her unique perspective to their world. And Papillon could teach Jayna that family was so much more than blood.

He kissed her over and over, wanting to surround her with his affection.

They moved together, her following his lead flawlessly as he eased them toward the bed.

He had to make her see they were perfect partners both in and out of the bedroom.

He could feel her breasts pressed against his chest and couldn't stand the clothes between them. Stepping back slightly, he tugged his shirt over his head and tossed it to the side. She unbuttoned her blouse and he was on her again, his hands finding warm skin as he pulled her close and kissed her. He managed to twist the clasps of her bra, tossing it aside and dragging her close. Warmth spread through him, and it wasn't all about how soft she felt against him. It wasn't merely sexual but a sense of home he felt whenever he was with her.

It had been mere days, but she'd become the center of his world, the sun he orbited around.

"I don't want to fight your family, baby. I want to get closer to them," he said. "But we're going to have to talk about mine."

"Not now, Havery."

She pulled away from him, and for a moment he thought he would have to fight for her to stay. Instead of running for the door, she slowly dropped to her knees in front of him.

"Baby," he began but his body was already tuning up in anticipation. He'd been the one to perform this particular act, loving the way she tasted on his tongue, but he hadn't felt her mouth on him before, and he tensed at the thought. "You're going to kill me tonight, aren't you? You're going to make me crazy."

Her hands went to the buckle of his belt, sliding it through the loop and unbuttoning his slacks. "You deserve it. The next time we're in court, I want this to be the only thing you think about."

She liked to play dirty.

But he didn't protest when she eased his slacks down his hips, dragged off his boxers, and then took him in her hand, manicured fingers stroking him. He didn't object when she leaned in and pressed a kiss on his most intimate flesh. He closed his eyes and enjoyed the feel of her mouth on him, lips and tongue moving over him, making him crazy.

Over and over she brought him to the edge and pulled him back. He slid his hands into her hair, smoothing it and watching as she lavished her affection on him.

It wasn't long before he couldn't take it a second longer.

He tugged gently on her hair. "Please, baby. I want to be with you."

Her head turned up and she held out her hand. "Only because I'm hungry and I get the feeling you're not going to feed me until you get what you want."

What he wanted was her with him always, but she wasn't ready for that. Not yet. He could be patient. The fact that she was willing to walk back out into the dining room with all the rumors that would be flying around now would have to be enough. "I'll get you anything you want. I really was planning on asking you to come out with me tonight. I wanted you to spend time with my friends. The sane ones. Take off your pants."

He was already kicking off his loafers and moving his slacks to the side. He retrieved the condom he now routinely carried because he'd turned into a constantly horny teenager around her. If she was willing, he would take her into the courthouse broom closet during their next trial. He watched as she shimmied out of her panties.

"You are so gorgeous," he said as he rolled the condom on. "Do you know how hard it is to concentrate when we're in court?" He moved in, his hands sliding around her waist to drag her close to him. "I lose my train of thought every time you look my way."

Her nose wrinkled. "It didn't seem that way when you objected to my line of questioning twenty-two times today."

He loved to work with her. He kissed her again, his tongue delving deep as her hands smoothed down his back. He hated the fact that they'd fought. "Forgive me. I can't stand that I made you think I'm not proud to be with you. I walk into that courtroom feeling like the luckiest man in the world. Don't you ever forget that."

He took her into his arms and gently tumbled on the small bed with her, spreading her legs and making a place for himself there. He stared down into her big brown eyes. They always pulled him in. This woman would forever be a mystery to him. He might unlock parts of her, but she would always be a challenge, a puzzle he desperately wanted to solve.

Jayna Cardet was the endgame for him. He accepted it in that moment when he thrust deep inside her body, making them one.

Her legs wrapped around his waist as she matched his rhythm, shifting it slightly so it wasn't his anymore, but uniquely theirs.

It wasn't long before she tightened around him, her climax sending him straight into his own.

Pleasure coursed through him along with all the unfamiliar emotions this one particular woman always brought out in him. Satisfaction. Love. Peace.

He fell on her, holding her close and praying he never had to let go.

chapter twelve

Jayna was warm, her body still pulsing with pleasure as Quaid wrapped his arms around her, and she realized she was on the edge.

She wanted Quaid but she wasn't sure she could trust him. Not that he would do anything to hurt her. He wouldn't. That was part of the problem. He was one of the nicest men she knew, and if he made a promise to her, he would do anything he could to keep it. Even sacrifice his own happiness.

"Tell me what I'm doing wrong?" He whispered the question against her shoulder, his lips still moving over her skin.

Oh, she wasn't about to let him think that. "You are perfect. It was fabulous, Quaid."

He chuckled. "I'm not talking about the sex. I'm talking about with you. Where am I going wrong with you?"

She tilted her head up so she could see him, take in his sandy hair. It was usually perfect, but now it was mussed and curling in every direction. Only she got to see him like this. "You aren't. It's about me."

"Always taking the blame." He was quiet for a moment. "I am willing to acknowledge that I should have been more patient and sat down with you this afternoon. I should have listened to why you wanted to take Paul's case and explained my position. Then I should have told you that I would back you up no matter what choice you made. But you made a mistake, too."

She wasn't sure what he was talking about. "I agreed to everything you wanted, Quaid."

"Yes, and then you walked away. Baby, we have to be able to fight."

Tears pierced her eyes because he was looking at her like she was something precious. Had anyone ever looked at her the way Quaid was now? "Fighting doesn't work."

"It didn't work with your ex because he wasn't fighting." Quaid's deep voice rumbled through the tiny room. "He was punching down. If we argue, it's because we're a couple and we're trying to work out our differences. I know I reminded you of him today and I promise I won't do it again."

Had that been it? Had she felt like he was manipulating her and shoved him in the same category as her ex-husband? When he'd ordered her to give him those contracts, hadn't she spent much of the afternoon thinking about all the times Todd or one of his cronies at the firm had ordered her to do something, like they knew better than she did? Todd hadn't considered that she was smarter than he was, had done better in school than him.

"You marginalized me."

"I did. It doesn't matter that it wasn't what I meant to do. All that matters is how I made you feel, and I am sorry, baby." He cupped her cheek, his gaze so sincere. "I will never again tell you to calm down, tell you that what you're feeling isn't real. I won't do it because I care about you. I won't do it because it's been done to me so often I can't even stand to hear the words."

There it was. There was his vulnerability, the one thing he'd demanded from her but withheld himself. The next few moments would prove if he really meant what he said. She thought about not asking the question, but she couldn't hold back. She wanted this intimacy with him, to share the burden of something he carried with him every day. "About Paul?"

His eyes clouded for a moment and she almost called back the question, but then he lowered his head down to her chest, hugging her like she was a teddy bear. "Always about Paul. He was my little brother. I knew him better than anyone, and my parents didn't want to listen to me when I said he had a problem."

"When did you know?"

"He was fourteen when I caught him smoking weed. I don't have a problem with it. It's legal in plenty of places, but a fourteen-year-old shouldn't be sneaking out at night to smoke," he said quietly. "I told my father because I was worried about the people he was hanging out with. Jayna, you should know that some of those people . . ."

Her heart clenched. There was only one reason he would say those words. She wouldn't have noticed what was happening back then. She'd been far too focused on her own future. "Did my cousins sell to Paul?"

"Yes. It was one of the reasons I didn't want to talk about it with you, but not the only one. I feel some shame when it comes to Paul. I feel like I should have been able to help him."

She sighed, so much of her anger fleeing when she heard those words from him. She hadn't realized what she'd been holding against him until his truth broke through her walls and let her feel compassion. "You tried. You did what you could. I know my aunt did, too, and it didn't work. Sometimes people do what they want no matter the consequences. My cousins didn't think of anyone when they decided to sell. They thought about money and getting out of the position they were born into. They didn't want to find another way. I guess in some ways, there wasn't another way for them. I got a scholarship. They had to drop out of high school because their dad got sick and couldn't work."

Then her uncle died and her aunt had struggled and her cousins had been eaten up by poverty and hopelessness and had tried to take down as many people as they could with them. Apparently Quaid's brother had gotten sucked in.

"He would have found it somewhere," Quaid said. "He was reckless. Our father paid more attention to me, and I think it started as a way to try to get his attention and then . . . well, then it was a disease he couldn't, wouldn't try to control. I often wonder if I'd tried harder to get my parents to take it seriously, if things would have gotten as bad as they did."

"That is not your fault." She sat up, cupping his face in her hands. "You can't be responsible for another person's choices. You did what you could. Your mom . . . she still doesn't listen to you about Paul, does she?"

"Paul is her baby and he always will be. He handles her perfectly. He knows exactly what to say and do to get her on his side. She doesn't want to see how bad the problem is so she gives him cash and sends him on his way."

"And expects you to sort everything out because you took over more than your father's legal practice. You took over your dad's life."

"Pretty much. For the most part it's not so bad, but the responsibility is starting to weigh on me. There are things I want to do that I can't because there's too much work to do. Having you here has been such a blessing in so many ways."

She'd been able to take on cases that would normally eat up all of his writing time.

Was that why he wanted her to stay? Was she a convenience for him?

Why did she have to ask all these questions? Why couldn't she stay in the moment?

"What's wrong?" Quaid asked quietly.

She shook her head. "Nothing. I'm glad I've been able to help."

"What's the 'but'? Because there's plainly a 'but.' I can see that big brain of yours working and I'm worried I won't like what you're thinking."

Did they have to do this? They'd ended one fight, and this felt like it would start another. "My mind's always going. It's nothing to worry about. I'm trying to live in the present for once in my life. I spent so much time worried about the future that I forgot to enjoy anything I had."

"And you're trying to enjoy me now?" The question came out ever so softly.

That felt like a trap, but there was only one real answer. "Yes."

"You need to enjoy me now because you won't be here to enjoy me later."

"That sounds selfish on my part, but yes." She got ready for the storm, for him to strike back, because she knew the last thing he liked her talking about was the fact that she was going to leave.

She had to, didn't she? Didn't she owe it to the kid who'd gotten out? The one who'd worked so hard to leave this town. The one who'd spent all her time in books, working toward a future that hadn't turned out the way she'd planned.

Instead, he sighed and reached out, tucking a strand of hair behind her ear. "It's okay, baby. You can be scared for a little while longer. You can tell yourself I'm just a rebound guy and there's nothing real between us. You can pretend this is all sex and that we don't belong together. You can say it all right up until the moment you need to decide whether you want to stay or go back to the city."

She didn't like how much he saw through her. "You think you'll be enough to keep me here?"

"No. I think you'll figure out what you want, what you truly want to do with the rest of your life, and then you'll either let me live that life with you or not. Because I will want to live that life with you. I won't change my mind or decide you're too difficult. I'm not with you because I want to rebel against my mother. I'm a fully grown man, and I know what's in my heart, and that's you, Jayna. You mean more to me than anything else. More than my family. More than this town. If you leave and you let me, I'll go with you. I'll make a life where you want to be."

She pulled away, taking the sheet with her. She wasn't ready for this. "You don't mean that. You're not going to leave Papillon. You have a business here."

He made no move to cover himself again, simply left his gorgeous, muscular body on display. "You mean more."

She shook her head, easing off the bed and putting some distance between them. "That's ridiculous, Quaid. You're not going to leave your home."

"What if you're my home?" He asked the question and then immediately held up a hand. "I'm sorry. I'm going too fast. It's all right. We still have time."

How much time? Weeks? A couple of months? She'd talked to the lawyer Quaid had secured for her, and she thought things would move fairly quickly. Apparently Todd and his family now wanted the whole thing done and over so they could focus on his new family. They wanted to forget she ever existed and move on, which would leave her completely free to do the same.

Did she want to move on without Quaid? Without Sienna and her nieces? She'd only recently figured out how nice it was to have an actual life that didn't revolve around working every minute of the day, that included eating boxed mac and cheese with giggling girls and spending long hours arguing with a sexy man who cleaned when she cooked.

But how could she stay here? If she did stay, where the hell would she go when Quaid inevitably figured out how impossible she could be?

He got up and walked to her, not hiding an inch of his gorgeous body. He moved right in and kissed the top of her head, the tender gesture nearly undoing her. "Stop worrying. I won't push you anymore. We're fine right where we are. Now let's get you some dinner. I would bet the dining room is starting to close down, but I assure you Remy will still feed us."

He stepped away and picked up his pants.

She stood there feeling like she'd missed some chance she hadn't even known she'd wanted, something infinitely precious slipping through her fingers but she couldn't quite make it stop. There should be something she could say that would make this all better.

But there wasn't and she didn't understand why. Why couldn't she accept that he knew what he wanted? Because it was too soon? What was the right amount of time? Was there some countdown clock she could check that would tell her okay, now it's all right to think the man knows his mind? Was there an alarm that would go off that let her know it was now time for her to accept the feelings she knew she had?

A knock on the door brought her out of those inner questions, making her remember that they'd basically told the whole town they were going to skip dinner in favor of having sex in an upstairs room.

It would be a story they would talk about forever. Her kids would hear the story of how their dad . . .

She'd just thought about having kids with Quaid Havery. Tears pierced her eyes because it wouldn't work. How could they have kids when their families were in such disarray?

When her own mom wouldn't talk to her? When his mom thought she wasn't good enough?

"Hey, you must have turned off your cell," Remy was saying. Quaid stood at the door, a crack letting him hear what his friend had to say. "The sheriff's office called and there's been an accident. It's Paul and your mom. You should get to the clinic fast. Lila is calling in a CareFlight."

She heard Quaid curse softly and then she dropped every worry she had along with that sheet as she dressed as quickly as she could.

It didn't matter that the town would know what they'd been doing or that his mother wouldn't want her there.

All that mattered was supporting him.

Quaid slammed the car into park in front of Lila LaVigne's tiny clinic that served as the only medical care for miles around. The Papillon Parish Clinic's lights were all on, a beacon on the darkened street. It was only nine thirty, but Papillon closed early on a night like this. Only places like Guidry's were still open. The town square was dark, the clinic's lights punctuating the fact that there was an emergency.

Jayna opened the door and slid out of the passenger seat.

When Remy had first told him the news, he'd thought she would want to stay out of it. He'd done a number on her by trying to keep her out of his family business, and now he realized how dumb an idea that had been. When the chips were suddenly down, he didn't want her to go back home and leave him to deal with the fallout, no matter how bad it was. The minute he'd heard his brother and mother were in trouble, he'd wanted Jayna to hold his damn hand and come with him.

And that was exactly what she'd done, no questions

asked. No arguments or *maybe I should stay behind*s. She'd dressed as quickly as she could and put her hand in his. She'd hustled out of Guidry's, and now she was moving to get inside the clinic as fast as he needed her to.

"Hey, Quaid." Armie stood outside the clinic's automatic doors wearing his uniform and there was . . .

He couldn't mistake that brown stain for anything but exactly what it was. Blood. Armie's shirt was stained with it, and it definitely did not appear to be his.

What was he about to walk into? Anxiety rose hard and fast, making his chest tight. He wasn't happy with either of the people in that clinic, but he also wasn't ready for either of them to no longer be here. God, he wasn't ready for any of this.

Jayna's hand found his. "What's happening, Sheriff? Remy didn't say much."

Quaid took a long breath, her solid presence beside him giving him the strength he needed. "All we know is a Care-Flight is on its way."

"I'm sorry to scare you like that," Armie replied, leading them inside. "There wasn't much time to explain. I couldn't get your cell, and I don't know Jayna's number. I found out you were at Guidry's earlier so I called Remy on the off chance you were still there."

The lights inside seemed too bright, the walls a clinical white that bounced that light all around. "What happened?"

"Paul had taken your mom out to dinner at Lucille's. When they came out after they finished, he was mugged in the parking lot. The attacker used a knife," Armie explained. "Roxie is still out there trying to find a witness and Landon is checking any and all cameras in the area, but you know how that goes."

They wouldn't find much if they didn't have an eyewitness. Lucille's was the only fine dining establishment for miles, so it was naturally the one his mother frequented. They had a camera on the entrances and exits but not the parking lot. It was a weeknight so there likely hadn't been a ton of foot traffic around the area. "Is he okay?"

"He was stabbed but the knife wasn't long. I would say it was something like a Swiss Army knife. Lila's already stitched him up and she's satisfied he'll be okay in a few days," Armie said, stopping in front of the intake desk.

A relief he hadn't expected flooded through him. Paul was okay. He didn't have to deal with that yet. God, how long had he been waiting for his brother to die? Dreading and almost accepting that it would happen. But deep down that dread was a raging fear that flavored every second of his relationship with his brother and possibly the whole damn world.

"That's good news," Jayna said. "So why did Lila call in a CareFlight? It doesn't sound like Paul needs one."

Armie turned and the grim set of his expression told Quaid that the worst wasn't over yet. "I'm afraid your mother is having a heart attack, but Lila thinks she caught it in time and she's stable for now. The CareFlight is my wife taking every precaution she can."

His own heart threatened to seize because he wasn't ready for that, either. He didn't wait for further explanations, simply started for the exam rooms where Lila would almost certainly have his mother while they waited.

Jayna didn't miss a beat. "Okay, do we know what hospital they'll take her to? Can Quaid ride with her and I'll drive Paul?"

She was asking the right questions while he was panicking. He didn't even hear Armie's answer, simply pushed through the closed door, and there his mother was, looking frail on the small bed, her arm hooked to an IV and Lila LaVigne monitoring her vitals. Her free hand was held in Paul's.

"Quaid," his mother said, her voice shaky. She held out the hand with the IV and Quaid moved to the right side of the bed, offering her his.

"Mom," he acknowledged before looking to Lila. "What's going on?"

"I thought it was a panic attack at first, brought on by the mugging." Lila had on yoga pants and a T-shirt. She'd likely been pulled from a relaxing evening, but that was what happened when you were the only medical authority for miles. "But I decided to be careful and did a test to make sure. She's definitely having arrhythmia. I've got her stable, but she needs an echo and likely surgery if there's a blockage the size I suspect."

"You're going to be okay, Momma." Paul brought her hand up and kissed it. "You have to be."

His brother was white as a sheet, his eyes red. He looked like hell, and Paul never looked less than perfect. He'd gone into damn rehab looking fresh as a daisy.

"I am now that I have my boys here." His mother looked over to where Jayna stood. "What is she doing here? My family is in a crisis. I need to be alone with my sons."

He was about to admonish his mother, but Jayna spoke up first.

"What I'm doing here is supporting my boyfriend, who happens to be your son. I'm going to stay here because Quaid needs me. I've arranged it with Armie and the CareFlight so he can go with you, and then I'll drive Paul to the hospital, where I will also stay and be of service to all of you whether you like it or not," Jayna replied with the no-nonsense tone she used in a courtroom. "I'll handle the hospital and all the other annoyances so your sons can focus on you and you can focus on recovering. I'll make calls that need to be made and arrange for you to be comfortable. I'll be pushy and obnoxious and get you everything you need so you and your sons can be sweet as pie and have all the staff love you. That's how it's going to be, Mrs. Havery. The other option is you fight with me and give your son the kind of grief he doesn't need right now. So it's your choice. Let me handle things and make you and your sons happy or tear him apart by making him choose."

His mother frowned for a moment, blinking as she stared at Jayna. "All right, then. I find this offer of aid acceptable. I'm going to need for you to call our housekeeper and let her know what's going on."

Jayna nodded and stepped back, but not before she winked Quaid's way.

Did she have any idea what she'd gotten herself into? He shoved the thought aside because Jayna did not need him to save her. She needed him to believe in her and support her and let her handle what she needed to.

She needed him to let her be part of his family. It was the "better or worse" part of the vows he eventually intended to share with her.

"I'm going to get everything ready," Lila said. "The helicopter should land in about ten minutes. Armie, help me make sure the pad is clear, and we'll need to get her in the elevator in a couple of minutes. Jayna, if you're serious, there's some paperwork you could look over. I would hate to send it with Quaid. He's got other things to worry about."

"I'm my mother's attorney of record, but Jayna and I work together so she can sign whatever she needs to." Quaid glanced down at his mother. It was time to see how much she was willing to change. "If that's what you want, Mother."

His mother started to open her mouth but then closed it again. "Whatever Quaid decides is all right."

"I'll take a look at it. I'd like to see the police report when it's ready, too." Jayna was calm and that allowed him to not be, to not shove down what he was feeling the way he normally would.

He hadn't had that since his father was alive. He'd been all alone in taking care of this family, this town, his whole world, and having someone he could trust completely lifted a weight off his shoulders he couldn't imagine not bearing. He released his mother's hand to go to Jayna and hug her close. "Thank you."

She went up on her toes and kissed him briefly. "Don't worry about a thing. I'll handle it all. I'll let the court know we might need a continuance with the nudity case. Though it goes heartily against my best interest, I'll agree to it."

"Your fans will be mightily disappointed," he murmured.

"So will yours. Don't think I don't see those women watching you. Court Cuties. More like Law Groupies." She pulled away and followed Lila and Armie out to the lobby.

Even in the midst of a crisis, she could make him smile.

"Law groupies?" His mother frowned. "Are there a bunch of women who come watch you try cases and attempt to get you to sin with them?"

He barely managed to not roll his eyes. "They come because Jayna and I are presenting an entertaining case. That's all."

"I've heard Noreen Driver from the Fillin' Station has a bet with Rena Tubbs that she can get you in bed." Paul just had to put in his two cents.

"Jayna better shut that down, and fast," his mother declared. "The law is a venerable institution. It shouldn't be used to ogle men."

Quaid turned back to his brother because the last thing he needed was a lecture from his mother on the immorality of folks these days. "Are you all right? I know you are physically, but that had to be a frightening experience."

Paul's jaw went tight as he nodded. "I'm fine. It was five stitches. Don't worry about me."

"Oh, Quaid, it was terrible," his mother said with a cry. "I thought that man was going to kill your brother right there in the parking lot. I threw him my purse, but he stabbed Paul anyway. I thought I was going to watch my baby die."

He held his mother's hand again, his mind working. That was twice Paul had been the victim of a crime in a town that had very little of it. It was curious, but that monitor started beeping again and he couldn't think about anything but keeping his mother calm. "It's all right now. He's fine."

"I'm fine, Momma," Paul agreed. "There's no need to worry at all. Quaid's going with you and Jayna will take care of me."

"Do you think we can trust her?" His mother's question was accompanied by the monitor going right back to a steady beat. "Maybe we should get a private investigator to send us a report."

She was calmer when she was thinking about how to get rid of his girlfriend. Apparently it was his mother's happy place. But suddenly that didn't seem so daunting. Jayna could handle his mother. "I would trust her with my life, and you should understand I won't accept you talking bad about her. I love Jayna. I'm going to do everything I can to keep her in my life, so you should start working your way through all the stages of grief you need to in order to be good to her."

His mother frowned, her eyes going to the door. "I suppose she is well educated. And according to the rumors, she did manage it all on her own. I was told there was no money saved for her college. There's something to be said for a girl pulling herself up by her bootstraps. She must be smart."

"Oh, she's really smart," Paul interjected. "And she mostly sees right through my bullshit, so she's not easily swayed by good looks and charm. It's good that she doesn't need a handsome, sparkly man since she's apparently ended up with Quaid."

He flashed his brother a death stare, but his mom's lips had curled up.

"Oh, your brother is charming enough," his mom said. "Maybe I can smooth out some of her rough edges."

"I like her rough edges," Quaid protested.

His mother nodded as though some diabolical plan had popped into her head. "Yes, once she gets Paul out of his terrible contracts, perhaps she and I should sit down and talk. There's a lot I can teach her about what it means to move in our world."

Now Quaid was the one who might need the CareFlight. "I thought you wanted *me* to look through Paul's contracts."

He didn't mention he'd already reversed that decision.

"Now that I think about it, she's far more ruthless than you are," his mother mused. "It's your polite upbringing. You were taught to be a gentleman, and she had to fight it out on the streets."

"Yes, the mean streets of Papillon," he deadpanned. His mother was making it sound like Jayna had fought her way through her childhood like a Dickensian character. Or more likely a kid in a Scorsese film who knifed her own sister to claw her way to the top of the Mafia.

"I think she might be one of those shark people." His mother proved she knew neither Jayna's history nor pop culture references. "You know, the kind who can sense blood in the water and don't mind taking down a fish or two. That's what your brother needs. He needs someone who knows how to fight dirty."

Paul nodded as though this had been his plan all along. "Yes, I think she's what we all need. You know our grandfather used to say that every generation needed an infusion of fresh blood to stay on top of things."

"Ideas," Quaid corrected. "Grandad said we needed fresh ideas. He was not talking about DNA."

"Oh, he was," his mother said with a sigh. "After Momma passed to her glory he tried to marry a stripper, and that was his excuse. That the family needed fresh blood. I think he was more interested in her boobs. I never told you this but I think she gave him a stroke. Or all that Viagra did it. Poor Daddy. Do you think we could get Jayna to grow out her hair? I know it's chic in the city, but here a woman needs her hair."

"I think Jayna is beautiful the way she is," Paul announced.

It actually felt a little nice for his brother to have his back for once. And Jayna's hair—which was perfect the way it was. "No one is going to talk to her about her hair. Her hair is fine."

The door opened and Armie and Lila were there again.

"Time to get you upstairs," Lila said. "Quaid, follow us. Paul, you can drive in with Jayna, but I'm serious about not lifting heavy items or doing anything physical until that heals. I don't want it opening up or getting infected."

"I've got Jayna. She can do all the physical stuff. I'll be around to amuse everyone." Paul stood and sobered. "I promise. I won't worry my mom any more than she already is. I'll be careful. When she gets home she's going to need me to take care of her."

Quaid wanted to believe him. Was there truly something different about his brother this time? He stepped aside to let Armie lift the side rail of his mother's bed.

"I'll see you soon, baby," his mother said as they wheeled her out.

He followed them toward the elevator that would take them to the helipad above. Jayna looked up from the paperwork in front of her.

"Thank you for everything." He kissed her, wishing she could come with him.

"Of course." She glanced over to where Paul stood by their mom's bed and lowered her voice. "And I'll figure out what's going on. I promise."

"You thinking what I'm thinking?" The bell dinged and they started to slide the bed inside. He would be taking the stairs. The elevator was too tight for three adults and a patient in a bed.

"That this has something to do with Paul's loan shark? Like his car did? Yes," she replied with no judgment in her tone at all. "I'll get that name out of him and you'll pay him off. This can't happen again. Do you want me to get the cops involved?"

Sadly, that might make things worse in the short term. "Not yet. Let's get the loan shark off our backs and my mother healthy before starting anything else."

Jayna's eyes lit up. "Then I can find a way to legally screw him over and possibly send him to jail for a long time?"

His mother was right. His love was a shark, and she enjoyed the kill. "Something like that. See you in New Orleans."

He hustled as Paul was coming back to join Jayna.

His brother was in good hands.

"Hey, Jayna, Mom wants you to know that she's got a tea with the Jaycees planned for two weeks from now and you're going to need to be properly dressed for it," Paul said.

"What does that mean?" Jayna asked.

It meant he might have just made a monster.

It also meant his mother would come around. Now he had to make sure Jayna did, too.

chapter thirteen

❧

Jayna drove, the night black around them with only the headlights to illuminate the way. Quaid would likely land soon and then he would text them any updates. She'd gotten all of the paperwork Lila needed done and now it was time to start the second part of the assignment she'd given herself.

To figure Paul out.

He'd been oddly quiet since they'd started the drive. He'd sat at the clinic after their mom had been taken away, only moving when Jayna had requested he come with her. She wasn't used to a Paul who didn't try to be the center of attention. The silent contemplation frankly scared her.

"So your mom is inviting me to the Jaycee thing?" She decided to go the easy route first. He hadn't gone sullen and silent until Quaid and his mother had been lifted into the night. "Do I dare ask who that is? I don't know a Jaycee, and I doubt you're talking about Jay-Z, though at least I know what he does."

"It's the Junior Chamber," he replied, staring out at the night. "It's a leadership organization for younger people."

"Oh, Quaid mentioned that but he called it the Junior League."

Paul snorted. "It's an entirely different organization. The Junior League is specifically focused on women in leadership. Mother has always sponsored the Jaycees group here. Quaid never paid much attention to the work she does. I'm fairly certain he would say it's all some rich people thing where they play at being charitable, but they've done some real good. Our mother's charities have raised millions over the years, money that she put into this town."

Paul had pretty much nailed how Quaid felt about the charities his mother dealt with. "Where did the money go in the town?"

There was charity, and then there was "people who liked things to be pretty" charity.

"The Jaycees hold business classes, and they sponsor many of our festivals. They also are responsible for the beautification projects around the parish," Paul explained. "I spent a lot of my high school years carrying planters around for my mother. She designed the gardens around the courthouse."

So "people who liked things to be pretty" charity. "Why would she want me to go to this thing? Is it some sort of trap?"

"It's not a trap. It's an olive branch," Paul replied. "You're in the right age range for the group, though they don't get many younger people, so you'll find they don't enforce that whole upper-limit age thing. Mom does what she knows. She tries to bring some elegance and class to the town."

"The town is fine." She was surprised at the actual level of disdain she felt at the thought that Papillon wasn't classy. It wasn't. She knew that, but Papillon was fine. "Do you know what Papillon needs more than flowers at the courthouse? A functional, modern library that isn't about to be torn down and sold off."

"You should bring that up when you meet them," was all Paul said.

She turned onto the main highway, though it was still a two-lane road, slightly wider and with less chance of her hitting a deer or getting attacked by a Cajun werewolf. She snorted at the thought because it meant she was settling back in. Or perhaps settling in for the first time. "I will."

Silence descended again and Jayna realized she was putting off the inevitable. She had a job to do, one she'd promised Quaid she would accomplish on the drive to New Orleans. Paul wasn't opening up to her so she had to find a way to crack him. Luckily getting people to talk when they didn't want to was kind of what she did for a living. "Are you okay?"

"I'm fine," he replied evenly. "It was only five stitches."

She'd expected him to deflect. He'd been doing it all evening, skirting around the real problem. She'd spoken with Armie, who'd told her Paul had said nothing beyond he was robbed. From what she could tell he still hadn't mentioned any trouble he had to the sheriff. "I wasn't talking about the stitches. I was talking about the fact that you got attacked tonight and it's probably the same guy who stole your car. You know, the guy you owe money to."

She found it was best to get the truth out there and let her client react to it.

Paul was silent for a moment.

She was handling him the wrong way. He was a reluctant witness, and she needed to get him to talk. Quaid had been playing bad cop with his brother for far too long. It might be time for a good cop. "I think it's admirable that you want to pay off the debt yourself, Paul. I really do, but we need to know if this thing is escalating. Your mom could have been the one who got stabbed."

"It's about me," Paul insisted. "I'm the one who owes money, not her."

He wasn't as selfish as Quaid imagined him to be. Or perhaps he truly was the changed person he claimed he was.

Addicts could make different choices when they were using, choices they wouldn't make when they had their heads on straight, when the drugs weren't clouding their judgment.

She was almost certain that was why her mom had made sure her dad wasn't in her life.

"But they'll use the people you love to force you to pay them back." He needed to understand the reality he was facing. She knew he'd been in some dicey situations, but she thought this was one he hadn't encountered before. He'd always had someone eager to bail him out, and he wasn't willing to fall back on his family again.

"I need more time. You said you thought the house contract was good, right?"

"Yes. I think it's fine, but the closing date is six weeks from now," she pointed out. "It doesn't feel like this guy is willing to wait for six weeks. I know you're trying to show Quaid that you can handle things on your own, but in this case, the more mature decision is to borrow the money from him and pay him back when the transfer from your house comes through."

Paul's head fell forward. "Then I'm the same person I've been for years."

"No, you're the person who genuinely needs help and will swallow his pride to protect the people he loves," she gently corrected. He wanted to be persuaded, wanted this burden off his shoulders. "You'll pay him back when your house sells, and you and I will deal with the production contracts. You'll stay with your mom and take care of her while she recovers. You'll sit down with me and your brother and figure out what your next moves are. What you're trying to prove can't be proven with a single act. It's the day-to-day living that will show Quaid you've changed."

"I thought it would be different. I thought I could come home and quietly deal with the mess I made, but it's all spiraling out of control again. Why did I come back at all? It would have been better if I'd stayed in LA."

"No, it wouldn't, because you wouldn't have your family around you. Look, Paul, you caused this problem and you have to be the one to get yourself out of it, and your best option is to make a deal with Quaid and hold up your end of the bargain. Then when you find yourself in a place where you have to make choices you aren't sure of, you ask for advice."

Paul sniffled, obviously trying to stay in control. "But I was sure of this investment."

"Well, then you should always ask Quaid for a second opinion moving forward."

"He's not an artist."

She practically growled Paul's way. "Yes, he is. He's a writer and a hell of a good one, but he hasn't turned that into his whole identity. You have to be more than an artist. You can't say you're an artist so that gives you some free pass to do whatever you want. You're also a son and a brother and a friend, and, Paul, you are also an addict. Say it." Now her bad cop was coming out.

"I'm an addict. I will die an addict. I do not have to allow that fact to ruin my life. I have a disease and I can choose whether or not I give in to it." He took a long breath. "Oh, I'm choosing it, aren't I? I'm setting myself up to fail."

He could learn. "Yes. You've put an enormous amount of stress on yourself, and it's going to push you to the edge. I know you want everyone to see you as cured or something, but you're not. You need to rebuild trust with them by showing them you are willing to put your recovery and sobriety first, way beyond your pride."

"His name is Patrick Whedon. I'll get you the information and the payoff amount," Paul promised. "I'll text him now and let him know he'll have the full amount tomorrow."

She breathed a deep sigh of relief as he brought his phone out. "I'm glad. This will put Quaid's mind at ease. He wants you to be safe."

"He wants me to be gone." Paul's voice shook a bit as he typed on his cell.

"You have to be patient with him."

"I spent an enormous amount of my life making my brother uncomfortable. Shouldn't I give him what he wants?" The sound of a text going out pinged through the car. "Shouldn't I honor his wishes?"

"He doesn't hate you. He's scared of you," she pointed out. "He's scared for you, and he's scared for himself at the thought of losing you. That fear comes out as anger. It usually does in men because you're taught it's not manly to be afraid or to have feelings that don't involve lust or rage. Deep down he loves you but he's afraid to feel it because if you die, he'll have to feel that, too."

"Do you think he still cares about me?" The question sounded like it came from a child afraid of being alone in the world.

But weren't they all just scared kids who wanted to make sure they were worthy of love and care? "Yes. But you have to care about him, too, and part of that is taking care of yourself so he doesn't worry."

Paul sat back and they were silent for a few moments. Another ping signaled a text, and Paul looked down. "He said that's fine. If he gets his money tomorrow, my luck should change. I always trust the wrong people. Like my production partner. That asshole did everything wrong and he's still suing me to take all the rights."

"Like what?" Her legal mind was whirling now.

Paul shook his head. "Everything. He was supposed to arrange for our insurance. He said he did and then I find out he never paid the company the premium. We did all that work and if anything had gone wrong, I would have been screwed. I still could get screwed if anyone found out about it."

Jayna tightened her grip on the steering wheel. "Is that in the contract? His duty to secure insurance for the production? It's written into the contract?"

"I'm pretty sure," Paul replied. "But I can't out him for that because it would make me look bad, too."

"Did he tell you that? Is that what he said?"

"Yeah. He's right, too. Who's going to work with me in the future?"

Oh, she was taking that guy down and getting Paul his rights back. "Everyone, because we're going to prove that not only did you attempt to be the responsible one, he then attempted to blackmail you to cover his own dereliction of duty. If I get this right, I might be able to void that contract. I need to talk to some entertainment lawyers, but we might have a way out."

"Really?" Paul sounded hopeful for the first time in hours.

"Really." She would have to prove that Paul didn't know it was going on during production, but she would bet these guys did everything through texts. "I'm going to need your text conversations with him and all your emails to and from him."

"Sure," Paul agreed. "You can have anything you need. I kept it all. My dad told me to always keep a paper trail, and at first I thought that meant I should print things out, but Quaid told me just not deleting things is enough. I keep everything. You might want to avoid any emails from a woman named Valarie. We might have been sending pics for a while now. You know. Fun selfies. Of parts that you probably should not see."

"I will not open anything that looks like it might contain

a venereal disease," she agreed, her outlook sunnier than it had been before.

"Jayna, do you think we have some time before Mom needs me?" Paul asked quietly.

"I think she'll be with doctors for hours. Why? Do you want some food?"

"I think I would like to go to a meeting. I think I need to."

There was always an AA or NA meeting somewhere. And they were heading into NOLA. She could find him one. "I'll get you there."

She drove through the night, certain she could make at least one thing right in her world. Whatever her world was.

The rest, she would have to think about.

Quaid ignored the stale coffee sitting on the table. The waiting room they'd sent him to smelled slightly bitter, and he wished he'd brought a sweater or jacket, because the whole place was cold.

The door opened and the world became infinitely warmer as Jayna walked through followed by his brother.

"Hey." She strode right up to him and wrapped him up in her arms.

He could breathe for the first time in hours. "I was getting worried about you. Did you have trouble on the road?"

She pulled back. "No. We made it fine. Just got waylaid. How's your mom doing?"

"Have you talked to the doctor?" Paul asked.

"She's having a stent placed right now." He glanced at the clock. "She's been back there for thirty minutes, so it shouldn't be long. He said it might take up to an hour, but it's a minimally invasive procedure. The blockage was bad, but the doctor says this is a routine procedure. She's going to stay here for two nights and then she'll have some rehab work to do. She's going to have to make some lifestyle changes."

"I'll call Lila in the morning and make arrangements for home health care and her rehab appointments," Jayna offered.

"And I'll talk to Caroline about eating healthier," Paul replied. "I wouldn't mind a change. I can't get paunchy."

Jayna shook her head. "That's good to hear." She yawned behind her hand. "I got us and Paul rooms at the hotel down the street. I'm going to go check us in and maybe catch a couple of hours of sleep before I go back to Papillon. I've already arranged for Rene to come up here tomorrow afternoon so you'll have a car."

"You have to go back?" He'd counted on her staying with him.

"I've got three meetings tomorrow," she explained. "I managed to get the court date moved two weeks, but unless we're shutting your office down, I should take those meetings. I can move them if you need me here."

His mother was going to be fine. There was no need for Jayna to stay up and rearrange her whole life when she'd already done that once tonight. She was right that they needed to keep things moving. "No, I'm okay. You've done more than enough. Thank you."

"I'll text you our room number," she promised. "And here are your keys. I'll catch a cab."

"No. We'll catch the cab. You take the car."

He hadn't said the words. He'd been about to, but he was surprised that Paul was the one who insisted. Paul rarely inconvenienced himself.

"And I'll walk you out." He wasn't letting her walk around a parking lot by herself at three in the morning. "I'll be right back."

They walked out to the parking lot, her hand in his.

When they'd made it to his car, he kissed her, wanting to put off the moment she had to leave. "Thank you for bringing my brother out."

She tilted her face up. "No problem, but you should talk to him."

"Why? Was he the reason you got waylaid?" They'd taken at least an extra hour more than they'd needed. "Did he try to go home and pack or something?"

"No. He called Caroline and she's going to pack a few things for him," Jayna replied. "I stopped by the apartment and grabbed you some toiletries and a change of clothes. They're in the car. Paul wanted to get here as quickly as he could, and you should know I'm going to need you to wire transfer a pretty hefty amount of money tomorrow."

A deep relief overtook him. "He told you where to send the money?"

She nodded. "Yes, I convinced him staying safe was more important than proving to you he's changed."

"Good. I'll send you all the info you need," he promised.

"I think he has." She looked up at him, a solemn expression on her face.

"Has what?"

"Changed. At least I think he's truly trying. I talked to him for a long time tonight and I think he's made some important choices."

"My brother is very good at playing out dramatic scenes."

She shook her head. "But they're not scenes. I know you don't understand him, and he's burned you before. You do not owe him another chance, but I hope you give it to him. I hope you at least hear him out. He's trying to find a balance that's hard to achieve on his own. I think I found a way to get his movie back. I've got to check into a few things, but I worry if he goes back to LA without settling anything with you, he'll lose his way again."

"If you get his movie back and he's got a little money, I assure you he'll be back in LA in a heartbeat."

"I don't think so. I think if you ask him to stay, he will."

"Why would I ask him to stay?"

"For your mom's sake. For his. Because he needs to be here for a while, maybe a long while. He needs to find himself again, and he can't do that out there in the world with no one to anchor him," she said quietly. "I think he needs his family. He needs his brother."

"Well, he got to you, didn't he?"

She sighed. "Like I said, I know you don't owe it to him, but I hope you'll at least talk to him."

"I'm giving him what? A quarter of a million dollars?" He resented the fact that they had to use the little time they had to argue about Paul, but then wasn't that what Paul always did? He put himself in the middle of everything so the spotlight was always on him.

"It's going to be more than a quarter of a million, but he's going to pay you back. I set the sale in motion," she replied.

"Sure he will. Maybe he does this time, but it'll happen again."

She opened the car door, her shoulders sagging. "Maybe, but if we don't have hope, I don't know what we have. I guess you're right. We make the same mistakes over and over again, and who can really put up with it? It's probably best to protect yourself when you know what's coming. Good night."

"Hey." He wasn't sure what she'd meant but those words had felt personal. "You don't make mistakes like that, baby. You're not selfish."

"My mother would disagree," she countered as she slid into the driver's seat. "If I don't see you before, I'll call you tomorrow and let you know when we're bringing the car."

She shut the door between them, and Quaid felt his fists clench.

He shouldn't have sent her with Paul. He should have known his brother would screw everything up for him. What line of bull had he been feeding her? Likely the same line he'd been feeding their mother for years.

He took the stairs up to the second floor two at a time, anger giving him a second wave of energy.

He stepped into the waiting room, perfectly ready to explain to his brother that part of taking the money he was about to give him would include his promise to stay away from Jayna.

Paul sat alone in the room, hunched over, head in hands, and his brother looked the very picture of weariness. Not of the body, but the aching tired that could only come from the soul.

What did he owe his brother? His family?

Maybe it was time to stop thinking about obligation and ask what he wanted. Truly wanted. Did he want to have a relationship with his brother? Did he want to try again? To set himself up for disappointment?

If we don't have hope, I don't know what we have.

Jayna had asked, and she hadn't been asking about Paul. She'd meant what hope was there for them. She was unsure about her place in the world and couldn't bring herself to believe he would always want her. Life had whispered to her time and time again that she wasn't enough.

What had life whispered to his brother?

He moved in and the minute he sat down, his brother's head came up.

His eyes were rimmed with red. "Hey. You missed the doc. He said she came through with flying colors. She's back in the ICU for an hour or so and then they'll move her into a room. I can call him back if you want. You'll probably want to talk to him yourself."

Because he wouldn't believe that Paul could even get that

much right. "No. It's good. We'll wait until she's settled in her room and then head to the hotel. How is your side?"

He'd been the one stabbed and yet Paul hadn't said more than a few words about it. The Paul of the last several years would have made the biggest scene, centering it around himself in every way.

"It's fine." He waved off the worry. "The asshole didn't want to kill me, just make a very specific point. I gave Jayna the name."

"She told me. We'll handle it in the morning."

"Thanks. I know you don't have any reason to believe me, but I'm going to pay you back as soon as the house closes." He went quiet for a moment. "And I'm sorry we were late. I asked Jayna to take me to a meeting."

"A meeting?" It struck him what kind of meeting they might find after midnight. "NA?"

"I'm sorry. I know you needed me here, but all I could think about was using and I can't. I can't." His brother's voice broke, and he had to take a deep breath. "I was under a lot of stress, stress that I put on myself, and when I'm stressed I don't deal well. So I had Jayna find a meeting for me. Luckily it's pretty easy to find one in the city. I'm sorry. It was selfish."

"No, it wasn't. It's the most mature thing you've ... ." He realized what he was about to say and how it would do nothing but add more weight to his brother's burden. If Paul was being honest, then he was hurting in a way Quaid couldn't understand. He knew he had every right to feel what he felt, but he could also show his brother a bit of grace for trying. "It was a mature decision. How are you feeling now?"

"It helped. I talked and got some stuff off my chest and listened to other people. I would never have imagined how much listening helps," Paul admitted.

"What do you do when you're in Papillon?"

"Oh, I've gone to a meeting almost every day I've been home." Paul sat back, a cup of that stale coffee in his hand.

"Really?"

"Yes. There's one at four every day at the library. It's held in one of the conference rooms off the main building. I've also got a sponsor who'll answer my calls, but he's back in LA. When I was there, we had coffee a couple of times a week to check in."

"You really do this?"

Paul nodded. "I have a schedule and reminders on my phone. It's my rehab, and I won't miss it. I know how slippery that slope is. I've seen the bottom, and I don't want to be there again."

He was quiet, thinking about what Paul had said. He had so many questions, but he wasn't sure what would be rude to ask.

But being polite hadn't worked for them. Maybe it was time to be frank. "Why do you think it will work this time?"

"I can't promise that it will. I can promise that I will do my best. I think that was what settled in me this time. The other times I thought I would go through the motions and check off the boxes and that meant I was cured. This time around, I realized I have to deal with this for the rest of my life. There is no magic button to push that will make me normal. I have a disease, and I am the only one who can make the decision to control it. I have to make the choice every day. Sometimes it's a minute-by-minute thing. But I want to live, Quaid. I want to make something of myself. I want to stand in front of our father one day and . . . I want him to be proud of me."

So much of his resentment lifted in that moment when his brother said what every child wanted. He longed for love and respect, for family and affection. Withholding those things wouldn't make Quaid feel safer, wouldn't make a loss less tragic. In fact, for him, it might make it worse.

He put an arm around his brother's shoulder. "I will help you in any way you want, brother."

Paul leaned in, tears falling. "I want to stay home for a while. I want to be here with you and Mom and Jayna. Do you think I could do that? I can get a job and earn my keep, but I want to be home for now."

He held his brother tight. "Of course."

Jayna had been right. They'd needed this.

"Mr. Havery?"

Quaid looked up. "Yes?"

A nurse stood in the doorway. "Your mom is being moved to her room now. You can come and see her, but very briefly. She needs her rest."

He stood, helping his brother up, and they went to see their mother.

Together.

chapter fourteen

Jayna set the phone down, perfectly satisfied with the way that call had gone.

If Quaid was all right with it, she had a lawyer lined up for Paul. He was a top-of-the-line entertainment lawyer who believed he could get the suit thrown out over breach of contract by the plaintiff. If there was no contract, there was no case, and the intellectual property reverted to Paul.

Her joy at solving the problem was tempered by the fact that she had a far more personal problem.

It had been a week since Mrs. Havery had been released from the hospital. Quaid had moved back to the house in order to help take care of his mother. Something had changed between him and Paul. Something good but perhaps a bit dangerous for her. They'd both tried to get her to move in. They wanted her at the big house, but she'd refused.

While they were in this building with its tiny apartment, everything seemed workable. She'd stood outside the big wrought iron gates of Havery House and felt like she was seven years old and didn't belong again.

"I'm here," Sienna called out from the outer office as the chime signaled her entrance. "Sorry I'm late. I had to talk to

Ivy's teacher. She got into a bit of trouble. She's been reading when she should be working."

Jayna stood and walked to the door. Luna had already bounded up from her big fluffy bed to greet Sienna. "Ivy didn't do her work? That doesn't sound like her."

"Well, she'd done it, but it wasn't time to turn it in yet," Sienna explained. "The rest of the class wasn't done."

Jayna knew that problem well. She'd gotten in trouble for stupid stuff, too. "So she gets punished for being smarter?"

Sienna's expression reminded her so much of their mom's. "The teacher doesn't want the other students thinking they can read whenever they like."

She'd heard that excuse, too. Luckily Ivy had an advocate, something Jayna herself never had. "Ivy wasn't reading whenever she liked. She was reading when she finished with an assignment, an assignment she likely didn't plow her way through without thought. What was her grade?"

Sienna frowned. "Well, it was a math test. She made a hundred."

She'd like to get that teacher in a courtroom to explain herself. "Uh-huh. So what is she supposed to do? Sit there and stare at everyone else? Put her head down and take a nap? I bet she'd get yelled at for doing that, too. She is being punished for being smart. She should be able to quietly read while she waits."

"I didn't think about it like that. She was reading a book on the reading list, too. So it was like she was still working on an assignment." Sienna put her purse down. "I'm going to talk to that teacher."

"Good." At least Sienna was growing. She was watching her sister bloom. She was more confident, more animated than she'd been in years. She was listening to the people around her and thinking about what they said.

"Did you talk to Quaid?"

She was also way more nosy. "I called him early this morning. I brought him up to date on everything I've worked on. We've got closing arguments on the *Oliver v. Abbot* case on Monday."

Sienna wrinkled her nose. "You know everybody else calls it the Geraldine's Boobs case."

"Well, everyone else doesn't take the law very seriously." Geraldine's Boobs weren't going to win. She was absolutely certain the judge would see that she was right. She feared a Papillon in which Geraldine's Boobs won and everyone started protesting other things by showing off body parts. She'd heard Herve and his brother were already planning a march to protest the twenty-five-cent price hike in chicken-fried steak at local restaurants. It would never end. First boobs, and then the men would bring out the big guns. Well, medium-sized and small-sized, too.

"I'll warn the café," Sienna said. "Your fans tend to go there after court adjourns to have pie and a lively debate about who won the day."

Yep, something else she didn't have in New Orleans. Fans. "Any chance they might not find out about the closing arguments?"

Sienna shook her head. "Not at all. Britney's sister is Team Quaid all the way."

She needed to make sure she knew exactly which one Britney's sister was. A talk was warranted to make sure everyone knew they could look but better not touch.

She had to stop thinking that way. How could she be with Quaid if she couldn't handle staying a night at his house?

The odd thing was that now that she and Mrs. Havery had their come-to-Jesus, they were actually getting along. She'd updated all the Haverys on Paul's case the afternoon before while they'd had lunch. The matriarch of the family had been very pleased. She'd asked Jayna some intelligent questions about her legal strategies and then moved the topic on to her upcoming plans for the tea she was still hosting.

Jayna was supposed to attend. In a suitable dress, of course.

How long would it be before her usefulness wore off and Mrs. Havery remembered how rough her upbringing had been? How long before Quaid's friends got offended by her rough edges?

"Oh, no." Sienna's eyes had gone wide as she stared out the window.

"What's wrong?" She moved in beside her sister as Luna started to bark.

"Is that who I think it is?" Sienna asked, pointing toward the square.

Jayna's ex-husband was walking down the street wearing one of his designer suits, his hair slicked back, and designer sunglasses covering his eyes. He looked up and down the street as though searching for something.

The man had to be looking for her.

Sure enough, he shifted his course, coming toward the building marked *Quaid Havery, Attorney at Law*.

Luna bounced in front of the door.

Todd might have been a crappy husband, but he'd played ball with Luna and taken care of her when Jayna couldn't.

He got a smile on his face when he saw her. He threw open the door and went down on one knee. "Hey, girl. Look at how big you are."

Luna enthusiastically licked his face as Todd took off the sunglasses that could probably feed a family of four for a week.

"What are you doing here?" Sienna asked, her arms over her chest.

Todd stood, managing to look hurt. "Well, hello, Sienna. Damn. You look good. Your mom told me you were at a new job. It suits you." He nodded Jayna's way. "Jayna. It's good to see you."

So they were being polite today. "What do you want?"

Well, one of them was.

Todd frowned. "I wanted to talk to you, and I thought it better to do it in person. I've never been here before but I looked up your mother's address. She told me I should come here because you were shacked up with someone named Quaid."

"I'm working here," she replied evenly.

"But she's also shacked up with him, and he is hot," Sienna added.

"Not helping," Jayna said under her breath. "Why don't you come into my office?"

Todd followed her, Luna at his side. "I was surprised to find out you came back here. Are you actually practicing here? I thought you swore to never set foot in this town again."

She probably had said something like that when she was younger. Lately she'd been thinking about the fact that perhaps she had been as ill-suited to serve her town when she was younger as it had been to serve her. She'd never fit in, but she'd also been quite rigid—especially as a teen. Now she'd seen the world, and every place in it had pros and cons. Papillon was no exception.

She slid behind her desk, preferring to keep a distance between them. "It's not so bad the second time around."

After all, this time she had fans.

"Because of this Quaid person?" He took a seat. "Havery. I think I've heard of the Haverys. They're old money down here, right?"

Naturally he would know all the people with money. "Why don't you get to the point, Todd? I've got things to do this afternoon."

She wouldn't tell him that she was planning on spending

a good portion of her day trying to save the library or that she also planned to do some pro bono arraignments so folks didn't rot in jail until they could get a judge to hear their pleas. Nor would she mention that she'd overheard a group of citizens discussing what to do with a raccoon once they caught him. Brian the Bandit, as they called him, had been spotted stealing various items out of purses and backpacks at the local park, and there were calls for his immediate apprehension and arrest.

Not like "catch the lil' guy," but arrest him. She was pretty sure that had been Ned Travers, who was bitter about his lost wallet that had contained an almost full frequent buyer card. He'd been one punch away from a free frozen yogurt and was certain that was why Brian had taken it.

Todd didn't need to know any of that.

Todd sighed in that condescending way of his. "Fine. I wanted to inform you that we've decided to drop the ethics case against you. The paperwork is being filed as we speak."

That was a surprise. She and Quaid had been planning to go into New Orleans to meet with her lawyer next week. They were going to stay at his friend's place and spend the weekend there. She'd been looking forward to the time with him despite the anxiety she had about the case. "Why?"

"Because it does nothing but keep people talking about something we would like to put behind us all."

Oh, there was something else in there. She could always tell when Todd was holding back on her. "Why, Todd? You know I'm going to do some research and find out."

One shoulder shrugged. "Fine, because it turns out you were right about the client."

"You knew I was right about him all along. I showed you the paperwork." She'd had an ironclad case against the man. Otherwise she wouldn't have brought it to the partners in the first place.

"Well, now other people have seen it, and apparently it's not as gray an area as my father thought," Todd admitted. "It's pretty black-and-white, and you actually saved the firm a lot of bad press because our name could have been attached to the client. The complaint will go away and all anyone will remember was that the firm did the right thing."

"You mean I did the right thing," Jayna countered.

"They probably won't remember you at all. You know how these things are."

"You are such an asshole."

"Perhaps," Todd allowed. "There are other reasons to drop the complaint. I think it will help us all to move on. And it's been stressing out my fiancée."

She huffed, an unamused sound. "You're already engaged. You've moved on."

"Have I? I suppose so, but in a way I'm merely doing what I'm supposed to do, what my parents want, what my future plans demand. I think you were my rebellion, dear."

"Rebellion?"

"I was always supposed to marry the right woman, and it was so clear you were wrong," Todd pointed out. "Oh, you had the right education and you brought something we needed to the firm, but you were far too aggressive to truly fit into our family. You were too career-oriented. It was obvious you wouldn't be a good mother."

She hated the fact that he could still hurt her. The words were stinging nettles, pricking and irritating her. "I tried to talk to you about kids. You're the one who put it off."

"Because you refused to even think about coming home to raise them, to be a proper wife." Todd's hands found Luna's fur, stroking down her back. "I'm thinking of running for Congress. I couldn't have some raging careerist at my side. I need to appeal to traditional family values."

"I think a mom supporting her kids is pretty damn traditional for a whole lot of us. I know my mom did." Her mom had worked hard. It was one of the reasons she hated the fact that her mom couldn't see that she did, too. Her mother had taught her the value of having a strong work ethic.

"I saw what your mother was providing. I wouldn't want any part of it. I truly understand why you never wanted us to visit here. You were ashamed."

Why should she have been ashamed? Maybe when she'd been younger. This time around, she'd found an odd comfort in the little trailer she'd grown up in. It wasn't special but it contained a lot of good memories, memories she'd somehow forgotten while trying to climb to the top of the ladder. "I knew how you would react, but you should understand that I'm certainly not ashamed of this town or the way I grew up. I had fun as a kid. I had some big dreams, and I couldn't fulfill them here. I think you were my rebellion, too. My mom and I had a rough go of it, and I knew you, in particular, would infuriate her."

"Ah, so you're saying you never loved me?"

She thought about that for a moment. "I thought I did."

"I did, too." He went quiet, the arrogance leaving his face for once. "I thought you could fix me, but I am who I am. I'll be honest, I thought you would be the one to divorce me. I never understood why you didn't."

"Now we've gotten to the part I was truly ashamed about." She'd come to realize it. She hadn't stayed because she wanted to make her marriage work or because she'd loved her job and hadn't wanted to leave. She'd stayed in an irrevocably broken marriage because she hadn't wanted the shame she'd felt at failing.

Because failing would prove her mother right.

Would she fail with Quaid?

"I can understand that. I truly can. I know all of this was hard on you and you won't believe me when I say this, but

I'm sorry, and that's why I'm here." He reached into his pocket. "I'm starting a new life with the right person for me. Amy is young and couldn't care less about having a career or who I sleep with as long as she has access to my money. Being my wife will be her job. You need more."

He handed her a card.

BRADFORD AND STONE
ATTORNEYS AT LAW

The card had an address in Dallas and a phone number. "What am I supposed to do with this?"

"His name is Mitch Bradford and he's the corporate half of the firm. Lea Stone runs criminal defense. They're a small operation with some very wealthy clients. Mitch has worked with us over the years. You'll find he's a straight shooter. He's looking to bring in someone to take some of the load off him. He's got a couple of kids he wants to spend more time with. Call him. If everything works out—and I know it will—he'll offer you a sweat-equity partnership. They're flush with cash but they need new people, and I told him you're one of the best."

She stared down at the card. "Why?"

"Because I owe you." He gave Luna one last pat on her head and stood. "Because I knew you would need more than I could give you, but I married you anyway. I'm not making the same mistake again. I don't think you should, either. Be careful with this Quaid person. Make sure he's worthy of you. I think you could be happy in Dallas. You can build something there. Give Bradford a call."

He moved for the door and then he walked away. It was mere seconds before she heard the bell chiming and then he was walking in front of the window and out of her life.

But he'd left one last land mine to blow everything up.

Why wasn't she calling? The Jayna from a couple of months ago would already have her phone in hand. She would already be making travel plans to meet with this guy in person.

The Jayna of today stared at the card like it was a snake that might bite her.

Was she thinking about staying? Quaid couldn't be the reason she stayed. She had to consider every angle, figure out what was right for her.

If she took a job in a city, she might never get another case of the naked grandma again. Cities didn't put up with such nonsense.

But nonsense could be fun. Nonsense was quintessentially human.

Jayna thought about putting on some music to quell the raging thoughts in her head. Stay and try or go and start over. Staying and trying meant she might fail again, and this time in front of everyone in town. At least in some anonymous city no one cared if she failed.

But her nieces wouldn't be in Dallas. Sienna wouldn't be there.

They could visit, of course.

She set the card down, her mind playing out all the possibilities.

The afternoon sun was warm on his skin as Quaid opened the door to the office for the first time in days.

Sienna was closing her laptop. She glanced up at him. "Hey, you're back. How is your mother?"

It had been a long week made infinitely easier by the fact that Jayna had handled everything. He hadn't been forced to worry about rescheduling court dates or keeping his appointments. Jayna and Sienna had handled everything. Even his mother. When she got stubborn about doctor's orders, Jayna simply talked about how one of her aunts or cousins or friends had the same problem and handled it so much better and suddenly his mother's competitive nature came out and she was following all the doctor's orders.

Jayna had poked and prodded and figured out how to get his mother to do what he needed her to do. She'd also worked wonders with Paul.

"She's good. She's taking her medications and not arguing with the health care workers who are helping her," he admitted. Luna poked her head out of Jayna's office and then made a beeline for him, her big tail wagging. Quaid got to one knee and greeted her while he continued talking to Sienna. "We have to change her diet and she's got a daily exercise regime, but the blockage was handled and she's feeling much better."

Sienna stood and reached for her bag. "I'm so glad to hear it. Jayna's at a meeting at city hall, but I expect she'll be back soon. Do you need anything? It's been weird without you here."

"Is Jayna doing okay?" He'd been told to keep an eye on his mother and let Jayna handle the office. She'd come out to dinner a couple of nights, but refused to stay over, saying she had to get back to Luna. When he'd offered to go out with her and bring Luna back to the big house, she'd come up with another excuse.

He was worried she was going to use this pause in their relationship as an excuse to run, and he wasn't sure what he could do to stop her.

Sienna seemed to think about how to answer that question. "She's handling everything here, if that's what you're asking."

His instincts started firing. Something was wrong, and

Sienna wasn't good at covering. He stood, Luna sitting back on her haunches at his side. "You know it's not what I'm asking."

"I don't know. She's gotten very quiet the last couple of days," Sienna admitted. "She's thinking something through, and I don't know if I'm going to like the outcome. Todd stopped by two days ago, and she's been quiet ever since."

"Her ex-husband was here?" They'd talked on the phone every night, and she hadn't once mentioned Todd showing up.

Sienna nodded. "Yes. He came by to tell her they withdrew the ethics complaint. He wanted to tell her in person."

His stomach felt like it was going to drop to his toes. "They withdrew the complaint? She didn't mention that."

Sienna flushed, her cheeks going pink. "I thought she would have told you."

"No, she didn't." She'd had plenty of chances. He tried to talk to her on the phone a couple of times a day. He'd seen her, but not once had she mentioned the fact that the biggest obstacle to her leaving was now gone.

She was slipping through his fingers, and he wasn't sure how to stop it. If he tried too hard to keep her, he would surely lose.

"I'm sure she was going to," Sienna assured him.

He didn't feel better. "If she meant to tell me, she would have."

Sienna gave him a sympathetic look. "I don't think it means anything. She's always been the one who has to think things through. The rest of us kind of flew by the seat of our pants, but Jayna was cautious."

"And she always wanted out." How long would it be before she had a sparkling new job in a city that could offer her the world? Not long, he would think. She was smart and hungry. She was exactly what he would look for in a partner.

She was also kind, and she challenged him and everyone around her to be better.

She was everything he wanted in a wife.

Sienna shrugged. "She did. You know most young people leave for more opportunity. There's not a lot here. I know you've got a ton of work to do, but that's mostly for the companies you work for. I worry she's going to need something more . . . challenging. But I don't think she's ready to go yet. I know I plan to work hard to persuade her to stay. I'm a little worried that if she doesn't, I'll end up listening to my momma and my own self-doubts, which might cost me and the girls the life we could have had."

"I think your momma is part of the problem. They haven't talked in weeks, have they?" He hadn't heard Jayna mention her mother in a long time. Even when he tried to get her to talk, she deflected.

Sienna shook her head. "No. When they dig their heels in like this, they can both hold a grudge forever. I don't know if they'll talk again. I'm fairly certain Mom wouldn't be talking to me right now if it weren't for the girls. We'll be fine because I'll keep going to her place and acting like she didn't make a jackass of herself, but Jayna won't."

If Jayna wouldn't fight for a relationship with her mom, why did he think she would fight for one with him? She'd told him that she would leave, and now she'd found her excuse to pull away.

He shouldn't have let her stay away for a week. He should have insisted on coming back to the apartment and sleeping with her. Paul could have handled their mother. Paul seemed more centered and focused since they'd paid off his debt.

Another miracle Jayna had given them. Paul had even insisted on a contract for the loan. She'd written it up and everyone had signed, and he'd seen some real pride in his brother's eyes as he'd passed it back. Paul was also going to regular meetings and he was looking for his next project.

Things were starting to work for his family, but none of it mattered if Jayna left him.

"I've got to ask," Sienna began. "If she does take that job, do you honestly still want me around? I know Cindy's coming back in a couple of weeks and there might not be . . ."

"Job? What job?"

"She didn't mention that, either, did she? Of course not." She shook her head. "I'm sorry, Quaid. She's my sister. I shouldn't have said anything. You're going to have to ask her about it."

"Of course." There was already a job offer on the table, and she hadn't mentioned that, either. Damn it. He'd started the day thinking it would be good to get back to work because he could spend time with Jayna, and now he had to wonder if she was even planning on being here in a week. It was too soon. He couldn't leave with her. It would take him months to get everything in order. He would have to find someone to take over his practice. He couldn't leave the town high and dry.

She wasn't going to ask him to come with her. He was making plans that he didn't need to because if she hadn't told him these very important things about her life, she wasn't about to ask him to share it with her.

And what could he say? She hadn't promised him anything. She'd told him the exact opposite, but he'd decided she didn't mean it. How could she not feel what he felt? How could this be one-sided?

"So should I look for another job?" Sienna asked quietly. "It's okay if you hired me to please Jayna. She can be persuasive."

"No, the offer was real. She might have been the one to think of it, but she was right. I need to start planning and honestly, having more hands around will help." He wasn't sure what to do. He wanted to walk out and find Jayna and get her in bed. She seemed to understand that they belonged together when they were in bed.

The door came open and Jayna walked through, carrying her briefcase and her heels. He'd noticed she'd started wearing a pair of bright pink flip-flops until she actually walked into court and then she slipped on her heels. He would bet she would never have prioritized her own comfort when she worked in New Orleans. She stopped when she realized he was standing there, and he got the feeling her surprise wasn't the good kind. "Hey, you're here. I thought your mom had rehab this afternoon."

"I'm picking her up in an hour." He'd been hoping he could convince her to come back with him.

Sienna settled her bag on her shoulder. "I'm going to lunch. I'll be back in a while. You two should probably talk." She winced her sister's way. "I'm sorry. I thought you told him about the job and the ethics case being dismissed."

Jayna's hand tightened around the strap of her bag, and she nodded her sister's way. "I was planning on talking to him when he came back to work next week. Don't worry about it. You have a nice lunch. I'll see you when you get back."

Sienna's gaze darted between the two of them as though she wasn't sure she should leave them alone, but she finally made her way out the door. It closed behind her and he was alone with the woman he loved, the one for whom his love might not be enough.

Had she ever given them a chance? Or had it truly all been about sex for her? Had he been some conquest, a way to get back at him for not noticing her when she was younger?

"I didn't expect you back in the office until next week."

"I thought I would come and see if I could take you to dinner later tonight."

"I've got a call this evening with the attorney I want to hire in LA," she replied, moving toward the stairs. "I was at city hall all day trying to come up with some kind of plan to save the library. The funds we have available can't match what a developer will offer, and I've met your client. I would definitely say she's not the reading kind. I came back to feed Luna and make that call. Did you look over the entertainment lawyer's credentials? Are you okay with hiring him?"

He followed Jayna and Luna up the stairs. Jayna had been working on getting Paul's movie back in his hands, and she'd found an excellent way to do it. He could have his movie on the festival circuit this fall if everything went according to Jayna's plan. "I trust you. Hire him. Do what you need to. I'll talk to my client about entertaining an offer from the city for the library land. Now can we talk?"

"I thought we were talking," she said, opening the door to the apartment and breezing through. Luna's tail wagged.

"The ethics complaint was dropped."

"Turns out taking revenge on me was making his new bride anxious, and we can't have the pregnant princess anxious, can we? So I'm off that particular hook, and I only owe you fifteen grand. I was worried we might get to six figures if it went on too long."

"I don't care about the money."

"It's easy for you to say because you have all the money."

"Jayna, I don't want the money back. I want you to talk to me."

"Fine. The ethics complaint is gone, and I have a couple of decent job prospects. Is that what you want to hear?"

"Prospects or actual offers?"

"One real prospect, but as long as the interview goes well, I've been assured the offer will follow," she admitted. "It's a small firm in Dallas. There are two partners, and they're looking for a third to take over corporate contracts. Apparently the man who runs the firm wants more time with his kids, and he's willing to consider letting me in for sweat equity in a couple of years if things work out."

Making partner at her age without having to buy in would be an incredible deal for her in a small firm. Although if she wanted a small firm, he wasn't sure she could get any smaller than his, and he would make her a partner right now.

"What's the pay?"

"It doesn't matter," she replied, opening the cabinet.

"What's the pay?" He wanted to know what he was up against.

"Six figures plus bonuses for new clients."

Nope. He couldn't offer her more than a stake in the business. His real money came from investments and generational wealth. Jayna was a woman who wanted to prove herself, and she couldn't do that by marrying into money.

"When would you start?"

"I still have to pass the Texas requirements."

"You could probably take that test tomorrow and pass it."

"I would ask for a couple of weeks to clear things up here," she explained. "If I decided to take the job. Quaid, you knew I was looking."

"I didn't know you'd already found." Somehow it felt like she'd kept this from him, like she'd hidden something important.

"I was going to tell you when you came back."

He was suddenly wondering if she'd meant to tell him in person at all. "Were you, or was I just going to come back to a note explaining you were done with me and the town?"

"It's not like that. Damn it, Quaid. I never promised I would stay. And I haven't made a decision yet, but you should know I'm going to Dallas tomorrow. I'll only be gone for a couple of days but I've got to do an in-person interview."

It felt like his heart was being pulled from his chest because she'd already made the decision. She could say whatever she wanted, but deep down she already knew she was going to leave.

"You aren't going to ask me to come with you, are you?" He might have to face the fact that his love wasn't enough.

She closed her eyes for a moment. "I don't think it would work."

"Why?"

"I don't think I fit in your world."

"You are my world. You don't have to fit in. You only have to be you."

She turned her chin up, and he knew he'd lost. "I'm going to Dallas. I'm going to check it out. I'd like to do it alone because I need some time to think. Is it okay for me to stay here or should we go to a motel?"

He moved in, and she didn't back away. He leaned over, putting his forehead against hers. "I don't ever want you to go. Anything I have is yours, baby. That won't change because you can't love me."

"Quaid . . ." she began.

"No." He kissed her forehead and stepped away. "If you're leaving, I'm not going to keep it in. I'm going to go to my grave loving you. I'll be here waiting and hoping that you can come back to me because I think deep down you love me, too. It's the wrong time and the wrong place."

"I'm coming back." She sniffled and her eyes were red. "We still have a case to try. Can we talk then? Please?"

"Of course." But he was fairly certain that the only thing they would be talking about was how to end it.

Quaid turned and walked down the stairs and away from the only woman he would ever love.

chapter fifteen

❧

Quaid sat down at the breakfast table, sliding his cell into his pocket with a sigh.

Paul looked up from his omelet. "Bad news?"

All the news seemed to be bad lately. "No, not really. Jayna texted me earlier that she was finally on the plane. She should be back in time for final arguments."

"Are you picking her up?" His mother had an egg white omelet with fruit and turkey bacon she claimed wasn't all that bad. Naturally Jayna had suggested the brand. "We could send a car for her if you need to prepare for your case."

"She drove herself to the airport and parked there. Her car was ready and while I offered, she said she wanted the time alone to think." She'd gone to Dallas to interview for the job with the law firm there. She'd stayed for a couple of days, and they'd had three stilted conversations over the phone that led to absolutely no conclusion.

She'd liked the small firm, liked the people there. She'd had dinner with the man named Mitch and his family. His wife had turned out to be Lila LaVigne and Lisa Guidry's sister. It was such a small world, but he feared it would be slightly too large for their relationship to survive.

His mother frowned. "There's no need for her to drive herself. We pay people to do that."

"I don't think Jayna considers herself part of the *we* yet, Momma," Paul explained. "I think we're a little intimidating to a woman who recently got burned by a family like ours."

"We are not those obnoxious new-money Shales," his mother said with a frown.

"No, we're worse. We're super old-money snobs," Paul replied. More and more often Quaid was seeing his brother push back against some of their mom's worse tendencies. Since that night in the hospital, Paul had shown he could take care of her, including in ways that made her angry with him. It had oddly led to what seemed like a deeper relationship between the two of them. In pushing back at her, fighting with her over her own health, his mother seemed to see that Paul truly loved her.

"I am not . . . All right, I will admit I have some work to do," his mother said. "I am an old dog but I can easily see that if I don't learn a few new tricks, I will be letting my sons down. I don't want to be the reason you lose Jayna, but I'll be honest. I don't understand what makes her uncomfortable about us. I've been nice to her lately. I've come to enjoy her frankness, and I had a little talk with Celeste Beaumont when she came to visit. She was open and honest with me about how having Seraphina Guidry in her family has made it stronger, not weaker. She told me I could change with the times or be a mean old biddy for the rest of my life. I thought that was put a bit rudely, but there's truth in it. I want grandbabies before I die. I want some young people around me again, and I don't think Paul is ready for that."

Paul put a hand over his heart. "I am still a child myself. Nope. That's going to have to fall on big brother. He's definitely the one with the biological clock ticking."

"I don't even know if Jayna wants kids." He did. They'd

talked about it and she'd told him how much she wanted a family that included a couple of kids, but he wasn't going to put pressure on her to make his mother happy.

"Well, at least she has those little nieces. They don't have fathers. They need more family," his mother said with a wistful sigh.

"They have fathers. They see them every now and then." Sienna had them almost all the time from what he could tell. Her ex-husbands weren't all that active with the kids. They had their mom and grandma and aunt and were happy and well adjusted.

"But that doesn't mean we can't love them, too. It doesn't mean we can't be a family. That's what Celeste made me see. We rely on blood, but what happens to the people who don't have blood families? What happens when your family is mostly gone?" His mother's eyes had gone watery in the early-morning light. "I only have my sister left, and we're not so close. She seems to tolerate me because we're family. It should be more. I miss your father. I miss my parents, and I can either spend the rest of my life wishing for something I can't have again, or I can make something new. I can either be the woman who looks down on everyone or the woman who helps people up again. I've lived in this town most of my life. It's about time I took care of it in a way that doesn't include planting flowers. Flowers are pretty but they die. Trees stay long after the one who planted them is gone. Trees provide shelter for generations. It's time for me to plant trees, Quaid. And Jayna needs to see that, too."

He reached over and covered his mother's hand with his own. "I hope she can, but I need you to know that I am proud of you for being open to this."

"That was good, Mom." Paul sniffled a bit. "Now I kind of do want a family."

"Not yet." His brother still had some growing up to do,

but it looked like he was on the right path this time. "I appreciate all of this, Mom, but she has more problems with Papillon than just being worried about fitting in here. If I had time, we could make her comfortable. But I don't think I can make her comfortable with her mother. They don't understand each other. They never have. I think deep down in the back of her mind she's still got this kid inside her who thinks she's failed if she's here."

"Well, that's ridiculous. She can have a perfectly nice life right here," his mother replied, her chin coming up. "She can see the world and then come home where her family is. Quaid, I'm beginning to think the problem is you. Have you not told her you like to travel? That you're not going to keep her cooped up here day after day?" His mother's voice went low. "Are you properly taking care of her?"

"I'm sorry, what?" She couldn't mean what he thought she meant. Not his mother. His mother would never speak of such things. Ever.

Paul snorted, his amusement plain. "I think she's asking if you know what women like."

"Now, you hush, you scamp," his mother admonished. "I'm asking if he knows what Jayna likes. Not all of womankind. I leave that up to you. And you better stay away from married women, Paul. I can still put you over my knee."

"You never put me over your knee."

"And that is where I failed," she announced. "Cavorting around town with married women. I hear gossip, too. That is how I know that Quaid has been sowing some oats, but those are forever oats, son. It's all right to sow them if you love those oats. But you have to know how to properly tend to your oats."

He was never telling Jayna his mother referred to her as forever oats. "Jayna and I are fine on that front. It's really about timing. I didn't get enough time with her."

"Dallas isn't so far away," Paul pointed out.

"No, but combine the distance with the fact that she'll be working all the time for the next couple of years and there's not much of a shot for us. I've thought about moving to be closer to her." He'd put the idea out there. He could get a place in Dallas and split his time.

"I would hate that, but I would also understand." His mother sat back.

"I'm not sure it would work. We needed more time." His heart ached at the thought of her taking that job. She might come back to Papillon to see her sister from time to time. Someday she would come home with a husband and kids of her own, and he was afraid he would still be alone because his heart was hers and he couldn't give it to anyone else. He would look out the window of his office and she would be walking by looking prettier than ever, the happy successful woman she'd always wanted to be.

He wished he could get her to see that successful had a million definitions, that the idea of it could change over time. What she viewed as success when she was eighteen didn't have to define her happiness now. She could find happiness in other places, satisfaction in a career that wasn't high-powered, peace in a place that had none for her before.

"I don't think it would work. Like I said, if she takes this job she'll be trying to make partner in three years," he explained. "She won't have time for anything but the job. She'll work weekends and late nights. She'll need to focus, and not on a relationship. The stakes feel higher in a firm like that. The judges in Dallas don't take Fridays off for fishing."

Everything moved so much faster when he left Papillon. They would be living in two different worlds, and he wasn't sure she would even look back. If she did, he would likely be a fond reminiscence, a memory of those months when she'd worked on weird cases and fell into bed with a small-time lawyer who'd loved her truly.

"I don't like this." Paul's brows had come together, a look of genuine consternation on his face.

"Well, I don't like it, either," Quaid replied.

"No, not the whole Jayna-leaving thing, though I don't like that, either. I don't like this new you. You aren't a man who lies down and takes what life gives him," Paul stated, putting his napkin on the table.

"Many would disagree." Over the course of the last few days he'd wondered if that wasn't their problem. He did take the path his father had placed in front of him. He'd done it with very few questions, and for the most part his life was a good one. Jayna had never accepted that her life was dictated by where she was born and the family she was born into. She'd fought it all her life. They were opposites in this. He'd loved writing his books, but he hadn't taken the leap to turn it into a real career because he couldn't let his town down. Jayna had given up everything to find the career she thought she wanted.

"I'm not talking about you taking over for Dad," Paul argued. "I'm talking about you laying down arms. You have gone after that woman with everything you have but one little pushback and you're planning the rest of your life without her. I can already see that you're working on your pining-for-her face."

"I am not."

"Yes, you are, son," his mother agreed. "It's a little like your I'm-about-to-be-sick face, but with more feeling behind it. And Paul is right. You're not fighting for what you want."

"How do I fight when she's not ready for what I want? I can't force her to stay here with me. I can't force her to let me go with her. I've offered her whatever she wants as long as I can be with her. What else do I do?"

"Well, it sounds to me like she doesn't know what she wants," his mother mused. "It sounds to me like she's jumping back into what she knows. I know it seems like I've changed overnight and you're worried that I'll revert to form, but seeing Paul nearly die and then nearly dying myself . . . well, it's like I lifted a veil that was covering my eyes for years. I didn't love your father the way he needed to be loved. I did all the things I thought were important for him, but what I never did when he was alive was ask him what he wanted. I didn't take the time to know him the way a husband and wife should. I'm not watching you make the same mistake. If you want her, fight for her."

"I don't know how to fight for her. There's no dragon to slay, no villain to beat up."

"Yes, there is," Paul insisted. "It's Jayna. She's the dragon. Well, her insecurities are. It's called a metaphor. I learned that in screenwriting class."

His brother was annoying but also right.

And so was his mother. He'd told her he would do whatever she needed him to do, but he'd been gentle about it. He wasn't going to overrule her and try to tell her how life was going to be, but he could make a damn fine argument for why she should stay here and give them a real chance.

Arguing was what they did best, after all.

She was up in the air right now, likely going over her closing arguments for the case that they had been duking it out over their entire relationship. She would be weighing every word she would say before she walked into that courtroom and tried to take him down. She would be so precise and focused.

What if he wasn't? Not the not-precise part. He intended

to be very precise about what he said. But he didn't have to have such a narrow focus. She was in every part of his heart and his life. Should this be any different?

Quaid stood, his mind rolling with possibilities. "I need to get to the office. I'm going to rewrite my closing on this case."

"And I'm going to have Paul take me to run a few errands in town before we head over to the courthouse," his mother announced.

Quaid frowned down at her. She'd never come to the courthouse for one of his trials, never gone to watch his father work. "Why would you do that?"

"I've been told it can be an amusing way to spend an afternoon," she replied.

"I'm going to make a sign. *Team Havery*." Paul was back to grinning. "But you should know I actually bet on Jayna to win. Hey, it was a little bet. Five bucks. Nothing more."

"Well, that's five bucks you're going to lose, brother." Quaid strode out of the dining room.

This was one case he was going to win.

Jayna stared at the courthouse steps, wondering how she was going to survive the next few days here in Papillon without crumbling.

Or she could actually sit down and figure out what she wanted to do with the rest of her life. She could be an adult and make a pros and cons list because there was more to living in Papillon than a boy. Her sister was here. Her mother was here, and it might be time to talk to her, to see if there was anything to be salvaged. If she stayed and it didn't work out between her and Quaid, she could still have a life here. It wouldn't matter that everyone was looking at her. She could stare right back. She wasn't a fifteen-year-old who didn't fit in. Somehow this place she'd grown up in had changed, or maybe she'd been the one to make the change. Maybe she'd needed to see the world to understand how warm this place was, how much she could do here.

She'd spent the weekend with Mitchell Bradford and his partner, Lea Stone. They'd been friendly. Well, the high-powered-lawyer version of friendly, which was aggressive with only a hint of fang.

She'd been surprised to find herself spending more time talking to Mitch's wife, Laurel. She would have told anyone who asked that talking business was her wheelhouse, but she'd found herself having a glass of wine and asking about what it was like growing up with Lila and Lisa. They'd had a lot in common, and she'd relaxed and even talked to her about Quaid.

Bradford and Stone was offering her everything she'd ever wanted. Dallas was a cosmopolitan city with restaurants that didn't also serve as gas stations or bait shops with Bibles on the side. The wildlife in Dallas didn't form criminal rings or slow down traffic because they needed to find a sunny spot to bask the afternoon away. She could shop in Dallas, and everyone would admire her expensive shoes. She could build a life in Dallas that would make everyone jealous.

Suddenly she didn't care if anyone was jealous. Maybe her life should be more than showing everyone around her how far she'd come.

Maybe what she'd done was come full circle, and there was a beauty in that.

"Are you going in?" a familiar voice asked.

She turned and Quaid's mother was standing on the bottom step, a leash in her hand. Luna tugged gently on it, getting to Jayna, her tail swirling around in excitement. "Hey, sweet girl. I thought I left you with Sienna."

Quaid had offered to take her dog out to the big house, but it seemed like too much to ask when she knew she could break the man's heart. That was the other thing that had settled deep inside her. Quaid meant what he said. He wouldn't lie to her, and he was old enough to know what he wanted. He loved her. She loved him.

Was it enough?

Mrs. Havery moved in. She was wearing a bright pink pantsuit with a white blouse and sturdy white shoes. "Sienna is inside with the rest of the town. It seems they've all turned out for closing arguments. I've heard it said if Geraldine wins, there might be a celebratory protest, and we should all hide our eyes. Lord. I know I'm supposed to want my son to win, but you need to get in there and save us all. My generation never got over Woodstock, I tell you."

What was happening? "So you took Luna?"

"I'm supposed to take walks a couple of times a day, and this girl needed to do her business." Mrs. Havery started up the steps. "Sienna was going to leave her at the office, but then she would be lonely. The bailiff tried to tell me Luna couldn't be in the courtroom, but I know his mother and I explained that I would call her up right then and tell her all about how her son was trying to keep a creature of God from witnessing one of the most momentous events in the history of Papillon. I've learned that if I keep talking with a righteous tone, most of the time I get my way. Not with you, of course. You just argue right back, but it works on most men. They fear women of a certain age, you see. We no longer care, as Geraldine is proving with her every breath."

Jayna hustled to keep up with her. "Well, I appreciate it. Luna is actually very well-behaved."

"That won't matter in Dallas. I bet that fancy new firm of yours won't let you keep her around," Mrs. Havery pointed out. "Poor thing will be in a kennel or worse. She could be left at one of the canine day care centers. You never know what kind of influences she'll be exposed to. You know, I think she likes it here in Papillon. She can go anywhere in town and no one will think anything of it."

"Except the bailiff." Had she fallen asleep on the plane and this was a dream?

"Who is very easy to deal with," Mrs. Havery countered. "I'm merely pointing out that there is a lot Papillon has to offer a woman like you."

"Okay, I'm confused. I thought you didn't want me around your son."

Mrs. Havery stopped at the top step. "Sometimes we think a person is a bad influence, but we're the ones who are wrong, Jayna. My generation can be quite rigid in our views, but we can learn. Just like you can. My son is in love with you. I thought he needed a proper wife. What I realized is what I think is proper is actually a long list of nonsense. What he needs is the right wife, and it's become clear that's you. So I have some work to do."

The only thing scarier than a Momma Havery who didn't want her around might be one who did. "What does that mean?"

"It means I need to give you a reason to stay. You think you can do good in the city, that the work there will be more important than anything you can do here," Mrs. Havery began. "You're wrong. You're wrong because this place needs you far more than Dallas does. Dallas has a thousand strong lawyers, many of them women. Papillon does not. You wanted to get out because you didn't see anyone like you here. There are other girls growing up right now who need someone to look up to, to point to and say 'I can be her.' I'm going to make a deal with you, Jayna Cardet. A deal that has no ties beyond you staying here. You don't have to marry my son, but you do have to stay and work here."

"A deal?" This whole conversation felt surreal.

"I purchased a large plot of land from the Hillyard estate this morning," she began.

Jayna knew exactly where that land was. "You bought the library land? The one they wanted to sell to developers?"

"I did. Now the way I see it, I can sell it to a developer like the Hillyards were going to or I could remodel that old library in honor of my late husband, but I would need a good lawyer to handle the project for me," Mrs. Havery explained. "I've heard the argument that everyone has books on their phones in this day and age, but that's not true. Especially for our people. Some of our people can't afford phones and fancy Internet hookups and they need a library. For some kids, the library is a haven. Isn't that true?"

"It was for me." How many times had she ridden her bike to that library and found refuge there? The library had been her lifeline, the librarian opening the gateway to whole other worlds she wouldn't have dreamed of. If they took the library, the town would suffer, and Quaid's mother had put it all on her. "That's not fair."

Mrs. Havery nodded. "Well, I don't play fair when I want something, darling girl. I don't play fair at all." She pushed inside the courthouse. The usually bustling space was oddly empty this morning. "Now, I expect you to be at the first meeting. We'll need to talk about a budget and fundraising opportunities. That library of ours is outdated. We need to modernize it but not lose the classic lines of the building."

Jayna found herself jogging to keep up. She wished she'd worn her flip-flops, but she'd just been in Dallas around all those put-together women. It was easy to fall back into habit, but her toes were protesting. "I didn't say I would take the job."

"Stubborn girl." Mrs. Havery shook her head. "You will in the end. You'll think about what you want out of this life and you'll come to the proper conclusion. Now, you should know there's a big audience in there, and Quaid is out for blood."

He always was when he was in a courtroom. Mrs. Havery pushed the doors to the actual courtroom open, and Jayna figured out where everyone was today. The courtroom was packed. She looked over the crowd and her breath caught.

Sitting in the front row next to her sister was her mom.

Tears blurred Jayna's eyes, and the world seemed to turn upside down.

"Your mother and I had a talk," Mrs. Havery said. "She's a stubborn woman, too, but I explained some things I've learned. Jayna, you are old enough now that you have to bend her, but she should have bent for you when you were a child. She didn't understand you. You were too smart and it intimidated her, so she tried to keep you closer to a person she could understand. You were her child. She should have been the one to compromise, should have done anything she could no matter how uncomfortable it made her. I made some of the same mistakes with my boys. She can't go back but she can try now. I can try now."

Her mother raised a hand, giving her a little wave as though she was unsure of her reception.

Jayna looked to Quaid's mother, and one of her worries fell away. If Marian Havery could try, could get her mother to try, then she could, too. "I love your son."

Marian's lips turned up. "I'm glad to hear it. I hope you can come to love us all because he's not the only one who needs you. I'm not going to be around forever. I would like to know my family is in good hands. Your hands are good, Jayna. They're strong hands. They're safe hands. Trust in them."

She was not going to cry here in the courtroom. She wasn't going to do it.

"Ms. Cardet, you are late," a deep voice said.

"Andy Brewer, you be nice." Marian pointed the judge's way. "You were not raised to be rude to a lady."

The judge sighed. "In this room she's not a lady. She's a lawyer, and I would like to get this over with. I'm tired. I got to fish more when there was only one lawyer in town."

"Thanks, Mrs. Havery." She had a job to do and then she needed to sit down and talk to Quaid. She rushed up the aisle as Marian joined Paul at the back of the courtroom. Jayna gave her mom a smile before placing her briefcase on the table and nodding her client's way. "I'm sorry I was late, Your Honor. My plane from Dallas was slightly delayed, and there was traffic on my way out of New Orleans. I appreciate how patient the court has been during this trying time."

It was trying because the judge really liked fishing.

"Are you ready to proceed?" the judge asked.

She finally looked over at the defense. Quaid was in his three-piece suit, looking devastatingly handsome. That man took her breath away. Was she a fool to even consider taking the job in Dallas? She'd left mere hours before, and Dallas seemed like it had happened weeks ago. Conversely, when she'd left Papillon for Dallas, all she'd been able to think about was being here again.

She moved toward Quaid. "Can we talk later?"

His lips turned up in a humorless smile. "We can talk about settling if you like. Does Abbot want to drop his suit? You should know Geraldine is thinking about filing a suit of her own."

"What?" The judge frowned fiercely, and suddenly there was a hum going through the courthouse.

"Geraldine is thinking about suing Jimmy again, Paw-Paw," Britney said.

"What?" Jimmy Abbot was on his feet. "Come on, Geraldine. This has gone far enough."

Geraldine shrugged a slender shoulder. "I find it kind of fun."

Jayna ignored the chaos around her. "Quaid, we need to talk."

He leaned over, whispering in her ear. "If you still want to talk after I pull apart your every argument, we can certainly do it. But you should think about what I say. You should understand that I mean every word."

She wasn't sure why he was so serious about this, but she couldn't ask him to explain because the judge pounded his gavel.

"Order in here. I'll kick the lot of you out if you can't keep it down," the judge promised. "Ms. Cardet, would you please present your closing arguments? If we don't get this done before lunch, the café is going to go under."

"No, I'm not," Dixie called out from the middle of the audience. "I have a new food truck ready. Well, it's more of a cart, but I'm prepared to feed the entire courtroom."

The judge sighed. "Just get this over with, Ms. Cardet."

She stared at Quaid for a moment, who stared right back.

"Go along, Ms. Cardet," he said, a bit of a taunt to his tone.

Had she lost him? Her stomach threatened to turn. Had she pushed him too far? Taken too long? He'd seemed so patient, but hadn't she always known it would be this way? She'd always known he would get tired of her issues.

This was exactly why . . .

No. She wasn't doing this to herself. "I'll want to talk to you after, Quaid." She wasn't going to let her insecurities make the choices this time. She was going to believe that she was worth the love Quaid had offered her. That had been the problem all along. Not Quaid. Her. Her fears. Her pride. Her past.

She wasn't going to let them rob her of a future.

She turned to the judge. "Your Honor, I believe I've

proven that Geraldine Oliver's protest parties, while not technically illegal, certainly have cost this community."

A loud *boo* came from the back of the room.

"You hush. My daughter is speaking," her mother yelled back. "I know that was you, Johnathon. I can take you."

It was good to know her mom was on her side.

The judge growled, and the bailiff moved to the back. "You may proceed."

"Community is a delicate balance," she continued. "My client had every right to take down that tree. He offered recompense to Geraldine Oliver not out of obligation, but out of his sense of community. But Geraldine Oliver demands more. Do we want to be forever known as the naked bayou? I assure you some reporter is going to pick this story up, and that's what we'll be known for. Geraldine Oliver absolutely deserves to feel safe and comfortable in her own home. But there are limits to our freedoms. What happens if Herve decides he doesn't need to close his blinds when he has a date? You know what will happen."

"I do like to push the boundaries," Herve said.

The judge's eyes rolled.

"Technically, she's doing nothing wrong, but she understands that she is harming the business behind her," Jayna continued. "She knew she lived behind a gas station and that she did not own the trees that acted as a barrier between her and the legal business. She knew that her fence was as high as the codes of the parish allow. Yet instead of trying to work with the city, she chose this method of protest. Judge, all we're asking is for a stop to the relentless nudity that is costing my client money. I hope you can see this is what is best for all of Papillon." She stepped back, resting her case.

And half the audience cheered while the judge tried to get them to calm down.

Jimmy leaned over. "You did real good. I think we could

win. But I'm also worried about how Geraldine is going to feel if we win. Do you think she'll be sad?"

"I think she'll be clothed," Jayna replied.

"Your Honor," Quaid began, "my opponent spoke about community. She talked about how my client understood what she was getting into, and now she has to abide by the unwritten rules of our society. She asked you what kind of community Papillon should be. This is an important question and one I think we should all ask ourselves. It's an important question, one almost as important as each of us truly questioning what we want out of life."

Where was he going with this? She sat behind the big desk and watched as he turned her way.

"What do you want out of life? Each one of you should ask this. What would make a successful life? So that at the end of it, you wouldn't look back with regret. Is it a life free of risk? One that stays in the middle and never experiences the highs or lows? A solitary life where work is the most important thing of all? What is work? Is it merely what we get paid for? What society values? I believe that work—our life's work—should be a blessing not merely to our bank accounts but to our families. To our communities. I believe that building a life with the people we love is the most important work of all."

Tears sprang to her eyes because he wasn't talking about the case. He wasn't trying to pull apart her argument.

He was making his case to her. He was fighting for her, trying to persuade her.

It was totally unprofessional and she would never, never let him forget it, but it was also the most romantic thing he could have done, and her heart swelled with love.

He was asking her to choose him, to choose a home and family. He was asking her to be brave.

His mother was offering her the good work her heart desired, the work that would truly satisfy the lonely child she'd been. She didn't have to be lonely. She could choose again.

"So I ask you, what do you want?" Quaid's gaze had turned warm.

"I want to go fishing," the judge replied.

"He's not asking you, Andy," Mrs. Havery said, her voice rising.

"PawPaw, I think he's asking the defense counsel what she wants." Britney seemed to be following the scene playing out in front of her.

"Well, I think she wants to win," the judge replied.

"It's a metaphor," Paul shouted.

It wasn't. It was actually very direct. She wasn't sure Paul understood what a metaphor was, but that was all right. She knew exactly what Quaid was doing.

He was making her face the real questions she needed to ask. She'd spent all of her time and effort making sure a bunch of people who didn't matter would be impressed with her success. That was what making it had meant to her younger self, but she saw the world through a different lens now.

There would be no job in Dallas. There would be work here in Papillon. Hard work. Good work. Work that would make her family proud of her.

Work she would never regret.

She stood and didn't care that she could feel tears running down her cheeks. "What do I want, Quaid? I want to spend time with my sister. I want to watch my nieces grow up and be there for them. I want to try to have a relationship with my mom because I think we have a lot to teach each other. I want to fight with your mom over that library because it is going to be this town's crowning jewel. I want to represent Brian the raccoon when he is inevitably apprehended. But most of all, I want to be your biggest fan. I want you to know that even if no one else ever reads a single page, that you have a crazy fangirl who will sleep with you for one more chapter. I want you, Quaid."

She moved toward him and then she was right where she wanted to be—in his arms.

"I want you, too, baby. I've missed you. I've missed you so much," he said as the courtroom erupted in cheers.

She went on her toes and kissed him.

"Are you done, Quaid?" the judge asked.

She thought Quaid gave the judge a thumbs-up, but she was too busy kissing him to be sure.

"Judgment for the plaintiff. Geraldine, keep your clothes on," the judge said. "I'm going fishing and I'm retiring if the two of you are going to keep this up. Case closed."

She got her man and she'd won the case?

That felt like a perfect day to her.

epilogue

Jayna looked out over the big crowd gathered at the fund-raiser and felt a deep sense of satisfaction.

She'd fought and the law had not won, the law in this case being Quaid's mom, who had insisted that a fundraiser should be elegant and not some family-style barbecue with a local band who was last scheduled to play at the opening of the zoo Herve tried to put in his backyard. She'd managed to get that project shut down and had found a new place for Herve to put his energy.

He was teaching automotive workshops for area youth, helping them try out the idea of being a mechanic so they would know if a trade school would be good for them. She'd worked with Sylvie Darois to use the rec center for a series of interactive classes about possible professions. Quaid had talked to students about law school and what it meant to be a lawyer. Celeste Beaumont was mentoring teens interested in business. Harry Jefferys taught basic carpentry.

She was already making a difference and she'd just gotten started.

"Hey, sweetheart, where do you want this potato salad? The café sent ten pounds but I'm not sure that's going to be enough. That deputy is here, and he can eat." Her mother had her hands full. "I swear I watched him eat two full meals for dinner the other night when we were at Lucille's."

Jayna gave her a big smile. They weren't perfect, but they were talking and getting along. They'd both apologized for the things they'd said the night of their big fight and were working on their relationship. Her mom had even come out to Havery House with Sienna and the girls for dinner several times. Her mother and Quaid's mom had found they liked to talk about how stubborn their children were. It was a bonding experience for them. "The café's booth is set up at the back."

Her mom winked. "All my girlfriends from the plant are coming out tonight. We even convinced management to donate."

That was good news, but then she'd managed to get several of the businesses around the parish to donate large sums of money. Between Marian's connections and her own belief in never giving up, they were going to get everything she wanted for the Wilson Havery Memorial Wing of the Papillon Public Library.

"Thanks, Mom," she said. "I'll join you and Sienna and the girls for dinner."

"We'll look forward to it," her mom promised. "And bring Quaid. You know I love to look at that handsome man."

Jayna laughed as her mom walked off. Her mom was definitely getting more comfortable with her future in-laws.

She was going to marry that man. There was no doubt in her mind that he would ask. After all, she'd gotten a peek at the new outline for the next Armand Landry mystery. Quaid had a plan to revise his books so that each included the police detective who suddenly looked a lot like her. Shannon now had short, chic hair and brown eyes, and she was trouble that Armand loved to get into.

And in the next book, Armand was going to ask her to marry him. A happily ever after for Quaid's hero was definite proof that her own was coming.

A big arm wound around her waist, and she couldn't help but smile. Speak of that Cajun devil. "Hey, babe."

"Hey, you," Quaid whispered in her ear. "I have crazy news for you."

She turned because that could mean anything. "Tell me Geraldine is happy with the trellis. I don't think Judge Brewer can handle another trial."

Despite the judgment, Jimmy had felt bad and worked with Harry Jefferys to build a beautiful trellis that skirted the parish's codes and blocked out the sight of the gas station. The community, it seemed, took care of its own no matter what the legal system claimed was due.

Quaid always looked relaxed now, even when he was knee-deep in legal briefs and would rather be writing. He never failed to smile for her and kiss her senseless before taking her to bed. "Paul sold the distribution rights to his film for twenty-five million dollars."

Jayna felt her jaw drop. "Are you kidding me?"

Quaid grinned. "I'm not. He's flying Mom out to spend a couple of weeks with him to celebrate. He wants us to look over the contracts, but it's basically a done deal. And he wants to talk to me about possibly producing the Armand Landry stories."

"That's amazing." She'd grown to genuinely enjoy the time she spent with Paul. His success would be hard-earned. "What do you think?"

"I think I would still like to try to get them published first, but we'll see what happens. I'm open to all possibilities." He let his hands find her hips. "Especially the possibility of getting you alone. We're not far from the office."

She missed the little apartment now that she'd moved

into Havery House. Every now and then they spent the night even when they weren't working late. They kept a bed and some food for Luna and locked themselves away from the world. "I might be able to slip away for a while."

"There she is. That's my aunt, and she will fix it. She won't let them hurt him," a quavering voice announced.

Jayna whirled around, and there was Ivy with some of her friends. She had tears in her eyes. "Honey, what's wrong?"

"Where's your momma?" Quaid started looking around the fair grounds for Sienna.

Ivy shook her head. "Momma can't help, but Aunt Jayna can. We want to hire her. We have nine dollars and eleven cents."

"Oh no. What happened?" Quaid asked.

Ivy's eyes went wide. "They caught Brian, and they're going to take him somewhere like a farm. That's what the animal control guy said. He said Brian would be happy on a farm, but I know what a farm means. Everyone knows what a farm means."

Animal Control Services needed to update their protocols on how to talk to children. Somehow she couldn't actually see Zep Guidry destroying a raccoon who didn't have rabies even if said raccoon was a menace to society. Still. The possibilities swirled in her head.

She could be a legal legend.

Or at least have a little fun. It had been a while since she'd indulged in Papillon shenanigans. She held out her hand and then two because that nine dollars wasn't merely in paper money. There were two ones, a five, and a bunch of coins. Those kids had pooled their resources and bought themselves a damn fine attorney. This would be a lesson in both civics and economics for the kiddos. "Done. I'll contact the court and file a stay. Brian is going nowhere. His arrest was likely illegal. I want to see the warrant."

Quaid's brows rose, the sides of his mouth tugging up in a way that let her know he thought she was slightly crazy and entirely amusing. "Uhm, I don't think they need a warrant to take a raccoon into custody, baby."

"That is for the court to decide, my love." She shoved the kids' retainer in her pocket. "Ivy, you're going to need to take care of Luna for me. She's with your mom and Kelly. Tell the mayor I had an emergency and I'll be back as soon as I can."

Her niece nodded and ran off to find her mom and Sylvie.

Quaid took her hand and started to walk.

Jayna glanced up at him, matching his stride. "I'm going down to Animal Services and then likely to the courthouse."

Quaid squeezed her hand. "And I will take the parish's position."

She grinned. "You are going to be the bad guy to every child in the parish."

He winked. "Yeah, but it's going to be fun, Counselor. You and me and a crazy court case. It's everything I ever wanted."

"Then let the games begin, baby."

Quaid would be at her side. Or across the table. It didn't matter as long as they were together.

She was ready for another round.

acknowledgments

I would like to thank the usual suspects. Thanks to Kevan Lyon, my agent, for championing this series and always being willing to talk a problem through. Much love to Kate Seaver and her staff at Berkley. To my team—Kim Guidroz, Maria Monroy, Stormy Pate, Riane Holt, and Kori Smith. Thanks to Jenn Watson and her Social Butterfly team. Special thanks to my family for being there through a rough year.

Ready to find
your next great read?

Let us help.

Visit prh.com/nextread

Penguin
Random
House